# BANDITS OF ROME

# by Alex Gough

To all my loved ones, human and animal,
living and no longer with us.

# CHAPTER I

## Italy, October AD 27

The wooden wheel on the cart hit another pothole in the road and Gurges swore aloud as the bump jolted up his backside and through his spine. From beneath the tarpaulin that covered the cart behind him, he heard an ominous tinkle. Already aching from the long journey, he felt his jaw clench and his head start to throb, and he thumped the mule driver seated on his left with a bony elbow.

"By Hercules, how many times? Watch out for the holes. Those aren't storage jars in the back there. Those statues are worth a fortune."

The mule driver grunted an apology, eyes set straight ahead. Gurges grumbled to himself. A spot of rain fell, then another, and he looked up at the grey sky with trepidation, knowing another soaking was on its way. Seated on his right, his new young wife drew her cloak more tightly around her. She never complained, but then why would she? He had found her as a destitute freedwoman, and given her a home, food, and now a new life growing inside her. Thinking of his unborn child, he called across to the head of the hired thugs that made up his bodyguard.

"How much further till we stop for the night?"

The large Gaul shrugged his shoulders, his long, matted blonde hair waving in the breeze. "We stop when we get there."

Gurges choked back a reply. This whole journey had been hellish from the start. The euphoria he had experienced when he made his original find in Rhegium had long since evaporated. He recalled the joy he had felt as he paid the uneducated farmer for the statues he had been using to shore up fences and hang washing from. Gurges had a keen eye for all things artistic, and knew that this collection consisted of genuine originals from the time when Rhegium had been a Greek colony, part of Magna Graecia. Bought for a pittance, these statues would fetch a fortune in Rome, enough to propel him at last into the ranks of the equestrian class.

The rain came harder, and the cart rattled over the cobblestones of the Via Popilia that connected Rhegium to Capua. He thought about the swiftness of a sea journey from Rhegium to Ostia, how by now he could already be drinking Falernian wine and eating the choicest sow's udders, before taking a slow stroll around Rome with his beautiful woman, to look for their new mansion on the Palatine.

But he would take no chances with this once in a lifetime find. A sea journey always bore risks. Pirates were uncommon these days, but storms and rocks and freak waves took their toll. The seabed along the coast of Italy must be littered with wrecks, and the bones of merchants unwilling to take the slow route. As the rain started to soak through to his skin, and his hair became plastered flat against his head, he consoled himself with Aesop's tale of the hare and the tortoise.

The small group, merchant and wife, driver and three bodyguards on foot, moved slowly along the Via Popilia. Other traffic on the road was sparse, just the occasional lone horseman or farmer transporting his goods. Their route continued between some hills. Roman engineers had cut the road into the slopes to avoid having a bend or steep incline, and low cliffs lined the way. Up ahead, Gurges thought he could see something lying in their path. He wiped the rain from his eyes and peered forwards, but couldn't make it out. He watched his head bodyguard. The Gaul had seen it as well, and was watching it closely as they approached.

The visibility in the heavy rain was so poor they were only twenty feet away before Gurges realised that what they had seen was a body, lying sprawled out, clothed in soaked rags. The Gaul held up a hand to stop the group, then motioned one of his men forward. The chosen bodyguard pulled his spear from his backpack. Suspiciously, he approached the body, weapon at the ready. The body made no movement, even when he prodded it. It lay face down, motionless.

The guard gripped a shoulder and heaved so the body rolled onto its back. He stared down in puzzlement.

"What is it?" called Gurges. The bodyguard turned back, and opened his mouth to speak.

The body sat up.

In shock, Gurges watched the body they had thought dead pull a long, curved dagger from beneath his rags. But his gaze was drawn to the man's face. It wore a mask, bronze, firmly secured by leather straps, the frowning face of a Greek tragedy actor. Gurges opened his mouth to call a warning, but no words came.

The Gaul was not paralysed like his employer. He yelled to his man to look out. It was too late. The guard started to turn, but the curved knife swung upwards, the still-seated man holding it double-handed, so it sank with force up through the bodyguard's groin and into his guts. The bodyguard let out a high-pitched scream and fell backwards, clutching between his legs in a vain attempt to stop the river of blood flooding out through the rent the knife had made. Gurges' wife let out a shrill scream.

With a roar, the head bodyguard drew his two-handed sword and rushed at the masked man.

An arrow took him cleanly between the shoulder blades, and he sprawled forwards, sword flying out of his hands. Gurges and the remaining bodyguard whirled to see the bowman standing in the road behind them. He too wore a bronze mask, this one the smiling face of a Greek comedian. The bodyguard only had time to draw his spear before the bowman let fly another arrow. It took his target in the throat, and the bodyguard went down, blood and air gurgling around the shaft.

Gurges remained frozen in shock. Beside him, his wife was silent, trembling violently, pulling the cloak ever tighter around her as if it would make her invisible. His driver jumped off the wagon and in blind panic started to run away from the bowman, down the road, head turned back, trying to see the arrow that might bring him down. He ran straight towards the tragedy-masked man, who took two swift steps to intercept him. The curved blade lashed out, eviscerating the mule driver. He let out a plaintive cry and dropped to the ground, trying to hold in the loops of intestine that spilled out onto the road.

Tragedy and Comedy advanced on Gurges. His whole body trembled, and to his shame he felt urine trickling down his leg. Tragedy grabbed Gurges' tunic and pulled him off the cart. Comedy kept the bow trained on the shaking merchant, while Tragedy went to the cart. He yanked off the tarpaulin, to reveal a number of delicately made marble statues.

Gurges found his voice. "The statues, they... they are priceless. Take them, they're yours. Just let me go, I won't breathe a word. They will make your fortunes, I promise…"

"Silence," said Tragedy. He reached down and unhitched the two-wheeled cart from the mules. He opened the back flap of the cart, then took the tow bar and hoisted it upwards. The cart tilted, and the statues tumbled out of the back and smashed into small pieces on the cobbles.

Gurges stared aghast at the wreckage. He looked back towards the man in the Tragedy mask. The grotesque frown on the mask chilled him to the marrow. Of the bandit, all he could see were the man's stony eyes, and they gave nothing away.

"Who are you?" said Gurges in a strangled whisper. "What do you want?"

"I'm Atreus," said Tragedy, "and this is Thyestes." The bowman gave a curt nod.

Atreus fixed his gaze on Gurges, studying him, and Gurges stared back, chilled from the rain and the fear, numb in his extremities, tremors running through his body.

The curved knife flashed out. It cut through skin and vessels and windpipe in one deadly slash. Eyes wide, Gurges sunk to his knees, then toppled forwards.

Both bandits looked down at the dead man. After a while, Thyestes, of the comedy mask moved to take hold of Gurges' cowering widow, and as he bound her hands, he asked, "The man asked us something. What do we want?"

Atreus, of the tragedy mask, regarded him through the eye holes. He thought for a moment before replying.

"That's a very good question."

Carbo bit back a groan as he stumbled into a pothole. His old wound complained, and his leg buckled slightly before he recovered his balance. Rufa held out a hand to steady him, but he waved her away.

"Don't be grumpy," she chided playfully, taking his arm against his protests.

"Hmm," he grumbled. He looked up at the skies, squinting against the rain that was drizzling steadily on them. "Remind me why we aren't in the dry in my tavern, drinking wine and eating hot food."

"Because," said Rufa, "Someone thought it would be a good idea to leave Rome and move to their little farm in the country."

"I seem to recall something about the warmth and sun of the south," said Vespillo from behind them.

"I thought you knew better than listen to Carbo," said his wife Severa.

"Hope sometimes overcomes experience, you know."

Carbo called out. "Well how was I to know the Nephelae would be dogging our journey?"

"We could have been a bit more sure of the weather inside your tavern."

"I like it," said Fabilla. The little girl was walking on the other side of Rufa, holding her mother's hand, looking around her in wide-eyed wonder. "I've never been outside Rome before."

Carbo looked over at the young girl. She had been through so much, and yet here she was mere weeks after the horrors she had endured, enchanted by hills and trees and wild rabbits and deer. He knew she wasn't completely unaffected, that most nights she crept into the bed he shared with Rufa, just to be held while the bad dreams faded. But during the day, it was as if none of the evil had ever happened. He caressed the hilt of his sword, vowing silently to give them the peace and safety they deserved.

As they headed south along the Via Popilia, the road entered a valley. Carbo could see it was carved into the hill by Roman engineers, and he admired the amount of effort that had gone into such a simple thing as avoiding a bend. As they got further into the valley though, a chill ran up his spine that had nothing to do with the cold rain.

The terrain here was different than the one in his mind's eye. In the German forests, it had been treacherously muddy underfoot. The path had not been cobbled, and the flanking hills sloped steeply away, in contrast to these sheer man-made cliffs. Still, he imagined he could see, dimly through the diaphanous curtains of rain, Germanic soldiers lining the clifftops, ready to pour down on them, screaming and hurling spears. He felt for his sword, gripped the hilt.

A hand on his shoulder made him jump.

"Easy, soldier," said Vespillo. "We aren't in Germany. This is Campania, safe as Rome itself."

Carbo raised an eyebrow at this. Rome? Safe? After everything they had been through there. His eyes unfocused, staring into the distance, as memories of flames, burning flesh, screams of the dying flooded over him. Severa, Vespillo's wife, back-handed him across the upper arm.

"Always saying the right thing, aren't you, my love?" Vespillo had the good grace to look abashed.

"Not all Germans are blood-thirsty barbarians," said Marsia, Carbo's slave, who walked just behind Vespillo and his wife. Carbo considered how many masters would punish a slave for being that outspoken. But Marsia knew where the boundaries were, and knew that Carbo wasn't capricious or cruel. Besides, they had been through too much together for pettiness.

"Not all," agreed Carbo. "Though I have only met one who wasn't."

Marsia let out a harumph. Fabilla tugged at Rufa's arm and pointed ahead.

"Mummy, what's that lying in the road?"

Carbo stopped dead, hand moving immediately to the hilt of his gladius. Vespillo almost bumped into him.

"What is it, Carbo?"

Carbo peered ahead at the shape lying in the distance. He looked around, up at the low cliffs, shielding his eyes against the rain.

"Carbo?" asked Vespillo again. Rufa was staring at him in mounting alarm, and Fabilla was plucking at Rufa's sleeve.

"I don't know," said Carbo. Vespillo stood beside him, squinting to try to bring the object into focus.

"Stay here with the women," said Carbo, and before Vespillo could protest, he continued cautiously forwards. His heart raced, nerves jangling, chest tight as he approached, constantly looking around for signs of ambush. The shape slowly came into focus as he got nearer, an upturned cart, smashed statuary lying around it. Carbo began to wonder if he was being ridiculous. How foolish he would look and feel, getting so concerned over a simple road accident. But as he reached the cart, he saw almost simultaneously, the body slumped against one wheel, and the other bodies spread out further down the road.

He drew his sword in one smooth motion, entering into a combat stance without thinking, balanced on the balls of his feet, knees bent to allow him to spring in any direction. He prodded the body by the cart with one foot and it slumped sideways. He had heard of bandits ambushing altruistic passers-by, pretending to be injured or in need of aid.

This one though was clearly beyond help. A huge rent gaped in the man's throat, and though the rain had washed some of the blood away, there was enough still lying around for Carbo to know the amount lost to be unsurvivable, even if he hadn't got the direct evidence of the corpse before him. Nearby was a second corpse, a larger man, a barbarian from his hair and clothes. This one had an arrow in the throat. Another body further on was full of arrows, yet another had had his guts spilled and a further man had bled out from some concealed wound. None moved or drew breath.

Carbo took one more look around, then beckoned Vespillo and the others to approach. Rufa kept Fabilla's eyes shielded as the small party arrived at the scene of the slaughter. Vespillo gazed around him in shock.

"It looks like an ambush," said Carbo grimly. His heart pounded, skin prickled, and his mind reeled. This was supposed to be a quiet backwater.

Vespillo nodded. "And recent too. Look how fresh the blood is."

"I wonder what they were after?"

Vespillo gestured at the broken marble statues. "These? They look valuable."

"Maybe once," said Carbo. "Not any more. I suppose they must have been destroyed in the fighting."

"There doesn't look to have been much of a fight. It looks like a massacre."

Carbo grimaced. "We shouldn't stay here. Whoever killed these men aren't long gone. And I reckon this was a merchant with three or four bodyguards. They are better equipped than us."

"You want to leave the bodies?"

"You can report it to the authorities when we get to Nola if you feel you have to. Let's get underway."

Vespillo hesitated. "Carbo, isn't it our duty…?"

"Duty can go to Hades!" snapped Carbo. "This is a new start. Rufa, Fabilla and me, we are putting everything behind us. I just want … no, I need, some peace. You can stay as long as you want, but I know your job will draw you back to Rome. For us though, this is it."

Vespillo studied Carbo for a moment, then looked at the frightened faces on the three women and the little girl and nodded.

"Let's go."

They continued onwards, Rufa still shielding Fabilla's eyes from her attempts to see what had happened. Carbo and Vespillo remained tense and alert, and everyone was silent, the only sound coming from the spatter of the persistent rain on the cobblestones.

The sun had not put in an appearance, but the deepening gloom told them they wouldn't reach Nola before night fell. They passed through a small village, only a handful of houses, a tavern and a couple of shops. By unspoken agreement, the cold, wet, bedraggled group filed into the inviting-looking tavern, where a fire was crackling in the hearth.

Vespillo approached the tavern keeper. A depression in the bar held a large pot which contained a gloopy, congealed slop of a stew. It looked warm and filling though, so Vespillo bought a bowl for everyone and joined them at a large table.

They ate quietly for a little while. Vespillo finished first, wiping his mouth with the back of his hand, which gained him an eye rolling look of disapproval from Severa. He let out a satisfied belch, breaking the silence.

"How far to Nola?" he asked Carbo.

"Nearly half a day. Then my farm is a few miles from there, maybe another hour or so."

"We stay here for the night, then," said Vespillo. It was not a question, but none were inclined to argue. Carbo looked around the table. The group seemed dispirited, eyes down, hair straggly with the soaking. Even the usually irrepressible Fabilla looked miserable, and she was shivering in her wet clothes. Rufa finished her meal, then put an arm around Fabilla and guided her over to the fire to warm herself.

Carbo went over to the tavern owner at the bar table.

"Do you have rooms for six for the night?"

The tavern owner grunted. "I have a room. I'm sure you could all squeeze in."

"Surely you have more than one room here?"

"I do. And they are occupied. Do you want to take it or not?"

Carbo pursed his lips, but passed over the coins necessary to pay the no doubt inflated price. It was obvious with the women and child and the foul weather that he was in no position to haggle. The tavern owner passed over a chunky iron key, and Carbo handed it to Marsia. She gathered up their belongings and carried them up the stairs the tavern owner had indicated.

"I'll take Fabilla to bed now," said Rufa.

Carbo nodded. "Marsia, you can go to bed now as well."

"And you, Severa. We still have some way to walk tomorrow."

Severa looked briefly defiant, but the tiredness seemed to overcome her resistance, and she dipped her head and followed the others to the bedroom.

Vespillo joined Carbo at the bar. "Drink?"

Carbo smiled. "I thought you would never ask."

Vespillo ordered two cups of wine, and they leaned against the bar table as they both took deep swallows. Vespillo looked into the cup reflectively for a moment.

"You know, that's not at all bad."

Carbo nodded his agreement. "Not quite as nice as that stuff from Mount Falernus."

"Of course not. Amazing how cheap you can buy Falernian if you are near where it is made. Of course once something arrives in Rome, its price automatically triples."

Vespillo took another sip. "No cold feet?"

Carbo looked up sharply. "What?"

Vespillo grinned at him mischievously.

"You're going to ask her to marry you aren't you?"

Carbo gaped. "How did you know?"

"Friend, it's obvious. You two dote on each other. And here you are, heading for your new home, your fresh start. Going to wait until you are settled, then ask her over a romantic meal?"

"I... hadn't quite worked out the specifics."

Vespillo laughed and clapped his friend on the back. "Congratulations. You two deserve each other."

Carbo looked around to hide his embarrassment. The tavern was quiet - a middle-aged couple arguing, a drunk snoring loudly in one corner and a small group of rough-looking men laughing and groaning as they played dice. At another table sat a smartly dressed young man, straight-backed and head erect, curly, dark hair cropped short and neat, sporting a light, youthful beard that he was trying to keep clean as he ate his sloppy stew. The tavern owner slouched against the wall behind the bar, looking bored and fed up. Carbo was happy to ignore him, but Vespillo was clearly in a more sociable mood.

"So do you get much banditry around these parts?"

The tavern owner looked up sharply, as the tavern became suddenly silent. The dice rolled to a stop with a clatter, but none of the gamers saw the score, all eyes turned towards the two strangers. The tavern owner picked up a cloth and started wiping down the bar table.

"Why do you ask?" he said, sounding like he was making an effort to keep his tone casual.

Carbo gave Vespillo a little shake of the head, but Vespillo continued oblivious.

"We came across a party on the road, a few miles back. All dead."

The tavern owner said nothing, concentrating on wiping a stubborn piece of dirt from the table.

"That doesn't surprise you?" pressed Vespillo. "Banditry is that common around here? So common that it occurs in daylight on a main road?"

"I don't know anything about that sort of thing," said the tavern owner sullenly. Carbo was aware that all eyes were on them, and he felt uncomfortable under the attention, but Vespillo was in his stride.

"Blatant lawlessness, in Italy, and no one seems to care," he said, his voice getting louder. "When I reach a bigger town, I will report what I have seen to the proper authorities, and I will make sure to mention the lack of interest from the locals here. I'm sure they will take that into account when they allocate their resources to protect the vulnerable citizens."

The barman said nothing, and Vespillo looked around the room. Only the young man in the corner met his challenging gaze. Vespillo shook his head.

"I am a commander of the vigiles. I have led freedmen and slaves and the poorest of the poor as they fought for their homes and their lives against criminals, against fire, against…"

Carbo put a hand on Vespillo's arm, giving him a strong warning look.

Vespillo shook his head. "Those slaves and freedmen are more Roman than any of you freeborn," he said contemptuously. "I'm going to bed." He stomped off. Carbo turned back to his drink, intending to finish it and leave. The buzz of low conversation slowly returned to the tavern.

A touch on his shoulder caused him to stiffen.

"I'm sorry to disturb you, sir. Your friend, he is right. I have been away from home, in Greece, for five years. Now I have returned, things seem different. No one will talk about it, but I am getting an odd feeling."

"What sort of feeling?" asked Carbo.

"I'm not sure. The people around here seem scared, somehow cowed."

Carbo looked around the tavern. Conversation was subdued, eyes downcast. The gambling had stopped.

"I don't know what the problem is," said Carbo, "But we reach our destination tomorrow, and that will be a relief after today."

The young man hesitated, then asked, "May I accompany you tomorrow?"

"Of course, if we are going the same way. Where are you headed?"

"To the villa of Gaius Sempronius Blaesus, near Nola."

"Nola? That's where we are going, to my farm."

The young man raised his eyebrows. "Then maybe we are neighbours. I am Quintus Sempronius Blaesus. Gaius' son."

Carbo reached out and shook his hand. "I suppose there are only so many places to stay for a night on this road, so it shouldn't be a surprise to encounter someone with the same destination. Very pleased to meet you though, Quintus. I'm Marcus Valerius Carbo."

"Likewise, Carbo. So you live near Nola?"

"Well I own a farm near there. Granted to me on discharge from the legions. I've never been there."

"So you decided to make a visit? To check it is being run correctly, make sure the steward isn't fiddling the books?"

"Sort of. We actually decided to move there. Rome... lost it's appeal. I invited Vespillo to accompany us too, though he will return to Rome in time."

"Is he always so outspoken?"

Carbo laughed. "He does sometimes get on his high horse. I think command can make some people like that."

"Command of a bunch of ex-slaves?"

Carbo frowned at this. "He was a centurion in the legions as well." His voice was low, and had a dangerous edge to it. Quintus noticed and back-tracked.

"I suppose it is a hard job, keeping control of a group of thugs." Carbo tensed, but let it go. How could someone who hadn't fought alongside the vigiles understand their sense of honour and pride at being taken from their lowly positions and given the opportunity to make a difference to their city, and to their families and households.

"How does he keep order?" asked Quintus. "Get respect and obedience from the likes of the men he commands?"

"He is a good leader," said Carbo, "And a good man. They follow him because he is in front of them. First into a burning house, first into a fight. And he treats them like Romans, not like shit on his shoes." He gave Quintus a penetrating stare at this, and Quintus had the good grace to look a little embarrassed. Carbo changed the subject.

"How long do you think it will take to reach your father's villa tomorrow? I think our journey will be just over half a day, if we don't tarry in Nola too long."

Quintus thought for a moment. "That sounds about right. It would probably be quicker if it was just you and me, but I presume your daughter isn't as fast a walker as a grown man." Carbo didn't correct the mistaken assumption about Fabilla.

"I have an injured leg, from the legions. She matches my pace pretty well."

Quintus smiled. "Well the road beyond Nola is not as well made as the Via Popilia. Just tracks, really. It will be nice to be home after so long away."

"I have to say I'm looking forward to seeing my farm. I hope my steward received the letters I sent on ahead asking him to be ready for me." Carbo yawned. "Well, if an early start is needed, I should go to bed as well. We will be ready to leave soon after sun-up. If you want to come with us, meet us in front of the tavern."

"Thank you, I will. Goodnight."

Carbo made his way up the stairs to their room. Vespillo was already snoring loudly, arms wrapped around Severa, lying on a blanket on the hard floor. Marsia had curled herself as small as possible in a corner, hugging herself for warmth. Rufa and Fabilla had the only bed. Fabilla was fast asleep, while Rufa lay awake, stroking her daughter's hair. By the dim light of a small oil lamp, Carbo saw Rufa look up as he entered, and smile. She gently drew Fabilla closer to her to make room for Carbo, and patted the bed.

As quietly as he could, he got onto the straw mattress, and pulled the single blanket over the three of them. He placed one protective arm over the woman he loved and her daughter, feeling contentment seep through him. But as sleep approached, his last thoughts were of blood, gaping neck wounds, and sightless eyes staring at the sky.

# CHAPTER II

The small company of travellers had assembled in front of the tavern promptly at sun-up. Carbo was pleased that no one had overslept, but not surprised. Vespillo and himself, used to rigid military timing from so many years in the legions, could not lie in bed with the sun up even if they wanted to. Marsia, Rufa and Fabilla, as slaves or former slaves, similarly had strict schedules that were ingrained. Severa kept her house with matronly efficiency, and pride would never allow her to sleep longer than Vespillo. Carbo had only doubted whether the little rich boy, Quintus, would be this disciplined. But he had been the first there, hair combed, tunic looking like it was fresh from the fuller, not grimed from weeks on the road. Around his waist he wore a long sword, seated in a scabbard, an ornate, silver-banded hilt protruding from the sheath.

A light mist hung over the road, but it was nothing like the previous miserable conditions, and they started their journey with rather more enthusiasm than they had managed the day before. Vespillo, more talkative than Carbo as usual, engaged Quintus in conversation.

"So what took you abroad then, Quintus?"

Quintus looked surprised. "Surely it is an essential part of any young man's education? Visiting the land of Aristotle and Euripides, Plato's Academy and the Theatre of Dionysus. Where better to learn about the world?"

Vespillo laughed. "Where better? In the legions, lad. Do you really think you can understand life by listening to some ancient Greek fellators? You know nothing, until you have shat yourself in terror as a barbarian army charges you, watched your friends' guts spilling onto the ground, heard the screams of women and children as their villages are burned around them. Isn't that right, Carbo?"

Carbo just grunted. Quintus wrinkled his nose as if he had smelled something foul.

"You may believe that. But why do those things? What drove you into battle?"

"A centurion with a bloody great stick, most of the time!" said Vespillo. Carbo chuckled. Quintus just shook his head.

"You fought, you suffered hardship and terror and deprivation, and yet you don't really know why."

Vespillo's expression darkened and his voice became hard.

"I know why I did it. I did it for my friends to my left and to my right. We fought for each other."

Quintus nodded at this. "Without friends, no one would choose to live, even if he had all other goods."

"Aristotle," said Carbo.

Quintus looked surprised, and smiled. "Aristotle indeed."

Vespillo pulled a disgusted expression. "You have been hanging around with Vatius for too long. I thought we had left all that rubbish back in your tavern in Rome." He turned back to Quintus. "So you spent your whole time in Greece sitting under plane trees and listening to assholes spouting crap?"

"Not my whole time, no. The mornings were philosophy, the afternoons were fitness, wrestling and sword-training in the gymnasium, and the evenings were drinking and fucking the best looking girls I could find."

Vespillo laughed out loud and clapped Quintus on his back. "Now that sounds more like my idea of fun." Severa glared at him. "In my younger days, I mean. When I was single, before I found my sweet wife..."

Severa didn't look mollified, and Carbo suppressed a grin as Vespillo went quiet, looking down at his feet.

They reached Nola in good time, but as it was still only mid morning, they decided not to stop for long. Vespillo however insisted on finding someone to report the bandit activity to, and wandered off in search of one of the decuriones who comprised the local council. Carbo approached an elderly street seller to buy some drinks and snacks for the others.

"Some of your dates and nuts, five cups of well-watered wine, and some fruit juice, please."

The reply that came was not in Latin, though it sounded similar.

"I don't understand," said Carbo.

The street seller repeated the same sentence.

Carbo looked around helplessly. Quintus smiled. "He is talking Oscan. The language of the Samnites. More people used to speak it in Italy than Latin. It's dying out now, but many people around here still speak it as their first language. This old fellow is obviously one of them."

"So what did he say?"

"He said, 'I'm deaf, can you speak up, please.'"

Quintus laughed as Carbo tried to get his head around the problem of a man speaking in a different language, who was too deaf to realise that Carbo didn't understand him. Quintus let him squirm for a while, before stepping in and speaking loudly and clearly in Oscan to the seller. The seller looked at Carbo in puzzlement, then understanding dawned. He smiled, and cupped his hand to his ear and Carbo signed back his incomprehension with an open armed shrug. Carbo then pointed out the food and drink he wanted, signalling quantities with his fingers. Quintus helped him bring back the provisions to where the rest of the group sat on the smooth paving slabs surrounding a fountain that was the centrepiece of a small plaza.

Carbo looked around him as they ate. The place had an air of decay about it, a hint of former glories to be seen in faded frescos and crumbling statues. People shuffled around, going about their business, and there was a downbeat air to them. Tempers frayed too easily, the crash of a falling pot or jolt of a cart in a pothole startled too much. Carbo was reminded of a dog that had been beaten too often, and now slunk about with its tail between its legs, trying to stay out of trouble and terrified of any raised hand. Quintus noted his gaze.

"This place used to be important, you know."

Carbo nodded. "It looks like it has seen better days."

"It has a noble history though. It is one of the oldest cities of Campania. Taken by the Romans in the Great Samnite War. Fought in three battles against Hannibal. Involved in the Social War and stormed by Spartacus. The divine Augustus died here."

"You seem proud of it."

"Proud?" Quintus considered. "Maybe. It's where I grew up. Not as big or important as Rome, but still, it's my home town, and that's what counts, isn't it?"

"It is," agreed Carbo, reflecting on his own attitude to the city of Rome. He had spent most of his life away from it, but fighting for it. When he returned home, he found a city of splendour and squalour, opulence and destitution. He found a repressed, poor underclass, almost completely ignored by the elite who ran the city. But he found those same poor people to have courage and integrity, and he had led them to fight for their homes against fire and madness. He loved that city, he concluded, for all its imperfections. But like lovers who had undergone a trauma together, and found they couldn't be together afterwards, he needed to be away from it, to start afresh.

"Your father," asked Carbo. "He is a Nolan too? Oscan through and through?"

"No, he is from Rome, like yourself."

"How did he end up down here, then? No offence to Nola, but not many who can afford to live well in Rome ever leave there."

Quintus shrugged. "I don't know. He never talks about Rome."

Carbo knew when a tone of voice told him to let a matter drop, so he checked on Rufa and Fabilla, found them nattering with Marsia and Severa, and so went back to eating in silence.

After a while, Vespillo arrived back, looking red-faced. Carbo tossed him a small bag of nuts.

"How did you get on?"

"Bloody incompetent officials. No one wanted to see me. Certainly no one seemed very impressed by my rank in the vigiles. I eventually got to see a junior clerk to one of the decuriones, who dutifully noted my report, said he would pass it on to the centurion of the stationares stationed here, and that was that."

"They aren't going to investigate? Send any men out into the countryside?"

"No. I don't know if it was apathy or fear, but they certainly don't seem to have any desire to rock the boat. The clerk just commented on stupid travellers going undefended."

"I didn't think we needed a fully armed century to move around the roads of Italy," said Carbo, frowning.

"Quite," said Vespillo, still looking like he wanted to strike something, or someone.

Carbo put a calming hand on his shoulder. "You've done your bit, friend. There's nothing else you can do."

"Of course there is. There is something very wrong here. You've noticed it too, I can tell. We can ask around, find out what's going on here. I bet you and I could smoke these criminals out, show them what Roman law means."

"No."

Carbo said the word flatly. Vespillo looked at him in surprise.

"No?"

"This is not my problem. I'm not a soldier any more. I'm just a veteran, retiring to his farm, with his new family. And you are not an official, you are a watchman of Rome, not Nola. You have no authority here, and no duty to do more."

Vespillo clenched his fists, jaw muscles working. Then he took a deep breath, and let it out. "You're right. Gods, though, if I ran this town, some of these lazy bastard officials would get a shock."

"Thinking of running for office? You, a politician?" Carbo chuckled.

"Don't laugh," said Vespillo. "Why not? A man of my integrity and honour, not to mention my experience of leadership. It's almost my duty to seek election."

Carbo punched him playfully in the upper arm. "You wouldn't last an hour among those snakes. Come on, let's get moving."

They headed out of the town, and once they were a little distance away, walking past the tombs outside the city boundaries, Carbo looked over his shoulder. The amphitheatre and the temple of Augustus were visible over the tops of the tatty houses that surrounded them. They looked shabby and uncared for. A city in decline. Carbo shook his head. Rome had its share of decrepit and run down buildings, but there was also a vitality to it, constant building and rebuilding, houses, shops, temples. Nola seemed tired, and scared. A place that had had enough, and was waiting to die. Or be killed.

Atreus and Thyestes had bypassed Nola. They had no need for provisions, and though without their masks they could be any traveller or Nolan citizen, there was no need for any risks. The detour, and the slow going away from the main roads had delayed them, but they were in no hurry. The weather was not as foul as the previous day, though the torrential rain had turned some of the tracks to little better than muddy swamps.

"A successful tour so far," said Thyestes. "Though I think we should have kept the merchant."

"He had jaundice," said Atreus. "Probably too much wine. He would have made us nothing. We made enough on his wife to make it worthwhile."

"The statues may have brought something, too."

Atreus shook his head. "Too bulky, too easily identifiable. Anyway, you know we mainly deal in human goods. Though that little collection of pearls we got from that Jewish fellow yesterday could come in handy."

Thyestes abruptly straightened. They had crested a hill, and the main road had come into view. In the distance was a small group of travellers. Atreus stood next to Thyestes, following his gaze. With a purposeful action, he slid his mask into place.

"Your eyes are younger than mine," said Atreus. "What can you see?"

Thyestes squinted. "Looks like…three men. Three women. Wait, I see a child."

Atreus considered for a moment. "We take them."

Thyestes looked sideways at him. "Haven't we done enough? Maybe we are pushing our luck."

Atreus pulled his mask on. "There is no such thing as luck, Thyestes. Just the results of our actions."

Thyestes smiled, and secured his own mask in place. Tragedy looked at Comedy, and they started towards the unsuspecting travellers.

As Quintus had predicted, the going became much tougher after they left Nola. For a short distance they followed the branch of the Via Popilia that led to Abella, but soon after this they had to leave the properly made road and head along donkey tracks. The recent rain had made it muddy underfoot, and they squelched along unhappily. Quintus thought he recognised Carbo's farm from the description, and it was in fact close to his father's villa. The young man was a useful guide, and Carbo realised that they could easily have got lost as they navigated the branching trails.

Carbo had to admit that, after a life spent either in Rome or in the northern parts of the Empire, this region was beautiful. Rugged but green hills looked down on them from the distance. The air smelled fresh after the rain, and the fruit orchards and olive groves still bore some fruit, despite it now being well into autumn. Up ahead, the path meandered through small but dense woods. Carbo peered forwards into the gloom of the trees, straining his eyes for signs of danger, still uneasy after their discovery on the road the day before.

Beside him, Vespillo's left foot hit a slippery patch of mud, and slid out from underneath him, causing him to flail his arms as he tried to keep his balance. Carbo started to laugh, just as the arrow glanced across Vespillo's skull.

Vespillo dropped like a beast stunned for sacrifice. A long wound had been opened in his scalp, and blood flowed freely. Carbo whirled, seeing a bowman on the path behind them. He was some distance away, but was clearly a good shot to have hit Vespillo from that far. He was already notching another arrow.

Carbo turned. The woods were only a fifty paces away.

"To the trees!" yelled Carbo, "Run!"

Rufa didn't hesitate, picking up Fabilla and running as fast as she could with the child in her arms. Severa and Marsia ran too, and Carbo was pleased to see the slave positioning herself behind the mother and daughter to protect them from any further shafts.

Carbo hoisted Vespillo up, grunting with the effort, pulled the injured man's arm around his shoulder and started to manhandle him towards the woods. The burden eased as Quintus took the other arm, and with Vespillo moaning incoherently, they moved as quickly as they could towards the safety of the trees.

A whistle came through the air. Carbo reacted instantly, pushing Vespillo and Quintus sideways, the shove propelling him in the opposite direction. The arrow whizzed through the space they had occupied just the briefest of moments before, and lodged in the mud ahead of them, shaft quivering.

Carbo grabbed Vespillo again, and they made a last rush for the woods. As they reached the first trees, Carbo dragged Vespillo sideways into cover. Another arrow hissed through the space they had been a moment before, and embedded itself deep in a branch, splinters of wood spitting out.

Carbo pulled Vespillo behind the thickest tree trunk he could find. It wasn't that wide, and Vespillo's broad shoulders protruded beyond the cover on either side, but his vital areas were protected, and if he took an arrow in the arm, he would probably live.

Carbo looked to the others. Rufa, Severa and Marsia were herding Fabilla deeper into the thickest parts of the woods. Quintus had gained cover and was standing with his back to a tree trunk. He had drawn a long sword, a spatha, Carbo noted, of the sort that was gaining popularity among the auxiliary cavalry. Carbo suppressed a shudder. He had been on the wrong end of one of those swords too many times during his service in Germany.

Quintus caught his eye, held the contact. Carbo returned what he hoped was a reassuring expression. No more arrows had whistled past, so Carbo risked a peek out from his cover. The bowman had closed the distance to the woods now. Carbo saw, in the instant available to him, that the bandit had an arrow nocked on his bow. Carbo heard the twang of the bowstring and ducked back behind his tree, feeling the wind from the arrow where his face had been a split heartbeat before.

He looked over to Quintus and held up one finger. Quintus nodded to show his understanding of the head count. Carbo mimed with his hands to indicate Quintus should head deeper into the woods to help protect the others. Again, Quintus nodded, and jagging like a hare, darted off into the trees. Understanding Carbo's plan, his retreat was noisy, as he thrust aside branches and crunched twigs and leaves underfoot.

Carbo followed a short distance, then veered off to one side, moving with remarkable stealth for a man of his bulk. He settled behind a large bush a short distance from the obvious trail of broken undergrowth that Quintus had left. As he waited, breathing slowly and deeply to calm his racing heart, something from his subconscious appeared in his thoughts. The glimpse of the bowman. There was something odd. Something about his face?

Carbo prayed to Mars that the bowman wouldn't find Vespillo, or if he did would ignore the grizzly watchman. Vespillo would clearly play no part in this fight, in fact looked dead at brief inspection, so the bowman would hopefully move straight on to pursue Carbo and Quintus.

Only a few more moments passed, before Carbo heard the sound of their pursuer, approaching quickly but without haste. Carbo kept himself hidden, estimating the right timing by sound alone. When he judged that the bowman had just drawn past his position, he leapt from behind the bush with a roar, gladius raised high.

The bowman whirled with incredible speed, and as Carbo brought his sword down to cleave the bandit's head in two, the man swayed to one side, bringing his own sword round in an arc to fend off the blow. Both men allowed their rotatory momentum to continue, giving power and speed to their sword swings. They both completed full rotations, and brought their swords together with immense power and an enormous clash of metal on metal.

Carbo was the larger, bulkier man, but even he winced at the shock of the meeting of the weapons. The other man staggered, but held tight. Carbo saw the bow had been discarded, useless for fighting in this terrain.

The bowman took a step back, and stared at Carbo, and Carbo was finally able to see what had been bothering him. The man wore a comedy mask, grinning insanely. From behind the mask, shrewd eyes assessed Carbo.

The effect was unsettling, like a bad dream, but Carbo had faced down German warriors dressed only in spear and shield before, and he put it swiftly from his mind. He could see the man's eyes, and that was all he needed.

A flicker of the pupils, a widening of the lids, and Carbo saw the thrust coming. Even so, he barely managed to parry in time. The man was fast, an accomplished swordsman. Maybe he had fought in more single combat than Carbo, who was more used to fighting with a man either side of him, the man on his right protecting Carbo's flank with his shield, while Carbo did the same for the man on his left.

Still, Carbo was a hardened veteran of twenty-five years in the legions, not to mention some hard fighting in Rome itself recently. Two more feints from the bandit were followed by another thrust. Carbo watched the eyes, and parried again, following up with a stabbing thrust of his own. The bandit parried, but the strength of Carbo's sword arm meant the gladius did not move sideways as much as the man intended, and the blade raked his ribs, ripping a bloody line in his tunic.

The bowman gasped and put a hand to his side, looking at his palm in amazement as it came away bloody. The mask still laughed at Carbo, mocking him. But

Carbo saw something different in the eyes. They held no mockery, only fear. Carbo raised his gladius.

Quintus quickly caught up with the three women and the little girl. Marsia, at the back of the group, rounded on him when she heard his approach, a short dagger in her hand. She relaxed a little when she saw it was him, but still clutched the knife tightly.

"Where's Carbo?" asked Rufa tensely, her arm around Fabilla's shoulders.

"Where's Vespillo?" asked Severa, more sternly. Quintus ignored them.

"Keep moving," he said, looking behind him anxiously. He ushered them forward, taking up position at the back of the group. Reluctantly, the three women continued onwards, Fabilla safely between Rufa and Severa. Marsia moved to the front, dagger outstretched, as she navigated between the fruit trees.

Quintus urged the group to hurry, as he guarded their rear, spatha at the ready. A large roar and a loud clash of weapons came from behind them, and Quintus glanced back, although he knew the sound was from too far away for him to be able to see anything through the trees.

A woman screamed.

He whirled, to see Marsia sprawled on the ground, bleeding from a wound to the side of her head, moaning and moving slowly. Severa and Rufa held Fabilla tight, staring in terror at the man who had just stepped out in front of them. Tall, unarmoured, a curved dagger in his belt and a long, unadorned gladius in his hand. And the mask of a tragedy actor on his face.

Quintus didn't hesitate. With his spatha outstretched, he shouldered past the women, and threw himself at the strange figure. Quintus was a passable swordsman, had trained with gladiators as a boy, and kept himself fit in the gymnasia in Greece on his travels. He gave his anger and fear their head, and attacked the bandit with a flurry of blows, screaming aloud as he did so. The bandit parried each cut and thrust with ease, the eyes behind the mask almost seeming to twinkle in exhilaration. Tragedy retreated step by step, letting the storm blow itself out.

Then when Quintus started to fade, when his sword arm started to burn, and his breathing came in rasps, Tragedy stepped forward. He striped his blade across Quintus' thigh, causing him to buckle and sink to one knee, then he slashed his upper right arm, causing the sword to drop to the floor.

He looked down at the young man, barely more than a boy. Quintus' head was bowed, breathing hard, shoulders slumped in defeat. Tragedy raised his sword for a finishing thrust. Quintus lifted his head defiantly, looked his killer straight in the eye.

Tragedy hesitated, stared. Quintus refused to tremble before his imminent death. Tragedy lowered his sword.

A loud scream reached them, distant in the forest. A man's voice.

"For Jupiter's sake, have mercy."

It did not sound like Carbo.

Tragedy stared off into the woods. Then he started to run in the direction of the scream.

Quintus sagged, then bent forward and vomited.

18

Carbo's gladius descended like a blacksmith's hammer. Terrified eyes stared out wide from behind the laughing mask, and for a moment, Comedy seemed transfixed. At the last instant, he threw himself to one side, and Carbo's sword swished through the air, missing a cleaving blow to the skull by a hair's breadth. Carbo staggered, unbalanced as the momentum of the swing pulled him forward. For a moment, his flank was unguarded.

But Comedy had snagged his foot on a root, and he sprawled sideways. His sword flew out from his hand as he sought to break his fall. He landed on his shoulder, then rolled onto his back, winded.

Carbo regained his balance, and looked down at the fallen bandit. Incredibly, his mask still remained in place, curly grizzled hair poking over the top, the smile now seeming to Carbo like the hysterical grin of a madman. He saw tears form at the corner of the bandit's eyes, overflow. He lifted his sword.

"For Jupiter's sake, have mercy," cried Comedy.

Carbo paused, narrowed his eyes. Mercy. He considered it briefly.

"Why?" he asked.

Comedy opened his mouth, stuttered. "I…because…"

"Will you cease your banditry? Give up killing? Make amends to those you have wronged?"

"Yes, yes."

Carbo looked down and shook his head sadly. "I wish I could believe you. Experience tells me I can't. There are too many like you in the world."

He gripped his sword in two hands and stabbed it downwards towards Thyestes' chest.

A crashing sound came from the undergrowth to Carbo's side, with an anguished scream.

"Noooo!"

Carbo looked to the noise even as his sword came down. Comedy saw the distraction and pushed hard with his legs, twisting his body at the same time. The sword missed its mark, the bandit's heart, instead sinking deep into the side of his abdomen.

A tall, slim figure wearing a tragedy mask burst out from the trees, sword high, emitting an incoherent scream. Carbo pulled his sword out from the fallen bandit's guts, heaving it upwards with both hands using all his considerable strength in time to parry a tremendous downswing. Swords clashed, the shock running down Carbo's arm. He pushed hard, opening up some distance between him and the newcomer in the tragedy mask. He had only a moment to fear for the safety of the rest of the party, before Tragedy attacked him with a frenzy. Carbo desperately parried each cut and thrust, forced backwards by the fury of the attack. His arms started to burn, the beginnings of fatigue, and he wondered how long his opponent could keep this up.

The onslaught showed no sign of abating though. Carbo took another step backwards, and his foot got caught in a rabbit hole. As he tried to retreat further, his ankle twisted and he stumbled. He managed to keep upright, but when he tried to put weight on his left foot, pain spiked upwards and his leg buckled.

He kept his weight to his right, favouring the injured leg, but the reduced mobility quickly showed. Tragedy saw his opportunity, pressed his advantage, and

Carbo found it increasingly hard to defend himself. He watched Tragedy's eyes, looking for any sign of weakness or fear. There was none, just a cold fury.

Carbo was forced backwards by another flurry of blows, and suddenly his back was against a thick tree trunk, and he could go no further. His arm felt like lead, and he found himself cut, across the chest, across the shoulder, then through his leg. None of the blows were crippling, but blood was flowing, and he knew he would weaken quickly now.

His sword arm started to sag, and he could see triumph in the eyes behind the mask.

"Stop!" came a loud voice, "Or I will drop you where you stand."

Tragedy hesitated. His eyes remained locked on Carbo's, still full of hate and anger. But he paused his attack.

"I have an arrow aimed between your shoulders. Step backwards."

Tragedy did as he was told, moving out of Carbo's reach before turning. Carbo was now also able to see beyond Tragedy, to where the voice had come from.

Vespillo stood unsteadily, blood flowing freely down his head, holding Comedy's bow, arrow notched and bow drawn, ready to shoot.

Tragedy seemed to consider him for a moment, head to one side.

"You look ready to fall."

"Not before I have placed an arrow into your heart."

"I wonder. Are you that good a shot? You seem to know the basics of how to hold a bow, but you lack a certain finesse. And you seem to be having trouble focussing. How many of me can you see? Which one of me will you aim at?"

"Want to try me?"

"Maybe. You will only have the choice to get off one shot, then I will be on you, and you will be dead."

"Then why not just leave us. That way we know that neither of us will die."

Eyes narrowed behind the mask, and the fury was still there, cold, controlled, but waiting to be unleashed.

"I can't do that." He lifted his sword.

"Brother." The word came out as a groan.

Tragedy looked across to where Comedy lay, still on his back, hands clasped to the bloody wound in his abdomen.

"Brother," he said again. "Help me."

Tragedy hesitated. He looked from Vespillo to his fallen brother. The arrow was starting to tremble as the weak Vespillo's arm started to tire. But the wounded watchman stubbornly kept aim at the bandit's chest. Tragedy spat out a curse. He lowered his sword, sheathed it and walked over to Comedy. He went down on one knee, stroked his brother's hair tenderly. He looked down at the wound, and Carbo thought he saw a slight shake of his head.

"Don't worry, brother. I'm here. I'll take care of you."

Comedy lifted a hand up to his brother's face. "You always did."

Tragedy put a hand beneath his brother's shoulders, another beneath his legs, and lifted him with an effort. He regarded Vespillo and Carbo coldly for a moment. Then he turned and walked away, back the way they had come from, back bowed from the burden.

Vespillo waited until the bandits were out of sight, then let the bow go slack. The arrow dropped to the ground, and Vespillo collapsed.

# CHAPTER III

When the sounds of fighting had died down, Quintus led the girls tentatively back through the woods. Nearing the place he thought the noise had been coming from, he gestured to the women to wait, and he crept through the brush. Rufa and Severa were only able to see his back as he peered out, and when they saw his shoulders slump, they had no way of knowing if it was relief or despair. But he turned, smiled, and beckoned them forward.

Rufa and Severa rushed past him. They found a bleeding Carbo slumped beside a recumbent Vespillo. Rufa threw her arms around Carbo, Severa ran to Vespillo. The two men allowed their women to tend them.

Carbo looked across to Vespillo as Rufa examined his wounds, and looked at his ankle. Vespillo met his gaze and smiled.

"How by all Vulcan's fires do you get me into these scrapes?" asked Vespillo.

Carbo smiled back. "Wasn't it you that wanted to do something about the bandits?"

Vespillo touched his head. "Was it? I think this wound has affected my memory." He grinned, then winced as Severa pressed a rag firmly to his head.

Carbo yelped as well when Rufa manipulated his ankle, but she nodded and said, "Nothing broken, I think. It should mend quickly."

Quintus distributed water to the two injured men, then turned to tend to Marsia. Her head wound was fortunately superficial. She made no complaint as Quintus probed it, then cleaned it with a damp rag. Fabilla looked at the injured men, eyes wide, mouth open and round. Carbo saw her and gestured her over to him. When she reached his side Carbo gripped her hand.

"Vespillo and I are tough bastards. It takes more than a couple of bandits to finish us off. We are fine, and you are safe. Always."

She nodded, a little uncertain, but at least partially reassured. Rufa smiled at him, then set about cleaning up his wounds.

Quintus was anxious to get underway, and while Rufa and Severa wanted the injured men to rest more, Carbo agreed with Quintus.

"We should get moving. We don't know if they will be back, or whether there are more of them lurking. And we certainly don't want to be out when night falls."

Severa and Rufa glanced nervously at each other at this thought, and reluctantly conceded the point. Rufa helped Carbo to his feet and Severa supported Vespillo. Quintus stayed close to the uncomplaining Marsia, though she shrugged off his offer of help. They made their way through the woods, Carbo intermittently cursing the uneven ground as his ankle twisted on roots, fallen branches and burrows. Before long, they had left the woods behind and were back on their path.

Their progress was slow, but as the sky started to become darker, they reached a fork in the track. Quintus stopped and turned to the group.

"Your farm is that way," he said, gesturing to the right. "My father's villa is this way. This is where we part company."

Carbo limped up to Quintus, gripped his shoulder.

"Thank you. You saved them."

Quintus looked embarrassed. "I was terrified. I was sick."

Vespillo laughed. "I shat down my legs in my first battle, son. You did well."

Quintus smiled hesitantly, and Carbo nodded his agreement.

"When you have settled, will you come to visit me? All of you?" He looked around them, and Carbo noticed that his gaze lingered on Marsia. "You would be very welcome."

"We would love to," said Rufa. "Thank you from me too. From all of us." Severa nodded her agreement, then after a short moment, Marsia did too.

Quintus looked satisfied. "Thank you all too. I wouldn't have made it through alone."

Vespillo shook his hand, and Rufa and Severa embraced him in turn. Fabilla ran up to him and gave him a huge hug around the waist. Marsia looked at him, then cocked her head to one side and gave him a slight smile. He grinned back, then reddened a little. Severa and Rufa exchanged knowing glances, and Quintus noticed.

"Goodbye," he said hurriedly. "I hope to see you all soon." He set off down the path to his home without a backward glance.

Carbo watched him go for a moment, then turned to the path towards his farm.

"Well, let's see what sort of a sumptuous estate the army has provided me with." The group of travellers set off towards Carbo's farm.

Atreus dabbed a damp rag over Thyestes' pale cheeks and forehead. His brother's face was screwed up in agony, and he screamed at regular intervals, shrill and piercing, as spasms wracked his body. Atreus felt helpless anger suffuse him. He had cleaned the wound, put pressure on to stem the bleeding. He had stopped Thyestes dying immediately.

But he had only delayed the inevitable. He was well aware of the slow, inexorable death that a gut wound would bring. He fixed the image of his brother's slayer in his mind, and cursed him again and again. He prayed that Fortuna would turn her face from him, that Apollo would bring him terrible illness, that Mars would bring him violence and that Jupiter would spear him with lightning.

Thyestes vomited, profuse dark granules within the vomitus that Atreus had once been told signified bleeding into the stomach. The vomit splashed over both of them, and Atreus wiped his brother's mouth, neglecting the staining and stench clinging to his own clothing. The effort of vomiting sent another intense spasm through Thyestes, accompanied again by an agonised howl.

The stricken man gripped Atreus' arm tight. "Brother, help me."

Atreus could say nothing. He stared down into his brother's anguished face, and his heart felt like it would break.

"It hurts so much," said Thyestes, his voice weak, barely above a whisper now.

After a while, Thyestes lost consciousness, and Atreus felt a guilty relief that he did not have to watch his brother suffering any more. He pulled out the knife at his belt, and ran his finger along the edge, checking it had retained its sharpness. He looked down once more at his brother and swallowed.

Was there really no hope? Should he not give his brother every chance of life? He shook his head. The wound was not survivable. To keep him alive to the very end would be a cruelty. He let the point rest lightly over his brother's heart, then with both hands pressed down hard.

His brother's eyes flew open, hands grasping at Atreus' sleeves. The dying man locked his gaze on his brother, and Atreus saw incomprehension and betrayal reflected there. Thyestes tried to speak, then slumped backwards. His body convulsed, once, twice, three times. Gods would it not stop? Then all was still and quiet.

Atreus leaned forward and buried his head in his brother's chest, and let the wave of grief overwhelm him.

When, after some time, his sobbing had subsided, he sat up. His face was set, hard. He thought about his prayers, and shook his head.

No, the gods should stay their hands. Atreus would play Nemesis himself. He would be avenged for this. A lightning bolt, a stab to the throat from some street thief, some illness causing his heart to cease its beating, these were too quick, too good for that man. Atreus would make sure that he suffered properly.

The exhausted and wounded group of travellers reached Carbo's farm as the sun disappeared behind the dark clouds that rimmed the horizon. The farm seemed to grow mainly olive trees, which to Carbo's non-agriculturally educated mind, looked a little neglected, in need of some pruning. Some of the trees were bare, suggesting they had been harvested, but others were still full of fruit, a mix of green olives and the more mature brown and black ones. On the ground around these trees, windfallen fruit rotted.

A path led through the trees to the villa, if you could give it such a grand name. The farm consisted of about forty iugera of land, if Carbo remembered correctly. He had been granted it for service to the legions by Germanicus himself, the former owner, one Trigeminus, having died and left it to Germanicus in his will.

Forty iugera of established olive orchards should not be hard to farm for the two slaves he owned here, plus occasional hired help, Carbo reflected, and decided he would spend some time investigating the running of this property. First though, they all wanted food, drink, bathing facilities and a rest.

They were met at the door to the villa by a tall, thin, bent old man, with long white hair, and a large, black dog that growled and snapped at the end of a lead.

"Be quiet, Melanchaetes," said the old man in a quavery voice. Melanchaetes paid him no attention, and continued to bark at the newcomers, lips peeled back and saliva dripping from powerful jaws. Carbo gestured for the others to stay back, and walked ahead of them, approaching until he was just out of reach of the angry guard dog.

"Are you Theron?" he asked, raising his voice to be heard over the noise from the dog.

"I am, and who might you be?"

"I am Gaius Valerius Carbo, owner of this estate, and your Master. Now would you please tie up that dog somewhere safe, so we can come in?"

Theron's mouth dropped open. "Master, I'm so sorry, I didn't..."

Carbo never found out what Theron didn't do, because at that moment the leather collar around Melanchaetes' neck broke, and the huge dog bounded forward. In two swift steps it was on Carbo, leaping so its forepaws hit him square in the chest. Despite Carbo's bulk, the sudden attack took him by surprise, and he tumbled over backwards, the dog landing on him heavily. He managed to force an arm under the dog's throat, and with all his strength kept the snapping jaws away. Canine saliva dripped stickily over his face, and the stench of rotting meat breath made him gag. He dimly heard Theron calling the dog off in a high-pitched, weak voice which made not the slighest difference, heard Fabilla screaming, Vespillo calling that he was coming, though he knew his friend was too weak to help.

Carbo felt for his gladius, felt it trapped under his body. He shoved upwards with all his strength, and eased the weight of the dog just enough that he could draw the sword. He pulled it back, getting ready to plunge it sideways between the dog's ribs.

"No, stop!" came a voice, high but commanding. "Mel, here, now!"

Carbo hesitated, and then felt a sudden brief increase in weight as the dog bounded off him, front legs using his chest as a spring board, making all the air leave him with a whoosh.

Slowly he regained his feet, to see a young girl of around twelve with her arms wrapped around the dog's neck, while the monstrous beast wagged its tail and licked her face exuberantly.

Carbo glared at Theron, who wrung his hands with excruciated embarrassment. "Master, I'm so sorry, it was an accident, he thought you were an intruder, I…"

"You were about to kill him," said the girl accusingly.

Carbo turned to look at her. "Yes, I was. It seemed to be him or me."

"He was just protecting us. He didn't know you were a friend."

"I'm not a friend, I'm your Master. Assuming you are my steward's daughter, Thera."

"At your service, Master," she said, with a lightness in her voice that made him doubt that was the case. "Come here Mel, say hello properly."

The now docile dog trotted over obediently, and sat before Carbo, looking up at him suspiciously. The ears were drawn back, eyes narrowed, but his mouth, so close to ripping Carbo apart a few brief moments ago, was firmly closed.

"Well, say hello back," commanded Thera.

Carbo paused, wondering if the changeable hound would take his fingers off if he tried to pet it. Then a little hand reached out from behind him and patted the dog on the head.

"Fabilla, no!" gasped Rufa, but it was too late. The little red-headed girl emerged from behind Carbo and started fussing and cuddling the dog, who sat and accepted the attentions with muscular tail thumping against the ground, his chest puffed out as if with pride.

Thera looked at Carbo defiantly. "See? He is a sweetheart. You two just got off on the wrong foot."

Carbo raised a hand to stroke the dog's head, and Melanchaetes let out a growl, so deep and low that Carbo felt rather than heard it. He pulled his hand away and looked around. No one else had heard, and given how the dog was tolerating Fabilla pulling its cheeks and looking in its ears, he felt foolish to make any further fuss. He wondered, though, why Theron needed such a fierce beast to protect them, and resolved to keep a close eye on the dangerous hound.

Theron approached Carbo, and started to attempt to brush the mud and leaves from his clothes, but Carbo gestured him away.

"We've travelled a long distance, Theron. We want food, wine and fresh clothes. See to it." He looked at Thera. "And you, tie that dog up, then get some hot water for the ladies."

Thera gave a little bow, which Carbo couldn't help but think had a touch of irony about it. She gave Fabilla a little wink, who grinned shyly back at the older girl. Before Carbo could say anything more, Thera turned, tugging on the rope she had wrapped around Melanchaetes' neck, to get him trotting away meekly by her side.

Carbo looked around at his friends and adopted family. They all looked away, attempting with more or less success to conceal smirks. Carbo frowned.

"Oh yes, it's all highly amusing. Poor old Carbo nearly gets ripped to pieces. But at least it was entertaining."

Rufa came up to him and took his arm. "Come on grumpy, let's get you inside. We all need some food and some rest."

Theron led the way, and the group entered Carbo's villa.

Thera and Theron waited on them as they reclined for the evening meal. The triclinium was tiny compared to the dining rooms of the wealthy, or cosy, as Severa termed it. Marsia reclined with the others, eating the simple meal of roast chicken with bread, and of course olives, that Thera had cooked. Marsia had tried to insist that her place was serving with the other slaves, but Rufa would hear none of it, and had attended to Marsia's head wound herself. The wound looked like it had been made when she was clubbed by the hilt of the knife, which Marsia herself confirmed, and Carbo wondered why the bandit in the tragedy mask had not killed her outright. Probably wanted to sell her and make some profit, he mused.

Carbo looked over at Theron. "You aren't a very curious sort, are you?"

Theron looked surprised. "Master? What do you mean?"

Carbo gestured around him. "My wounds. Marsia's bruise. The cut on Vespillo's head. You don't want to know how they happened?"

Theron squinted and peered at Marsia and Vespillo. He walked up closer, and then his eyes widened.

"Oh my! Master, I'm sorry. My eyes, they are very dim these days."

Carbo looked more closely at Theron and realised that his pupils were indeed cloudy. Clearly the old man was not blind, but his vision must be quite restricted.

"How did your friends get these injuries, Master?"

"Bandits," spat Vespillo, twisting his mouth like he had a bad taste. "We were ambushed."

"Bandits?" gasped Theron. "In these parts?"

Carbo nodded. "Not two hours travel from here."

Theron shook his head. "We don't have much trouble with bandits around here."

Thera looked at him in surprise, opened her mouth, then shut it again. Carbo looked at her curiously.

"Thera?"

"Yes, master?" she said, not meeting his gaze.

"Do you know something about banditry around here?"

She looked at her father for help, but he remained impassive.

"People... talk. When I go to the market, I hear stories."

"Go on," said Carbo.

"They talk about men with masks," she said hesitantly. Theron shot her a warning glare.

"That was who we encountered," confirmed Carbo.

"We saw them off though," said Vespillo. "The one who thinks he is a comedy actor in a Greek play won't be accosting innocent travellers any time soon."

Thera looked surprised. "You have done what many others have not then. These men have been spreading terror around here for years. People robbed, murdered, disappearing."

"Why have the authorities done nothing?" asked Vespillo tetchily.

"They say they don't know where to look," said Thera. "But the farmers and merchants at the market say they just can't be bothered. I think maybe they are frightened."

"Ignore my daughter," said Theron. "She is young, and doesn't know what she is talking about."

Vespillo looked angry. "Why is everyone so scared of these men? The local authorities should send out parties to capture them. They should be crucified."

Theron shook his head. "Our leaders aren't interested in that sort of thing. The council just look after their own interests, and the stationarii seem to think they are only needed for crowd control."

Vespillo glared at Theron. Carbo put a hand on Vespillo's shoulder. "It isn't Theron's fault," he said gently.

Vespillo narrowed his eyes at Carbo, then relented. "I'm sorry. I'm tired, my head hurts like stink, and I'm embarrassed I got taken out by the first arrow that was fired." He took a deep drink of his wine. "Well, we are here now, safe. Let's enjoy our time here."

The dry clothes that Theron found for Vespillo, together with the wine and food, improved Vespillo's demeanour considerably, and he spent much of the meal teasing Fabilla, while Rufa looked on indulgently. Fabilla's giggles often split the room as Vespillo told another tall tale, or simply tickled her mercilessly.

When they had finished eating, Theron and Thera cleared away their plates. They all sat companionably, sipping at their wine, or grape juice in Fabilla's case, and picking at the dates that Thera had provided as after dinner snacks. After a while, Theron emerged from the kitchen.

"Is there anything else you or your guests require, master?" he asked.

Carbo indicated a couch. "Join us, Theron. Your daughter, too."

Theron and Thera exchanged surprised glances, then settled themselves onto the couch.

"Tell me about yourselves then, Theron. I know you by name, I was told you ran the place for Trigeminus before me. I know nothing of Thera."

Theron looked a little tongue-tied, clearly not used to company, let alone having to speak before this many guests.

"I'm not sure what you might find interesting, master."

"Anything you care to share, Theron."

Theron nodded and collected his thoughts. "Well, I was born into... into my current status. My parents were slaves before me, captured in Greece and brought to Rome when they were just children. Trigeminus purchased me when I was a young man, a little more physically capable than you see me now."

Carbo took in the man's slight frame and arthritis-twisted joints, and found his thoughts drifting towards his own mortality. Aching bones, a slower recovery from exertion and injury than in his youth, a general tiredness with life, not to mention the cuts he had received in the recent battle that stung like a swarm of bees every time he moved. He felt himself getting old.

Vespillo snorted. "Nothing wrong with you, man. A fine specimen. Carry on."

Theron smiled. "Well, I worked the farm for Trigeminus, but I had learned some letters and numbers from my parents, and Trigeminus saw my potential and promoted me to be steward of this…estate."

Calling the farm an estate was as appropriate as calling this house a villa, Carbo reflected, but he allowed Theron to continue without interruption.

"When Trigeminus was at his richest, this farm consisted of nearly two hundred iugera. He owned a domus in Nola, a fuller's in Abella and a warehouse in Rome to store his exports."

"I thought when he died, this house and its forty iugera were all he left in his will to Germanicus," said Carbo, puzzled.

"That is correct, master," said Theron. "Trigeminus fell on… hard times." He fell discreetly silent.

"What happened?" asked Vespillo, clearly not prepared to let Theron draw a veil over the matter.

Theron sighed, then continued. "Trigeminus' wife had died in childbirth, giving him a son. Raising the boy to be a good Roman was Trigeminus' only interest in life. But the gods took the boy away."

Rufa reached out and put a protective arm around Fabilla. Severa looked over to Vespillo, and squeezed his hand.

"Just a fall, when Trigeminus and his son were out hunting together," said Theron. "Not even a bad one, but he took a deep injury when a stick impaled his thigh. The wound festered, and the fever finished him." Theron shook his head. "Trigeminus was never the same again. He had nothing left to live for. He drank, gambled, whored around. He stopped investing in his properties, let them fall into disrepair. He sold off his assets to pay his debts, until all he possessed was this place. He died a few years ago."

"Did the drinking kill him?" asked Vespillo.

"Only the gods know. He went to bed one night in a stupor, and did not awake the next morning."

There was a momentary silence as everyone reflected on the sad story.

"So Trigeminus had left the place to Germanicus in his will?" asked Vespillo.

"Yes, in one of his more optimistic moments, he was considering moving to Rome, and attempting to better himself. He thought that Germanicus would make a good patron, if he informed him that he had changed his will to the general's benefit. He died not long after this."

"And Germanicus died just a few months after that," said Carbo, "but not before he had passed the place on to me, after a particularly brutal engagement."

"I have served you some ten years, master," said Theron, "to the best of my abilities, though I had never met you."

"I thank you for that," said Carbo, sincerely. "You have been a faithful servant, and I have never had reason to doubt the accuracy of your accounting."

Theron inclined his head to accept the praise.

"And Thera's mother?" asked Rufa gently. "She died too?"

Theron shook his head angrily. They waited for him to speak, but he said nothing.

Thera instead spoke up. "Trigeminus sold her," she said matter of factly.

Theron's face twisted, but Thera continued. "Mother was considerably younger than Father. Not that I remember her. But she was still young enough to be a valuable stake at the dicing table."

Tears now rolled freely down Theron's cheeks. "He never even told me what he had done. Not till they turned up, and dragged her away screaming for me to stop them from taking her away from Thera."

Rufa got up and walked over to Theron, and put an arm around his shoulder. The old man started to sob uncontrollably, burying his head in Rufa's chest. She stroked his bald pate as his body shook. Carbo and Vespillo looked at each other in surprise, unsure how to respond. Carbo opened his mouth to speak, but Rufa's look was forbidding, and he shut it again. He knew Rufa herself had been sold into slavery by her uncle to pay gambling debts, and Carbo could think of nothing he could say to ease the situation.

After a while, the sobs settled down. Thera moved to her father and gently prised him away from Rufa, helping him to his feet. Theron looked stricken with embarassment.

"Master, honoured guests, I'm so sorry, I don't know what…"

"Think nothing of it," said Carbo, in what he hoped was a sympathetic tone.

"Come, father," said Thera, guiding him towards the door. She glanced back at Carbo. "With your permission of course… master." The word came out as if it was a foreign word, unfamiliar on her tongue. Carbo realised that for all the life she could remember, she had never had to answer to anyone but her father.

"Of course, Thera. And then you can retire yourself as well. We will make our own sleeping arrangments."

"Thank you," said Thera, and led her father away.

An uncomfortable silence settled on the room. Fabilla looked from adult to adult, aware that something sad had been related, but not quite able to grasp the full significance of the story she had heard. After a moment, she blurted out, "Mother, may I sleep in Thera's room tonight?"

Rufa looked at her, taken aback, then let out a light laugh. "Of course, if Thera doesn't mind."

Fabilla looked confused. "But you can just tell her to let me, can't you? She is a slave."

Rufa's expression darkened. "As were you, a few short weeks ago. Have you forgotten so quickly?"

Fabilla looked crestfallen. "I'm sorry, mother, I didn't think."

Rufa tousled her hair. "Go, find her. But make sure you ask permission. I will see you in the morning." Fabilla gave Rufa a kiss and rushed off, then came rushing back, and threw her arms around Carbo. "Good night mother, good night Carbo. I love you both." And she was gone.

The solemn atmosphere broken, the small group continued to drink and chat. But the events of the day soon caught up with them, and very soon Vespillo and Severa made their apologies and left. Marsia looked exhausted too, and Carbo dismissed her for the night.

"Just you and I," said Rufa, a mischievous smile on her lips. "A little time alone together."

Carbo looked at her with mock horror. "Do you really think I am up to anything energetic? After today?"

She laughed, and kissed him firmly on the lips. Carbo encircled his arms around her, held her close as he kissed her deeply. As she took his hand and led him towards the master bedroom, he reflected, as he so often did, how this woman had saved him, made him whole again. He didn't know where he would be without her.

# CHAPTER IV

"Welcome to my little home," said Quintus.

Carbo gaped, looking around him in amazement. They were only in the atrium, but it was still easily the most spectacular room he had ever been in. The walls were lined with beautiful bronze statues of fauns and nymphs, marble busts on ornate pedestals and delicately carved statuettes of male and female youths carrying pitchers of water and sheaves of wheat. The impluvium was deep, wide and immaculately clean, the surface of the water reflecting the sky above. It was surrounded by eleven statues of what looked like satyrs, though they appeared more horse-like than goat-like.

Quintus noticed Carbo examining them. "Sileni," he explained. Carbo had once seen a comedy that involved a drunken Silenus, the tutor to Dionysus, and supposed these figures were related in some way, but decided not to reveal his ignorance by enquiring further. He looked at the walls, covered with bright, colourful rustic scenes. Even to the rough ex-centurion, the room was a place of beauty. Having risen to hold high rank in his legion, he had hobnobbed with his noble and patrician commanders, and even been invited to dine with them. But the field quarters of a military commander, no matter how wealthy, could never compete with a purpose-built leisure villa in Italy. Even a sumptuous domus in Rome, like the priestess Elissa's, where Rufa had been a slave, did not have the space in that crowded city to spread out into such a palatial dwelling as this.

Rufa gripped his hand as she too stared. She let her fingers trail over a bronze statue of a faun playing pipes, and Carbo smiled as he saw the look of wonder in her eyes. Then she wrinkled her nose, and Carbo followed her gaze. He saw the cause of her disgust, a bronze statue of a goat lying on its back, legs in the air, while Pan copulated with it. The statue left nothing to the imagination, and he raised his eyebrows at Quintus. Quintus just shrugged his shoulders. "My father has rather… eclectic tastes. I'm told this statue is considered the height of sophisticated humour. Besides, Pan is a god. Sex with animals, that's just what they do isn't it?"

Carbo recalled that the Greeks believed that Jupiter had seduced women while in the form of a swan, a satyr and a golden shower. And as for the origin of the minotaur… He shook his head and thanked Aphrodite that his tastes were more conventional.

"This way," said Quintus. They followed him into a beautiful peristylium. Carbo glimpsed various rooms leading off the peristylium, some of which he couldn't guess the purpose of, others such as a large tablinum decorated with frescoes and busts, a bit more obvious. Quintus led them through an exit in one corner of the peristylium and Carbo came to a halt, stunned.

They were in a garden, fully enclosed by a portico colonnaded by dozens of fluted columns made from stuccoed brickwork. It must have measured over two hundred yards, end to end. Down the centre ran a long ornamental pond, full of lilies and fish, with a fountain at the far end in the shape of a water nymph. Intricate topiary took the form of birds and wild animals. More busts and marble statues rested in recesses along the walls. There was a delicate, fresh fragrance in the air of flowers and dew. The sky had cleared, the weather no longer foul as it had been a few days before, and the autumn sun, shining down at an oblique angle, cast aesthetic shadows.

"This must be what Elysium is like," whispered Rufa. Carbo couldn't help but agree with her. He had seen more of the world than her, but this was beyond anything he had experienced.

Quintus smiled indulgently. "Please, take a seat. What would you like to drink? Some wine? Fruit juice?"

"Wine for me, please," said Carbo. Rufa said nothing, still staring around her. "Rufa?" prompted Carbo.

"What? Oh, sorry. Anything, thank you."

Quintus flicked his fingers, and Carbo noticed how he didn't even turn to check the slave he had summoned had hurried to his side. This was a young man born to privilege, and used to obedience, Carbo realised. A tall, reedy slave, little more than a boy, bowed to Quintus.

"Yes, master?"

"Three cups of wine please. Falernian for our honoured guests. And take their cloaks."

"Of course, master." He took the light cloaks from Rufa and Carbo and hurried away.

"Falernian?" said Carbo. "Really, that's not necessary."

"Don't be absurd. We have fought together. Nearly died together. You are my friends and guests. Now please, be seated. My father and brother will want to meet you soon."

Rufa and Carbo sat next to each other, and Rufa's hand slipped into Carbo's lap, where he gripped it reassuringly. He knew she felt overawed and out of her element. To some extent, he did as well, but hoped he was hiding it better. Their wine arrived quickly, in beautifully engraved silver cups.

Carbo tried to remember the etiquette that had been passed down to him from the patrician legates and tribunes that he had served with. He looked into the cup and swirled it, watching the amber-brown liquid move. He took a sniff, noting the delicate scent, and then took a small sip. He let the wine rest on his tongue for a little, and although it was sharp, there was none of the roughness he was used to. He swallowed and nodded at Quintus with a smile.

"Twenty year old dry Faustian Falernian, mixed in equal measures with spring water. Does it meet with your approval?"

Carbo took a deeper draught. "It certainly does."

Rufa, who had been watching Carbo, now shyly took a drink. She savoured it, swallowed then grinned at Carbo.

Quintus took a seat himself, drinking and chatting to his two guests about the improvement in the weather, the countryside, how they were settling in at Carbo's farm. Despite the gulf in their classes, Carbo found Quintus to be a considerate host, and he found himself quickly growing at ease, as his respect and liking of the young nobleman grew.

A loud voice broke their conversation. "Please stand for Gaius Sempronius Blaesus."

The man who emerged from the house immediately struck Carbo as being a little frail. He was tall, with a rim of short-cropped white hair around a bald pate. He stooped, and he was supported at the elbow by an athletic looking young male slave, the one who had announced him. He walked with short, measured steps down the garden towards Carbo and Rufa, appearing stiff and arthritic. Carbo sympathised, twenty-five years in the legions made him feel like an old cart that had been on the roads too long. This man must have fifteen years on him, but he doubted he had trod the cobbles in his caligae with sixty pounds of legionary's pack on his back, or gone hand to hand with battle-maddened Germans, so was likely better preserved than Carbo.

Carbo and Rufa stood, and Quintus sprang to his feet with a beaming smile.

"Father." He walked straight up to the older man and gave him a crushing hug, and then a kiss on both cheeks. Blaesus seemed to wince a little at the strong embrace.

"Quintus, a very good day to you." His accent was refined, his voice a little high and weak. He turned from Quintus, and looked at Carbo. His eyes narrowed, and a shadow seemed to pass across his face.

"Carbo, this is my father, Gaius Sempronius Blaesus," said Quintus, brightly. "Father, This is Gaius Valerius Carbo. The man I told you about, who saved us from the bandits. Former pilus prior in the XIIIth Gemina. Lately of Rome. And a hero."

Blaesus gave Carbo an appraising look. "I see." He extended his hand and Carbo shook it, noticing the weak strength in the grip, as Blaesus continued. "You are very welcome, y… y… y… young man."

The stutter took Carbo by surprise and he glanced involuntarily at Quintus. Quintus gave a slight shake of the head, keeping his expression neutral. Carbo quickly turned back to Blaesus.

"Thank you for honouring us by allowing us to visit your wonderful home. Your son does you credit, he also fought honourably and well when it was needed."

Blaesus gripped Carbo's hand tighter at that, and Carbo was surprised at the real strength suddenly there. Blaesus' eyes seemed to flash. Then the hand dropped away, and Blaesus looked down.

"That is good to hear. Too often my son has been a di…di…disappointment."

Quintus' smile vanished, and there was an uncomfortable silence, broken only by birdsong and the tinkling of the fountains. Blaesus sighed and shook his head, then let the slave guide him to a bench. He settled himself down stiffly.

"So, Carbo. Tell me what brings you to these parts?"

"Carbo owns a farm nearby…" began Quintus, but Blaesus held up a hand, cutting Quintus short.

"Carbo," he said again, emphasising the name. "What brings you to these parts?"

Carbo flicked a glance at Quintus, who looked crestfallen. "I…ah…own a farm nearby."

"Really," said Blaesus. "I didn't know that."

"Well, no," said Carbo, feeling disconcerted. Was this how noble families always dealt with each other? He knew that the father was the head of the family, the paterfamilias, with absolute power of life and death over everyone in his household. But he had always assumed it was more of a concept than an actual thing. He thought that fathers still loved their sons. Blaesus was showing little evidence of love. "I have never visited it before. I inherited it from my commander."

"Hmmm, that place used to belong to Tri…Tri…Tri…" Blaesus stopped, making a disgusted face. He flicked his fingers and the slave offered him a cup of wine.

As he drank, Quintus helpfully supplied the name. "Trigeminus, father."

"I know who it was," snapped Blaesus. He took another deep drink from the cup, then spat. "This is a rather poor vintage of Falernian, boy."

"Yes, master," said the slave.

"Well, take it away and get something at least halfway decent."

The slave bowed, and hurried away with the cup.

"Should we have the slave punished, father?" Rufa had remained quiet throughout all this, but she looked down at the mention of punishment of the slave. Blaesus, though, ignored the question.

"And you, dear," said Blaesus, addressing Rufa. "You are our hero veteran's wife?"

"No, master, I'm just…"

"Just his fancy woman, huh? And I'm not your m… m…, I don't own you."

"No, master, sir, um…"

Blaesus let out a low laugh.

"Rufa is a freedwoman, father," said Quintus, still trying to be helpful. Now it was Carbo's time to throw Quintus an annoyed glance, but Quintus seemed not to notice.

"That explains it. And not long freed, unless I am much mistaken."

"Rufa was born free, and is free now," said Carbo firmly. "I believe that is all anyone needs to know about her."

Blaesus gave Carbo a long, appraising glance, and for a moment Carbo feared he had crossed a line, insulting the nobleman. But Blaesus merely nodded.

"Very well." He looked around. "Where is that s…slave? Quintus, is it time for dinner yet?"

"I'm sure it must be, father. Shall we head for the triclinium?"

"Yes. Take my arm boy. Carbo, Rufa, please join us for dinner."

Carbo inclined his head as he stood. "It would be an honour."

Blaesus took the central place at the top couch, and invited Carbo to take the place on the same couch to his right. To Carbo's surprise though, Quintus was relegated to the couch that ran at a right angle to the top one. He settled himself in on Carbo's right hand side, and when Carbo shot him a questioning glance, he simply gave a resigned shrug. One of the slaves ushered Rufa to the left couch, so she reclined opposite Quintus.

Blaesus gestured at the slave who had assisted him earlier.

"Pharnaces, food and drink."

Pharnaces bowed, his dark, wavy hair flopping forward as he did so, then hurried to give orders to the serving girls to fetch drink, and organised the attendant male slaves to start serving food. Carbo noticed that some of them gave him resentful looks, and he wondered at the youthful Pharnaces' apparent position of responsibility. Could he be the old man's lover?

As the serving girls arrived with wine and water, Blaesus stared pointedly at the empty space next to him.

"Pharnaces, where is my son?"

Pharnaces glanced at Quintus. "You mean, Publius?"

"Of course I mean Publius," snapped Blaesus.

"I… do not know, master."

"Please request his presence."

"Is uncle Lucius joining us tonight?" asked Quintus.

"No," said Blaesus, harshly. "He has gone away. A trip."

"A trip?" said Quintus, looking surprised. "Where? For how long?"

Blaesus ignored him. "Pharnaces. Immediately!"

Pharnaces bowed and hurried out. An uncomfortable silence fell over the room, broken only by the sound of Blaesus drinking deeply from his cup of wine. Quintus sipped with more restraint, and Carbo followed Quintus' example. Rufa looked anxious, separated as she was from Carbo, and Carbo gave her what he hoped was a reassuring smile.

Presently, another young man entered the room. He was tall, broad-shouldered, with curly, dark hair like Quintus. Carbo estimated him to be in his mid twenties.

"Publius," said Blaesus, and Carbo saw the man smile for the first time, a broad beam full of affection. Publius embraced his father, and settled himself in the space Blaesus had reserved for him.

"I'm sorry I am late, father. I was exercising, and I needed to bathe."

"Of course, of course," said Blaesus. "It is no inconvenience. We have only just settled ourselves."

Publius looked around the room, and his gaze settled on Carbo, narrowing his eyes. "You must be this Carbo that Quintus keeps gushing about."

"Pleased to meet you," said Carbo, carefully.

Publius turned to Rufa, who reclined to his left. "And who is this beauty?" He smiled broadly and took her hand, kissing it gently. Rufa looked like a rabbit hypnotised by a fox.

"This is Rufa," said Carbo. "She is my…" Jupiter, what was she? She wasn't his slave, and she wasn't his wife, not yet. He couldn't call her his lover. Feeling a surge of jealousy as the young man looked into Rufa's eyes, he used the same term as Quintus. "She is my… freedwoman."

Even to his own ears, it sounded weak, and the frown that Rufa shot his way made his heart sink. She was so much more to him than he knew how to describe. Soon, when the moment was right, he would ask her to marry him.

Carbo felt completely out of his depth. It had seemed like a good idea, when Quintus had invited them. Meet an influential local dignitary, maybe make a powerful friend, possibly a patron, that would make life easier. And maybe find out more about the local banditry. How safe were they here really?

But the sumptuous setting, the delicately flavoured, incredibly tasty food, presented in styles he had never encountered, the clearly fabulously wealthy host, all unsettled him. He couldn't even reach a hand under the table to receive a reassuring touch from Rufa. Publius was still favouring her, making suggestions as to what morsels she should try next, even feeding her, and what was worse, Rufa was smiling and laughing at his comments. After a couple of cups of wine, Carbo was feeling a little less diffident, and decided to try to initiate some conversation himself.

"So, um, sir…"

"Call me Blaesus," interrupted Blaesus.

"Thank you… Blaesus. You have a beautiful home here."

"You are most kind," said Blaesus.

"You have a house in Rome, too?" Carbo was aware that many of the super-rich elite kept town houses on the Palatine and holiday homes in the countryside.

"No, Rome is a stinking cess pit. I never go there."

"But, you don't attend meetings of the Senate?"

"I'm not a S...Senator," snapped Blaesus. "Firstly, I have no interest in the affairs of state. Rome can burn to the ground, for all I care about her. Secondly, even if I did care about Rome, why would I want to be a Senator? Senators have had no power since before Caesar's time. Rome is run by one man."

"Tiberius," said Carbo, nodding.

"No, you idiot," said Blaesus, sounding exasperated. "Sejanus. That snake, running the Empire like it was his own personal kingdom."

Quintus looked concerned. "Father, I don't think you should talk like that."

Blaesus looked surprised. "Do you think we have an informant amongst us? Maybe our guest Carbo here, whom you hold in such high regard? Your brother? Pharnaces?"

Quintus looked down, chastened, while Publius grinned at his brother's discomfort.

Carbo tried again. "You have lived here a long time then?"

"I quit Rome some twenty years ago. Soon after Quintus here killed my wife."

Quintus reddened but said nothing.

"He was too big, or too twisted, or something wrong. They r...r...ripped her apart, getting him out. If I had known, I would have sacrificed him in a heartbeat. But the doctors told me they could save both."

Blaesus shook his head. "So much loss." A tear gathered in the corner of one of his eyes and rolled down his cheek. Then he looked up again and glared at Carbo. Carbo looked down, embarrassed at the display of grief. Quintus too looked close to tears.

"I'm sorry," said Carbo, tentatively. "You aren't tempted to go back to Rome? Nola seems too small for someone of your wealth and rank."

Blaesus fixed him with a steely stare. Then shook his head derisively. There was a dragging silence.

Carbo decided to change the subject.

"We ran into some bandits on our travels," he said.

"So my son tells me," said Blaesus.

"I got the impression that they have been causing a lot of trouble around here lately. Is the region safe?"

Blaesus shrugged. "The locals and the travellers seem to have their loin cloths twisted about something. Fuss about nothing as far as I can see. There is always a low level of banditry in the countryside. It is as inevitable as the fact that the poor stink and the rich are corrupt. So, you helped my Quintus out of a hole? Trust him to need someone to save him."

"Quintus fought bravely," said Carbo, eyeing Quintus.

Blaesus grunted dismissively. Carbo felt a surge of anger.

"He took wounds," he said, trying to keep his voice steady. "To the front. Protecting ones I care about."

Blaesus looked at him with renewed interest. "You have people you care about, Carbo?"

Carbo was taken aback by the question. "Of course. Don't you?"

Blaesus shook his head. "Sometimes, I wonder if I really care about anything. Have you heard of Hegesias of Cyrene?"

"I'm afraid my schooling was quite limited."

"More a man of action than learning, I suppose. Hegesias said that happiness is impossible to achieve in life. Wealth, poverty, freedom, slavery, none of it matters. It brings no more pleasure than pain. Therefore the only worthwhile pursuit in life is to be free of pain and sorrow."

Carbo thought of the pain and sorrow he had experienced, and the happiness with Rufa it had led him to.

"I don't think I can agree with that. Happiness is possible."

"I think you delude yourself. So who is it you care about?"

Carbo shot Rufa an involuntary glance, and she blushed and looked down. Blaesus looked between the two lovers, a thoughtful expression on his face.

"I'm prying. S… say no more, Carbo."

Carbo nodded, grateful to extricate himself from the embarrassing subject. Rufa gave him a surreptitious wink, and Carbo grinned inwardly. He would be alone with her again soon, and his heart leapt at the thought.

After that the conversation became fragmented. Blaesus grew quiet, and drank steadily. Publius too became drunk, and started to grow even more forward with Rufa. Carbo watched the two of them, wondering whether to intervene, but Rufa was no longer flirting back, and was firmly deflecting both his suggestive remarks and his wandering hands.

The courses grew ever more extravagant, to the point of absurdity. A whole roast pig was brought in, spit so it was in a standing position, and when its belly was slit by the chef, sausages tumbled out, mimicking intestines. Fried sow's nipple, camel's heels and flamingo's tongues were followed by cheesecake and fruits drenched in honey. Soon Carbo was feeling bloated and nauseous, while next to him, Blaesus picked at the banquet idly, eating a little and leaving much.

Pharnaces organised the entertainment, starting with a tumbler and a pair of jugglers, which barely drew a glance from Blaesus. Two dwarfs came out next, and proceeded to tell jokes.

"I was beaten by my father yesterday," said the first.

"Why was that?" asked the second.

"He caught me sleeping with my grandmother."

"Was he very cross?"

"Yes, but I said, why are you so angry? You have slept with my mother many times. I have only slept with yours once."

Publius guffawed and slapped Rufa on the shoulder who winced. Carbo smiled thinly, it was an old joke. Quintus looked shocked. Blaesus picked up a fig and inspected it like the comedians weren't even there.

Next Pharnaces sent slave girls in, clad only in tassled skirts, to dance and twirl. When even this raised no interest from his master, Pharnaces summoned the final act, a hunchback and a bearded lady, who proceeded to have noisy sex in front of them all. Blaesus puffed out his cheeks and let out a sigh. The hunchback loudly emptied himself into the hirsute woman, and then Pharnaces hustled them away.

Carbo felt some relief that the entertainment was finished, and sipped with restraint at his wine. Quintus chatted to Carbo about Nola, olive growing and banditry, and questioned him about life in the legions. Carbo listened attentively, though volunteered little of his own past. The evening dragged and Carbo wished the time away until he could escape back to his own environment, and feel in control once more.

Finally, Blaesus rose, drunkenly. "I have partaken of enough pleasure for this evening. Wine, food, and…" he looked at Carbo, "interesting company. Pharnaces. Accompany me."

Carbo stood respectfully as Pharnaces helped Blaesus out of the room.

"I'm for bed too," said Publius. "Carbo, would you mind if I asked your freed-woman to accompany me?"

Carbo opened his mouth to speak, but Rufa smoothly interjected.

"I'm afraid I have commitments elsewhere."

Publius frowned. "I insist."

Carbo clenched his jaw, his fist closing involuntarily.

"You may insist all you like, young sir," said Rufa, giving Publius a placating smile. "But I am afraid my patron, the one who freed me, has first claim on me. And he looks like he wants to leave."

Carbo's face was thunderous, but when he opened his mouth, Rufa gave him a stern look. He closed his mouth, swallowed, then nodded.

"Rufa is right, the hour is late, and we have some way to walk home."

"Of course," interjected Quintus before his brother could reply. "I will escort you as far as our boundaries."

Publius looked as if he would take the matter further, and he locked his gaze with Quintus. Quintus appeared to shrink back, but did not break the stare. Publius shook his head, and spat on the floor in disgust.

"Then goodnight to you all." He pointed at a young female slave. "You, come to my bed chamber. And bring your sister."

The girl looked stricken, but bowed and went to do her master's bidding. Publius stormed out without a backward glance.

Quintus sighed and let his shoulders slump as he, Rufa and Carbo found themselves suddenly alone apart from a single attentive slave.

"I should have known better than to invite you here," he said

Carbo bristled. "I'm sorry that we were a disappointment. We have not had the benefit of your cultured upbringing."

"No, no," said Quintus hastily. "You misunderstand. I am the one who is apologising. My father and brother, they can be challenging company. I believe my father has never been the same since he left Rome."

"He left after you were born? After your mother died?"

Quintus nodded. "Around then. One of the older slaves told me a long time ago, that father and uncle Lucius had left Rome suddenly, bringing Publius and me here when I was still a baby. We have lived here ever since."

"And you don't know why?" asked Rufa.

"He will never talk about it. He's a moody old bastard at the best of times, and that is one subject guaranteed to raise his temper." Quintus stood. "Come, as you say, it is getting late. I will walk with you a way." He flicked his finger towards the attending slave. "Their cloaks."

The slave bowed, and fetched the cloaks, helping them put them on. Quintus showed them out, and they walked together in silence down the cobbled path that led to the track towards Carbo's farm. When they reached a stone marking the boundary of Blaesus' grounds, he offered his hand to Carbo.

"Thank you for coming. I don't suppose you will want to come again."

"It seems… awkward," said Carbo. Quintus looked despondent.

"But you are most welcome to visit us," said Rufa. "For as long as we are staying."

Quintus brightened.

"Really?"

"Of course," said Carbo, shaking his hand firmly. "Comrades in arms are always welcome."

Quintus grinned and returned the shake enthusiastically, then gave Rufa a light kiss on the cheek.

"I will see you soon then," he said, and turned to walk back to his father's villa.

Carbo let out a breath as he found himself alone with Rufa. He shook his head, and Rufa laughed, a light, beautiful laugh that caused his heart to miss a beat.

"You weren't tempted by Publius' proposal then?"

"Of course I was," said Rufa. "Young, handsome, wealthy."

Carbo frowned at her. "So why did you turn him down?" he asked gruffly.

"Unfortunately he was also a complete horse's backside."

Carbo laughed. "Besides," she continued. "I had a better offer."

She proffered Carbo her arm, and he took it, smiling as he pulled her close. They started to walk back to Carbo's farm.

CHAPTER V

Carbo sighed and looked up at the sun, trying to judge the time from its position in the sky. It was a bright, fresh, late October day, without a cloud above them, and though the blue sky gave Carbo's spirits a lift, they were currently being thoroughly dampened by the interminable shopping trip with Rufa.

"How about these ones?" she asked, holding up a pair of copper earrings.

"How are they different from the last ones?" asked Carbo wearily.

Rufa wrinkled her nose at him. "Because, these ones have a left-hand twist in the pendant portion. The last ones had a right-hand twist."

"Of course, so unobservant of me."

"Don't be such a grouch. Which ones?"

"These ones," said Carbo, gesturing to the earrings she held.

"But you said you liked the other ones!"

"Fine, the other ones then."

"Now you are just making it up."

Carbo exchanged an exasperated look with the market seller, then gazed around him. It was a nundinae, a market day in Nola. At dinner the previous evening, when Rufa had told Fabilla what they were doing, and after she had complained about not being allowed to come, she had asked why it was called a nundinae. Vespillo had explained the name came from the nine day week. Fabilla then asked how many days there were in two weeks. Vespillo thought about it for a moment, then told her seventeen. Fabilla had furrowed her brow, then declared that in that case there could only be eight and a half days in one week. Vespillo had looked confused at this, and his attempted explanation of the inclusive method of counting that Romans used was just met with the flat comment from Fabilla, "That doesn't make any sense." Carbo chuckled to himself now at the memory of Vespillo's offended expression.

The town forum was packed with market stalls, and crammed with traders and buyers. It was nothing compared to Rome, the density of the crowd, the variety of goods, even the intensity of the stench were all less in this smaller conurbation. But there was more than enough to keep Rufa occupied. Hawkers screamed to make themselves heard, advertising dresses in the latest fashions from Rome, exotic spices and jewellery, as well as the more mundane fare from the surrounding farms, olives, cabbages, onions, pears, grapes, cheese and bread.

The sun was past its zenith, Carbo was sure, and he was starting to get hungry as well as footsore. He wondered why it was so much more tiring accompanying a woman on a shopping trip than marching with the legions. He thought about attempting to persuade Rufa to stop for some lunch, then saw her face light up as she spied some new trinket. Despite himself, he smiled, and felt warm inside, watching the woman he loved enjoying herself.

Something caught his attention, a movement at the corner of his eye. He turned, sure that someone had been watching them, but he was surrounded by people, and there was no one that stood out as he scanned the crowd.

Suddenly uneasy, he put his hand to his gladius. This wasn't Rome, there was no law in the provinces about being armed, and for travellers from the countryside to the town, it was positively encouraged. Especially, he suspected, in Nola. The familiar hilt felt reassuring in his palm. He turned his attention back to Rufa, who had not noticed his sudden alertness.

"I think it's time to make a choice, Rufa, so we can stop bothering this poor man."

Rufa pulled a face at him, then selected the first set of copper earrings.

"May I have these ones please, Carbo?"

The jeweller named a price which caused Rufa to gasp.

"Oh Carbo, I'm sorry they are too expensive. Never mind."

"Don't worry," said Carbo. "I'm sure I can beat him down." He looked at the jeweller. "Or beat him up," he said pointedly.

The jeweller immediately halved the price, and with a little more haggling, they agreed a sum. Carbo paid him and gave the earrings to Rufa. He helped her to put them on, and she shook her head to make them swing from her earlobes, smiling broadly. She put her arms around him, and kissed him firmly, then hugged him. As her arms wrapped around his neck, he saw a man in the crowd, a diagonal scar across one cheek, clearly watching them. When the man noticed Carbo had seen him, he retreated back into the throng.

The nagging feeling of worry grew. He gently extricated himself from Rufa's embrace.

"Come on," he said. "Let's find a tavern that looks like it doesn't serve roast rat and piss." As they walked away he looked back, but the scarred man was no longer in sight.

He wasn't sure he had accomplished the first part of his mission as he looked down at the shapeless chunks of meat in the stew he had just bought, and when he sipped the cheap wine, he was sure he had failed the second part.

Rufa chewed some tough, stale bread heavily, trying to look like she was enjoying it. Carbo watched her, feeling a contentment inside her. He had been impressed with how she had handled herself a few evenings before, at the dinner with Blaesus. It was such a short space of time since she had been a slave, her life and the life of her daughter in terrible danger. Yet already, he was seeing the return of the vivacious, self-assured, independent girl he had known when she was the free child of his commanding officer.

At night, when everything was quiet, and there were no distractions to occupy her mind, he sometimes caught her trembling, or found her cheeks wet with tears when he kissed her. He knew that feeling, the way the memory of terror could creep up on you unexpectedly, and overwhelm you. He knew also that it was possible to get past it, or at least to cope with the feelings. He was starting to, with Rufa's help.

The tavern was packed, despite the poor fare. Presumably the market day improved custom for all the taverns and guest houses. He couldn't think of a reason for this place to be so busy, unless everywhere else was full. He looked around at the clientele. An unremarkable mix of townsfolk and farmers, likely both slaves and free, though they were hard to tell apart. He couldn't see the man who had been watching earlier, nor anyone else paying them undue attention, and he wondered if he had been over-reacting.

Rufa pushed her bowl away, less than half eaten.

"I'm feeling rather full today," she said. "I think the banquet at Blaesus' is still sitting heavily."

Carbo smiled at her, both of them knowing that no matter how filling the banquet, too much time had passed since then for it to be a factor, and in fact it was the atrocious food that had dented her appetite.

"I'm sorry," said Carbo. "I don't think you would get food this bad, even in the Subura."

Rufa laughed. "Don't worry. I will buy some vegetables and some fresh rabbit today, and cook us something tasty."

"You don't have to cook, you know. We do have slaves to do that."

"A German barbarian, an old man and a young girl. Which of those do you think cooks better than me?"

Carbo shook his head, knowing this was an argument he couldn't win.

"Come on then," he said with as much enthusiasm as he could muster. "Let's do some more shopping."

Rufa smiled happily, and they left their partly consumed meals behind and headed back to the market. Rufa browsed the meat and vegetable stalls. They found a place with dozens of rabbits strung up by their back legs. Rufa prodded and sniffed four plump specimens, pronounced them fresh and haggled a good price with the seller. She then found stalls selling carrots, onions, cabbages and courgettes, and they rapidly filled the two cloth bags they had brought with them. Carbo started to feel like a pack mule as the bags got heavier.

Finally Rufa seemed satisfied, and at Carbo's pleading, agreed that they could return home. Carbo looked around, suddenly aware that he had lost his bearings in this unfamiliar place. He took Rufa's hand, and walked purposefully in a direction he hoped was correct, as he looked out for a familiar landmark. The thick crowds slowed his progress, and he became frustrated. His height allowed him to see over most of the crowd, but the densely packed market stalls made it hard to see any buildings.

Carbo squeezed between two booths, one selling farm tools and one selling clay pots, and found himself in a small square, rimmed with stalls and carts stocked high with produce.

Lounging against a stall, a dozen yards from them, were three men. Carbo was instantly alert. They looked out of place. They were showing no interest in buying goods, nor were they attempting to sell anything themselves. His hand moved to the hilt of his gladius. One of the men looked up, and Carbo recognised the man with the diagonal scar who had been watching them earlier. Carbo put a hand on Rufa's upper chest, and stopped her. She looked at him questioningly.

"Let's go back," he said to her in a low voice.

The three men started to approach them, and Carbo turned to go back the way they had come. Behind them, three more men had appeared, and they stood shoulder to shoulder, blocking the exit from the little square. Curious glances from passing marketgoers turned into alarmed stares. The square suddenly emptied of stall holders and customers, until only Carbo and Rufa and the six men remained. A few of the braver and more curious citizens peeped over the tops of the stalls and carts from a safe distance.

"Carbo," said Rufa, panic creeping into her voice. "What's happening?"

"I don't know. Stay calm. They probably just want our money."

The three men blocking their exit behind them were not moving, so he turned back to the first three who continued to advance on them.

"What do you want?" he shouted. "You're making a mistake if you are looking for a fight."

The three men stopped a short distance in front of them, spreading out so they were completely boxed in. Six men, varying sizes, but all looking tough, all carrying a weapon of some sort, a club or a knife.

"You may take me down," said Carbo, feeling anger rise inside, "But some of you will die too. Walk away. It's not worth it."

The three men in front of him suddenly looked past him and smiled. Carbo turned to see what had caught their attention. The men blocking the exit parted, and allowed two more men to come through. The newcomers wore masks.

Tragedy.

And Comedy.

Carbo stared in disbelief at the two masked men.

"You," he said, looking at Comedy. "I killed you. You couldn't have survived that wound."

Comedy was silent, the grinning mask giving nothing away. Tragedy regarded Carbo steadily as well, eyes unblinking through the eyeholes. Carbo drew his gladius and pointed it towards them. Beside him, Rufa was breathing raggedly, and Carbo recognised the symptoms of an attack of panic gripping her.

"Get out of my way," said Carbo, keeping his voice calm, with an effort.

"Do you understand loss, soldier?" said Tragedy. As before the mask muffled the voice, the words hard to make out.

Carbo said nothing, keeping his sword arm steady. Behind him he heard the three men come closer and he waved his gladius towards them threateningly. "Stay back," he said.

They looked to Tragedy, who nodded, and they retreated a few steps. A young couple, arm in arm and laughing, stumbled drunkenly into the square. One of the men showed them his knife. "Fuck off," he said, and they retreated in alarm.

"I asked you a question, soldier boy," said Tragedy.

"Let us pass," said Carbo, his voice holding as much threat and menace as he could muster.

Tragedy sighed.

"You won't answer? Then I must conclude that you do not. And I will teach you. Menelaus." He gestured to Comedy.

Comedy drew a sword from its scabbard, then pulled a curved dagger from his belt. He leaped forward, impressively light on his feet. He thrust out with his blade, and as Carbo fended it away with his own sword, brought the dagger round in an arc towards Carbo's throat. Carbo swayed back, feeling the wind from the dagger's passage against his cheek. He countered with a two-handed swing, and when Comedy parried, Carbo twisted his arms so his blade slid down his opponent's. Seeing the threat, Comedy spun to the side, and the thrust grazed his chest, tearing a rent in his tunic, but drawing no blood.

Comedy took a step back.

"You have some skill with the sword, soldier boy," called Tragedy. "But just a legionary's skill. You don't know how to fight like a gladiator, one on one." Comedy sprang before Tragedy had even finished speaking, launching a flurry of one handed thrusts and sweeps. Carbo parried each one with ease, but was unable to find a counter, and at the end of the sequence, the dagger flashed out again, catching his sword arm and opening a superficial skin wound. Carbo felt no pain, but saw the blood run freely down towards his elbow to drip onto the dusty ground.

Now Carbo went on the offensive, using his superior strength and reach to push Comedy backwards. Comedy retreated, one slow step at a time, back across the square. Carbo feinted then gave a thrust towards Comedy's midriff, which the masked man barely turned aside in time. Carbo saw alarm in the man's eyes, and thrust again, pressing the advantage. Comedy wove his sword with skill and desperation, keeping Carbo at bay, but Carbo's power began to tell, and he saw the man start to fatigue.

As Comedy backed up against the men blocking the exit, he thrust his gladius towards Carbo's chest. Carbo let the sword pass to one side, then trapped it with his arm tight against his chest. Too close to stab, he slammed the heel of his fist into the centre of the mask, rocking Comedy's head back, then twisted his arm in front of his body, the armlock forcing Comedy to drop his sword.

A woman's scream came from behind him. He turned, realising too late that Comedy had been leading him away from Rufa. Tragedy held Rufa, one arm pinned behind her, knife at her throat. Steady eyes regarded Carbo from behind the mocking mask. Carbo pushed Comedy away from him with a roar, and raised his sword to charge at Tragedy.

A massive blow connected with the back of his head, a club wielded by one of the thugs. Carbo staggered to his knees, the periphery of his vision turning black, bright specks of light dancing in front of him. He looked up, and saw Rufa struggling against her captor. The knife bit deep into the side of her neck, but she didn't stop her efforts to escape. One of the thugs cuffed her hard across the side of the head, and she cried out, and stopped her struggles.

Carbo tried to regain his feet, feeling the world spin around him. His sword had flown out of his hand, and was out of reach. He managed to get his legs underneath him, but they felt as weak as a reed, barely supporting his weight. He tried to walk towards Rufa, but felt a hand grasp the hair at the back of his head, pulling him backwards. He staggered, fell against the man behind him, and found Comedy's knife pressed into his back.

"Stand still," hissed Comedy.

"Carbo," cried out Rufa, helplessly. Her eyes were filled with panic, and brimming with tears.

"Rufa, don't worry, everything will be all right."

Tragedy laughed aloud.

"Oh soldier, you don't seem to understand. I told you I would make you understand loss."

"No, please," said Carbo. "Kill me. Let her go. She is innocent."

"An eye for an eye, the Jews say. A loved one for a loved one. Yes, she is innocent. But killing you will not inflict the same pain on you as you inflicted on me. Killing her will. And maybe it will make all these cowards hiding behind their stalls and carts understand what happens when someone defies me."

"Carbo," cried out Rufa hysterically.

Carbo lunged forward desperately, but another blow to the side of his head sent him sprawling, his face thudding into the cobbles. He groaned, got to his hands and knees and started to crawl towards Rufa. Comedy's mocking laughter followed him. The few short feet separating him from Rufa seemed like a mile.

"It's time," said Tragedy. "Watch, Menelaus."

Carbo held out a pleading hand.

Tragedy looked him straight in the eyes as he dragged the blade across Rufa's throat.

Blood spurted out from the great vessels in her neck, filled her mouth, overflowed down her chin. She stared at Carbo, eyes wide in terror and pain and despair as she sank to her knees. He crawled the last few feet towards her, caught her as she toppled forwards.

"Rufa, gods, no," he whispered, as he cradled her in his arms.

She looked up into his eyes, and tried to speak, but only bubbles and blood came from her mouth. His hands and arms and clothes were soaked with the sticky red fluid. She gasped and gurgled as her lungs filled with blood. He gripped her tight as he watched her eyes drift away from him, unfocused. Her body spasmed, jerked, then went still. He buried his face in her hair, and howled.

He didn't know how much time had passed when he felt hands on his shoulders, roughly yanking him from Rufa's warm body. He shook them off, hung onto her, but more grabbed him, and when he resisted, lashed out, a blow from a blunt object knocked his head sideways. Numbly, he let himself be pulled away. Two stationarii, legionaries seconded to police duty in the provinces, picked him up, supporting him beneath his arms. The thugs were gone, and the braver souls who had witnessed the crime had been joined by a larger crowd who stood a few feet away, gawping in morbid fascination at the blood-soaked man, and the murdered woman at his feet.

A man from the crowd bent down beside Rufa, taking in her blank, staring eyes, still chest, and the huge volume of blood pooled on the cobblestones. He looked up at the legionaries, and shook his head. Carbo lunged at the man, thrusting him backwards.

"Leave her alone!" he cried.

One of the stationarii put a hand on his shoulder, and Carbo rounded on him with a hard punch to the centre of his face, breaking his nose and causing blood to spurt.

The other stationarius was on him in an instant, pinning his hands behind his back, and the injured soldier stepped forward and punched Carbo hard in the side of the head, dazing him.

"You need to come with us till you calm down," said the legionary holding his arms.

Carbo shook his head. "I can't leave her. She needs me."

"We'll take care of her," said the man kneeling beside her. "Go with the soldiers."

All fight gone from him, he allowed his hands to be tied behind his back, then let himself be led away. He turned his head back as he walked, seeing them cover Rufa with a blanket, then respectfully lift her body onto a cart.

They took him to the statio, the local police station, a small group of children and curious market goers trailing behind. Inside, they unbound him and gave him a bowl of cold water and threw a cloth at him to clean himself. He put his hands into the bowl, and rubbed, seeing the congealed blood fall off in sticky sheets. He dampened the cloth and wiped his face, then put the cloth back in the water and watched the water turn crimson. He stared into the bowl, eyes unfocused, uncomprehending.

"Come with me," said the stationarius with the broken nose, the words muffled and resentful.

He led Carbo to a small office containing a cluttered desk, at which sat a centurion, with his optio standing beside him. Carbo was marched forwards. The centurion looked up from the document he was perusing, and his eyes widened at Carbo's gory appearance. Composing himself, he spoke in well-accented Latin.

"I am centurion Lucius Ambrosius Asellio. This is optio Lutorius. What's your name?"

Carbo opened his mouth to speak, but no words came out. The stationarius stepped in front of him, and punched him hard in the abdomen. Carbo, not expecting the blow, doubled forward, gasping for air.

"The centurion asked you a question," said the stationarius.

"That's enough," said the optio. "Get out and leave him with us."

"Yes, sir," said the legionary, saluting and turning to depart.

"Well, man?" said Asellio.

"Gaius Valerius Carbo, pilus prior centurion of the second cohort of the XIIIth Gemina," said Carbo, responding to the military tone of voice by force of habit. Then he added, "Retired."

"I see," said Asellio, putting his hand to his chin thoughtfully.

"Sir," said Lutorius, tentatively. "There was a Carbo in the XIIIth that had some notoriety…"

"There was, wasn't there?" mused Asellio. "Lutorius, help him get cleaned up, then let him leave."

"But sir," said Lutorius, "Shouldn't we be asking him some questions. A woman has been murdered, isn't it our duty to…"

Asellio held up a hand to stop his optio. "Lutorius, you haven't been stationed here many months. I have been here years. Unfortunately, Nola is a dangerous place. These things happen."

"But right in the centre of town? In broad daylight? Shouldn't we be out on the streets, tracking down these murderers?"

"By all means, keep your ears open. But experience tells me you will hear little. The murderers will never be found, and that is the end of the matter."

The words penetrated the fog of Carbo's mind like a distant light, guiding him back to the present.

"You aren't going to make enquiries?" he asked, incredulous. "Find these bastards?"

Asellio looked down at his desk, reading some notes on a wax tablet. He waved a dismissive hand. "Lutorius, please escort him out."

Carbo stared and was gripped with a sudden rage. He lunged across the desk, grabbed the centurion by the tunic, pulled his face close.

"You have to do something!" he yelled. "She's dead. The murderers can't be allowed to go free."

Strong arms grabbed Carbo from behind, pulled him off. Asellio rearranged his clothing, an air of offended dignity on his face.

"Put him in a cell until he cools off."

Lutorius and two other legionaries led Carbo away. He looked back at Asellio as he was dragged out of the office, incredulous at the centurion's lack of concern.

Lutorius led him to a wooden door with a small barred window set at head height. He opened it, and ushered Carbo forwards. Carbo stepped through the door, to find himself in a small cell, about six foot square, containing a low bench and a bucket. The door slammed shut behind him, and he heard a key turning in the lock.

Carbo looked through the bars. Lutorius regarded him sorrowfully.

"I'm sorry about this, sir. You will be out of here in no time."

He turned and left.

Rufa was gone. It was impossible, but he had held her as she died. He sat at the bench, and put his head in his hands. Tremors shook his body. Then he started to wail.

# CHAPTER VI

There were no windows in the cell, and the corridor beyond was dimly lit. Carbo sat in almost complete silence and darkness, replaying the scene over and over in his head. He kept finding flecks of Rufa's blood embedded in the cracks and calluses of his weathered hands, and picked at them, trying to rid himself of the gore, then feeling guilty for the disgust the blood engendered in him.

Rufa was gone. She had left him, alone. The one he loved, the one he needed, the one who had made him whole again. And then there was Fabilla. His heart missed a beat at the thought of telling the little girl her mother was dead.

He felt empty. Numb. How could life ever be the same? How could it even be worth carrying on?

He thought about the fight, ran over the sequence of events in his mind. How could he have saved her? What could he have done differently? So many things, he supposed. Never gone to the market. Never gone to Nola. Never left Rome, and encountered those bandits.

The faces of the two masked men swam before him. In the darkness, where the eyes and the mind could play tricks so easily, he could swear for a moment they were actually there.

Within him a spark appeared. Tiny at first. But something. He focused on those masks, the eyes behind them. The spark flared into a little flame. He remembered Rufa's terror in her last moments, the mocking laughter of the thugs, the cold look in the eyes of her murderer. The flame roared into an inferno, and he now knew what the fire was. It was rage.

He thrust himself to his feet and screamed aloud. He punched the walls, bloodying his knuckles. He picked up the bench and threw it across the cell, splintering it into firewood. He kicked the door, rattling it in its hinges, dislodging small pieces of plaster and brickwork from around the frame.

"Hey, big guy, calm down," came the voice of Lutorius.

Carbo continued to give rein to his fury, and two more stationarii came down, peering through the small window.

"He's going to hurt himself," said Lutorius.

"He's wrecking the cell," said one of the others.

"We should go in," said Lutorius.

"Screw that," said the third. "You must be insane if you think I'm going in there with that raging madman."

The three stationarii looked on, wincing in unison at the heavier blows that damaged the cell structure as much as Carbo's fists and feet. Slowly, the storm blew itself out. The blows became weaker, and the tears started to flow. Carbo sunk to his knees, put his head in his hands, and started to cry.

"I'm going in," said Lutorius.

"Rather you than me," said one of the others.

Lutorius cautiously opened the cell door. Exchanging a nervous glance with his comrades, he entered the cell. Carbo didn't move. Lutorius knelt beside him and put a hand on his shoulder. Carbo looked up at him but seemed to be looking straight past him. Lutorius could see his knuckles were bruised and red raw, and he was amazed that there were no obvious broken bones. Tears flowed freely down

Carbo's face, making clean trails in the mud and blood that still grimed his cheeks.

"I'm going to kill them," said Carbo, his voice low and quiet.

Lutorius nodded. "Who did it?"

"I'm going to rip them apart with my bare hands."

"Who?" asked Lutorius.

Carbo now focused on Lutorius, seeming to see him for the first time. He looked down at his bloodied fists, flexed his fingers tentatively and winced.

"You don't care," said Carbo.

"I do. Some of us here have a greater sense of duty than their superiors."

Carbo shook his head. "I don't know who they were. Two men. They wore masks. But I will find them."

Lutorius looked at him sharply.

"Masks? What sort of masks?"

"Those masks that Greek actors wear. One for comedy and one for tragedy." Carbo saw Lutorius' thoughtful expression. "What is it? You know these men?"

Lutorius shook his head. "No. But I know of them. They have become rather notorious around these parts."

"How so?"

"They have been terrorising travellers for years. Often just the two of them, the comedy mask and the tragedy mask, but sometimes accompanied by local thugs to provide numbers and muscle."

"They are just simple bandits?" asked Carbo, his tone contemptuous.

"Far from simple. They are skilled and ruthless. They defeat parties that have superior numbers, with armed bodyguards. Sometimes they take money, but often they take people."

"For what?"

Lutorius shrugged. "Draw your own conclusions."

Carbo considered for a while, then said, "We met them before. In the countryside, near the via Popillia towards Abella."

Lutorius' eyes narrowed, and he waited for Carbo to continue. Carbo weighed up whether to tell the story, then decided he had nothing to lose. He related to Lutorius how they had been attacked, how they had managed to fend the two bandits off.

"But I killed one of them. The one that wore the comedy mask."

"You killed him?" said Lutorius, surprised. Then he frowned. "But you said two masked men attacked you today."

Carbo shook his head. "I know. I don't understand."

"You saw the one in the comedy mask die?"

"No, he was still alive when his comrade dragged him away. But I was in the legions for twenty-five years. I know when a wound is mortal. I killed that man, I'm certain."

"Yet the same man attacked you today."

"I can't explain it," said Carbo, forlornly. "Maybe if I had made sure, not let them escape, Rufa would still be..." The sentence choked off.

Lutorius put a hand on Carbo's shoulder sympathetically. Carbo swallowed.

"And there is no one who knows who they are?" he asked.

"They refer to each other by names, but they are probably aliases."

"What names?"

"Atreus and Thyestes."

Carbo thought about this, then shook his head.

"No, that's not right. Today, they used the name Atreus. But the other was called…" Carbo shut his eyes, picturing the horrible scene. Watch, Menelaus, he had said. And then the knife…

Carbo squeezed his fists together tight, took a deep breath.

"The one in the comedy mask was called Menelaus."

"You must be mistaken," said Lutorius. "We have lots of witnesses from previous crimes who say that their names were Atreus and Thyestes."

Carbo thought back to the fight in the woods. The man in the comedy mask then had been about the same height as the one today. Their voices were muffled, so he couldn't tell if their accents were the same. But the build. As he thought about it, he realised that Comedy from the woods was thicker set than Comedy from the town today. Different too in the way they moved - the one from the woods seeming more self-assured, confident, the one today more hesitant, more subservient to Atreus.

"I did kill him," said Carbo.

"What?"

"The man with the comedy mask. In the woods. I killed him. The one today was a different man."

Lutorius considered this. "So you killed Thyestes. And now Menelaus has replaced him."

"There's something else," said Carbo. "Atreus and Thyestes called each other brother."

Lutorius sat back and let out a low whistle.

"You killed Atreus' brother? No wonder he was mad at you."

Do you understand loss, soldier? Atreus had asked him. I will teach you.

"Let me out of here," said Carbo.

"It's not that easy," said Lutorius. "The centurion won't let you out until he knows you aren't a danger. Do you have someone who can vouch for you?"

Carbo looked at him coldly. "Go to my farm and fetch Vespillo."

Lutorius knocked on the farm door and waited. It had started raining again, and he was thoroughly soaked. He cursed himself. What was he doing, running errands for the prisoner? The centurion had laughed at him and called him soft when he had told him the prisoner's request, and then told him to go if he felt the need.

The door opened, and a huge beast leaped out, knocking him over backwards. A large foul-breathed maw dropped saliva on his face.

"Melanchaetes. Off!"

The dog backed off and stood a few paces away, hackles up, lips drawn back to reveal large stained teeth.

A young girl held out a hand to him. He took a deep breath, then let the girl help him up.

"I am sorry, sir. Melanchaetes is a, um, dutiful guard."

Lutorius scraped ineffectually at the mud on his back, scowling at her.

"Can I help you, sir?"

"Is this Carbo's farm?"

"It is, but I am afraid he is not here at the moment."

"I know," said Lutorius. "I'm here to see Vespillo." A sudden thought struck him. "Are you...are you Fabilla?" Carbo had told him the name of the murdered woman's daughter.

"No, sir, I'm Thera, the steward Theron's daughter."

Lutorius let out a sigh of relief.

"Fabilla is inside, sir. Shall I summon her?"

"No, no," he said hastily. "Just let me see Vespillo."

"Of course, come in out of the rain. I will tell him you are here."

Lutorius followed Thera through the door, and took a seat in the atrium, while Thera went off to search for Vespillo. There was a small lararium, and Lutorius offered a quick prayer to the household gods, to help him through the next few moments.

Presently, an older man, short and stocky with a grizzled beard entered the atrium and Lutorius stood.

"I'm Vespillo," said the man, looking at Lutorius suspiciously.

Lutorius offered his hand.

"Lutorius, stationarius, on detached duty in Nola."

"Carbo isn't home," said Vespillo.

"I know," said Lutorius. "He sent me to fetch you."

Vespillo's face creased in concern. "He is in trouble?"

Lutorius hesitated, then nodded.

"Rufa too?"

Lutorius said nothing, but his expression was anguished.

"Sit down. Tell me everything," said Vespillo in a strained voice.

"Carbo and Rufa were attacked in the market in Nola."

Vespillo looked grim but said nothing.

Lutorius took a deep breath. "Rufa is dead."

Vespillo closed his eyes. His head slumped into his hands, and he remained like that for a few moments, motionless on the stone bench he sat on. Lutorius waited. Vespillo looked up at him, and his eyes were bright with tears.

"Carbo?" he asked, in a whisper.

"Carbo is unhurt, more or less. He is being held in a prison cell for violent be-haviour. We need someone into whose care we can release him, who will vouch for him."

"Gods," said Vespillo, face creased in anguish. "Poor Rufa. Poor Carbo. Oh Jupiter Optimus Maximus. Fabilla."

"Carbo is asking for you."

Vespillo nodded. "Who did this?"

"Bandits. Carbo thinks it was the same bandits that attacked you when you were travelling down here."

"The ones with the masks? I thought Carbo killed one of them."

"We think there has been a replacement. Besides, there were other men today. Local muscle."

Vespillo looked grim. "So what is your next move? Legwork? Hitting the streets and asking questions?"

Lutorius shook his head sadly. "My centurion won't allow much in the way of resources to be allocated to this. He says it is a fact of life in Nola, and we won't find anything out."

"What? But it's his duty!"

"You don't have to tell me about that. I want to find these criminals too. What does it say about us as Romans, as legionaries, that we let these bastards get away with this evil?"

"It's you and me, then," said Vespillo, voice firm. "I need to speak to my wife, then we should get moving." He stood abruptly, and his knees buckled. He put his hand against the wall to steady himself, head bowed. Instantly, the young girl was at his side, supporting him.

Vespillo looked up. "Thera." The girl's cheeks were soaked with rivers of tears. "You heard everything?" asked Vespillo.

The girl nodded wordlessly. Vespillo bent down so his eyes were at the same level as hers.

"Thera, listen to me. I know you and Fabilla have become good friends. But you must not tell her any of this."

Thera looked uncertain. "This is important, Thera. I will tell her when the time is right. We need to break the news to her very gently."

"I...understand," said Thera hesitantly.

Vespillo held her gaze a bit longer then nodded. "Now go and fetch Lutorius some warm wine and fresh clothes. Lutorius, as soon as I have spoken to Severa, we will get on the road."

Carbo stared at the wall of the cell blankly. Emotions churned inside him. Anger. Hatred. Loss. Fear. He felt a familiar tremor in his limbs, an increase in his heart rate, a cold sweat across his skin. The thought of life without Rufa was terrifying.

But the panic did not overwhelm him, like it would have in the past. Maybe that was Rufa's enduring influence. More likely it was his fury. His breath was short and fast, and he clenched and unclenched his fists. He focused on the masked men, trying to recall every detail about them, their voices, their build, the way they moved. He would find them, he vowed, and he would make them suffer.

He thought too about the thugs that had helped them. Without those men, he would have had a fighting chance. He could have saved Rufa. His hatred was voluminous enough to encompass them as well. They would all pay.

He had no idea how much time had passed. There were no external windows in the cell, the only illumination a lamp just outside, sending a tiny beam of light through the barred window in the door. It must be night time, he thought. It had been hours since Lutorius had left. That made sense though. It would take hours, for Lutorius to reach his farm, talk to Vespillo, and return. That's if there were no hold ups. Like being accosted by bandits.

Footsteps came from outside the cell door. There was a jangle of keys and the door swung open. Vespillo's short, stocky figure stood, outlined in the dim light. He swayed, steadied himself against the door frame for a moment, then entered the cell.

Carbo got to his feet, and for a moment they simply stood, looking at each other. Then Vespillo took two swift steps forward and put his arms around Carbo, and Carbo sagged against him, burying his head into his best friend's shoulder, and letting the tears flood out in sobbing gasps.

After a short while, Vespillo started to weaken under Carbo's weight, and guided him back to the stool that Lutorius had earlier allowed Carbo to have after extracting a promise he wouldn't destroy it. Carbo sat, head bowed, shoulders slumped. He tried to speak, but the sight of his friend's anguished face blocked the words in his throat.

Vespillo looked around for Lutorius. "Can you get me a seat, too?"

Lutorius, who had been standing in the door, nodded and hurried out, returning quickly with another wooden stool. Vespillo took it and placed it in front of Carbo, and sat facing him, placing one hand on his shoulder.

"There is nothing I can say, friend. Nothing that will bring her back, or ease the pain. All I can do is be here for you. And I am."

Carbo nodded and covered Vespillo's hand with his own.

"I'm going to kill them all, Vespillo. Every one of the cunni."

Vespillo shot a glance towards Lutorius, but the soldier was pretending not to have heard.

"Let's get you out of here. Lutorius, is he free to go?"

"If you keep him under control."

"He'll be no trouble. Will you, Carbo?"

Carbo shook his head, but his eyes were blazing.

"Lutorius is going to help us find them," said Vespillo. Carbo looked at the optio, eyes narrowed.

"The centurion may not be interested in justice, but that doesn't mean we all feel the same," confirmed Lutorius. "Can you tell us anything from today that might help?"

Carbo closed his eyes. It was hard, picturing those scenes. His mind's eye kept being drawn back to Rufa, collapsing in gouts of blood.

"Before it happened, I thought I was being watched. Maybe a scout, or someone co-ordinating it all. He had a diagonal scar across his face."

Lutorius put a hand to his chin.

"Sounds like Febrox."

"Who is Febrox?" asked Vespillo.

"A local thug, nasty piece of work."

Vespillo nodded. "It's a start."

"Well, it would be if we knew where to find him."

Vespillo looked thoughtful. "We can work on that."

# CHAPTER VII

Lucius Ambrosius Asellio sat behind his desk, arms folded. Carbo stood before him, with Vespillo and Lutorius behind, one at each shoulder.

"Sir? Do I have your permission to release Carbo into the care of his friend, Lucius Vedius Vespillo?"

Asellio inspected Vespillo with an air of faint contempt.

"Is he an upright citizen?"

Vespillo bristled. "I am a tribune of the vigiles in Rome," he said. "Centurion," he added, trying to keep the sneer out of his tone. "I believe that qualifies me as upright. Moreover, it qualifies me to ask what you intend to do about this awful crime committed on your doorstep."

Asellio sighed, and looked to his optio.

"Do you remember, Lutorius, when our cohort was posted to Egypt? They had their own police force. Professional men, kept everything in line, investigated crimes."

"I remember, sir, it was very odd wasn't it?"

"And how are things done in Italy, Lutorius?"

"Well, Rome has the vigiles..."

Asellio let out a contemptuous laugh, and Carbo felt Vespillo stiffen beside him.

"Really, Lutorius. I'm sure the vigiles are well intentioned, but everyone knows they are a bunch of freedmen whose main job is to fight fires, and occasionally beat up a burglar if they catch one in the act. Tell me how it really works, Lutorius."

"The people police themselves."

"Of course they do. They honour the way of their ancestors, they fear the legions, the duumvirs and decurions and aediles sometimes get involved, but mostly they will dish out their own justice to anyone they think has done wrong."

Lutorius looked at Carbo apologetically.

"Sir, I will be assisting Vespillo and Carbo in tracking down these bandits."

Asellio sighed. "On your head, then Lutorius. Don't blame me if it is all an entire waste of time. Or worse, you end up dead in a market square with a slit throat."

Carbo paled, jaw tightening. Vespillo put a warning hand on Carbo's shoulder.

"Carbo," said Asellio. "You are free. You can go."

"Not without Rufa."

Asellio's eyes narrowed.

"What?"

"I am taking my woman with me."

"Carbo," said Vespillo, hesitantly, "I'm not sure..."

"Take me to her," said Carbo firmly.

Asellio threw his hands up in the air.

"Fine, fine. Just go. Lutorius, show him the way. And see if you can keep him out of trouble. "

"Yes, sir," said Lutorius.

"And don't let your...investigations get in the way of your duties."

"No sir, thank you, sir."

He gave a salute, and then turned to Carbo.

"Please follow me, sir."

"It's Carbo, not sir," said Carbo as he followed Lutorius out of the office. "I'm retired."

Carbo looked down at Rufa's body, shrouded in a plain woollen blanket, laid out on a table in the basement of the statio. He hesitated, looked at Vespillo, then nodded to Lutorius. Lutorius pulled the shroud back solemnly.

Carbo drew his breath in sharply. They had done their best to clean her up. They had respectfully cut away the bloodstained clothing, and wrapped her in a white sheet. They had mopped up the blood that must have spilled down her chest.

But they couldn't disguise the gaping wound in her throat, now filled in with dark, congealed blood. The perfumes they had anointed her with could not disguise the smell of fresh death. And what could anyone do about the dead eyes, wide open and staring at nothing?

He wished she looked serene, at peace. But her expression, frozen in mortality, was terrified.

Carbo swallowed. He had seen death many times before, on the battlefield, on the streets of Rome at night. He thought himself inured to it. But this was a woman. His woman. Grief rose within him, threatened to overwhelm him.

A hand touched his shoulder, making him jump. Lutorius was looking at him with deep sympathy graven on his features.

"You can take her now," he said gently, pulling the blanket back over her face.

Carbo lifted the stiff, cold body and hugged it close to him.

Word of the horrific murder had got quickly round the town, and a small crowd had gathered outside the statio, a few holding torches shedding a little light. Some watched curiously, some saw the gathering as a social occasion and caught up on gossip with friends, others shouted for justice. Two armed stationarii stood on duty at the statio entrance, fidgeting nervously as the crowd slowly became more restless.

When the doors of the statio opened, the crowd turned as one. Lutorius was first to come out, and he stood on the steps of the station house, and held his hands up for quiet. A reluctant hush fell over the crowd.

"People of Nola. A terrible crime was committed this afternoon, near the market. A man was assaulted and a young woman was murdered. We have witnesses who tell us that it was the work of a group of thugs, who we have not yet identified. If you know anything about this horrible deed, please come and talk to me or one of the other stationarii. Whatever you say will be held in strictest confidence."

The crowd seemed collectively to look away and shuffle their feet.

"Now, please make way for the wronged man, Carbo of Rome."

Lutorius stepped to one side, and Carbo emerged from the doors. In his arms, he carried the body of Rufa, wrapped in a blanket, her face and neck exposed. Rigor mortis made her expression even more terrifying, and the deep wound to her neck was clearly on show. As one, the crowd took a collective gasp. Carbo stood for a moment, tears streaming down his face. Then he walked down the steps of the statio, and the crowd parted for him.

As he walked through them at a slow, dignified pace, angry murmurings began, and picked up in volume. At first it was unclear who they were directed against.

Then the murmurings became clearer. Some people clapped Carbo on his back. A woman came and embraced him. A young girl came forward and placed a flower in Rufa's hair.

"Get them, Carbo," shouted one man.

"Find the bandits," shouted another.

"Death to the bandits," cried a third, and the shout was taken up as a chant.

A woman stepped in front of him, elderly face streaked with tears.

"They took my son, sir. Please find them, avenge him. The people of Nola want to be free of this evil."

Carbo stopped, spoke in a loud, clear voice. "People of Nola."

The crowd was silent, watching and listening hopefully.

"You people." He spat on the ground. "You stood back, fled, cowered away while these thugs attacked me and killed my woman. You did nothing. You cowards!"

The crowd seemed to flinch back.

"You people deserve everything you get."

He walked on to the edge of the crowd, where Vespillo was waiting for him with an ox cart. He respectfully laid Rufa in it, and then got up beside her. Vespillo waited until he was settled, then struck the ox with a cane to get it moving. Slowly, the cart with its grim burden made its way out of Nola, leaving the shocked, scared population behind.

Melanchaetes' barking alerted the household to the arrival of Carbo and Vespillo, so when they reached the front of the farmhouse, Theron, Thera, Marsia and Severa were waiting for them. Melanchaetes seemed to sense the mood, and lay down, watching the cart pull up with his head on his paws.

Carbo stepped down from the cart. Marsia moved quickly to assist him with the body, but he shrugged her away. The small group could only watch as Carbo picked Rufa up, her light body appearing to take him no effort to lift. Gently, he laid her on the ground before the house, the traditional parallel with the birth rites, when the infant child was placed upon the earth. Then he sat beside her, staring into her eyes and stroking her hair.

Severa took Vespillo's arm, looked at him questioningly.

"Leave him," said Vespillo, quietly. Then his frown deepened. "Fabilla?"

"Asleep," said Severa. "Thank Somnos for that."

"She needs to be told, before she sees her mother like this."

"I will tell her," said Carbo in a flat voice. "No one else."

"When?" asked Vespillo gently.

"As soon as she wakes, fetch me. I will talk to her."

Carbo returned to stroking Rufa's hair. Rain started to fall, fat, solitary drops at first, but soon turning into a downpour. Theron and Thera were first to go back inside, then Vespillo and Severa. Carbo remained where he was. Marsia hesitated, then sat on the ground, just behind Carbo and to one side, not touching him, not saying a word. He looked at her, then nodded, and returned his attentions to the dead form of the woman he loved.

Atreus sat in a corner of a busy tavern, and watched his son curiously. Menelaus took a small sip from his cup of well-watered wine, and returned the stare impassively.

"What is it, father?"

"I was wondering how you were feeling, that's all."

Menelaus shrugged. "How should I feel?"

"Well, you took part in your first murder today. Maybe you should feel something."

"How did you feel, father, the first time?"

Atreus' eyes lit up. "Avenged!" he said.

Menelaus nodded. "And did you feel avenged today?"

Atreus looked thoughtful. "Maybe. Or maybe I should have killed him too. I'm not sure yet which makes me feel better. How did the mask fit?"

Menelaus glanced to the bag on the floor that contained the comedy and tragedy masks. Without them on, they were just ordinary market goers getting a drink at the end of the day. Even the thugs they had paid to help them today would not recognise them. But when they wearing them, they were feared by all for miles around. Well, maybe not all. Menelaus recalled the expression on the big veteran's face as his father slit his beloved's throat. He suppressed a shudder, born from the memory of excitement and fear.

"It fits well. You never did tell me why the actors' masks."

"It was your uncle's idea," said Atreus. "When we started this adventure together, he thought the idea of us as actors, playing out tragedy and farce, was somehow fitting."

"Was the adventure his idea too?"

Atreus shook his head. "All mine." He looked Menelaus straight in the eyes. "Have you ever felt so bored that you feel your soul is shrivelling inside you like a prune? So alone, despite the people around you, so grief stricken for a lost past, that you would do anything to just feel alive. Shout, scream, hurt yourself. Hurt someone else."

Menelaus was silent.

"Of course not, my son. You are sheltered. Still, it feels good to share this with you, my own flesh and blood. Even if you are a replacement for someone I dearly loved." Atreus sighed. "Ah, listen to me. Sentimental old man."

Menelaus sipped his drink again, expression betraying nothing. He had his own reasons for joining this so-called adventure, he reflected, and they had nothing to do with boredom.

Rufa's body lay on a pyre, firewood and kindling spread over a shallow pit. Carbo stood with a burning brand in his hand, staring at the small, wrapped bundle that represented the last sight he would have of his beloved. Beside him stood Fabilla, little hand gripping tight to Severa.

True to his word, Vespillo had fetched Carbo inside from his all night vigil as soon as Fabilla had stirred in the morning. Carbo remembered the expression in her eyes when he entered her bedroom. He must have looked in a state, soaked through, with a haunted expression. She had immediately ran to him, hugged him and asked if he was all right.

Carbo had gently peeled her arms from around his waist, squatted on his haunches so he was looking up into her eyes, and squeezing her hands tight, told her that her mother was dead.

Her reaction had surprised him. There had been no hysterics, screaming, beating of fists against his chest. Her lower lip had quivered, and she simply asked how. Carbo had told her that her mother had been murdered, and then as he started to tell her how sorry he was that he couldn't save her, he had broken down into tears himself. Fabilla had put her arms around him and comforted him while he wept, until Severa had entered and taken Fabilla away.

The tears for Rufa arrived later, when she was helping Carbo prepare the body. The trigger had come when Fabilla was anointing Rufa's hair with perfume. She had told Carbo that the perfume was a gift from her mother, that Rufa had liked the smell on Fabilla, and she was glad that her mother could take the nice scent with her. Then it was Fabilla's turn to weep and howl, while Carbo held her, and Vespillo, Severa and Marsia looked on with heartbreak on their faces. Behind them, looking solemn, stood Theron and Thera.

Carbo now turned to Fabilla. He wished she was too young to understand anything, or old enough to understand everything. Still, he was amazed by her strength and maturity. She looked up at him. Her eyes were red, but there were no more tears. A few drops of rain fell.

"Are you ready?" he asked her. She nodded silently. He held out the burning brand, and she put her hand above his. Together they lowered the flame to the kindling, then let it drop.

The wool, dry grass and tiny twigs caught quickly. More rain fell, and Carbo looked up at the sky nervously, suddenly terrified that the flame would be doused, the firewood soaked, the whole ceremony delayed until the conditions were better and more dry wood could be gathered. He wasn't sure he had the strength to do this again. A panic started to build up in him.

The fire roared into life, life of which Rufa had been robbed. A wave of relief swept through Carbo, for which he felt immediately guilty. Fabilla's hand found its way into his, and he squeezed.

The flames quickly obscured the body, and thick smoke from the newly damp wood billowed out, stinging his eyes and forcing him to take a step back. Only weeks before, he had saved Rufa from a fire that engulfed a large part of Rome. Now here he was, watching the fire take her away from him for the last time.

The rain fell harder, dampening the mourners, but the fire was too strong to quench. They all remained, heads bowed, silent. Carbo could not tell who was crying freely and who simply had rain pouring down their faces.

Eventually, the flames died down, the rain having stopped shortly before. When the ashes were cool enough, Carbo picked up a small trowel to gather them into a pottery urn. He bent down, and saw bones in the grey powdery remains. The fire had burnt away the flesh, but had not been hot enough to consume the skeleton. If this had been Rome, professionals would have taken care of this. Carbo cursed himself for botching the job.

Carbo hesitated, looked to Vespillo. Vespillo stepped forward, and saw the problem. He signalled to Severa to take Fabilla further back, then squatted beside Carbo.

"Let's take some ashes back to Rome, then bury the rest. Then she can rest with your mother in the columbarium, and at the same time be here in the countryside, a free woman for ever."

Carbo gave Vespillo a grateful look, and collected some of the ashes into the urn. He moved a partially burnt log to take another sample, and found himself staring at Rufa's blackened skull. He gasped, stepped back, eyes transfixed by the sight. Even stripped of flesh, he could picture Rufa's face, the cheek bones, the smile, the soft skin clothing the bare bone.

His chest tightened, his breathing quickened, his heart started to race. He wasn't as superstitious as many Romans, but he had a healthy respect for the manes. He whispered a prayer of appeasement to the restless spirits, but still could not look away, as he felt the familiar panic and terror rise inside him.

A touch on his arm made him cry out loud.

"It's enough, Carbo," said Vespillo. Carbo nodded, and stood. He turned, facing the mourners. They were starting to shiver in their wet clothes, now the heat of the fire had receded. He looked down at the small pot in his hands, containing the remains of the only woman he had ever loved, then looked back at the onlookers, his friends and the members of his familia. His eyes fell on Fabilla, tired, cold, but resolutely seeing the ceremony out to its end. He knew there should be a eulogy, he should be heaping praise on Rufa, crying his love for her to the skies.

He opened his mouth, but his throat seized up. He could not think of a single word to say. Anything he considered sounded trite in his mind, too feeble and insincere. He closed his mouth again, feeling embarrassed and useless.

Vespillo put an arm around his shoulders, and led him towards the house. The rest of the mourners followed at a respectful distance.

"How is he?" asked Quintus.

"He doesn't speak," said Vespillo. "Barely eats. Alternates between drinking heavily enough to pass out, and not touching a drop."

They sat in the small peristylium, under the covered colonnade, watching the rain trickle off the roof. Quintus stared at a puddle into which a stream of water poured from a hole in the guttering.

"Have you talked to him?" he asked.

"I've tried," said Vespillo. "But what can I say? I'm not sure if it even helps that I have been through exactly the same thing. Well, worse, though it wouldn't do to point that out."

"No. Well, I suppose these things take time."

Vespillo looked at Quintus. So young, so little life experience. No, 'these things' didn't take time. They stayed for ever. You just learned to cope. Vespillo didn't chide the young man, though. He knew that he meant well. He just clearly had no idea what this really felt like.

"Will he see me?" asked Quintus.

"Yes, but don't expect much."

Vespillo led Quintus to the triclinium, where Carbo lay on his back on a couch, arms folded over his chest, eyes closed, breathing slowly. On the table was a meal of bread, nuts and olives, which looked untouched. Near Carbo stood Marsia, anxious to be of service, though her service clearly wasn't required. She looked up when Vespillo walked in, then smiled when she saw Quintus. Quintus smiled shyly back at her, then turned his attention to Carbo.

"Carbo," he said, softly. Carbo didn't stir. He said his name a little louder. Carbo opened his eyes, turned his head towards Quintus, then turned back to stare at the ceiling.

Quintus glanced to Vespillo for guidance, but Vespillo simply shrugged. Quintus cleared his throat.

"Gaius Valerius Carbo," he said in a formal tone. "I come to offer my condolences on the passing of your...loved one." Carbo betrayed no reaction, so Quintus continued.

"My father, Gaius Sempronius Blaesus commands me to tell you how sorry he is for your loss, and my brother, Publius Sempronius Blaesus also sends his deepest sympathies."

No reaction. "Curse you, Carbo, say something!" Quintus bent over to shake Carbo roughly by the shoulder.

Instantly Carbo grabbed Quintus' hand, rising in one swift movement, pulling Quintus' arm up behind his back, and propelling him against the nearest wall. Quintus managed to get his free hand in front of him just in time so his face merely squashed against the brickwork rather than smashing into it. Marsia gasped, her hand flying to her mouth.

"Like what?" Carbo hissed.

"Carbo?"

"What would you have me say, Quintus? What little speech of thanks for your concern should I give, that would let you leave here, duty done, so you can get on with your life?"

"Carbo, you're hurting me."

"Do you think I care? Do I care what you or your drunkard brother or your morose father think? Do I care what anyone thinks? Do I care if I pull on this arm harder so it rips out of your shoulder?"

"Enough," said Vespillo. "Let him go."

Carbo turned, keeping his grip on Quintus. The two friends locked eyes in a battle of wills. But Carbo's moment of arousal was gone. He let go of Quintus, who stumbled out of reach, then turned his back to the wall and slid down it, until he could hug his knees and bow his head.

Quintus stretched his abused arm. He threw Carbo an angry stare, then marched for the door. From behind him came the sound of gut-wrenching sobs. He hesitated, turned back. He looked towards Vespillo, but the older man offered no guidance. He walked over to where Carbo squatted, head buried in his crossed arms, body spasming with grief, and sat beside him. Vespillo sat on the couch and watched.

For a while no one said anything. The sobbing subsided, and Carbo sat still, face still hidden.

"I care," said Quintus. Carbo didn't move, but Quintus could tell he was listening.

"Maybe you don't care what I think, or my stupid brother, or my melancholy father. But I care. I care about how you are feeling. I care about Fabilla, and the other people around you. I cared about Rufa. And I care about finding out who did this."

Carbo looked up at this last statement, surprised.

"You didn't think I would let them get away with this did you? Comrades in arms, you said that, remember?"

Carbo nodded hesitantly.

"We are going to find them, and make them pay, Carbo," said Quintus, and there was iron in his tone.

Carbo looked to Vespillo. "He's right," said Vespillo. "It's time. The grieving will never stop. But the next phase has to begin."

"The next phase?" asked Carbo.

"Retribution."

# CHAPTER VIII

The narrow street was deserted, and dark as a mine. The moon appeared intermittently from behind black clouds, just enough so Marsia could see where she was
going. She glanced behind her, but could see nothing. The purse of coins at her
waist clinked, as loud as the clash of arms in this silent street, to her ears. Every
door was locked, every window shuttered. She hurried along, breath quick, heart
pounding, trying hard not to regret being in this position. It had been her idea, after
all.

She thought she heard footsteps behind her, and stopped, straining her ears.
Nothing. She carried on, heard them again. She stopped, but this time the footsteps
continued. She peered into the dark, could make out two large shapes approaching,
not twenty feet from her.

She turned and ran. The footsteps were loud behind her, leather shoes slapping
against the cobblestones. She rounded a corner, kept running. Brought up in Ger-
mania, amongst barbarians as the Romans called them, she was no weakling. Still
she cursed her lack of masculine strength and speed, cursed that she had not been
born a man.

The pounding steps behind her came closer, gaining. Another corner approached, and she sprinted, gasping breath into her lungs, legs burning with fatigue. She could hear the heavy breathing of the men close behind her. She turned
the corner, with the men nearly upon her.

She was going at such a speed, she nearly collided with Quintus, who was
standing in the centre of the street, a short way round the corner, feet planted apart,
his sword held casually, angled towards the ground. She stopped, stood behind
him and to one side, and turned to face her pursuers.

The two men stumbled to a halt as they rounded the corner and came face to
face with Quintus. They hesitated, and Quintus held his ground, expression stern.
The two thugs took in Quintus' youth and slight frame, looked at each other, and
laughed.

"Get out of the way, boy," said one. "We just want the money."

"And the girl," said the other.

"Well, of course, and the girl. Not going to all this effort of chasing her down,
without having some fun with her too."

Quintus didn't move, and the thugs looked uncertain.

"You can have her afterwards, if you just get out of the way now," said the first
thug. Quintus raised his sword.

"You asked for it." Both thugs drew out short swords of their own.

"Drop them," said a voice from behind the thugs. They turned as one. Behind
them, an armoured legionary stood, gladius drawn.

"There's still only two of them," said the first thug. "We can take them."

"Think you can take all four of us?" said a new voice. From black doorways on
either side of the street emerged two more men, one short and squat, the other tall
and muscular. The thugs looked around them in disbelief.

"Pluto's foreskin, what is this? An ambush?"

"That's exactly what it is," said Lutorius.

"Put your weapons down," said Vespillo.

The first thug rushed at Quintus, sword out, before any of them could react.

"Quintus," cried Carbo in alarm. The thug lunged forward, to thrust at Quintus' abdomen. Quintus sidestepped neatly, let the sword pass him, then stabbed his sword viciously through the thug's rib cage, all the way to the hilt. The man opened his mouth, and blood poured out. He toppled forwards and was still.

The other thug let his sword fall to the floor and held his hands out to the side. "What do you want with me?"

"We just want to talk to you," said Vespillo. "We want some information."

"I don't know nothing about nothing."

"We haven't asked you anything yet," interrupted Lutorius.

"I won't tell you bastards nothing."

Carbo grabbed the man's tunic in both hands and thrust him backwards. The thug's head hit the wall behind him with a dull thud.

"Who do you work for?"

"What? I..."

Carbo punched him in the abdomen, pulling the force of the blow, but still hard enough to double the thug up as the air rushed out of him. Carbo pushed him upright.

"Who do you work for?" he repeated.

"H...him," gasped the thug, gesturing to the man on the floor.

Carbo looked round at the thug who lay still in a huge pool of blood.

Vespillo stepped up close to the man Carbo held.

"And who does he work for?"

"I... couldn't say."

Vespillo drew a knife and pressed the tip into the thug's neck.

"Lutorius here is a stationarius. His job is to uphold the law. He would have to arrest you, try you. I am a tribune of the vigiles of Rome. If this was Rome, I would have to do the same. But here in Nola, I have no authority. So that means, when Lutorius turns his back, I can simply cut your throat, and then we can all walk away."

"Please, he would kill me."

"Be in no doubt, we will kill you right now if you don't tell us what we want to know."

The thug looked around at the grim faces staring back at him.

"There is a man, he is... sort of in charge around here."

"What do you mean, in charge?"

"Well, if anyone...um... comes into some money, they had better give him a cut of it, or they will get a visit from him or one of his men."

"So he is the one you go to if you need any muscle around here, then?" asked Vespillo.

"That's right."

Lutorius nodded. "We know there is a big fish in Nola. I think Febrox, the one with a scar who followed you, he works for him. Everyone we have arrested though has clammed up about him. He must be pretty scary."

"His name?" asked Vespillo, pushing the knife in a little deeper.

The thug swallowed. "Rabidus."

"Lovely name," muttered Quintus.

"And where do we find him?" asked Carbo.

"You don't. He finds you."

"I think we've got all we're going to," said Vespillo.

Carbo nodded, and released his grip on the thug.

"Listen," said Lutorius. "We are going to let you walk away. But we will be watching and listening. If you tell anyone what has happened here tonight, we will let it be known that you snitched on Rabidus. Then I wouldn't want to be in your shoes."

The thug shook his head vigorously. "I won't say a word."

"Very well." Lutorius looked around at the others. "Are we done?"

"Yes, let's go," said Carbo, turning to leave.

Quintus stepped forward and punched the thug hard in the face.

"That was for what you planned to do to Marsia, you scum."

The thug held his nose, as blood poured down his face. Quintus put his arm around Marsia, and followed the others out of the alley.

Carbo sat in a shadowy corner of the tavern with Lutorius, head bowed, unnoticed by the increasingly drunk clientele. The man responsible for the contagious inebriation was standing at the bar, racing a wiry, tough looking patron to down a full cup of wine, then turn it upside down on his head to prove it was empty. Though the tough guy finished first, his cup was not quite empty, and red wine soaked into his hair and poured down his face, to the delight of the onlookers.

"Barman, two more cups," cried the man at the bar, pulling out a large purse bulging with coins. "Who's next?" Another contender stepped forward. The onlookers roared as the two men raced to finish their drinks, the competition ending by consensus as a draw.

The generous man pulled out some more coins. "More," he shouted over the noise of loud conversation, cheering and singing.

The tavern door opened, and a man stood framed in the doorway, darkness behind him, his face lit by the flickering glow of the brazier and the oil lamps. A diagonal scar on his cheek stood out livid against his olive-skinned face.

Carbo tensed, and made to rise. Lutorius put a hand on his chest, gently pressing him back into his seat. Carbo reluctantly settled back.

Some of the patrons of the tavern noticed the scarred man, nudged their neighbours and gestured towards him subtly with nods of the head or pointed elbows. Slowly the cacophony of the crowd diminished and faded away, until only the man at the bar, oblivious to the newcomer, was making any kind of noise, singing a bawdy ballad, out of tune and at the top of his voice.

The scarred man walked through the crowd, which parted, making a clear corridor for him, despite the crush. The newcomer sauntered with an arrogant assuredness up to the bar, and sat next to the singing man who was clearly well on the way to being fully drunk.

The drunkard's song trailed off and he turned to the scarred man. He put an arm around him and held up a cup of wine.

"Will you drink with me?" he slurred.

The scarred man tensed at the familiarity, and firmly removed the arm from his shoulders.

"You look like a man who has just come into some money," said the scarred man.

"Maybe," said the drunkard, winking and tapping his nose in an over-elaborate enjoinder to secrecy. "Name's Hilarius." He stuck out a hand with a smile. "It means cheerful."

The scarred man looked at the hand contemptuously.

"My name is Febrox," said the scarred man. "It means fierce."

Carbo felt disappointed. He had been hoping this was going to be Rabidus. It couldn't be that simple. He looked across to Lutorius, who held out his hand, palm down in a calming gesture.

Hilarius smiled. "Febrox?" He stroked his chin. "I had a dog called Febrox once. Cute thing, loved to be rubbed just behind its ears."

A low chuckle went around the onlookers, which was immediately quelled by a look from Febrox.

Febrox fixed Hilarius with a dagger stare, to which Hilarius seemed oblivious.

"I hear you have been shouting your mouth off all evening, talking about your good fortune."

Hilarius waved his hand. "Oh, you know. I had some luck."

"Tell me about it."

Hilarius looked around, then leaned in close to Febrox.

"Don't tell anyone," he said in a slurred whisper so loud the whole tavern could hear, "but I mugged someone."

Febrox's eyes narrowed.

"Really?"

"Yes," said Hilarius. "Some old nobleman, walking the streets without his bodyguard, silly man. Huge purse at his belt. I don't normally do this sort of thing, but it was so easy. I just showed him my knife, and he begged me not to kill him. He litul... littreral... he litterelurally threw the purse at me. Then he ran away, little skinny legs sticking out from under his toga."

Febrox put a hand on Hilarius' arm.

"That's not how things are done around here, friend." The word friend sounded anything but friendly.

Hilarius looked confused, then mild alarm settled on his features.

"Oh no, you aren't one of those stashlio... stationarii are you? Are you going to arrest me?"

Febrox chuckled humourlessly.

"No. I work for someone else. You are going to need to speak to him."

"Why?"

"Because you owe him."

"I'm not from around here," said Hilarius looking confused. "I don't owe no one nothing."

"You owe him," repeated Febrox firmly. He pulled his cloak back to reveal a long dagger at his belt. "Now come with me."

Looking concerned, the tottering Hilarius allowed himself to be led out of the tavern. Gradually, the conversation restarted.

"Do you think he will be all right?" asked Lutorius.

"Vespillo is always all right," said Carbo firmly. Then he looked doubtful. "I just hope he isn't really as drunk as he looks."

Lutorius shook his head. "Come on, we don't want to give them too much of a head start."

Vespillo let Febrox lead him down the dark street. Although nowhere near as busy as in daylight hours, this part of Nola had enough taverns, guest houses and brothels that there was a regular stream of passers-by. Febrox kept a firm grip on Vespillo's arm, nodding to anyone who looked at them curiously, showing his knife to anyone who looked twice.

Vespillo's head was spinning. He could hold his wine, years of keeping up with the other centurions in the legions, and after that with the vigiles, had hardened his constitution. Still, that didn't mean he was completely immune to the effects, and he had drunk a fair quantity that evening while making sure all and sundry knew about his new found wealth. His staggering gait was only partly exaggerated for appearance. He hoped that Carbo and Lutorius were not far behind. He was very unsure of his ability to fight his way out of trouble.

Nola had a surprisingly twisty collection of narrow streets and back alleys. Unlike the more modern colonia and other new settlements, started from scratch with an efficient grid pattern of streets, the more ancient Nola had developed haphazardly, like Rome itself. Consequently, Vespillo with his blurred senses found it hard to track his route. A few more turns, and he was convinced he was lost.

Febrox led him to a nondescript house, nestled close to its neighbours. Its only unusual characteristic were that its walls were free of graffiti, unlike most of the other vertical surfaces in Nola. Febrox banged on the door. After a few moments of silence, the heavy wooden door swung open with a deep creak.

A bulky porter looked Vespillo up and down slowly, then stared questioningly at Febrox. Febrox returned the look silently, eyes narrowed. The porter patted Vespillo down roughly, checking for concealed weapons, then stepped aside, and Febrox gripped Vespillo's upper arm and pulled him through the door.

Two scruffy men, both holding long knives in loose grips at their sides stood in the atrium, watching Vespillo with little interest. Despite the tatty exterior, the inside of the house was well decorated, with bright murals, and a well-tended lararium, the little deities of highly polished silver surrounded by offerings of food and coin. A third man stood before Febrox, not even acknowledging Vespillo's presence.

"Is this him?"

Febrox nodded.

"He is expecting you. Go on through."

Febrox led Vespillo through to the triclinium. The room was sumptuously decorated, marble statues, elaborate chandeliers, ornate oil lamps, delicate carved wooden furniture with fur upholstery.

Reclining alone on the couch, closely attended by a voluptuous and scantily clad slave girl, was an enormously obese man. His jowls hung low in folds of flesh, and his bald pate, rimmed by a thin line of grey hair, was shiny with sweat. He wore a toga, which hung loose enough to reveal a fleshy chest, covered in large moles. The man took a deep glug of wine, and looked from Vespillo to Febrox.

"Well?"

Febrox gave Vespillo a hard shove in the back, and with his unsteadiness, he didn't have to pretend to lose his balance, as he fell to his knees.

"This is the one my source mentioned," said Febrox.

"What's your name?" demanded the obese man.

"Who are you, first?" said Vespillo, defiantly.

The man laughed. "Febrox, tell the little cunnus who he is dealing with."

Febrox pulled his blade and touched it to Vespillo's throat. He let the point dig in then drew it in a curve, in a half circle around his neck. It dug in just deep enough to draw a thin line of blood. Vespillo tensed at the sting, keeping stoically silent, then remembered his role and allowed himself a little cry.

Febrox lifted the blade to his mouth, and licked the blood off it. "This, cunnus," said Febrox, "Is Rabidus."

Vespillo looked confused. "I'm sorry, I… I'm not from round here." He stared up at Rabidus, letting a little of the fear he was feeling appear in his eyes. "I don't know who you are."

"I am the one who is going to teach you some respect." He nodded to Febrox, who without warning punched Vespillo in the side of his head. Vespillo sprawled sideways, stunned. Febrox was instantly on top of him, rolling him onto his back and straddling him, pulling his hair back. The thug leaned down, putting his face close to Vespillo's, while he placed his blade just underneath Vespillo's eye socket.

Vespillo froze. The foul breath of rotting teeth and spicy food washed over him, and he suppressed a gag. Febrox's cheeks flushed red around the livid scar. Some saliva gathered at the edge of his lips, and dripped onto Vespillo's face.

"Let him up," said Rabidus. Febrox sneered down at Vespillo, then rolled off him. Vespillo righted himself uncertainly, but judged it best to remain on his knees. Rabidus laughed.

"That's a bit better. Now, I could just keep calling you cunnus, but there are so many cunni in Nola, it would get confusing. Tell me your name."

"I'm Hilarius," said Vespillo.

"And I believe you owe me something."

"I don't know…" Febrox flashed the blade near Vespillo's eyes. "I mean… yes, I do, I do. I just don't know the exact… nature of the debt."

Rabidus took a mouthful of a fruit tart, chewed slowly, then washed it down with some more wine, draining his cup. He passed the empty vessel to the slave girl, and as she turned to fill it, he put a hand on her backside and squeezed painfully, causing her to flinch.

Rabidus wiped his mouth on the sleeve of his toga, then belched loudly. The smell of the expelled gases reached Vespillo, who tried not to betray a physical reaction.

"Understand something, Hilarius," said Rabidus, getting louder. "I run this town. Not the duucuntmvirs, not the decurions, not that idiot Asellio who commands the sons of slave whores who make up the stationarii." He slammed his fist down on the table in front of him, causing the freshly-filled cup of wine to jump in the air, then roll off to smash on the floor. "Me!" he roared.

"Yes…master," said Vespillo.

Rabidus took a deep breath, partially mollified by Vespillo's deference.

"There is a tax, payable by all businesses in Nola. Legitimate and not so legitimate. Twenty per cent of all takings is payable to me." Rabidus smiled. "And not to those masked bastards," he added. Vespillo noted some of the thugs exchanging concerned glances.

"I apologise sincerely, master," said Vespillo. "I didn't realise."

"Your apology is accepted. And since you are new in Nola, I will not punish you."

"Thank you, master Rabidus."

"So, how much did you steal."

"Ten aurei."

Febrox whistled through the gaps in his teeth.

"A fine yield," said Rabidus. "And a very careless rich man. I will take my tax of twenty per cent."

"Absolutely," said Vespillo, fishing in his purse for two solidi, and placing them in Febrox's outstretched palm.

"Good. However, this doesn't compensate us for the inconvenience of having to track you down. For my colleague's time. And of course, the fine for late payment."

"Of course," agreed Vespillo, anxious now to be away from this odious man and his mad lieutenant.

"Ten more aurei."

Vespillo's jaw dropped. "But, I only stole ten in the first place. And I spent at least half of that in the tavern tonight. I don't have any more."

"Then you had better find someone else to mug. You have until tomorrow night. Ten aurei. Bring them to me here. Now, out."

Rabidus turned to his slave girl, putting an arm around her waist and pulling her onto his lap. He kissed her deeply, and her eyes widened as his tongue entered into her mouth. After a long, breathless moment, he let her go, and she pulled back, gasping, distressed, before remembering to smile, and gently stroke his cheek.

Febrox pulled Vespillo to his feet and led him to the door.

"Oh, and Hilarius."

Vespillo turned.

"If you do rob someone, don't forget to pay my tax this time."

"No, master Rabidus," said Vespillo. Febrox dragged him away as Rabidus lost interest in him again. He pulled him past the guards in the atrium, past the porter who opened the door, and pushed him out in the street. Vespillo sprawled onto his face. For a moment he lay there, head spinning, neck stinging, one side of his head throbbing.

Two pairs of strong hands gripped his arms and pulled him upright.

"Come on, friend," said Carbo. "Let's get you sobered up, and you can tell us what you learned."

Carbo passed a cup of water to Vespillo, who took it gratefully. A thin scab ran around his neck, and one side of his head was swollen. He drained the cup, then looked at Lutorius through narrowed eyes that spoke of an intense headache.

"I don't suppose there is anywhere around here that could do me some fried canary at this time of the morning?"

They sat in a corner of the mess hall of the quarters of the stationarii. The room was empty, dimly lit by the very first rays of sun.

"We will see what we can find," said Lutorius.

"First," said Carbo. "Are you up to telling us what happened yet?"

Vespillo nodded, then winced at the effect of the sharp movement on the pain in his head. He recounted what had happened, like a soldier reporting after a battle. Carbo let him finish before asking questions.

"Tell me about Rabidus. What did he look like?"

"Fat. Ugly. Old."

"Apparently he is also completely ruthless," said Lutorius. "He may not look like much, but no one would dare cross him."

"It's not him, is it?" asked Carbo. "He isn't one of the masked men? Comedy or Tragedy?"

Vespillo shook his head, then groaned again. "Gods, that hurts. No, there is no way he is up to banditry. He clearly has men to do that for him."

"Could the masked men work for him?" asked Lutorius.

This time Carbo disagreed. "They were their own men, that was clear. The thugs that attacked Rufa and me were working for them. If Tragedy and Comedy weren't their leaders, then they must have paid for their help."

"So Rabidus must know their identities."

"I don't think so - he mentioned them but not by name. And I get the impression there was a little fear beneath the bluster."

"So what now?" asked Lutorius.

"We gather up your men and arrest Rabidus," said Vespillo firmly.

Lutorius laughed. "Are you kidding me? All the men are terrified of Rabidus. Why do you think he is allowed to carry on doing what he is doing?"

"Even Asellio?"

"Asellio turns a blind eye. It makes life easier."

Vespillo shook his head in disgust, then slammed a fist into the wall to distract from the pain. "By Hermes' scrotum, why do I keep doing that?"

"So the stationarii won't act," said Carbo. He held the other two men in a stern gaze, one after the other.

"In that case, we do it ourselves."

# CHAPTER IX

Carbo sat on a stone bench behind the farm, thinking hard. Melanchaetes wandered up to him, and Carbo absent-mindedly scratched the huge dog behind the ears. Melanchaetes sat, cocking his head to one side, and making a scratching movement with his hind foot, which thumped against the wet earth rhythmically. His tongue moved in and out in little laps with pleasure at the attention.

There were just three of them, and Rabidus had a gang. Frontal assault was clearly out of the question, so some sort of subterfuge would be necessary. Vespillo could obviously get near to Rabidus again, when he went to make his payment that night, but he would be searched for weapons like before. Carbo couldn't work out how to turn the situation to their advantage.

He stood up and paced, and Melanchaetes trotted along behind him, clumsily treading on Carbo's heels. Carbo turned angrily and lifted a hand and the dog shrank back. He sighed, and knelt down to give the beast some fuss.

"Maybe you should pay some attention to Fabilla too."

Carbo looked up. Vespillo was watching him. Carbo flushed. He hadn't seen the little girl since they had come back from town that morning. He told himself it was because he was busy, that he had too much to think about and do, but he knew he was fooling himself. He stood.

"She's in the tablinum with Thera." Vespillo's expression was sympathetic but firm.

Carbo walked into the atrium, and looked into the small tablinum that was supposed to serve as an office, if Theron had been that organised. Fabilla sat at a chair pulled up to a low table, and Thera sat opposite her. Their attentions were focused on a board with three concentric squares, with dots at the corners and the mid-points of each side, and lines connecting the midpoint dots. Small pebbles sat on various dots, and each girl had a collection of pebbles at her side. Carbo recognised the game of merelles, and continued to watch.

Fabilla reached into her pile of pebbles and placed one on one of the dots. Thera quickly placed one of her pebbles to make a line of three. She snatched one of Fabilla's pieces off the table, and smiled triumphantly. Fabilla simply looked at her blankly, then let her eyes drift to the wall, where they remained, staring unfocused at the colourful fresco there.

"Fabilla. Fabilla? It's your turn." Thera placed her hand on Fabilla's which seemed to bring her back to herself.

"Oh, sorry," said Fabilla. She turned back to the board, but made no move. Then Carbo saw her little shoulders start to shake, watched as she folded her arms on the table and buried her head in them, crying silently. Thera stood and walked to Fabilla's side of the table, and put her arms around her, just holding her.

Carbo stared, helpless. Then cursing himself for his cowardice, he turned to tiptoe away.

He walked straight into Severa, who blocked his exit from the atrium with folded arms.

"Please let me pass," said Carbo in a low voice.

"She needs you," said Severa.

"No she doesn't. I failed her. Her mother is dead because I couldn't protect her.

She should hate me."

"She doesn't hate you. She wants your strength and comfort."

Carbo looked to one side, struggling with his own emotions. "I have none."

Severa continued to glare at him, and he felt himself withering under her gaze. "I will serve her better by avenging her mother," he mumbled.

"No, that is how you serve yourself."

He pushed past Severa, and stomped out of the farmhouse. Vespillo stood when he saw him, but Carbo marched straight past him, walking off into the olive groves, unaccompanied except by Melanchaetes who padded along behind and to one side. Images of Rufa flashed through his mind, passionate, happy, scared, dying. He clutched at his hair with both hands, dropped to his knees, and howled at the sky like an animal.

After some time, he returned to the house. Vespillo was waiting outside for him, but said nothing, just regarded him with concern.

"I'm fine," said Carbo tersely. "But we need a plan for tonight."

"Can we kidnap him?"

Carbo shook his head. "There is no other way in apart from the front door, and he has too many men to force it."

"Lure him out?"

"He rarely goes out in public, Lutorius tells me."

"What if I took Marsia, and she had a concealed weapon?"

"Do you think they would neglect to search her? They would take great pleasure in it, I'm sure."

"What then?" said Vespillo helplessly.

Carbo smoothed his hair with one hand, musing. "Marsia. Maybe that would work."

"You said they would search her."

"Yes, but maybe she could have something on her that they would expect to find, that wouldn't concern them."

Vespillo looked puzzled.

"Come on," said Carbo, "Let's go and talk to her."

Vespillo stood before Rabidus, sober this time, and more scared because of it. To his side, Marsia looked composed, though angry from the overly thorough frisking the porter had given her. She looked beautiful, made up for the role, Vespillo reflected. Her dress was long and flowing, her eyes darkened with kohl from Severa's make up kit, her face whitened with white lead, then her cheeks lightly rouged, and her long hair pinned up stylishly. She looked every inch the pleasure slave she was intended to play.

Rabidus looked Marsia up and down with undisguised lust, grinned at Febrox who was lounging against a wall with another thug, then turned to Vespillo with curiosity in his expression. He looked at the purse of coins at Vespillo's belt.

"You have my money, I see," said Rabidus. "Why bring the girl?"

"I had a modest haul today, master. Just enough to pay what you need, with a little left over. I purchased this one from a passing slaver, for my...entertainment. I think though, maybe I am developing a taste for a life of banditry. I was thinking of continuing my, ahem, work. So I brought Marsia to you this evening. To see if, by offering you first use of her, as a gift, you could maybe see your way to allow me to go about my business in Nola, unharmed. With the proper taxes paid to yourself, of course."

Rabidus' eyes narrowed, looking at Vespillo with suspicion.

"I don't like freelancers on my patch," he said.

"Then maybe I should work for you," said Vespillo, hastily. "Or you may tell me you will not allow it, in which case I will accept and move on. Whatever you decide, Marsia is for you to enjoy tonight."

Rabidus thought for a moment, then beckoned her over. Marsia, walked over to him, hips swaying seductively, and every man in the room watched her move. Rabidus reached up to stroke her face gently, and Marsia smiled. Then he grabbed the front of her dress at her neckline and ripped harshly downwards. Her ample breasts tumbled out for all to see.

Vespillo couldn't see her cheeks colour underneath the makeup, but he knew how the proud slave must be feeling. He suddenly realised how his own attitudes to the feelings of slaves had changed, in the short time he had know Rufa and Fabilla. Before that, the slave's discomfort would have meant nothing to him.

Febrox whistled. "He's brought you a fine one there, boss, to be fair to him."

Rabidus reached up and grasped a breast, squeezing painfully, while Marsia kept her face inviting. He grabbed her and pulled her onto his knee and kissed her deeply. Marsia reached up into her hair, pulled out the hairpin that had kept her hair up, letting the hair tumble free, then stabbed the pin into Rabidus' leg.

Rabidus howled and cuffed Marsia around the head, the force of the blow sending her sprawling across the floor. He leapt to his feet, pointing an accusing finger at Vespillo.

"What is wrong with your slave whore?" he roared. "Febrox, kill them both."

Febrox drew his knife and advanced on Vespillo, while the other thug grabbed Marsia by the hair and put his dagger to her throat.

"Wait," said Vespillo, desperately. "Kill us and you are dead."

Rabidus laughed, but raised a hand to stay his men.

"Who is going to save you? The stationarii? The townsfolk."

"You are," said Vespillo, trying to keep his voice even.

Rabidus cocked his head on one side, a broad leer on his face.

"Now why by Juno's tits would I want to do that?"

"Because if you don't," said Vespillo, "You will never get the antidote to the poison that was on that pin."

The ruddy colour drained from Rabidus' face, and his jaw dropped. Febrox looked at Rabidus uncertainly, still brandishing his knife in Vespillo's face.

Rabidus slowly got to his feet. It took considerable effort to get his prodigious frame upright, and he reached down to rub the site of the prick in his leg, from which a tiny trickle of blood was seeping. He stepped forward, and then with a speed that was startling for a man of his size, he grabbed the knife from Febrox, seized Vespillo around the throat, and pressed the blade up under his chin, forcing his head back.

"What," Rabidus said, slowly and menacingly, "are you talking about?"

Vespillo hissed his reply, the powerful hand at his neck choking off his air and the blade forcing his mouth closed.

"The hairpin," he spluttered. "It had been dipped in extract of Pan's Bane."

Rabidus looked uncertain. He gripped Vespillo's neck harder. "What's Pan's

Bane?"

Vespillo felt his air supply cut off, felt his head start to swim, blackness appear at the periphery of his vision.

"Can't...speak," he gasped.

Rabidus relaxed his grip, but didn't let go. Vespillo sucked air into his lungs, head slowly clearing.

"What," repeated Rabidus, quiet and threatening, "is Pan's Bane?"

"A rare poison," said Vespillo. "Known only to priestesses of a certain obscure cult of Isis."

"What does it do?"

"At first, very little," said Vespillo, voice hoarse. "Just a tingling sting around the entry wound."

Rabidus kept the knife under Vespillo's chin, but reached down with his other hand to rub his thigh. Vespillo could see concern on his face.

"Then, chills start to run down your spine. Next, you start to sweat, you feel out of breath, and you can feel your heart beat faster."

Vespillo looked into the gang boss's eyes, saw them becoming wider, heard his breathing quicken. He put a hand to his chest.

"In some people, their bowels tighten. For others, they loosen and shit all over the floor."

One of the thugs laughed, then fell silent at a deadly glare from Rabidus.

"Some feel like they are going to be sick. Then comes weakness in the legs, faintness, a tightening of the throat, a gasping for air...then death."

Rabidus looked completely panic stricken now.

"How quickly?"

"Quick. Maybe half an hour once you start to feel the first effects. You can feel them already can't you? I can tell. The way you are holding your leg, it is stinging like a swarm of wasps have been at it. I can see you sweating, hear your breathing getting fast."

"There is a cure? An antidote?"

Vespillo nodded. "There is. It usually works. Although," he added, feeling now that he had the upper hand and starting to enjoy himself, "I must warn you that the after effects of the poison will leave you impotent."

"What?" roared Rabidus.

"Unless," said Vespillo raising one hand in gesture of conciliation, "You have regular doses of the antidote."

"Give me the cure, now!"

"I would be a fool to bring it with me, wouldn't I?"

"Get it, or you are a dead man."

"That threat doesn't really work, does it? Kill me, and you die too. I am your only hope."

Rabidus gestured to Marsia. "I will kill your slave," he threatened, weakly.

Vespillo shrugged. "She has served her purpose. It makes no difference to me." Vespillo ignored the glare Marsia was giving him that he could see from the corner of his eye, wondering if he would pay for that comment later.

Rabidus let the knife drop away from Vespillo's throat, and his shoulders slumped. A wave of pain broke across his face and he gripped his leg. His breath came short and panicked.

"What do you want?"

"I want you to leave me alone. If I give you the cure, I owe you nothing, nor will I owe you anything in the future, whatever my activities."

"Agreed. Now give me the cure."

"Come with me then. Marsia will lead the way."

Rabidus looked across at the thug holding Marsia, and nodded at him. The thug released Marsia. She shook herself free angrily, then turned and spat in his face. The thug lifted his hand to strike her across the face, but Rabidus roared him down.

Marsia headed for the exit, and Vespillo gestured for Rabidus to follow her. Febrox started to accompany him, but Vespillo put a hand on his chest.

"Alone," he said.

Febrox started to protest, but Vespillo cut him short. "We don't have much time Rabidus. How is the leg feeling?"

Rabidus rubbed the leg, wincing. "Stay here, Febrox. This fool could never best me."

Febrox looked doubtful but bowed his head in acquiescence. Rabidus limped heavily after Marsia, and Vespillo walked behind, eyes straight ahead, ignoring the dagger glares from all the thugs who had gathered in silence to watch him take their leader away.

They reached the doorway that led from the atrium into the street, and Vespillo longed to be out of the gang's hideout. The large porter stepped into their path. Marsia locked eyes with him, but he returned her stare implacably. She turned back to Vespillo.

"Get out of the way," said Rabidus.

"Boss…" said the porter, a pleading quality in his voice. "I don't want you out there alone."

"Rabidus," said Vespillo. "The water is running out of the clepsydra."

Rabidus pushed past Marsia and shoved the porter out of the way, opening the door himself. He held it open for Marsia and Vespillo.

"Come on," he said. "Hurry."

Lutorius lay on his back on the bed, covered in a light sheen of sweat. The woman next to him was panting, her eyes half shut. She sighed and half turned, so her arm and upper body was draped over his, her ample breasts against his bare chest. He stroked light finger tips down her back, enjoying the post-coital glow, the sensation of closeness these moments brought.

She looked up at him, kissed him firmly on the lips, her tongue exploring his mouth brazenly. He reflected on where her mouth had been just moments before, but put it from his mind and kissed her back passionately. He wondered if he was falling for this woman. He certainly liked the need she felt for him, the almost desperate nature of her passion. She clearly wasn't getting what she wanted from her husband.

He leaned towards her, placing a hand on her breast, feeling the nipple harden against his palm. He squeezed and she sighed, her leg moving across his body, so his thigh was pressed firmly against her. She started to grind herself against him in a marvellously wanton way, and despite having only just finished one performance, he was surprised to find himself hardening again.

She reached down to discover this for herself, and smiled at him, then bit him lightly on the neck. He responded, rolling over and between her legs. He entered her smoothly with one thrust, looking down into her eyes as they flew open in pleasure. She wrapped her arms and legs around him as he thrust firmly in and out, crying loudly, to his slight consternation. Fortunately, he knew her husband was elsewhere, in a brothel on the other side of town. He hoped the household slaves were discreet.

He lasted longer this time, much to his lover's pleasure, but his climax still arrived quickly, the beautiful woman below him clutching at him as her own climax washed over her. He collapsed on top of her, exhausted now. She gasped below him, as he lay, all thoughts banished from his pleasure flooded mind.

Slowly, awareness of the present came back to him. He looked at the guttering oil lamp, fuel nearly gone. Sudden panic seized him.

"Merda, how long have I been here?"

She stroked his face. "Relax, my husband won't be back for hours."

"I know, but there is somewhere else I need to be."

She pouted at him as he hastily threw on his clothes, pausing only to blow her a kiss from the doorway. He knew she would be irritated with him for the hasty departure, but he really did have somewhere else he had promised to be, something he would hate to be late for.

Still, it was definitely worth it. The affair was still new, but he was in no hurry to end it. She was an amazing fuck. And there was the added bonus of the fact that he got to cuckold his arse of a commanding officer.

Carbo looked up with annoyance at the approaching figure.

"You're late," he snapped.

"Sorry," said Lutorius. "I'm here now."

Carbo peered down the dark street, eyes straining for movement.

"How much longer can he be?" he asked anxiously, turning back to Lutorius.

"I've no idea," said Lutorius, sitting on the edge of the fountain they had agreed as their meeting point. "I still don't understand why you are so confident he will come."

"You'll see," said Carbo. "As long as nothing has gone wrong."

"We are all in the hands of the Parcae," said Lutorius.

Carbo shot him an irritated look.

Lutorius spread his hands in a conciliatory gesture.

"Better in the hands of the Fates than the Furies."

"When I find out who killed Rufa, they will wish for the vengeance of the Furies rather than what I will do to them."

Lutorius opened his mouth to reply, thought better of it, then squinted over Carbo's shoulders. He pointed. "There. That's them."

Carbo turned to see two shapes emerging from the darkness, one short and broad-shouldered, the other bulky and rotund. Another shape appeared behind them, a muscular woman. As they drew close, their faces became clear, Marsia, Vespillo and a grotesquely obese man who was panting and sweating.

"Rabidus?" Carbo asked Vespillo.

"The same."

Carbo put his hand out to Vespillo, then slapped him on the back.

"Well done, friend." He faced Rabidus, looking him up and down with contempt. "We're going to have a talk."

Rabidus looked uncertainly at Vespillo.

"Who is this? Where is my cure?"

"This is Carbo," said Vespillo. "Your men assisted in the murder of his woman."

Rabidus looked back to Carbo, eyes widening. "That was you?"

Carbo returned the gaze, face impassive.

"Are you going to kill me?" said Rabidus, a tremor in his voice.

"Bring him," said Carbo to Vespillo, and spun on his heel. The four of them, Carbo, Vespillo, Lutorius and Marsia, with Rabidus in the middle of them, walked a short way down the street to a small temple. Carbo entered and looked around. An oil lamp gave just enough flickering light to make out a drunkard and two homeless urchins lying near the altar. Carbo kicked them awake, and told them to leave. They protested until he half drew his sword, then quickly exited, spitting curses behind them. Vespillo and Lutorius pushed Rabidus into the room.

"The cure," he said, breathing heavily.

Carbo patted a pouch at his belt. "In here. When you have answered my questions."

"Please," said Rabidus. "I can feel it, the Pan's Bane, in my blood. My heart feels like it is going to burst."

"Who hired you? Who paid you to send men to help them attack me?"

"Give me the cure," gasped Rabidus. "It's getting hard to speak. Can't think properly."

Carbo undid the pouch, pulled out a small stoppered flask and held it up. Rabidus reached for it, but Carbo put a hand on his chest and pushed him backwards, feeling his hand sink into the rolls of fat as he did so.

"Who?" he said.

"I can't tell you," said Rabidus. "These aren't people you double-cross."

"How's your heart doing?" asked Vespillo.

Rabidus paled. "Please. They will kill me. They are completely ruthless."

"From you, that's high praise," commented Lutorius.

Carbo remained motionless, the flask outstretched but out of reach. "Names."

Rabidus rubbed his chest and shook his head. "If I tell you, no one must know it came from me."

Carbo raised one eyebrow.

Rabidus shook his head. "Their names are Atreus and Menelaus."

"Greeks?" asked Marsia. Lutorius looked at her in surprise.

"She's surprisingly educated," explained Vespillo.

"I don't think they are Greek," said Carbo. "They don't sound Greek."

"We know those names. But what are their real names?" asked Lutorius.

"That's all they have ever gone by, to me at least."

"What do they look like, then?" asked Carbo.

"But...you've seen them," said Rabidus confused.

"I mean without their masks, obviously."

Rabidus looked around the faces confronting him, surprised. "I haven't seen them without their masks. No one has. Do you think if I knew who they were, I would let them get away with what they do in my territory?"

Carbo looked away and cursed.

"There must be something else you can tell us about them," said Vespillo. "How did they find you? What did they sound like?"

"They approached me initially. They pay well and they are merciless, so I don't complain. As to what they sound like, their masks muffle their voices." Rabidus was gabbling now, gasping breaths as the words flowed out in a torrent. "Though Menelaus doesn't say much, not like Thyestes used to."

Carbo looked over at Lutorius. "I told you I had killed Thyestes. That this Menelaus was someone new."

"Ah," said Rabidus. "You killed Atreus' brother. That makes sense." Then he let out a wheezing cough. "You know killing your woman was just the start. He wants you to suffer, but ultimately he wants your life."

Carbo exchanged glances with Vespillo. Lutorius looked disgusted. "So this has been a waste of time."

"Not a complete waste," said Carbo. "This piece of shit gave Atreus the men he needed. They would never have been able to kill her if it wasn't for him. I can at least end him."

Carbo drew his gladius and pressed it to Rabidus' neck.

"Wait, wait," gabbled Rabidus desperately.

"Give me a reason not to kill you."

"I can bring you to them," he said.

Carbo said nothing, but held still.

"We have a way of meeting. If we need to see each other, we leave a piece of graffiti on a certain wall. Different words mean different times and places."

Carbo looked across to Vespillo and Lutorius.

"What do you think?"

"Sounds like our best chance," said Lutorius. Vespillo nodded agreement.

Carbo considered for a moment then stepped back, lowering his sword.

"Fine. Set it up."

"The cure," said Rabidus. "I can't help you if I'm dead."

Carbo hesitated, then passed him the flask. Rabidus grabbed it from him and drained it rapidly, being careful not to spill a drop.

"How quickly does it work?" he asked when it was gone.

"More or less straight away," said Vespillo. "You will find your heart rate starting to slow, your breathing becoming easier. A sensation of calm will come over you, and the tightness in your guts will ease."

Relief flooded over Rabidus' features.

"Yes, yes. I can feel it working. Thank you, thank you."

"Get out of here," said Vespillo. "Send Febrox to the tavern where I first met him, tomorrow night, with details of the meeting."

Rabidus hurried to the door.

"And remember," said Vespillo. "Every month you will need the cure, or you will be permanently impotent. I will make sure Lutorius always has it for you."

"I understand," said Rabidus, and the sour look he gave Lutorius suggested that he did. With that, he hurried out.

Vespillo walked to the door, looked out to make sure Rabidus was gone, then turned back to the others and doubled over, howls of laughter erupting from him. Lutorius stared at him in surprise, then over to Marsia, who was grinning broadly.

"What is it?" he asked, confused.

"Pan's Bane?" asked Carbo. "How did you come up with that name?"

"Oh," said Vespillo, trying to compose himself. "I thought it sounded good. And played on the fear of any man, especially a fat, ugly one like that. Everyone knows Pan is famed for his sexual prowess, so Pan's Bane would emphasise one of the effects I was claiming."

"Your mention of impotence was very clever, Master," said Marsia. "You could see the terror in his eyes when you mentioned that."

"Thank you, Marsia," said Vespillo. "And now he belongs to Lutorius - if he doesn't come back monthly for the cure, he will believe himself to become permanently impotent. Lutorius, I'm sure you can come up with all sorts of ways to use that to your advantage."

Understanding dawned on Lutorius. "It's fake? There is no such thing as Pan's Bane?"

Carbo laughed and shook his head. "Not that we know."

"But, when he finds out that he isn't impotent in a month's time?"

"He won't risk it," said Marsia. "And even if he does, the fear of impotence will probably make him impotent anyway."

Vespillo roared with laughter at this, although Carbo's smile faded. Carbo had been unable to be intimate with a woman after his experiences of torture at the hands of German priestesses, until Rufa had come along. She had shown him it was still possible for him to be a man, in all ways. And now she was gone.

"But," Lutorius still sounded confused, "he thought he had been poisoned. He could feel it."

"The needle was laced with simple acetum, vinegar. That ensured it stung like a hornet from Hades. After that, the symptoms I told him were just those of a man in terror. Fast heart rate, fast breathing, cold sweats, clenched bowels. Taking a very fat man for a brisk walk afterwards is only going to worsen that."

Lutorius shook his head in amazement. "You and Marsia walked into Rabidus' lair armed with nothing more than a hair pin dipped in vinegar?" He looked at Carbo accusingly. "Why didn't you tell me?"

Carbo found his smile again. "Where's the fun in that?"

# CHAPTER X

Carbo and Vespillo sat at the kitchen table in the farmhouse, eating some bread and olives for a light lunch. Marsia poured them some water, and Carbo took a sip, a faraway, pensive look on his face.

"What are you thinking?" asked Vespillo.

"How I'm going to kill them," said Carbo, flatly.

Vespillo nodded.

"And? How?"

Carbo focused on Vespillo. "You want to know the details?"

"Yes," said Vespillo. "I loved Rufa too, you know. And I see your pain every day. And Fabilla's."

Carbo ignored the mention of Rufa's daughter. He had avoided her again today, and hated himself for it. He cursed himself as a coward, but was struggling too much with his own pain to feel he could be helpful to the little girl.

"I'm going to string them up. A rope around their neck, until they are half hanged. Then slit them open, and let them see their guts fall out." He stroked his chin. "Or maybe burning? That's supposed to be pretty painful, isn't it?"

"It is," confirmed Vespillo, the vigiles commander, who had seen many men burn in his time fighting fires in Rome. He regarded Carbo with sympathy, and some alarm. He had seen his friend go through a lot, but he had never seen him so coldly and viciously angry. But he couldn't fault him for it. He knew, from his own past, exactly how his friend felt.

Melanchaetes started barking, a deep and booming noise that alerted the farm's occupants, while intimidating visitors. Theron appeared from his quarters and slowly and stiffly went to answer the door. Shortly he returned with Quintus.

"Quintus Sempronius Blaesus to see you, master," said Theron.

"Thank you, Theron, I can see who it is," said Carbo, then regretted his terse tone. "Go and have some lunch yourself."

Theron inclined his head and backed out.

Carbo stood and extended his hand. "Quintus. Good to see you."

"And you, Carbo. Vespillo." Quintus shook hands with both of them, then accepted the seat Carbo offered him.

"How are you?" Quintus asked Carbo. Carbo opened his mouth to speak, and couldn't find anything to say that didn't sound either overly emotional or too cold. He closed his mouth and shrugged. Quintus nodded, eyes expressing sympathy.

"You, Quintus?"

"I'm well, thank you."

"Your brother and father?"

"My brother seems unlikely to change. Bored, frustrated, wanting more from life but not sure what. Maybe Rome would hold more interest for him than Nola."

"He wants to start a political career?"

Quintus laughed. "Ha! Publius? No, he has no ambitions beyond his own amusements. I was thinking that Rome, with its festivals and chariot races and gladiatorial contests and an endless supply of whores would be to his liking."

Vespillo smiled. "So why doesn't he go?"

"My father won't allow it. He gave me a small amount of money to sustain myself on my tour of Greece - I think he liked the idea of being rid of me for a few years actually - but he has made it clear that Rome is forbidden to us."

"Do you know why?"

Quintus hesitated. "I'm... not supposed to."

"But?" prompted Vespillo.

"I don't suppose you have something to drink? I'm parched from the journey over."

"Of course," said Carbo. "Apologies for my poor hosting. I'm not really used to visitors. Marsia!"

Marsia came into the kitchen, and Carbo opened his mouth to speak, then noticed something odd.

"Marsia, are you wearing make up?"

Marsia blushed furiously, something Carbo had never seen before.

"I was just...Thera said I could borrow..."

Carbo frowned in confusion, then waved his hand dismissively. "Get Quintus a drink."

"Yes, master." She turned to Quintus "What may I serve you, sir?"

Quintus smiled at her, and they locked eyes for a moment, before Marsia looked down, embarrassed.

"Water will be fine, thank you, Marsia."

"Yes, sir." Marsia hurried over to a pitcher standing on a table by the wall and poured Quintus a cup of water from it. She brought it over to him, and as she passed it, her hand trembled and a few drops fell into Quintus lap.

"Marsia, what's wrong with you?" barked Carbo.

"I'm so sorry, master," she said, and before Quintus could protest it was nothing, she had fled from the room.

"What's got into her?" wondered Carbo.

Vespillo laughed. "Oh dear. Apologies, Quintus, I think Carbo's slave rather likes you."

"Really?" asked Quintus, looking genuinely pleased. He turned to gaze at the door through which Marsia had just retreated. Vespillo grinned at Carbo, who raised his eyebrows.

Vespillo gave a little cough, which seemed to bring Quintus back from a daze.

"You were telling us about your father and Rome, I think?"

Quintus nodded.

"Like I say, I'm not supposed to know. This goes no further than this room, agreed?"

"Of course not," said Carbo and Vespillo nodded emphatically.

Quintus took a deep breath. "There is much I don't know. Some things I can only guess. But my brother, he is older than me. He remembers more, and when he is drunk, he lets things slip, things that father has clearly told him should remain secret."

"Like?" asked Carbo.

"Like the night our family fled Rome." Quintus sipped from his cup, and Carbo noticed that he was gripping it tight enough to whiten his knuckles. He hoped it wouldn't break.

"I was a baby. I mean really tiny. Days old. My mother... she had just died. Giving birth to me. My father has told me about this, many, many times. How I was presented in the wrong position, how my mother screamed in agony for hours trying to expel me. How the Roman and Greek physicians were helpless, and how, as my mother's strength faded, he found a Jewish doctor who claimed to know the procedure by which a baby could be taken from the womb through a hole in the mother's side."

Carbo looked surprised. "You were cut from the womb? Under the Lex Caesarea?"

"The Lex Caesarea dictates a baby must be cut from the womb when the mother is dead. My mother was still alive and the Jew claimed to be able to save her."

"He failed, then," said Carbo sympathetically.

"At first the operation seemed to be a success. He seemed very skilled, and I know that among the Jews in Rome, many women do survive the procedure, though the Greek and Roman doctors swear it is impossible. I was pulled alive from the side of my mother, while my father held her down and tried to keep her still as she thrashed about. Afterwards, I'm told, she fed me, and smiled, and promised to love me as long as she lived.

"It seemed like the operation had worked. On the first day she seemed to grow stronger. Then suddenly she started vomiting, became delirious. The Greek and Roman doctors smelled the wound and pronounced, with some satisfaction apparently, that it had putrefied. In her last lucid moment, she made my father swear to look after me. She died within hours."

Quintus looked down into his cup, swirling the water around, lost in thought.

"I'm sorry for your loss," said Vespillo.

Quintus looked up. "Can you count it a loss, a woman I never knew? And yet I feel it as a loss. My father was insane with grief apparently. My brother remembers him raging, punching walls, breaking furniture, while my uncle tried to calm him. My brother says he swore vengeance on the one who slew his mother. I don't know who he meant - the Jewish doctor I suppose. The next night my father and uncle left the domus. When they returned, they were covered in blood. That same night, the whole familias, father, brother, uncle, slaves, left Rome with as many possessions as they could take, and my father's fortune in gold. None of us have ever been back."

The three of them were silent. Carbo struggled to keep his own emotions in check. He knew exactly how Quintus' father had felt, and found himself feeling that maybe he shared a bond with the cantankerous old man. Blaesus certainly seemed to have reacted the same way Carbo had. He had obviously exacted vengeance on the one he thought responsible for his wife's death, just as Carbo had so sworn.

"Justice never sought your father then?"

Quintus shook his head. "My father is rich. I'm sure he knew who to pay to prevent a prosecution or a private vendetta from the family of whoever he killed. But he also knew that it would be foolish to remain in Rome, that the authorities would not tolerate the presence of a murderer among them. So he took himself into a voluntary exile, and the rest of us with him."

"It was so long ago, though," said Carbo. "Surely you could return now?"

"My father won't discuss it, won't hear of it. He is paterfamilias. He has the power of life and death over his family. Even if I'm sure he wouldn't kill me for going to Rome, he would cut me off and leave me destitute, I'm certain."

"I'm sorry," said Carbo. "You are trapped by events that happened when you were a baby."

"It's not so bad. I like Nola, it's my home. I like the people. And I have travelled. I would like to see Rome, and maybe I will one day. For now, though, all I really want is for my father to…" He stopped. Carbo knew what he had wanted to say, but was too embarrassed. All he wanted was for his father to love him. Carbo feared that if after eighteen years, his father still blamed him for the death of his mother, that situation would never change.

"Would you join us for some lunch, Quintus?" asked Carbo after a few moments.

"I would be honoured," said Quintus. Carbo yelled for Marsia again, and she appeared, seeming to be more in control of herself. She entered the room stiff-backed, and Carbo noticed the makeup had been removed.

"Fetch Quintus some bread and cheese and olives." He looked at Quintus. "Will that suit you?"

"That would be fine," said Quintus. "Thank you, Marsia." He smiled at her, and she bit her lip, blushing as she prepared the food. Theron returned, and picked up the plates that Vespillo and Carbo had emptied.

"May I begin preparations for the evening meal, master?" he asked.

Carbo nodded, and Theron busied himself at the kitchen work surface with peeling, chopping and dicing vegetables.

"So what brought you out here, today?" asked Carbo.

"I wanted to see how my comrade in arms was doing," replied Quintus. "And whether you had made any progress in catching… them."

"Maybe," said Carbo. "Have you heard of a man called Rabidus?"

Theron hurried out of the farmhouse. Carbo had shown little interest when he had told him that he had to go to town to get some more ingredients for the evening meal, and now he was on the road to Nola. His old bones protested at the pace he forced on them, but he had to do what he needed to do, as well as actually return with some produce to avoid arousing suspicions.

He felt guilty. He liked Carbo, and the poor man had been through so much. But he would not risk his safety, and more importantly the safety of Thera, to protect the man. When the thug had cornered him in the marketplace, threatened him and his daughter unless he gave them the information they needed, there was no doubting he would agree.

The thought of Thera caused his throat to close. He loved his daughter more than sometimes he thought he could bear. So like her mother, intelligent, vivacious. What a waste that she was a slave, when she could have made such a wonderful wife and mother to some worthy man. Still, she had as much freedom as a slave could have, as the daughter to the steward of the farm. Or she had until Carbo arrived. Not that he was a bad master. But he was still their master.

None of that mattered though. Things could have been normal, stable, if only Carbo hadn't encountered the bandits, if only Rufa hadn't been killed. Now, Carbo was on a collision course with a deadly adversary, and Theron was right in the middle of it. He wished fervently that he could just disappear with Thera, run away. But he knew what happened to runaway slaves.

Besides, his master was not the only one he feared.

Atreus would expect to be told what Theron had just heard. If he found out that Theron had been holding out on him, he would kill him and his daughter.

Theron increased his pace.

"Tell me, Menelaus. What do you understand by the term otium?"

"Rest. Relaxation. Leisure."

Atreus rubbed his face thoughtfully.

"Yes, many think of it like that. Tibullus for example. Have you read him?"

"No, father."

"No, I suppose you wouldn't have. I must see to your education as well as your martial skills. Tibullus' poems are full of praise to love and leisure, to the simple joys of the farming life. He wanted to live in a simple world, with no wars, no conflict. Just relaxation, a little agricultural labour.

"'Give, if you will, for gold a life of toil!
   Let endless acres claim your care!
While sounds of war your fearful slumbers spoil,
   And far-off trumpets scare!
To me my poverty brings tranquil hours;
   My lowly hearth-stone cheerly shines;
My modest garden bears me fruit and flowers,
   And plenteous native wines.'"

Menelaus listened to the verse with apparent attentiveness, though Atreus knew he had no interest in poetry.

"Very pretty lines, father," said Menelaus.

"Tibullus was a fool," said Atreus. "Do you know what I think another term is for otium? Boredom. I have all the leisure time I could want. I have all my worldly needs, all the entertainment that this backward part of Italy can provide. But I am bored! No chance to prove myself in politics. No military campaigns. Just leisure."

"I understand, father."

Atreus narrowed his eyes and looked at his son.

"Maybe you do. But understand or not, I am glad you are here with me now. Helping me relieve the boredom of endless otium. And of course making money at the same time."

They sat on damp ground a few miles from Nola, sheltered from the road below by an overhanging rock, watching the traffic. It was late afternoon, and pedestrians, laden donkeys and ox-drawn carts passed their position regularly, but not frequently.

"How about that one?" asked Menelaus.

Atreus looked down at the horse and rider and shook his head.

"Imperial courier. We don't want to attract that sort of attention. Besides, he would be gone before we could strike, those horses are fast. No, we have our information, we wait for the merchant our little spies in the town tell us they are expecting."

They let the courier trot on by, and waited quietly a little longer. The sound of cloven hooves and the rumble of iron rimmed wheels on the cobbles alerted them to the next traveller before they came into view. Soon they saw an ox-cart driven by a weathered looking merchant, who was drinking from a large flask. By his side was a younger, larger man, facial resemblance suggesting to Atreus this was the merchant's son. The son carried a large axe sideways across his lap, gripping the haft tightly at the end and near the head. The cart was full of expensive clothing from Rome. Atreus knew though, that after he had sold the clothing in Nola, the merchant's main business was to buy locally made jewellery and sell it back in Rome at a huge profit, and that he had a large amount of money with him to make the necessary purchases.

Atreus smiled and pulled on his tragedy mask.

Menelaus fastened the comedy mask around the back of his head with its tight leather straps, wincing as the buckle caught in his dark, curly hair. Just before the cart reached their position, Menelaus vaulted off the overhanging rock, and landed agilely in front of the travellers. The oxen looked up in surprise, and stopped plodding along. The merchant and his son gaped at the man wearing the comedy mask who had come from nowhere to appear in front of them.

"It's him," gasped the merchant. "That bandit they are all talking about."

"The world will be less one bandit soon," growled his son, and jumped off the cart, hefting the axe in both hands. Menelaus drew his sword and stood his ground, feet placed a little apart, eyes staring out intently through the holes in the mask. The merchant's son swaggered towards him, his bulk and heavy weapon lending him confidence.

"Careful," warned the merchant. "They say they fight well."

"Let's see if his puny sword can stop my axe then," said the son, and swung the axe high, then brought it down towards Menelaus' head. Menelaus dodged easily, and gave the off balance axeman a shove, sending him staggering to one side.

The merchant's son regained his balance, let out a roar and charged towards Menelaus, shoulder down. Menelaus side-stepped again, leaving a foot out to trip the axeman, causing him to sprawl forwards on the road. Menelaus laughed as the man slowly regained his feet. He was now side on to the cart, from where his anxious father looked on. More cautiously now, he swung his axe, from left to right, from right to left. Menelaus swayed out of the way, not even moving his feet from where he had planted them.

A gasp came from the axeman's left, from the direction of the cart. He turned, and saw his father staring at him, wide-eyed, mouth hanging open. Then blood started to pour out of his father's mouth, and he now saw the tip of the knife protruding from the front of his father's neck. Rising up from behind the cart was the man who had wielded the knife, a man wearing a tragedy mask.

"Father," cried out the axeman in distress, and took a step towards the cart.

There was a swish through the air, and the axeman's head leapt sideways away from his body. Blood spurted high from the severed vessels in the neck, and the body crumpled as the head hit the ground and rolled, eyes blinking a few times, before all was still.

Atreus pulled his mask off, and Melenaus did likewise. He reached into the cart, pulled out a bright red dress and held it up against himself.

"I wonder if my bed slave would like this?" he said out loud.

Menelaus shrugged, and Atreus tossed it aside.

Menelaus patted the still bleeding merchant down, and drew a purse out from under his tunic. He opened it and smiled. "Not bad, father. Maybe enough for a new statue?"

"Or a new bed slave?"

Menelaus cocked his head on one side. "Maybe you should be more careful with your pleasure slaves, father. How many more bastards should you sire?"

Atreus laughed. "As many as I damned well please." He looked along the road, saw no one.

"No slaves this time," said Menelaus.

"Sadly not. They were going to be too much trouble to subdue. Don't worry, I'm expecting a good catch soon. Something to keep Zosimus and Durmius happy."

Menelaus smiled. "I look forward to it."

"Let's get going, before someone comes along. Besides, I need to check the message drop location I gave to Carbo's steward, Theron. I am expecting him to be quite useful."

Atreus and Menelaus entered the plaza from the east. A bright moon cast shadows from the surrounding buildings. For once the sky was clear. Atreus noted the tough looking men positioned at each corner where the two streets making this crossroads intersected, armed with knives, clubs and bows. There were few people about at this time of night, but Rabidus' thugs were making sure this meeting, as always, would be undisturbed.

Atreus paused, and Menelaus halted at his right shoulder. He looked around, scanning the rooftops for the possibility of ambush, checking the windows of the buildings facing onto the square were all shuttered for the night. Satisfied, he carried on towards the fountain in the centre of the plaza, where Rabidus sat, flanked by two of his thugs, who stood a discreet distance away, backs turned to the oncoming men.

Atreus stopped a couple of paces before Rabidus, and looked at him from behind his tragedy mask. Rabidus did not stand, and for a moment, both men were silent, as if speaking first was losing some sort of battle of wills.

Rabidus broke first. "You saw my message, then."

"Indeed," said Atreus. "We were attending to some business nearby, today, and as we returned through Nola, naturally I checked our message board. You asked to meet, and here I am. I hope it is worth my time."

"Atreus you are such a prick sometimes. Fearsome with a sword, ruthless, cold-blooded and arrogant as a Parthian prince. Such a shame you don't work for me."

Atreus inclined his head.

"I will take all that as a compliment."

Rabidus smiled. "It was meant that way."

A moment's silence. Then, "Well?"

"Well," said Rabidus. "I have information for you. On the man who killed your brother."

Atreus said nothing. Rabidus continued, looking a little flustered. "I know your revenge on this Carbo is not complete. That when my men helped you kill his woman, that was just the start."

No response.

"Well, um, you can't do anything unless you know where he is. I can tell you."

"I see," said Atreus. "And where is he?"

"Here," said Carbo, spinning from Rabidus' shoulder where he had been imitating a silent guard. As he turned he drew his sword in one smooth motion, and swung it with fine control so it rested lightly against Atreus' neck.

Menelaus whipped his sword out with lightning dexterity, but hesitated at the sight of the blade at Atreus' throat.

Atreus did not so much as blink. He simply let out a sigh.

"Oh, Rabidus, you are a fool."

"What?" gasped Rabidus, taken aback by the calmly spoken words.

"A big, fat, stupid fool," said Atreus, saying each word slowly and clearly.

Rabidus rose to his feet now, anger suffusing his features.

"Oh, I am a fool am I? This, from a man who has walked into an ambush, and now has a sword at his throat held by a man who has sworn vengeance on him."

"Sit down, Rabidus," growled Carbo. "You've done your part now."

"Oh yes," said Atreus, "You have done your part, that's for sure. And why is that? What is it that induced you to betray me?"

"I...they...that's none of your business," blustered Rabidus.

Atreus shook his head, as far as the edge biting into the skin of his neck allowed.

"Pan's Bane, Rabidus? Really?"

Doubt shadowed Rabidus face.

"What are you talking about?"

"Didn't you think to consult a Greek quack? There is no such thing as Pan's Bane."

"But how did you know... wait, what do you mean, no such thing?"

"They made it up. It was just vinegar to give you a sting and a fright."

Carbo pressed the blade more firmly into Atreus' neck.

"Shut up," he hissed.

"Is this true?" yelled Rabidus, his voice becoming high pitched and squeaky.

"Fine, it's true," said Vespillo, who had been pretending to be the other guard flanking Rabidus. He pulled a short knife and held it against Rabidus back, briefly hoping the blade was long enough to reach through all the fat rolls to reach the gang leader's kidney. "I thought I was quite convincing."

"Not that it matters," said Carbo. "You are mine now, masked man. Atreus, or whatever your name is. And it's time to make you pay."

"Pay? For what? For finishing off that little whore of an ex-slave you liked to play with? Are you telling me you didn't enjoy it when she begged you to save her? When she screamed, when I slit her throat, and she bled out over the cobbles."

Carbo pulled his arm back to strike.

"And how are you going to get out of here alive, now?" asked Atreus calmly.

Carbo hesitated.

"Rabidus' men surround you," said Atreus. "Menelaus here will gut you as soon as I am dead."

"He can try," growled Carbo.

"He can, and will probably succeed, but even if he doesn't Rabidus' men are covering you with bow and arrow."

"They won't fire on us while we hold Rabidus hostage," said Vespillo.

"Yes, you are right," said Atreus. "Febrox," he called out.

"Yes, master," came the call back from the far end of the square.

"Kill Rabidus."

"What?" cried Rabidus in shock.

"Sorry, master," called Febrox, from where he stood with two bowmen. "Atreus pays better." He pointed to Rabidus, and said to the men flanking him, "Do it."

Two arrows flew out, whistling in the quiet night air. It was dark, the bowmen were not skilled, but the distance was not great. One arrow flew low and to one side, grazing Vespillo's outer thigh, making him cry out. The second buried itself in Rabidus' chest.

Rabidus gripped the shaft protruding from him, eyes wide, gasping. With a guttural cry, he ripped it free. A dark spurt of blood emanated from the hole it left. He stared at Atreus with hate in his eyes, then pitched forward, and fell with a heavy thud to the flagstones.

Vespillo stepped back, looking at the ground in horror, his human shield and exit strategy lying dead at his feet. Carbo stared, trying to adjust to the sudden change in their situation.

In that instant of hesitation, Atreus took a rapid step backwards, at the same time bending his knees. The sword blade sliced against the skin under his chin, but blood flowed only in a trickle from the superficial wound.

Carbo swung his gladius two handed in a stroke designed to bite deep into Atreus' neck, but it was stopped short in a clash of metal on metal by the counter-stroke from Menelaus. The shock of the heavy blows ran up both their arms and shook them. Carbo recovered first, twisting his sword away, then thrusting for Menelaus' midriff. Menelaus moved quickly. His build was slim and he appeared young, even though his face was concealed, so he was agile. The blade slid by him harmlessly. Carbo thrust again, and Menelaus parried, then countered. The counter was swift, but there was no great strength behind it. Carbo batted the sword away with superior force, putting Menelaus off balance, then swung a blow that sliced Menelaus' arm. Menelaus hissed in his breath at the sting, but his low stance didn't change, and Carbo recognised someone who was a trained fighter.

But training was no substitute for strength and experience, and Carbo battered Menelaus backwards. A driving blow forced Menelaus to his knees, and Carbo raised his sword arm.

"Enough," said Atreus in a loud voice. Carbo placed his sword tip over Menelaus' heart, then half-turned to Atreus, keeping Menelaus in his field of view.

Febrox had Vespillo in a stranglehold, one arm wrenched painfully up behind. Two bowmen stood either side of and just behind Carbo, arrows triangulating on his back. Carbo froze, like the subject of a mural, the heroic legionary poised to strike the cowering barbarian. But there would be no strike. Febrox twisted Vespillo's arm higher, causing an involuntary cry to escape from between the grit-ted teeth of his friend. Atreus moved up close behind Carbo and stroked his neck just below his ear with a sharp knife, neatly but shallowly incising the skin.

"Put the sword down, Carbo," said Atreus. "This ends now."

Carbo let the sword drop from his fingers, the noise loud in the stillness of the plaza. Numbness and cold spread through his body. His shoulders slumped, his head drooped. Lutorius, you bastard, where were you?

The end. Defeat. No chance to revenge Rufa. Oh Rufa, I'm so sorry.

He didn't feel the blow from Atreus.

The world faded to black.

# CHAPTER XI

Lutorius lay beneath his commanding officer's bed, trying not to sneeze. Piles of dust irritated his nasal passages, along with rat droppings and scurrying cockroaches. Calidia must not have very good control of her household slaves, he thought. From above him came the sound of grunts and groans as the portly Asellio bounced on top of his wife. Calidia's personal slave had warned them of his unexpected return, bursting in on them while Lutorius was in the very position that Asellio occupied now. They had just enough time for Calidia to throw on some night clothes and feign sleep, and for Lutorius to dress, then scramble under the bed at the heavy sound of approaching footsteps.

Asellio was drunk, and had demanded his conjugal rights without preamble. Lutorius cursed his luck. He knew he had no right to jealousy, but he still hated the idea of this drunk, fat, old man with his lover. The only consolation was that Calidia made none of the noises of passion with Asellio that she made with him. He wondered how she must be feeling right now.

He cursed Fortuna, then rather more fairly, himself. His new friends had been relying on him for back up tonight, and if Asellio hadn't turned up unexpectedly, he would have finished his business and been away with plenty of time. They didn't really need him, he reflected, if everything went according to plan. But how often did that happen?

Asellio let out a guttural groan, then was still. He waited a while longer, until intermittent splutters and snorts indicated that Asellio was snoring. Then he gently eased himself out from under the bed, and quietly stood. Asellio was draped over the naked Calidia, fast asleep, his poor wife pinned in place by his dead weight. She looked at him with an anguished expression. He shrugged helplessly at her, then turned tail and left as quickly and quietly as he could.

Lutorius ran down the quiet, dark streets from his commanding officer's house towards the plaza where Carbo and Vespillo were planning to meet the two masked men. With Rabidus terrified for his life, bound to Vespillo to get the antidote to keep him alive and more importantly virile, they should have no problems overpowering and capturing the two bandits who had been terrorising the area. Still, he was uneasy, didn't like the thought of it all happening without him observing from the rooftops, as Carbo and Vespillo would be expecting.

He wasn't sure what the plan was after that. Trial, conviction, death by crucifixion or beheading, depending on whether they were citizens. That was what Lutorius had in mind. He suspected Carbo was thinking along different lines.

He rounded a corner, saw the building he had been heading for. External stairs led to the upper flats and the roof. He mounted them two at a time, up two stories, then pulled himself onto the gently pitched roof, up to the crest, and looked down onto the plaza below.

A cold hand gripped his heart.

The tableau that confronted him held him, frozen in place. Carbo was standing, head down, sword at his feet, with the masked Atreus holding a knife against his neck. Behind, Vespillo was being restrained by Febrox. And Rabidus. Rabidus was stretched out on his face, lying in an enormous pool of blood, an arrow clutched in his hand.

What could have gone so horribly wrong? By what sequence of events could Rabidus have ended up dead? His head spun, as a tremendous weight of guilt descended on him. If he had been here watching as he was meant, would he have been able to intervene? Would his presence have made a difference?

As he watched, gripped in indecision, Atreus brought the hilt of his knife down hard on the back of Carbo's head. Vespillo yelled out incoherently. Carbo pitched forward and was still.

Lutorius drew his sword, but still hesitated. He counted six opponents. Atreus and Menelaus, Febrox, and three thugs. Two of the thugs were armed with bows, one with a club, and Febrox had a knife at his waist belt. What could he do, that wouldn't be suicidally stupid?

Atreus' voice carried in the quiet, cold night air.

"Febrox, I'm going to take one of your men. He is going to help me with this brute, in case he wakes up."

"Where are you taking him, master?"

"None of your business," snapped Atreus. Then, relenting slightly, "Let's just say, his end will not be a merciful one."

Febrox smiled. He nodded to one of the bowmen. At Atreus' prompting, he bound Carbo's hands behind his back with thick rope, then hobbled him.

Atreus nodded at Vespillo. "Have whatever fun you feel the need for with that one," he said to Febrox. "Then kill him." He beckoned Menelaus and the bowman. "Come, let's find a cart to throw this lump of meat into."

Menelaus and the bowman then picked Carbo up, under the arms and by the feet, and followed Atreus out of the square.

Febrox's two remaining men stepped forward to take Vespillo from their leader, pinning his arms behind him.

Febrox pushed his face up close to Vespillo, and Lutorius could imagine the stench washing over Vespillo from the man's rotting teeth. Vespillo had stopped struggling, despair written clearly across his face. The new leader of the gang of cutthroats and muggers leered at the veteran watchman.

"So, how does this feel?"

Vespillo returned his stare coldly, saying nothing.

Febrox punched him, a hefty roundhouse blow to the jaw. Vespillo sagged, blood dribbling from the corner of his mouth, then lifted his head to stare wordlessly at Febrox again.

Finally shocked into action, Lutorius crept forward, lowering himself off the edge of the roof onto a ledge, then quietly down into the plaza.

Febrox growled at Vespillo. "So brave, so stoical. I'll get some noise from you when I start to cut you up. I'll show you what happens to someone who tries to make a fool out of me."

Vespillo spat a bloody gob into Febrox's face. Febrox flinched, wiped his face with the back of his hand, then punched Vespillo hard in the midriff. Vespillo doubled forward, a whooshing sound accompanying the air leaving his lungs.

"You've got balls, I'll say that," said Febrox. He drew his knife slowly from his belt. "Not for much longer though."

Lutorius let out an incoherent roar. He charged the short distance from the shadows of the building at the edge of the plaza. All three thugs left in the square turned and stared.

"Febrox, you cunnus!" he yelled, sword waving.

The remaining bowman let Vespillo go, fumbled for his bow which lay on the floor. He stepped forward, and with surprising speed, he notched an arrow, and let it fly. The hasty aim was untrue and the arrow flew well wide. Lutorius dropped a shoulder and barged into the bowman, sending him flying backwards, bow clattering away, winded. Momentum barely checked, he carried on towards Febrox.

Febrox took a step back, alarmed, suddenly realising he had brought a knife to a swordfight. Lutorius thrust at him, a deadly stab lacking entirely in finesse, aiming only to penetrate flesh, to kill. Febrox writhed wildy to one side, and Lutorius swung, making him jump back further.

Vespillo reacted quicker than his captor. Short and stout, he was able to twist in the grip of the thug who still restrained him. A little fuzzy as he was from Febrox's blows, he was still able to grab hold of the thug's wrists, preventing him from reaching the club that hung from a loop on his belt. The two men wrestled, grunting. They were evenly matched. The thug was younger and fitter, but Vespillo had more brawn and more brains. He slowly pushed the man's arms backwards, then brought his head forward sharply, forehead connecting with a crunch squarely in the middle of the thug's face.

The thug yelped and stepped backwards, but rather than clutch his nose which was now pouring with blood, he stepped forward in rage and swung a two handed blow at Vespillo's head. Vespillo ducked, but not enough, and the blow glanced off the side of his temple, staggering him sideways. The thug pressed forward, aiming a kick at Vespillo's middle which connected, knocking the breath out of him. The thug dived on him, and they rolled on the floor, each searching for a lethal grip.

Febrox tried to parry Lutorius' sword with his little knife. The blow nearly flicked it from his hand and he barely managed to keep his grip. He attempted a thrust of his own, but he didn't have the reach and Lutorius swept his sword across Febrox's forearm. The swing had little power and momentum, and his sword did not have the razor sharp edge of a gladius belonging to a legionary on active duty. Still, it bit into muscle and tendon, and Febrox's knife fell from suddenly useless fingers.

The bowman hit Lutorius in the back, pitching him forward onto his face, his own weapon now going flying as he brought his hands up to break his fall. The bowman had obviously recovered his wind, and knelt across Lutorius' back, punching him on alternate sides of the head with heavy blows that sent a ringing through his skull. He bucked and rolled, the bowman falling sideways. One of Lutorius' hands, scrabbling for an advantage, found the bowman's eye socket and pressed. He heard a scream as the soft globe gave way beneath his thumb. Then the bowman brought his knee up, a lucky blow between Lutorius' legs, and Lutorius doubled up in gasping, intense pain. He looked up through tear-streaming eyes as the bowman picked up a fist-sized stone, and kneeling over Lutorius, raised his hand.

A hefty kick caught the bowman in the side of the head, and he went down, unmoving. Lutorius' eyes focused on the panting, bloodied face of Vespillo. Beyond him, the other thug lay still, tongue lolling, face blue, where Vespillo had strangled the life out of him.

Vespillo held out his hand, and gingerly, still bent at the waist, Lutorius gained his feet. He looked around the plaza. Febrox had fled. Only he and Vespillo remained in the square both conscious and alive

Atreus was gone.

Menelaus was gone.

And Carbo…

Vespillo and Lutorius stared at each other helplessly.

Quintus sat in the small farmhouse kitchen, watching Marsia scrubbing at a large copper cooking pot. The previous night's stew had congealed, and she was working hard using water, sand and her fingernails to prise off the grime. Her brows were knitted as she concentrated on the task, but Quintus knew her mind was elsewhere.

"When did you say you expect them back?" asked Quintus again, for want of breaking the silence as much as hope that the answer had changed.

"I do not know, master. They said it would be last night or this morning."

The sky was grey, but brightening. Quintus had arrived not long after dawn, intending to visit Carbo and Vespillo and find out how their evening went, but also hoping to see Marsia. Her long, dark hair was held back with a functional, plain grip. He surveyed her face, her broad nose, her blue eyes framed by thick dark eyebrows, lips full, chin stronger than was considered beautiful among Roman women. She was dressed simply in a beige tunic but though this did nothing to flatter her figure, he could clearly make out her thin waist, wide hips, ample bust and broad shoulders.

No, she was no delicate Roman beauty. So why did she entrance him so?

She looked up at him, gave him a stern look that admonished him for staring. He looked away, embarrassed.

The last time he had seen her, she had put on make up, smiled at him, blushed. Now she seemed irritated by his presence. Had he offended her somehow? He shook his head. She was worried about her master. A man she genuinely loved, not like him, someone she had just flirted with for diversion.

What was wrong with him? A Roman nobleman, heir to a fortune. He could have his pick of the nubile equestrian girls, maybe even a poorer senator's daughter. He dreaded to think what his father would say, if he found out he was mooning over a slave.

"May I have a drink, please, Marsia?" asked Quintus.

A brief pursing of the lips showed Quintus he was putting her out, before she nodded.

"Of course, master." She brought him a glass of water. He reflected that that brief expression would have been enough to get her beaten in many a household. Carbo obviously gave her more latitude than most masters. But then, if she was his, so would he.

He sipped his glass, returning to watching her work.

"Why do you stare at me so, master?" asked Marsia.

Quintus spluttered into his cup.

"I…I'm not."

"Yes, master," said Marsia in a tone of complete acceptance, which her expression gave the lie to.

"I mean, yes, I was watching you work. There is precious little else to do in this house, while waiting for Carbo's return."

"I see," said Marsia.

"Good," said Quintus, and took another drink. Why did he feel so small in front of her? He had slept his way through half of Greece, with the appetite and stamina of a young man. He had had matrons and young girls, even the occasional older man, and he had displayed the confidence and arrogance of a noble Roman coming into his manhood. Yet this slave made him feel like a boy again.

"Do you think they will be back soon?" he asked.

This time she actually sighed. She opened her mouth to speak, and Melan-chaetes started his deep, resounding bark.

Marsia stopped what she was doing, looking towards the door as if she could see straight through into the atrium. Quintus stood and made to leave. He saw Marsia hesitating, and realised she knew it was not her place to leave her work and rush to the door to greet her master.

"Come, Marsia," he said. "Your master and his guests will have needs to attend to."

Marsia nodded gratefully and followed him.

Theron was holding the door open, as first Vespillo, then Lutorius entered. They looked tired and bruised, and there was fresh blood on both of them. Quintus looked out of the door, but no one else followed them in.

Vespillo nodded to Quintus. Lutorius didn't meet his concerned gaze. He opened his mouth to speak, but Marsia beat him to it.

"Where is my master?" The question was loud and hysterical.

"Marsia, please calm yourself," said Vespillo gently.

"Vespillo, sir, please. Where is he?" Her tone was anguished and pleading now. If Quintus had harboured any doubts about the devotion Marsia felt towards Car-bo, they were extinguished now.

"It's my fault," muttered Lutorius. "All on me."

"No," said Vespillo. "Even if you had been there on time, the outcome would not have been different."

"It might have been."

"What are you talking about?" asked Quintus. "What outcome? Why was Luto-rius late?"

Vespillo suddenly looked old and tired.

"Please, masters, come and sit," said Theron. "Have a drink and let me fix you ientaculum. Give me your cloaks."

Lutorius and Vespillo allowed themselves to be guided to the tablinum, where they slumped onto padded benches. Marsia and Quintus followed them in, Quin-tus taking a seat, while Marsia remained standing, wringing her hands, eyes wet with tears.

"Sirs, please tell me. Is my master dead?"

Vespillo looked at Lutorius, then shook his head.

"I honestly don't know, Marsia."

Marsia let out a stifled sob, putting a fist into her mouth and biting her knuckles hard.

Severa came into the room, rushed straight over to Vespillo and threw her arms around him. Then she pulled back, looking at the blood stains on his clothes, the dark congealed mess on his face and hands.

"Husband, are you hurt?" she asked anxiously.

"Nothing serious," he replied. She turned to Lutorius. "And you, sir? Are you injured?"

Lutorius shook his head, staring at the floor.

Quintus reached over and touched a hand to Vespillo's arm.

"Vespillo?" he prompted.

Vespillo looked around at the expectant faces staring at him - Theron, Severa, Quintus, Marsia.

"Somehow, the man with the tragedy mask, Atreus, he knew everything. He seemed to have expected us to be there. He even seemed to know the poison wasn't real."

"How is that possible?" asked Quintus.

Vespillo shrugged. "The poison, maybe he just asked a quack. He mentioned to Rabidus that is what he should have done. That it was an ambush? I think it must have been Febrox. I don't know how widely Rabidus discussed the plan, but Febrox was his second in command, so it would make sense that he was informed. And Febrox was in league with Atreus."

"What? He turned against Rabidus?"

Vespillo nodded. "He said that Atreus paid more than Rabidus. I suspect there was an element of coercion as well. Rabidus was feared, but the respect of his men must have plummeted when they saw how Marsia and I had so easily defeated him. Atreus on the other hand, everyone seems to be terrified of meeting him."

"You said Febrox was Rabidus' second in command," said Quintus. "Is Febrox dead then?"

"No, Rabidus is."

Quintus shook his head in confusion. "What happened, Vespillo?"

Vespillo took a deep breath. "The plan we told you about, Rabidus had agreed to it. Partly because of the threat of withholding the antidote, but partly too I think because he feared Atreus, and wanted to end the threat to his authority."

"I'm sorry I wasn't there for you," said Quintus. "My father sent me on an errand, but it didn't sound like you needed me."

"We shouldn't have," agreed Vespillo. "We shouldn't even have needed Lutorius to help us. And the more of us there, the more likely Atreus would have been able to detect a trap."

Quintus didn't look satisfied, but he let it pass and waved a hand for Vespillo to continue. Vespillo explained how they had confronted Atreus and Menelaus, how the ruse had seemed to work, until Febrox turned against his boss, and ordered Rabidus slain. How Carbo had been about to kill Atreus when Menelaus intervened, and how Vespillo had been overpowered, allowing Atreus to force Carbo to surrender.

"And where were you?" Marsia asked Lutorius, her social status completely forgotten, her face flushed red with anger.

Lutorius looked devastated. "I was...delayed. By the time I arrived, Carbo had already put his sword down. If I had charged in then, it would have been suicide, and Carbo and Vespillo would have been dead before I could do a thing. So I... waited, until the odds had evened up."

"And how did that happen?" asked Quintus.

"Atreus, Menelaus, and two of the thugs...left."

"Empty-handed? Why?"

Lutorius shook his head. "Not empty-handed. They…took Carbo with them."

There was a silence as the small group took in the information. Then Marsia stepped forward and slapped Lutorius hard across the face. Lutorius didn't flinch, didn't raise his hand to the welt on his cheek as it slowly turned red.

"You hid," hissed Marsia. "While they took my master, to torture and death. You let it happen. You cowardly cunnus. I hope you suffer in Tartarus for eternity."

She turned and fled the room, sobbing as she left.

For a moment no one spoke. Then Vespillo reached out to put a hand on Lutorius' shoulder. "You can't blame yourself, friend," said Vespillo.

Quintus frowned. "And why is that, Vespillo? We haven't heard why he was delayed yet."

Vespillo looked to Lutorius, waiting to see if the man would defend himself. When no explanation was forthcoming, he spoke for the stationarius.

"There was an incident with a woman. A liaison that was interrupted by the return of her husband."

Quintus gaped. "You have got to be joking! Lutorius was late because he was fucking another man's wife? If that's true, it's despicable. It's beneath contempt."

"What do you mean, if it's true?" asked Vespillo in a low voice.

"How do we know Atreus got his information through Febrox? He has money, he can scare people into obedience and betrayal. What if Lutorius is his source?"

"Take that back," said Vespillo, standing. "You have no right to make those accusations."

Quintus stood too, raising his voice. "Isn't it just a little convenient? He arrives just too late to save Carbo. Only intervenes once Atreus is gone?"

Vespillo stepped forward and hissed between gritted teeth into Quintus' face. "He risked his life to save mine. He fought against Febrox and his thugs."

"And where is Febrox now?"

"He escaped," said Vespillo, slightly more subdued.

"And where are Atreus? Menelaus? Carbo?"

Vespillo looked doubtfully across to Lutorius, who sat with his head in his hands, saying nothing.

Quintus pointed at Lutorius. "There is your traitor!" he cried.

"Where is Carbo?" asked a little voice.

They all turned, to see Fabilla standing framed in the doorway. Her face was pale and drawn. Her dark eyes were dry, but sunken. She had been losing weight, and her cheekbones were prominent on her face in a way that a little girl's should not be. She clutched a small rag doll that Thera had given her to play with.

"Oh, Juno," whispered Vespillo.

"Is Carbo coming back? Or have the bad people killed him, like they killed mummy?"

A lump formed in Quintus' throat, all anger evaporating from him instantly.

Severa rushed over to her, wrapped her up in her thick arms and crushed Fabilla to her chest.

"No, little darling. The bad people haven't killed him. Carbo will be coming home." She stared over the child's head at the men in the room, and challenged them to keep her promise to the little girl. They stared back at her helplessly.

"Come, sunbeam. Let's go and find Thera and see what games we can play."

She ushered Fabilla out of the room, leaving silence in her wake.

At last, Lutorius spoke, his voice low and quiet. "I'm not a traitor," he said. "I'm many things. An idiot, an adulterer. Maybe even a coward. Maybe I should have thrown myself into the fight even when it was hopeless. But I would not betray my friends."

Quintus paused, regarding the dejected man with suspicion. Then he turned away.

# CHAPTER XII

Carbo woke with a start. He found something across his face, gasped in some breath and found material sucked into his mouth, cutting off the inflow of air. He tried blowing the material away, only for it to suck back against him when he breathed in. He tried to bring his hands up, and found they were tied behind his back. His heart raced, stomach clenched in the familiar grip of fear and panic.

He tried to breathe more slowly, and the reduced airflow stopped the material from sticking to his face with each breath. Recently, whenever panic had gripped him, as it still often did, he had taken to picturing himself in Rufa's arms, her fingers stroking his hair, her warm body soothing against his. But as Rufa's image appeared in his mind, he felt panic and grief flood him again, threatening to drown him. He tried to concentrate on Fabilla instead, but the misery that was the loving little girl's existence now made him even worse. In desperation, he fixed on the image of Marsia. Marsia, always there for him, calm, strong, brave. Even beautiful.

He shook his head at the thought of attraction to the slave. Not because a slave was below him, he had rid himself of that notion when Rufa had come back into his life. But because it felt disloyal to Rufa's memory.

Rufa's memory. Is that all she was now? A memory.

With an effort, he brought himself back to focus on the present. A little more in control of himself, he assessed his situation. He was lying on his side, wrists and ankles bound tight enough to numb his hands. He flexed his fingers and toes, which pumped a little blood into tingling extremities. The material on his face felt like cloth, rough against his stubble, and smelled of must and wheat. A sack on his head then. He expected to be able to see light through cloth, and yet his vision was black. So it was night, or he was being held somewhere without windows or lamps.

The memories of the fight in the plaza returned, and with it a throbbing ache centred on the back of his skull that radiated throughout his head. As his mind became less fogged, questions started to crowd in.

How had it all gone so wrong? That was the main one. It had all seemed to have worked so well. Atreus and Menelaus, there at his mercy. Rabidus in his power, Rabidus' thugs leashed and obedient to their merciless leader. It had seemed to be all over.

And then, what? Atreus had been in control all along, it seemed. The thugs were his. Rabidus was cut out, impotent, and not from the fake poison. Atreus had to have been forewarned. He knew about the poison, and had had the foresight to co-opt Febrox. Maybe Febrox had always worked for him, maybe that was a new event, but Atreus and Febrox could not have controlled the whole gang until that moment, or Rabidus would long ago have been forced out.

Carbo blinked his eyes hard, shook his head to clear it, despite the headache. So who had warned Atreus? And where, by Juno's dry cunnus, had that irrumator Lutorius been? A horrible suspicion swelled in his gut. Surely not. Lutorius had seemed such a straight man. An optio. Trustworthy. But what did he really know about him? Legionaries came in all shapes and sizes, and a variety of concepts of honour. Carbo had fought alongside plenty of men who would die without hesitation for the men in their contubernium, as well as many who would sell them into slavery for a copper as.

Anger at the betrayal gripped him, as he convinced himself that Lutorius was working for Atreus. Then a worse thought struck him. Maybe Lutorius was Atreus. The man responsible for Rufa's murder. A stream of curses erupted from him, and he struggled violently against his bonds, his body bucking, legs spasming.

A door flew open with a crash, and a flicker of light from an oil lamp penetrated the cloth sack.

"What's all the noise?" A deep voice, Greek accented.

"Let me go," growled Carbo. His voice grew to a roar. "Let me go right now, you irrumator, or I will rip your balls off and stuff them down your throat!"Calm yourself, Carbo," said another voice, one he recognised. "You are going nowhere. Well, that isn't quite true, but we will get to that. What I mean to say is your bonds are quite secure, I tied them myself."

"Atreus?" asked Carbo, trying to peer through the translucent sack. His voice was low and dangerous. "Atreus, I will kill you. I swear it, to Jupiter Optimus Maximus, to my mother, to Rufa who you murdered, on my very honour!"

Atreus let out a low chuckle. "Zozimus, are you ready to sail?"

"Within the hour, Atreus."

"Excellent. Thank you for taking this extra piece of cargo at short notice. You will make sure he reaches his destination?"

Zosimus let out a deep booming laugh. "Of course. As soon as he is on board, he will be locked up with the others. Even this big old hulk won't be able to break out of iron chains."

"Very well. Could you fetch some men to get him loaded? But give me a short while alone with him first."

"As you say," said Zozimus, and Carbo heard the door open and the Greek man depart.

The lamp light flickered through the sack, and for a moment, all Carbo could hear was his own breathing. Then abruptly the sack was pulled off his head. He looked up into the mocking tragedy mask that he had now seen too many times.

Fear and anger warred inside Carbo. He considered making a lunge at Atreus, but his struggles earlier had already shown him the ropes would not easily break, and that it would be futile.

"What are you talking about?" asked Carbo, trying to keep his voice even. "Where are you sending me?"

Atreus squatted down in front of Carbo, the mask close to his face. Carbo could see the eyes through the slits, blue irises, the whites shot through with red veins. The skin around the eyes was slack, lined. Carbo suddenly realised, Atreus was old.

"You didn't answer me," said Atreus.

Carbo's eyes narrowed in confusion. He was still disorientated, from the blow to his head and from recovering in captivity in an unfamiliar place. Had he missed part of the conversation.

"What?"

"I asked you a question and you never replied."

"What question?"

"The second time we met, I asked you if you understood loss. Maybe at the moment I asked it, you didn't. The gods know what dark turns your past journey has taken. Regardless I think you appreciate it better now."

"You took my woman's life, in exchange for my killing of your brother. Yet my act was self defence, yours was murder. And you did not love your brother the way I loved my woman. Or maybe you did, you seem to have some pretty unnatural pleasures."

Carbo mentally stiffened for a blow at the insult, but Atreus simply continued to gaze down on him.

"I know the loss of a woman, too, Carbo. My life has been all about loss. My family is cursed I believe, just like the Atreides. The loss you inflicted on me was one more in a long line. But I am avenged on you, as I was on the one who took my wife."

"I'm not dead yet."

"And why is that, do you think? Do I seem merciful?"

Carbo was silent.

"I could let you find out in time, I suppose, but I wouldn't get to see your face. Tell me, what is the worst punishment that the authorities will inflict, apart from execution?"

Carbo considered for a moment, unwilling to play along, but desperate to find out what Atreus was thinking. "Exile?" he guessed.

Atreus shook his head. "Ah, I see your confusion. Yes, a Roman citizen convicted of a major crime is likely to be executed, exiled or fined. But you, you are now a slave. So that doesn't apply."

Carbo's eyes opened wide. "What do you mean?"

"To Zosimus, you are just part of his cargo of slaves. I am actually going to get paid for you, which is gratifying. I will buy a fine Falernian and toast your memory."

"You can't do that," Carbo said, aghast.

"Hmm. The facts suggest otherwise. Anyway where were we? Ah yes. Punishments. So many possibilities for a slave. Roman society uses its full imagination when it comes to slaves. We can brand you, break your bones, crucify you, whip you. Really whatever we like. But most of those things are either too quick, or too minor. If I crucify you, you will be dead in a couple of days. How does that honour my brother? No, I have a much slower way for you to die. You are going to Sicily to work in the lead mines."

Carbo blanched, felt his skin go cold and clammy.

"Ah, I see you understand the significance of that. So many people in my world don't understand what horrors, what sacrifice of human flesh and spirit goes into providing the luxuries they love so much. The marble quarries, the vineyards, the garum factories, all staffed by hordes of slaves, working themselves into early graves, tossed out when they are no longer of use, at which point of course they cannot support themselves, and so starve to death.

"And the worst of all? The mines. It's why slaves are sent there as a punishment. The weakest slaves survive there only for days. A strong one like you might make it for months or more, assuming you don't get murdered by a sadistic guard, or die in a cave-in. You will die though, one way or another, worn out, broken, knowing that everything you have worked for in your life has come to this. Exhaustion, agony and death, so that some rich Romans can have silver cups and water flowing into their fountains in lead pipes. And I will have both my revenge, and a decent payout for a strong specimen like yourself."

Carbo shook his head, but his throat was frozen. He wanted to argue, to plead, forgetting his pride to avoid the fate Atreus had manufactured for him.

Atreus' eyes narrowed, the corners crinkling with the suggestion of a smile. He nodded.

"Yes, I think that will do nicely. Goodbye, Carbo. We won't meet again."

Atreus turned to leave.

Carbo found his voice.

"Wait," he cried out desperately.

Atreus turned back, head cocked to one side.

"Who are you?" asked Carbo.

Atreus considered for a short moment, took hold of the bottom of his mask, then shook his head.

"I like the idea of you dying with that question on your lips."

"I will kill you," spat Carbo.

"No, you won't. You will fall apart in a Sicilian lead mine."

Zosimus knocked and entered, three bulky sailors with him.

"You can load him up now," said Atreus. Zosimus nodded, and approached Carbo.

"Pleasure doing business with you, as always, Atreus."

The three men sat around the kitchen table, faces downcast, not meeting each other's eyes. They chewed laboriously at the salted bread and figs that Theron had brought them for their ientaculum. No one spoke.

Presently, Marsia came back in. Her face was streaked with tear trails, but her eyes were dry, and her face set.

"Would any of you like me to serve you a drink? Some water, or some wine?"

"Water, please," said Quintus, attempting a smile in her direction. She bowed her head and filled his cup from a jug.

"Marsia," said Vespillo. "I am not your master. I'm not clear who is in charge of you in Carbo's absence, unless it is Fabilla. Nevertheless, you should apologise to Lutorius."

Marsia stiffened, but said nothing.

"Marsia," said Vespillo again, voice low. "You know how badly punished you could be, a slave striking a free man. I'm sure Lutorius would overlook it this time. We know how devoted you are to your master, and it can be put down to an emotional over-reaction."

"It doesn't matter," mumbled Lutorius, not looking up.

"It does," insisted Vespillo. He locked eyes with Marsia and she stared back, unblinking. Vespillo recognised the power of Marsia's will at that moment, the iron inside that had allowed her to survive being ripped from her homeland to serve strange masters in a foreign country. Vespillo knew his way around wilful subordinates though, and he did not flinch. Eventually, Marsia looked down.

"I'm sorry, master Lutorius. I was wrong to strike you."

"And…" prompted Vespillo.

"And," said reluctantly. "I was wrong to say the things I said."

Vespillo noted to himself that this was not the same as admitting the things she said were untrue. But it would do.

Lutorius looked up at Marsia, and Vespillo saw his eyes were wet.

"I am sorry, too, Marsia," said Lutorius. "Truly I am. If I could go back a day, start afresh…"

"It would have made no difference," said Vespillo, firmly. "We have been over this. Now, Marsia, I will have some water too, and pour some for Lutorius."

Marsia did as she was bid. Vespillo looked around at his dejected companions.

"Come on," he said, trying to inject an enthusiasm into his voice he didn't feel. "We are behaving like Carbo is dead. That man is a fighter and a survivor if anyone is."

Marsia looked up at Vespillo, and gave him a grateful half smile.

"But even if he is alive, he is in captivity, suffering the gods only know what," said Quintus. The smile disappeared from Marsia's face as quickly as it had appeared.

"Then let us start thinking how to help him," said Vespillo.

"What could we do?" asked Lutorius.

"It would help if we knew who this damned Atreus was. And his son, this Menelaus," said Vespillo.

Lutorius shook his head. "The names are false. I have enquired enough in the past. No one by the names of Atreus or Thyestes live in these parts. They must be like the names gladiators take for themselves for the arena."

"Then their names don't help us at all," said Quintus.

"Well, where did the names come from?" asked Vespillo. "Why did he pick Atreus?"

"Atreus was the king of Mycenae," said Marsia. "He was the father of Menelaus and Agamemnon."

All three men turned to stare at her.

"How do you…never mind. Thyestes? Who was he?"

"He was Atreus' brother."

Lutorius nodded. "Not random names then. We know our Atreus and Thyestes were brothers. That is what led to this whole problem in the first place. So, Menelaus is Atreus' son?"

Vespillo nodded. "It seems likely."

"So all we need to do is find a family that includes a man and his son, in which the man's brother has died. There must be hardly anyone like that in Campania."

"Sarcasm isn't going to help," said Vespillo. "Marsia, I know Agamemnon and Menelaus from the Iliad. Greek kings who sailed against Troy. Agamemnon was killed by his wife I recall, and Menelaus had his wife stolen by Paris, which triggered the whole thing. But Menelaus is a recent creation, I am guessing. He has only made an appearance since Thyestes died, and may have taken the name simply as he is Atreus' son, so the name Menelaus may have no significance beyond that. But why Atreus and Thyestes? What makes them special?"

The three men looked at Marsia expectantly, and she blushed lightly at being the centre of attention.

"Well," she began hesitantly. "The house of Atreides is said to be descended from Tantalus."

"The Tantalus?" asked Lutorius. "The one who fed his son to the gods and now lives in Hades with fruit and water forever just out of reach?"

"So it is said," said Marsia. "The House of Atreides was cursed by a charioteer who had been double-crossed after helping the father of Thyestes and Atreus win a chariot race and claim a kingdom."

"Is this really getting us anywhere?" asked Quintus. Vespillo shot him an angry glance, and Quintus threw up his hands in mock surrender. Vespillo nodded to Marsia, who was turning redder all the time.

"Atreus and Thyestes were twins who were exiled by their father for killing their half brother Chrysippus. They fled to Mycenae and took the throne there. Their mother fled with them, and hanged herself. Atreus and Thyestes soon fell out. They fought over who should rule, and eventually Thyestes was banished. After this, though, Atreus discovered his wife was Thyestes' lover. In revenge he killed Thyestes' sons and tricked their father into eating them."

The men looked at each other in distate.

"Thyestes then fathered a son off his daughter. His ashamed daughter abandoned the son, called Aegisthus, and eventually killed herself, but he was raised by Atreus, until Thyestes revealed the truth - that he was the boy's father and grandfather. Aegisthus then killed Atreus. Atreus' sons, Agamemnon and Menelaus were exiled to Sparta, where they married Clytemnestra and Helen."

"I know what happened after that," said Vespillo. "The Trojan war. And when Agamemnon returned, Aegisthus who was now Clytemnestra's lover murdered him."

Marsia nodded. "The family curse doesn't end there. Agamemnon's children, Orestes and Electra eventually killed Aegisthus and their mother Clytemnestra in revenge for their father's death. What happens next depends on whether you read Euripides or Aeschylus, but in one version Orestes is judged by the gods, and when they found his actions were justified, the family curse was lifted."

There was a momentary pause as the men present digested the story Marsia had told.

"Incest. Rape. Murder. Cannibalism. What a pretty tale," said Lutorius.

"So what are we saying here?" asked Quintus. "That Atreus is somehow modelling his life on the Atreus of myth? That he killed his nephew and fed him to his brother? That his brother had a son from raping his own daughter? This is ridiculous."

"It does sound far-fetched," admitted Lutorius.

"Every word of the story doesn't have to fit," said Vespillo. "But we do know the names are assumed, that they must have chosen them. Atreus and Thyestes, the original ones and the ones we met, were brothers. Menelaus was Atreus' son. What else could be true? What elements of what Marsia has told us are possible?"

Lutorius considered for a moment. "Well, the cannibalism seems unlikely. Possible but unlikely. The conflict between the brothers doesn't ring true either, our Atreus seems to have loved his brother."

"The incest?" asked Vespillo. He shrugged at the disgusted looks he received. "I'm only asking."

"What about the exile?" asked Lutorius. "They could have come from somewhere else. Maybe even Rome."

Vespillo nodded. "That's possible. Many people are exiled from Rome for a range of crimes."

"Anything else?" asked Lutorius.

"The curse," said Quintus. They all looked at him. "Maybe Atreus believes his family is cursed."

They digested this for a moment.

"Well, what next?" asked Quintus. "Has this really got us any further forward?"

"We could start looking for someone who is not native to Nola, someone who isn't poor. Someone whose brother died recently and has a son."

"Well that really narrows it down," muttered Quintus.

"Have you got any better ideas?" snapped Vespillo.

Quintus looked sheepish, then shook his head. "I'm sorry. It's just so frustrating. Rufa dead, Carbo taken, and no real leads on where to find him."

"And why is it you care so much?" asked Vespillo suspiciously.

"Because I fought alongside him. Because he treated me as an equal. A comrade and a friend. Unlike…" He trailed off. Vespillo regarded him for a moment, then nodded, satisfied.

"Fine. But if you want to help, then you need to show it. Not just criticise and accuse."

Quintus hung his head, then looked up, into the eyes of first Vespillo and then Lutorius.

"I apologise. To both of you, Vespillo, Lutorius. What would you have me do?"

"We need to ask questions. Lutorius can use his contacts and his colleagues. You can talk to your acquaintances. I can talk to… well, the sort of people who might not want to talk to a stationarius or an equestrian."

Lutorius nodded, but Quintus looked doubtful. "I don't really have many acquaintances. I have been gone from the region for a long time. And when I was younger, my father was hardly the most sociable person. My circle is not large. Still." He took a deep breath. "I will do what I can."

"We should pay Febrox a visit too," said Lutorius. "I don't know what he knows, but it isn't going to hurt to question him."

"The hideout is well defended," said Vespillo.

"I can ask the centurion for some men to help."

Vespillo nodded.

"Good," he said. "Then the task before us is to rip those masks off. However we can manage it. Once we know who these thugs are, things will be very different. Then we will get Carbo back, and we will be revenged."

The ropes chafed his wrists, and the hobbles that shortened his stride bit into his ankles, and made the pain from his old leg wound more pronounced. The cart driver trundled away, and Zosimus gestured to the guards to lead Carbo towards the docks. Carbo had never been to Neapolis before, but he recognised the type of place, the smell of fish and salt in the air, the shouts of dock workers and sailors busy loading and unloading their wares. Officials wandered up and down with airs of superiority, as they inspected cargoes and ticked off checklists on their wax tabets with their styluses.

Carbo had been hidden beneath a tarpaulin for the uncomfortable journey in the back of the cart from Nola. Now he was in the open, being led towards the ship that would take him to his enslavement and death. This might be his last chance.

The ropes were thick, the bonds were tight, and there was no way he could overcome the four guards that accompanied him, especially bound and unarmed. He looked around him desperately, trying to find an official face, a legionary or dock official to whom he could appeal. One of the guards gave him a shove in the back, and the hobbles stopped him getting his leg beneath him to keep his balance. He sprawled forwards, bringing his hands up just in time to prevent his nose smashing into the cobbles, but still receiving grazes on his forearms and mud across his tunic and face.

The guards laughed, and hauled him unceremoniously to his feet. Zosimus frowned at the delay, and reprimanded the guard who had pushed him.

"Don't damage the goods, idiot."

The guard bowed his head in mock contrition.

Carbo continued to scan the workers on the docks, looking for anyone demonstrating the slightest bit of authority, but all he saw were slaves and labourers, and scruffy, tough-looking sailors. He was led towards a cargo ship, and started up the gangplank.

"Zosimus."

Zosimus turned, and so did Carbo. Behind them was one of the dock officials, wax tablet in hand.

"Have you declared all your cargo?" asked the official.

"Late addition," said Zosimus. "I was just loading him, then was going to come and find you."

"I'm sure you were. Slave for the mines?"

"Yes," said Zosimus.

"No!" cried Carbo.

Zosimus and the official looked at him in surprise.

"Sir, I'm a free man. My name is Carbo, I'm a veteran of the legions. I was abucted in Nola. I am not a slave. This man has illegally kidnapped me."

"I see," said the official. "These are serious allegations, Zosimus."

"All lies. These slaves will say anything to avoid their just fate."

"Even so, maybe I should investigate." The official stroked his chin and cocked his head to one side.

Zosimus frowned. "I already paid you once, you greedy bastard."

"That was for the rest of the cargo. Like you said, this is a new addition."

Zosimus sighed, reached into his purse, and took out some coins. Carbo gaped as the dock official took them, then made a mark on his tablet and said, "Everything seems to be in order here."

"No," said Carbo. "I'm not lying, you corrupt felator."

The dock official raised an eyebrow, then said to Zosimus, "Safe journey. Oh, and I recommend you gag that foul-mouthed slave till you reach your destination. You wouldn't want him spreading those lies too widely."

## CHAPTER XIII

A wooden pole ran lengthways along the compartment within the hold, fixed to the walls at either end. Metal chains ran between manacles on Carbo's wrists and ankles, and another chain looped around them to secure them to the pole. Carbo sat on the damp wooden floor, unable to fully straighten either his back or his legs. A twisted strip of cloth had been forced between his teeth and tied tightly behind his head. The dark hold, lit only by cracks in the boards above them, was filled with several dozen other captives, chained as he was, though no others were gagged. Carbo smelled tar, urine, sweat and pungent farts.

The marked degree of the pitch and roll of the boat told Carbo they were far out to sea. Carbo was not a seasoned mariner, but he had spent some time on river boats on the Rhine when serving in Germany, and a little time in sea-faring boats when on secondment to other units. A couple of hours had passed since he had been loaded aboard like a piece of heavy freight, dumped below and left with his fellow passengers.

He had half-heartedly tested his bonds, and found them secure as he had expected. He had kicked the pole, but the wood was thick oak, not yet softened by age or soaking in brine, and he just bruised his heel. Then he had slumped forward, fighting the nausea the boat's motion induced. Despite the discomfort, his predicament, his grief, he suddenly felt overwhelmed with exhaustion. He closed his eyes and within a few heartbeats was fast asleep.

A sharp pain in his leg woke him. He opened his eyes in time to see a guard lift his foot back and kick him again.

"Wake up, slave."

Carbo lifted his head and glared at the guard.

"Dinner," grunted the guard, and threw some bread at Carbo's feet. He watched it soak up the bilge, like a sponge thrown into a chamber pot. He looked up at the guard and gestured to his gag. The chains were too short to allow him to reach his mouth with his hands. The guard shrugged and moved to the prisoner to Carbo's left, throwing another small piece of bread down. The prisoner scooped it up rapidly and hungrily tried to cram it into his mouth. He was brought up short by his own chains, and only managed to eat by rolling onto his side, angling his face towards the sky and dropping the bread into his open mouth.

Carbo stared at the skinny man. His clothes were rags, and through holes in the tunic Carbo could see the marks of a recent whipping. The prisoner continued to eat without any show of obvious self-consciousness. Carbo shook his head and looked down at the bread between his feet. Nausea, misery and fear leant him no appetite, even if he could stomach the filth-soaked food.

Carbo suddenly felt he was being watched, and turned. The prisoner to his right was a slight, young girl with long dark hair. She regarded him with unblinking, curious eyes. As he watched, she tore a small piece of bread off her portion, tossed it into the air and caught it deftly in her mouth. Then she cocked her head on one side, winked, and gave him a cheeky smile.

Despite himself, Carbo found himself, for just a moment, smiling back. Then he felt abruptly stupid, and turned his head away from her, gazing into the gloom of the hold, trying to empty his mind of thoughts of Rufa, of Fabilla and Vespillo, of

Rome. From the corner of his eye, he saw the girl's smile fade.

Carbo's head nodded forward, and he drifted in and out of sleep. A sudden jar to the hull as the boat ploughed into a particularly deep trough startled him awake. The prisoner to his left was fast asleep and snoring. Sounds of creaking timbers were interspersed with a few quiet sobs and moans. Carbo realised he was losing track of passing time. Glancing up, the bits of sky he saw were dark grey, but it was not yet night.

The prisoner to Carbo's right fidgeted, shifting from buttock to buttock, pressing her knees together. When she saw that Carbo had looked in her direction, she glared at him defiantly. Then a more anguished look came into her eyes.

"I need piss," she said. The voice was light and melodious, incongruous with the statement. Carbo could not place the accent. Not quite Germanic, not Greek. Carbo glanced around him. No guards were in sight, and from the ammoniacal smell, Carbo guessed that trips to lavatory facilities were probably not allowed on this cruise. He shrugged at her.

She glowered at him for a moment, then said, "You turn away."

Carbo turned his head. There was a pause, then he heard her sigh. After he felt enough time had elapsed, he looked back at her. The lower part of her tunic was soaked, even where it wasn't in contact with the bilge water. Her glare was defiant, but even in the gloom he could see the redness burning her cheeks, and the tears in the corners of her eyes. Carbo thought for a moment. He was going to need to relieve himself soon too, he realised.

He raised one finger, then relaxed. It was harder than he expected, being watched, even in these circumstances. Soon though, he felt the flow warming the inside of his thighs, and his eyes unfocused at the transient pleasure of emptying his bladder. When he had finished he glanced down at his dark-stained lap, looked at the girl, and shrugged. She followed his eyes, and as realisation dawned, she smiled broadly at him, and again Carbo found himself, against the odds, smiling back.

"I am Sica," she said.

Carbo grunted through his gag.

"Why your mouth tied?" asked Sica.

Carbo raised his eyebrows, and Sica laughed, suddenly realising the absurdity of her question.

"So I have to do speaking for both?"

Carbo nodded.

"I not speak Roman well."

Carbo shrugged.

"Not good for us talking."

Carbo shook his head. The girl went silent, and Carbo stared off at the dim walls. The distraction ended, dark thoughts crowded back into Carbo's head. He tried to empty his mind, tried to think about happier times, army days with his comrades, but always the anger and fear and crushing grief forced them out. As he stared into the gloom, figures appeared, solidified. Vespillo, bleeding from a head wound. Elissa the priestess, laughing amid soaring flames. A man wearing a mask, that as he watched, swapped from the grotesque smile of the comedian to the sinister grimace of the tragedian. His heart started to race, and he breathed more heavily through his gag, trying to suppress the small cries of anguish that kept escaping him.

The figures faded away like mist in the sun, and his breathing started to settle, his heart started to slow.

Rufa's face appeared directly in front of him. Her eyes searched his, looking for answers. But her beautiful face was white, as if daubed with the lead that the society ladies used for foundation. And below her chin, her neck gaped wide, slashed open, blood still flowing in torrents down her chest.

Carbo screamed aloud, terror gripping him. He kicked his feet, trying to put distance between himself and the lemur before him. The chains brought him up short. He tilted his head back as the face swam nearer. Rufa's lips opened, puckering for a kiss as she had so many times before. But now bloodstained her teeth and ran from the corners of her mouth.

Carbo's cries became formless and incoherent. He tried to turn his face away, but he couldn't avert his eyes from the spectre. Rufa's lips approached his.

A sharp pain radiated through his right arm. His eyes flickered to one side, then were drawn back to the dead face. The pain came again, and he turned to look for the source. Sica was looking at him with concern. His eyes drifted forwards, and he saw Sica lean across and headbutt him in the arm again.

"Look at me," she said. He looked at her uncertainly, and she held his gaze with large, wide, green eyes. His eyes flickered, and she said sternly, "Look at me." She extended her hand, but her chains prevented her from reaching him. He hesitated, then reached out his own hand, the length of his chains and hers allowing their fingers to touch.

He could hear the smack of Rufa's lips, feel her cold breath on his skin, hear her respiration, smell her perfume. But he stayed focussed on Sica. The presence at his periphery receded, the scent fading, the soft breath noises diminishing. Sica stretched, took hold of his hand. He could see the effort was making the chains bite deep into her wrists, but he needed the contact and he selfishly gripped her hand tight.

Then it was gone. He swallowed, then braved a look. Just dark walls again. He looked around. The other prisoners were all staring at him, some with curiosity, some with suspicion, fear or hostility. He looked back to Sica. Her eyes searched his, concerned. He squeezed her hand one more time and let it drop. He nodded to her, and attempted a smile. She didn't smile back, but the anxiety in her expression lessened.

Carbo took a deep breath, let it out slowly. His stomach churned, and he knew the nausea wasn't from the rolling seas this time - he had experienced fear, from threats real or imagined, often enough to know how it felt afterwards. He willed his muscles to relax, felt some of the tension drain away.

"We all have had bad things happen," said Sica, and her voice betrayed sympathy, not reproach. "Everyone here." She gestured around her.

The skinny prisoner to Carbo's left grunted. "Ain't that true," he muttered.

Carbo nodded. He hoped his face expressed contrition, but he was no actor, and he had no idea what message he was conveying. Sica seemed to have relaxed though. She reached out again and Carbo touched her fingertips with his.

"Sleep," she said. "Long journey. Nothing else to do."

He shook his head, but tiredness suddenly overwhelmed him again, and Somnus took him.

Lutorius nodded to the stationarius, who brought the heavy axe down hard. Wood splintered from solid door. With a tug, the stationarius freed the axe, brought it down again. Three blows were enough to break a big enough hole in the door for Lutorius to reach in and heave the bar out of the way. Another stationarius then hefted a large hammer and smashed at the door lock. Door and frame splintered, and another blow smashed it wide open. The door flew back on its hinges, crashing against the wall.

"I think they know we are here, now," said Vespillo.

Lutorius grimaced. "After you?"

Vespillo drew his gladius and entered the atrium of the thieves' hideout. Lutorius and the detachment of ten stationarii followed behind him. A surprised sentry stood at the far end of the room. He turned tail and ran deeper into the building at the sight of them.

"Let's go," yelled Vespillo, slipping into a command role easily, though he had no authority here. The stationarii followed without question, and ran behind him, weapons drawn. They entered the triclinium where Vespillo, posing as Hilarius, had met the unfortunate Rabidus. Two men stood there, weapons drawn. One looked terrified, knife gripped in shaking hand. The other, who Vespillo recognised from his previous visits, gave a defiant yell, and charged him.

It was over in an instant. A street thug was no match for a veteran of the legions and commander in the vigiles. Vespillo parried the blow, sidestepped, and ran the thug through his chest, skewering him side to side. He tugged his weapon free, watching the spurt of heart blood ejecting through the hole he had made with satisfaction. He turned to the other thug, who threw his weapons onto the ground and sank to his knees, hands clasped before him.

Lutorius stepped up beside Vespillo, putting a hand on his shoulder and looked around.

"Is this how you remember it?"

Vespillo shook his head. "This place was full. And there were statues, tapestries, silverware. It looks cleaned out now."

Lutorius pointed to the kneeling thug with his sword.

"You. Where are the rest of your friends?"

The thief shook his head. "I don't know."

"What do you mean you don't know."

The thief closed his mouth tight and looked down.

Lutorius sighed. "It's going to be like that is it? You sure you aren't prepared to talk before this gets messy?"

The thief trembled, but said nothing.

Lutorius turned to his comrades. "Let's get him back to the station, and get some answers."

"We should have expected it," said Vespillo. "Febrox would have moved immediately when he knew the location of his hideout was no longer secret. It's a shame we couldn't have raided the place sooner."

He punched the prisoner in the abdomen. The thief was suspended by his chained wrists from metal loops on the wall, feet dangling off the ground.

"It was a long shot," agreed Lutorius, punching the man square on the nose, cartilage crunching beneath his fist. The thief cried out.

"Stop, for Clementia's sake, please."

Vespillo punched him in the gut again, driving the air out of him and cutting off his pleading.

"You know how it can be in the military," said Lutorius. "Asellio hesitated for an age before he let me get this group together." He nodded at the hanging thief. "Should we ask him again?"

Vespillo considered the prisoner for a moment. "I suppose we can try." He addressed the quietly weeping man. "Where is Febrox?"

"I don't know, please believe me. Wait!" he yelled as Vespillo pulled his fist back. "I'll tell you everything I know."

Vespillo paused. "Why do I have a feeling that won't take long?"

"The gang moved out the day after we had that fight in the square. Transferred all the loot, weapons, everything."

"Where to?"

"I don't know, I swear. The two of us were left behind to guard the old place, and to report daily so Febrox knew whether the hideout had been raided."

"How did you report?" asked Lutorius.

"We just had to make a chalk mark on the wall of the hideout once a day. That was it. I guess he sent someone to check it."

Lutorius looked over at Vespillo. "What do you think?"

"Maybe," said Vespillo. "Febrox may have planned to go back to using that place one day, so it would make sense to keep it guarded. And he would also want to know whether he was being pursued, whether he still needed to keep his head down. If he was expecting the raid, or at least worried there would be one, he wouldn't have told anyone he left behind where he was going."

Lutorius nodded. "Then this has been pointless, hasn't it?"

"Wait a moment," said Vespillo. "You said, 'the day after we had that fight.' You were there?"

The prisoner nodded. "I didn't hurt anyone, I promise. I was only doing as I was told."

"What happened to Carbo?"

"Carbo? You mean the big guy? I don't know."

Vespillo drew back his fist.

"Febrox said something to that guy, the one with the frowny mask, something about slaves, and the docks at Neapolis. That's all I know. Please stop."

Vespillo stroked the whiskers on his chin.

"It's a start," said Lutorius.

"Maybe not completely pointless then," agreed Vespillo. "I'll do some asking around."

"Why do you care about this man?" asked Asellio, expression sour.

"Does it matter?" said Lutorius. "Isn't it our job to help find him?"

"Really, Lutorius. You still have to ask that question? No, it isn't our job to investigate crimes, or to search for missing citizens, or to help old ladies get their pussies out of trees. The emperor stationed us here to keep order, and make sure the taxes are paid. If we have to crack a few heads, or crucify some criminals, fine.

But using our limited resources on a manhunt? I thought you knew better."

"He is a good man. He stood up to the bandits that have been preying on the travellers around Nola. You know, the ones that we have failed to catch, despite their effect on commerce and tax revenues in Nola."

Asellio's eyebrows drew close together, eyes narrowed to slits.

"Watch yourself, Lutorius. I will not have you questioning the job I do here."

"I'm sorry, sir. We have some information. He may have been taken to Neapolis. Illegally sold into slavery. I'm only asking for a few men to help…"

"No."

"Sir?"

"I said no. I have given you plenty of leeway to help this Carbo. But enough is enough. We have spent sufficient effort on this. Time to move on."

"But sir, we can't just abandon him."

"He is not our responsibility, Lutorius. You will return to your duties. I want you to take four men and patrol the market. The traders keep asking for more presence from us to deter thieving."

"You want me to spend my time stopping children stealing apples and trinkets?"

"I want you to obey my orders, optio!"

Asellio's face was red, round cheeks blowing in and out as he breathed hard through clenched teeth.

Lutorius stood to attention and snapped an overly formal salute.

"Yes, sir! Am I dismissed?"

"You are."

Lutorius wheeled and marched for the door.

"Lutorius," called Asellio after him. Lutorius paused at the door, turned.

"Sir?"

Asellio seemed to be wrestling with something. His mouth worked, but no words emerged. He clenched a fist, then relaxed it and sighed.

"Just get out."

Quintus looked slyly at the woman walking beside him. His insides were taut, and he struggled to find words. He didn't understand. He was no virgin, he had had his share of whores and farm girls and slaves since he had reached manhood. He had even had a brief dalliance with an older man during his stay in Greece. He had had him do things no respectable Roman man would do. He still felt chagrined about the way he let himself be dominated in the man's bed, the way he had become the giver of pleasure instead of the receiver. But he couldn't regret it, he had taught him so much.

Yet he had never felt like this around anyone before. Stumbling over his sentences, uncertain as to whether to offer an arm, or keep his distance, or even have the woman walk behind him. A flush on his cheeks that his sparse beard couldn't hide.

And all over a slave.

Marsia was shorter than him, though tall for a woman. She was broad-shouldered, almost mannish in her upper frame, although her sizeable bust would leave no one in doubt as to her gender. Her long black hair was tied back tightly in a simple pony tail, giving her face a severe appearance, and her strong facial features would never lead anyone to class her as a classical beauty.

But she captivated him, and he didn't know why.

They strolled in silence, walking along a goat path which skirted a hill a short distance from the farm. Broken clouds allowed the sun to appear intermittently, and the weather was cool but not unpleasant. When Quintus had asked Marsia to take a walk with him, she had betrayed no surprise, simply inclined her head as a slave should. Vespillo had said nothing, just watched them leave with interest.

"How come you know so much?" asked Quintus, then, as Marsia turned her gaze on him, he cursed his clumsiness. Where was the boy who had studied elocution and rhetoric under experts in Greece, when he needed him?

"So much for a slave, you mean?" asked Marsia.

"No," said Quintus. "I mean, the other day, you knew more than anyone in that room about the old legends. How did you acquire such knowledge?" That was slightly better put, he thought.

"I was taught," she said.

Quintus considered, then, surprising himself at how much courage this took, he said, "No, Marsia, that's not good enough. Give me a more complete explanation."

Marsia raised her eyebrows, and was silent for a moment. Then she said, "Why do you want to know?"

In other circumstances, Quintus might have had a slave beaten for such impudence. But he detected a genuine interest in her question, rather than mere defiance. Besides, he couldn't imagine letting anyone hurt Marsia.

"Because you are amazing," he said, then clamped his mouth shut. He turned his head forward, no longer able to meet her eyes, face now burning. "I mean," he said, still not looking at her, though feeling her gaze boring into him. "You are a remarkable woman in many ways. Your bravery when we were attacked, your intelligence, your…"

Her hand slipped into his, and he marvelled at how neatly they fitted together, and how the touch of her skin on his sent a little flood of satisfaction through him. He looked back at her, and she was smiling. She stopped, looked around, and pointed to a flat rock sticking out from the hillside. "Let's sit."

She sat, and he settled next to her, and after a moment's hesitation, he slid his arm around her waist. She leaned into him and rested her head on his shoulder, and he held still, savouring the sensation, completely confused about his feelings for this slave, but at that moment not caring one bit.

Time passed but he lost track. Was it racing or standing still? The sun barely seemed to have moved in the sky and yet he felt like he had been holding her an age when she looked up at him.

"I was taken from my people when I had seen twelve winters. My father was a good, strong man, high in the tribe, but he had enemies. One of them kidnapped me, in revenge for what, I never knew. I was purchased by slavers, who sold me in a market in Rome, with all the other goods and produce."

Quintus watched her as she spoke. Her voice was calm and dispassionate, but he could read the heavy sadness in her eyes.

"The master who bought me was old, and kind. He ran a welcoming household. He was wealthy, but a widower, with no heirs. The other slaves were mostly friendly, and they taught me to sew and clean and cook, and comforted me when I cried for my homeland.

"The master was an intelligent man, and he saw something in me that he loved. Not the way a man loves a woman, or even a father loves a daughter. More, how a teacher loves an able pupil. He liked teaching, and I would keep him company for hours, while he talked. I learned from hearing his stories, and as I grew older and he realised how much I was absorbing from him, his lessons became more formal, and more in depth.

"He taught me Latin grammar, rhetoric, oratory, mathematics, law. He taught me about the Greek and Roman gods and the stories of the heroes of olden days. He read to me the poems of Homer and Hesiod, the histories of Herodotus and Xenophon, and the philosophy of Plato and Aristotle. He even took me to see plays by Sophocles and Aeschylus. I drank the knowledge like a thirsty dog drains a bowl of water. I like to think I taught him a little myself, about the language and customs of my people, and some of it he wrote down and shared with his friends.

"And then he died, very suddenly. His estate was divided among a number of beneficiaries. One was his chief steward, a slave called Publius Sergius. Publius was a competent, if unimaginative man, and he was rewarded in the will with his freedom, some money, and a slave of his choice. He chose me. I wondered for a long time why I had not been freed, not given any reward from my master who I thought cared for me. Later, Publius told me that my master had been talking about changing his will before he died, though he didn't tell him what the changes would be. I like to think if he had not been taken away so suddenly, he would have given me my freedom. But thinking about what might have been doesn't change what is.

"So Publius chose me, and bought a tavern in the Subura. I helped him run it, and Publius used my intelligence and education to help with the accounting and the general running of the business. But I no longer discussed philosophy, or went to plays, or read histories. Life became a drudge of cleaning and serving."

Quintus squeezed Marsia's hand.

"Those were your only duties?" he asked tentatively.

"I was never whored," said Marsia. Quintus let out what he hoped was a quiet sigh of relief. "My first master had stipulated in his will that none of his slaves may be sold on into prostitution. I had the usual pinches and gropes that a serving slave expects, but Publius was very honourable about upholding my status, though he had offers."

"And he never made use of you that way himself?" asked Quintus, surprised.

"Of course he did," said Marsia. "I am a slave, he is a man. I serve in whatever way I am ordered."

Quintus flushed and looked down.

"Does it disappoint you?"

"No, no," he stammered. "I just... I would never order you to do that, if you were mine."

"I am not desirable, sir?" asked Marsia.

"No, it's not that, it's not that I wouldn't want to, I just..." He looked up to find Marsia smiling at him, and he cursed for allowing himself to be teased. He laughed, and pinched her backside, and she yelped, then laughed too. Then she grew somber.

"There was a time, when it nearly happened. Publius ran the tavern badly, ignored my advice. Local thugs extorted money from him, and it crippled him. One of them decided he was going to make use of me, and Publius could not or would not stop him.

"That took Carbo."

Quintus looked at her in surprise, then understanding dawned. "He saved you?"

"He faced down the thug, then when Publius decided to flee from the inevitable retribution, he bought the tavern, and defended it against the local criminals. He put me in charge, and he respected me and he cared for me and he still does."

"Did," corrected Quintus gently.

"Does!" said Marsia angrily, pushing Quintus away from her.

"Marsia," said Quintus, voice soothing. "He was taken. If he is in Atreus' hands, and still alive, then he won't be for much longer."

Marsia stood abruptly. "Then why are we taking walks, and talking like lovers? We should be looking for him, before it is too late."

"Marsia, please," said Quintus, alarmed by the sudden change in her demeanour. "I…like you. I wanted to spend some time with you."

"I am a slave, Quintus," she said coldly. "If you wish to take me for your pleasure, that is your choice, though you will have to answer to my master for the use of his property without permission. Otherwise, I would like to return to my master's farm."

Quintus stared at her, trying to work out what had gone wrong. For a brief, blissful moment, he had been holding this woman who had been constantly in his thoughts these last days and weeks. Now that moment was gone, popped like a bubble in a fountain. He slowly got to his feet.

"Very well. Let's return." He stomped off in the direction of the farm. He didn't look back, but he heard Marsia following him, and he thought he heard a stifled sob.

Vespillo looked up as Marsia marched into the atrium, and straight through into the house, then turned back to his conversation with Lutorius. Moments later, Quintus knocked and entered, face like a thundercloud. Lutorius opened his mouth to ask what the matter was, but from the corner of his eye caught Vespillo's slight shake of the head. Instead, he addressed Quintus as if he had noticed nothing amiss.

"Quintus, we interrogated that prisoner from the thieves' hideout."

Quintus composed himself, then inclined his head.

"What did you learn?"

"Not much," admitted Lutorius. "But he mentioned slavery, and the docks at Neapolis."

"You think Carbo may have been sold as a slave?" Quintus shook his head. "That's pretty bold, enslaving a free citizen and a distinguished veteran like Carbo."

"I don't think this will be his first time," said Vespillo. "To carry that off, you have to have contacts in the slave industry who won't ask questions. Lutorius, do you know any slavers we could talk to?"

Lutorius shook his head. "We tend not to cross paths. They aren't criminals, and we wouldn't meet socially."

"My father entertained local businessmen and merchants from time to time," said Quintus. "I remember one he had to dinner recently, a sea captain who shipped slaves. What was his name? Zosi… something. Zosimus, that's it!"

Vespillo smiled. "Sounds like someone I need to meet."

Carbo was able to track the time by the light coming through the cracks in the boards above him. Twice since he had been brought on board, cloudy grey sky had given way to complete blackness. With no moon or starlight, the hold was black as the tar that gave the ship one of its distinctive smells. Sweat, urine and brine was now being overwhelmed by the stench of faeces, as some of the prisoners could no longer hold their bowels. Carbo himself hadn't felt the need. Sometimes fear caused the guts to tighten, sometimes to loosen. Right now, Carbo knew he couldn't evacuate himself if he had half an hour in a latrine with Caesar's Gallic Wars to read.

Worse was the hunger. They hadn't taken his gag off at any stage, and the corners of his mouth were sore, agonies shooting through him when his facial expressions changed. He had stopped smiling when Sica attempted to boost his spirits. He hoped she could see why.

Thirst was a problem too. Here at least the guards had displayed a modicum of compassion, or at least sense, when it came to looking after the cargo, and each time they had come round they had poured some water onto his face. Some he had managed to swallow, some had soaked his gag, which he had been able to suck dry. It wasn't much, and he felt parched most of the time, but it was sufficient to sustain him.

Two days was not long enough for most diseases and contagion to spread, Carbo thought, but at least two of the prisoners were showing signs of ill health already. One was coughing up copious phlegm, and his wheezy breathing filled the room at night. The other, a middle-aged woman, two bodies down from Carbo, was vomiting, and passing watery, mephitic motions. She had been moaning continuously over the past day, but for the last couple of hours, she had gone quiet and limp. Her chest still rose and fell, but Carbo suspected she would not survive these conditions long. He had seen disease spread through a camp, he knew how quickly it could take hold and how much damage it could do. And that was under the discipline of the legions, with their dedicated latrines, and their carefully controlled supply of nourishing, if not appetising food.

He wondered how long this journey would be. Atreus had mentioned Sicily. What was that, two days sailing? Three? They must be getting close. Maybe not close enough for the woman, but enough for the rest of them. That, of course, would just be the start of their suffering, though. Carbo had been dwelling on the recent past, to the exclusion of the future. But there was nothing he could do to prevent what awaited him. And he wasn't really sure he wanted to. He had failed Rufa and she was gone. He had failed to avenge her. Only shame and loss remained for him.

Rufa had visited him twice more, each time her face looming suddenly out of the darkness, making him gasp and shrink back. On each occasion, Sica had reached out to him, and the touch of her fingertips had been enough to bring him back from the edge of the abyss of madness and terror that he was teetering over. When Rufa's visage had receded, he was overcome by relief and guilt in equal measures. He should be treasuring her visits, yet they terrified him. He had wept without restraint. When he had finished, the other prisoners regarded him with fear and suspicion. Except Sica, whose eyes held only compassion.

In the times between Rufa's visits, in those rare moments when he was not dwelling on the tragedy of his recent past, or the trauma of his more distant past, or the misery of his present, or the terror of his future, he wondered about Sica. What had she done to earn her place on this journey to punishment and death. Maybe it was their mutual predicament, maybe it was the little touches, physical and emotional, that showed him her kindness, maybe he just needed someone to care for and protect. Something he had so badly failed to do for the one he had loved most. Whatever it was, he felt a bond growing between them, despite the fact that he had never spoken a word to her, and that she said little. He supposed, when he was at his most lucid, that in extremes of despair the mind took tiny crumbs of comfort wherever it found them.

It was early morning, Carbo estimated. Patches of blue and light grey were shining through the cracks above him, and had been for an hour or so. His gag itched, and his tongue felt ulcerated. He was thirsty, famished and his back ached with a dull, intense pain that he could not relieve by shifting his position. He sighed, and looked over to Sica. She gave him a serious stare, then crossed her eyes and stuck her tongue out, attempting to lick the end of her nose. Carbo watched her clownish efforts and surprised himself by chuckling. The smile that accompanied this made him wince in pain, but Sica had seen she had amused him, and gave him an impish grin.

"So, big Roman knows how to laugh."

Carbo nodded, keeping his mouth in its least painful, neutral position, but crinkling his eyes at her.

"Think we will need to remember how to laugh, soon." Her voice was now solemn. Carbo looked at her, undoubtedly a woman, but not long ago a child. He realised her bravery and high spirits covered a fear as deep as any. He looked into her eyes, then extended his fingers. She touched the tips, as she did whenever he needed reassurance. He held the touch, and nodded to her. The moment passed between them, wordless, but overflowing with meaning.

A loud, hacking cough came from the prisoner with the breathing problems, who then spat, the phlegm making a wet splat on the floor. Sica rolled her eyes, and Carbo grinned, then winced again.

Cries came from above them, the sound of hands shouting instructions to each other. The flapping noise of sails being hauled in reached them. The prisoners looked at each other questioningly.

"We've arrived," said the man to Carbo's left.

Shortly after, a gentle impact juddered through the ship as it docked. The hatch to the deck above them opened. Brightness flooded in, making Carbo squint. A ladder dropped down, and two guards climbed down. They went along the prisoners, unlocking the chains that attached them to the pole, but leaving the ones that bound wrists and ankles in place. With kicks and liberal strikes with a cane, they roused the prisoners to their feet.

They all cried and groaned as they stood, stiff spines and elbows and knees protesting in agony as they unbent for the first time in a couple of days. Carbo didn't wait to be struck before he stood, but he felt the pain keenly in the joints that twenty-five years of service in the legions had abused. He gritted his teeth, biting on the gag to prevent himself from crying out. Sica, with her young bones, didn't suffer as badly, but even she stretched and flexed and extended as best her chains would allow.

The prisoner who had been vomiting did not stand. One of the guards started to beat her repeatedly with his cane, until the other one held up a hand.

"She's dead, you idiot. Move on."

When all the surviving prisoners were on their feet, the guards wasted no time in herding the prisoners to the ladder. It was a slow process, getting the stiff, chained prisoners, some of whom were elderly or infirm, onto the deck. When Sica's turn came, she went up with the speed of a squirrel up a tree. Carbo followed her more slowly, one step at a time, trying to get feeling and strength back into his limbs. He clambered out onto the deck and took his place in line with the other prisoners.

The port was busy, thronged with legionaries, sailors and dock workers. Just like any other port Carbo had ever been in, although he could see Italy a few short miles away across the Straits, the lighthouse on the peninsular side of the Straits just visible.

The ship was docked, thick ropes tying it to a wooden jetty. A gangway was lowered, and a bald, hook-nosed man with a broad smile came on board with four burly guards. He shook the hand of the captain vigorously.

"Good morning, Zozimus. You have made excellent time."

The captain shook his hand with enthusiasm, clapping him on the back. "We had a good following wind, Durmius."

"Wonderful, wonderful." Durmius looked over to the prisoners congregated on the deck. He approached, walking up and down the line, squeezing a leg here, pulling a mouth open there. When he got to Carbo, he looked up and whistled, feeling the width of his upper arms appreciatively. Then he looked at Sica, and shook his head.

"Bit of a mixed bag, captain. Any dead?"

"Just one," said Zosimus. "A fat old woman, no great loss. But we had a last minute extra anyway." He gestured to Carbo.

"Yes," said Durmius. "He does look like he might do good service. But the rest of them…" Durmius swept an arm to indicate the other prisoners. "Really. How long do you think they will last?"

Zosimus shrugged. "Not really my concern," he said. "You work them till they drop. These are the scummiest of the lowest of all slaves, they are all marked for death. That's why they are so cheap."

"About that," said Durmius. "I think the price is still too high."

"We've done our negotiating. Pay me, and they are yours. Otherwise I dump them in the Strait of Messana."

Durmius laughed. "You wouldn't. Come, I think we should consider at least a discount of a twelfth for this rotten bunch."

Zosimus stepped up to the prisoner who had been on Carbo's left for the journey. He grabbed his chains, jerked him to the seaward side of the boat, then tipped him unceremoniously into the water.

The prisoner's cry was cut off as he hit the water with an impact that winded him. Briefly, he struggled to keep his head afloat, gurgling and pleading. But the weight of the iron chains was too much, and he disappeared under the waves. The prisoners stared in horror at the frothy patch of water that marked their comrade's fresh grave.

"You have one less slave now," said Zosimus. "The price is the same."

"Don't be ridiculous, you will have to at least refund me for that one."

"Our negotiations are done, Durmius." He grabbed Sica, and pulled her to the edge of the boat. She cried out and struggled ineffectually. Carbo tried to yell through his gag, and made to move towards her, but a guard kicked him in the back of his legs and he collapsed to his knees. Zosimus dangled Sica over the side, her midriff balanced on the railing, head down towards the water, legs kicking in the air

"Fine, fine," said Durmius. "Point taken. I will honour our original deal. Just think yourself lucky that I am so desperate. Production is down due to the recent level of...losses among the workforce."

Zosimus hauled Sica back into the boat and threw her to the deck, where she lay, trembling and sobbing. Carbo shuffled over to her awkwardly and took hold of her hand. She squeezed it tight.

"Though you might as well have thrown that one in too," said Durmius nodding to Sica. "I don't think she will be with us long."

Durmius pulled out a purse full of money and handed it to Zosimus. Zosimus opened it, and carefully counted it, before nodding, satisfied.

"They are all yours," he said.

"A pleasure doing business as always," said Durmius. "Guards, let's get them moving."

Carbo and Sica struggled quickly to their feet to avoid the kicks and blows they would have received if they had remained down. As they shuffled onto the gangplank, Eutropius indicated Carbo.

"Why is the big one gagged?"

"He is mouthy," said Zosimus. "I think you might want to watch him."

"You don't need to worry about that. Right let's get this sorry bunch to the mines. Move on everyone."

Carbo walked down the gangplank, and onto the island of Sicily. It was a place he never expected to leave.

# CHAPTER XIV

Vespillo wandered along the docks in Neapolis. Marsia was by his side. She had insisted on coming, and though he felt it wasn't right to be giving in to a slave's demands, he did feel sorry for the young woman. She was as distraught as any of them at Carbo's disappearance. The cooling between her and Quintus had become pronounced and she seemed glad to be away from Carbo's farm, and doing something active to help. Quintus himself had offered to come, but Marsia had coldly suggested he had more important things to do, and Quintus had taken the hint.

This part of the waterfront smelled of fish and tar. The docks here tended to industry, whereas further along were the seafront villas for the wealthy. This whole region catered to the nobles who wanted to escape Rome for some luxury, especially in the summer months, and Puteoli to the north and Stabiae to the south were popular holiday destinations. Neapolis was a bit more cosmopolitan, and Vespillo had seen poor and rich quarters, Greek and Roman influence, as they had travelled here from Nola.

Now he questioned dock workers, porters, sailors and ships' captains, asking if they remembered a large man, a prisoner or a slave, being transported from here a few days previously, or knew of a captain called Zosimus. He was met mainly with blank looks, and even the offer of coin seemed to jog no memories. It was unsurprising. The docks heaved with activity, all manner of goods and cargo being loaded and unloaded. One ship sat low in the water, laden with garum. Another disgorged a seemingly endless supply of miserable and vomit-stained slaves from its hold.

Despondently, Vespillo walked up to the captain of the slave ship. The man was tall, with a ruddy, weathered face.

"Captain, may I ask you a question or two?"

"You can ask," said the captain, his accent suggesting to Vespillo Phoenician or other semitic heritage.

"I'm looking for a man who passed through these docks about three or four days ago. He may have been a prisoner, or a slave."

The captain looked at the lines of slaves shuffling down the gangway of his ship onto the dock. "You might have to be a bit more specific."

"This is a tall man. Strong, broad. Pitch black hair. Walks with a limp, and covered in battle scars. We're also looking for a captain called Zosimus."

The captain frowned. "And why do you want to know?"

"That's my business," said Vespillo.

"And the cargoes of ships are the business of their captains, and the merchants that pay them, and no one else."

"Please, master," said Marsia "If you can help us, we would be so grateful."

The captain looked Marsia up and down. "How grateful?"

Marsia flushed, then looked down. "With my master's permission, I would reward you in any way I could."

"That's not necessary," said Vespillo. "We have coin," he said to the captain.

The captain chewed his lower lip. "I'd like to see that coin," he said.

Vespillo drew out a jangling purse. The captain put his hand out, but Vespillo tossed it in the air and caught it, so the captain could appreciate its weight without getting hold of it.

"I saw your friend," he said.

Marsia gasped. "Please tell us where, master."

"Do you always let your slave speak for you?"

"Marsia, be quiet. Captain, would you tell us what you know?"

The captain held out his hand again. Vespillo hesitated, then dropped the bag into his palm. The captain opened the drawstring, peered inside, and drew out a silver coin, holding it up to the light to inspect it. Satisfied, he tied the purse to his belt.

"The other night," he said. "They were loading cargo onto the boat next to me. A fairly rotten looking bunch of slaves if you ask me. Unruly. Not sure they would be worth much. Anyway, your friend was among them. Tall, muscly, scarred. Stood out from the rest. Looked like he didn't belong. Funny thing was, they had him gagged."

Vespillo looked at Marsia, whose face had lit up with hope.

"Where were they headed for?"

"I'm afraid I didn't ask. I wasn't that curious."

Vespillo felt his heart sink. Knowing where Carbo had departed from was useless if they didn't know the destination. The boat could have taken him anywhere in the vast Empire.

"Strangely though, the captain was called Zosimus. He is due back in two or three days. I remember because he said he planned to catch the chariot races, and we had a wager. I'm a big supporter of the blues, he favours the whites."

Vespillo shook the captain's hand. "Thank you. You have been a big help."

The captain patted the purse at his belt. "My pleasure."

"Welcome to our establishment," said the overseer. "I am Durmius, and I will be your host for... well, the foreseeable future. We have all the modern amenities that you would expect. Your cells, I mean rooms, are furnished with luxury straw to give you a comfortable night's sleep. A corner of each room is allocated as a latrine, and there are only eight of you per room. Regular meals will be provided at no extra cost, almost every day. As for the entertainment...no, I won't spoil the surprise."

Sica looked at Carbo with incomprehension.

Carbo shook his head. "Great, he's got a sense of humour." The words came out thickly - his tongue was swollen and his mouth and lips ulcerated from the gag that had only been removed when they arrived at the mining compound. Speaking and swallowing were painful. The overseer heard the comment, and nodded to one of the guards. The guard took a step forward and flicked out his whip, the stinging blow landing on Carbo's chest. The speed of the punishment took Carbo by surprise, and he bit down to stifle a cry, then cried out anyway as his teeth closed on his tender tongue.

"We do have one or two house rules to follow," said Durmius. "Some minor chores to earn your keep as well. You'll pick it all up as you go along. But enough of me, you'll be dying to get settled in, I'm sure." He chuckled to himself, and nodded to the guards.

The line of prisoners shuffled forward. Their ankles were chained so they could not take a full stride, wrists were chained close together, and iron neck collars were chained to the prisoner before and behind them. The slow march to the mines from the dock had taken most of the day, during which they had not been fed, although had been given short breaks for rest and water. Carbo had watched carefully for an opportunity to escape, but had quickly realised it was hopeless. The guards were competent and numerous, and the chains were heavy and unbreakable. A bud of optimism that his best chance to get away would be during the transfer from ship to mines had withered and died in a short space of time.

They were led to a group of long stone buildings, divided up into small cells, and they were split into groups of eight. Carbo and Sica were herded in with six others adjacent to them in the line, and the door behind them was slammed shut and barred from the outside.

There were no windows, but there was a large hole in the wooden roof that let enough light in, once Carbo's eyes had adjusted, for him to take in his surroundings, and the sorry group who had become his roommates.

As the overseer had said, there was a little straw on the floor, less than you would give a horse in a stable, and one corner in particular reeked of urine and faeces, suggesting a designated latrine area. The walls were damp, but with little graffiti, which surprised Carbo given what he had seen of cells in the past.

And that was it. His new home.

He looked around at the other prisoners, who were staring around them with unanimous misery. They were a mixed group. In addition to Sica and himself, there were two other women and four other men. Both the women were middle-aged, one younger than the other, and they clung to each other. From their resemblance, Carbo speculated they were sisters. Three of the men had the physiques of manual labourers and bore stigmata branded onto their foreheads, two of them reading 'FUG' for fugitivus, meaning they had escaped in the past and been recaptured, and one reading 'FUR' for fure, meaning he was a thief. The fourth man, a boy really, appeared more delicate, with soft hands and poorly developed muscles, and his expression showed stark disbelief at his circumstances.

Carbo sighed, and shuffled towards one corner. Sica moved with him, but the prisoner on his right, the boy, did not, and when the chain between them grew taut, Carbo gave it a little tug. The boy seemed to startle out of his daze, and once Carbo had some play in the chain, he slumped against the wall and slid to the floor.

Clumsily, the other slaves found ways to sit or lie that afforded them the best comfort they could achieve. Carbo closed his eyes, trying to keep from thinking.

A warm body nestled into his left side, and he opened his eyes to see Sica grinning up at him. He hesitated, then placed an arm around her and drew her closer. She laid her head on his shoulder, relaxing into him.

"You, big guy," said the man branded as a thief. "Do you speak Latin?"

"Pretty well," said Carbo.

"Good. These two don't." He gestured at the two fugitives, who glared at him, realising they were being spoken about, but not understanding.

"I do, too," said the boy.

"Did I ask you?" asked the thief. The boy opened his mouth, then thought better of it and closed it rapidly.

"Looks like it's up to you and me to run this group then," said the thief.

"Does it?" Carbo's tone was non-committal.

"Yeah. Now you look like you can handle yourself, so I don't want to fight you for the top spot. But I know a dirty trick or two myself, so you really don't want to tangle with me either."

"I see."

"So we are agreed? Both of us in charge."

"I think the overseer believes he is the one in charge."

"Not in here, not when we are locked in together and the guards are outside."

"I see your point."

"Good. So first we need to draw up some sort of rota."

"Rota?" asked Carbo. "For what?"

"For who gets to fuck the women, obviously. You and me get first choice of course. But we probably need to let these two lumps have a go, or they will be trouble. The boy looks like he would prefer a cock up his own arse anyway, so we can ignore him. Now, do you want to take it in turns, or would you rather have your own woman. That girl curled up to you is the prettiest one here, but as a gesture of goodwill, you can have her if I have those other two."

Carbo felt Sica tense against him, though she didn't move or speak. The two older women started to wail, holding onto each other tightly.

"No," said Carbo.

"No?" said the thief. "You prefer to swap things around? Or maybe you want one of the older women instead?"

"No," said Carbo. "We are all in this together. No one touches anyone else here."

The thief looked at Carbo in surprise. "What are you talking about?"

"Be in charge, if that's what you want. But you will not lay a finger on anyone else in here."

The thief started to tremble in indignation.

"You do understand where we are? You know we are likely to survive only a few weeks or months down there? And you won't let me take any small crumb of pleasure before I am worked to death?"

"I won't allow anyone else's misery to be worse than it has to be."

The thief glared at Carbo, but Carbo did not blink. Eventually the thief looked away, face flushed with anger.

"This isn't over," he said.

The two fugitive slaves who were chained next to each other had watched the argument with interest, if not comprehension. When it finished, they turned to each other, embraced, and started to kiss. One of them reached down into the other's lap, and started to stroke gently up and down.

"Juno's tits, that's just what I need," muttered the thief, and turned away as the two men forgot their situation in a small moment of pleasure.

Sica relaxed against Carbo again, giving his arm a squeeze, then fell asleep.

Rufa visited Carbo once in the night, waking him from a disturbed sleep with a touch on his face that made him gasp. Sica was instantly awake at his side, and when she saw him staring into space with a look of horror on his face, she reached up to him, grasped his chin and turned him towards her. As before in the ship, she made him concentrate on her, until he sensed the apparition had vanished. He looked around to check Rufa was gone, then pulled Sica to him, waiting for his racing heart and his breathing to slow back to normal. Soon Sica was asleep again, and her gentle, deep breathing helped Carbo also to drift off.

They were woken at dawn by the door flying open. Eight loaves of bread and a jug of water were dumped into the cell and then the door was slammed shut and barred again.

The thief was the first to react, grabbing three of the loaves for himself.

"There is one each," said Carbo.

"Look," said the thief, "Fine if you don't want the women fucked, though I can't understand why. But surviving in this place means staying fit and healthy. That means eating enough. If the weaker ones can't fight for their food, well, the stronger ones have more of a chance. And the weak ones won't survive long anyway."

"One each," repeated Carbo.

The thief clutched the loaves to him defiantly, but one of the fugitives reached forward, and before the thief could react, slammed his head backwards into the wall. The loaves dropped to the floor as the thief howled. The fugitive had obviously held back, or the thief would be unconscious or dead, but the thief put his hand to the back of his head and brought it in front of his face, staring in disbelief at the blood he found there.

"I'll kill you for that, you cock-sucking barbarian," said the thief.

The fugitive simply picked up two of the loaves and passed them to Carbo, then offered the other loaf to the thief. The thief snatched it out of his hand and started to chew it hungrily.

Sica passed around the other loaves and the jug of water, and everyone ate and drank. The meal was over in moments, and it was in no way satisfying. Carbo knew the amount was not sufficient for a man of his size, and wondered if there would be other meals during the day or in the evening. He hoped so, or he wouldn't last long.

"What each names?" asked Sica. The other prisoners looked at her. "I Sica," she said, pointing to herself.

"Carbo," said Carbo.

The two fugitives smiled in comprehension. "Phraates," said the first, the one who had assaulted the thief. "Orobazes," said the second.

The names and accent reminded Carbo of slaves captured in battle he had encountered during his time in the legions. "Parthians?" he asked. The men recognised the Latin name for their people and nodded.

"I'm Meru," said the boy. "My father was an Egyptian, my mother Greek. I shouldn't be here."

"I from Dacia," said Sica. "I should not be here either. Not my fault I had to cut off my master's cock to stop him raping me."

The other slaves looked at her in surprise for a moment. Sica pointed at one of the women.

"I'm Pamphile," said the one Sica indicated. "And this is my older sister Agamede." Her accent had a tinge of Attic. "We were hairdressers to rich matrons in Nola. Freeborn. We don't belong here either." Carbo could see tears glistening at the corner of her eyes.

Sica stared at the man with the thief brand, who looked back at her defiantly.

"You aren't going to tell us your name?" asked Carbo.

"Why should I?" asked the thief stubbornly.

"Oh there are a few reasons. I might say, 'Sica would you like this bread that the guards have brought?' Or Pamphile may say, 'Meru, would you like me to massage the ache away from the day's work?' Or I might say to you, whatever your name is, 'Would you like me to stop punching you in the face?' Of course I would need to know your name to be able to ask you that question."

The thief spat. "Fine. Call me Curtius."

"Pleased to meet you, Curtius."

The door flew open again, and a guard poked his head in. He wrinkled his nose at the smell of their night's excretions, then barked at them. "Everyone out."

The prisoners rose to their feet, slowly stretching out aching joints, trying to co-ordinate their movements so they didn't get tangled in their chains. When they were up, they exchanged glances, none of them in a hurry to be the first one out.

Sica shrugged, and stepped outside, and Carbo had to follow her. One by one they all emerged into the cold, bright early morning. By their order in the links of the chain, Orobazes was last out. Four guards faced them as they stood uncertainly outside their cell. Each was armed with a club, stowed in a belt, and one of them held a whip loosely, its leather straps trailing on the ground. This one, apparently their leader, walked behind Orobazes, and laid the whip firmly into his back. Tiny bits of gravel picked up from the ground added to the bite, leaving a row of dots of blood beading up through the rip in his tunic that the whip had created.

"Next time, be quicker, or you will all be whipped. Now follow me."

The eight prisoners shuffled after him, a guard flanking them on either side, and one bringing up the rear. They walked over rough ground a short distance. They rounded the rock face that skirted the path on one side, and Carbo saw the mine works for the first time.

Wooden huts ringed a large dark hole. Above the hole a pulley was set up, the ropes of which were being hauled on by a small group of slaves. As Carbo watched, a large bucket of grey-black, shiny stone appeared, which was manhandled into a cart. When the cart was loaded, it was hauled away by oxen towards furnaces which belched black smoke and pungent fumes.

The whip cracked near Carbo's head, the tip slicing the skin on Agamede's shoulder, who screamed, then bit her lip.

"No dawdling, move it," yelled the guard. The prisoners walked on in their line to the huts. Durmius was screaming at a thin, elderly man, who lay curled up on the ground, to get up. The tremoring man made no attempt to stand, just babbling incoherently. The overseer began to kick him, blows of such severity with hob-nailed boots, they sent blood spraying wherever they fell. After what seemed an eternity, during which the prisoners watched in silence, the overseer stopped. He wiped the sweat of his exertions from his head, and looked down at the dead man at his feet. He gestured to two nearby guards.

"Dump him in the burial pit." The guards hurried to obey, lifting the emaciated body easily and carrying it away. The overseer turned to the guard that had escorted Carbo's group.

"Let's get the newcomers started then. Get the four men picks and aprons, they will work at the rock face. We cracked a new one yesterday. The boy and the young girl can be loaders, and the old ladies can work the Egyptian screw. The water level is getting a bit high after the recent rain."

Guards came forward and unlocked the prisoners' chains. Agamede and Pamphile were led away, chattering miserably to each other. Carbo rubbed his wrists, examining the red skin where the iron had chafed. One guard handed a pick to each of the adult male prisoners. Carbo hefted it thoughtfully in his hand, testing the weight of the head, the balance of the shaft. He looked up and noticed a guard watching him closely, hand hovering near his sword, and Carbo let the pick hang loosely at his side.

"Right," said Durmius. "Most important rule. You will do as I say without question or you will be severely punished. Is that understood?" The prisoners nodded, the ones who didn't understand following the example of the others. "Good. Now, all of you strip."

The prisoners hesitated and looked at each other. A whip cracked out, opening a red stripe on Meru's upper arm. Hastily, they all shed their clothes, the two fugitives copying the others in confusion. Soon they were all naked, using their hands and arms to cover themselves as best they could. The air was cool, and they all shivered.

Durmius smiled with obvious enjoyment of their discomfort and humiliation. His gaze lingered on Sica, who stood with her legs tightly pressed together, one arm across her breasts and a hand covering the area between her legs. She gazed back at him defiantly and he chuckled unpleasantly.

"You probably think I made you do that for fun. That's only partly true. You will be thanking me soon, though." He turned to the guards. "Give the men aprons. Give the boy and girl baskets."

The guards handed leather aprons to Carbo, Curtius and the two fugitives, and woven baskets to Sica and Meru. The aprons covered their fronts, reaching down just below their knees, and fastening with leather straps behind them. Carbo felt a little more covered and less vulnerable, though he was aware that Sica behind him had a good view of his buttocks. Sica and Meru did not get any protective clothing.

"Right, you men, you will be hacking ore out of the rock face. It has already been broken up by fire cracking. You'll find out more about that in time. Well, if you live long enough. You two, the boy and girl, you will be collecting the rock pieces they mine and carrying them to the buckets to be hauled to the surface. You will keep working unless told you may rest. Anyone who stops working without authorisation, anyone who works too slowly, any idleness of any sort will be punished severely. There are no excuses. Understand?"

They all nodded.

"We'll see. One or two of you look like you might still have some defiance in you. Maybe that's why you got sent here in the first place. Let me make it clear. Your only hope of survival here is to work hard and obey. There is no other choice." Durmius beckoned over a slave who had been hovering nearby. The slave, bent-backed and stiff, limped over.

"This is Amasis, he will show you the ropes. Obey him like you would me. Amasis, take them down."

Amasis shuffled off towards the hole, and the six prisoners followed them. When they reached the edge, Carbo saw a ladder leading down into the darkness.

"Follow me," said Amasis, wearily, climbing onto the ladder and starting to descend. Phraates and Orobazes followed Amasis, and as Carbo waited his turn, he tried to make out anything in the darkness. Far below, he could see flickering lamps. A sudden creaking noise startled him, and the rope down the centre of the hole started to move around the pulley as nearby slaves hauled on it. A huge iron bucket slowly inched its way upwards, filled with pieces of dark grey-silver rock. When it reached the surface, it was hauled to the edge of the pit, and with difficulty tipped into a waiting wagon. Once it was empty, the wagon was pulled away by mules, and the bucket lowered down again.

Carbo's turn came and he clambered onto the ladder. He was aware of a long drop and gripped each rung tightly. The climb was long and slow. He could see little below him. When he looked up, he saw Sica's bare legs.

Eventually they reached solid ground, and Carbo stepped onto rough rock. Sharp pebbles dug into his bare feet painfully. He had soles hardened by long marches, but always protected by caligae, and he knew that much walking on this surface would soon leave his feet blistered and sore.

They were in a large cavern, six shafts leading away in different directions. Small oil lamps set in niches in the walls shed a low-level illumination. Amasis was already walking slowly but purposefully down one, and the others followed him. The shafts were much lower than a man's height. Even Sica had to bend her head to avoid banging it, and Carbo had to stoop right over, the highest point of his back scraping the ceiling if he didn't bend enough. The low ceiling was supported by stone pillars that had been left in the original rock when it was originally excavated, with wooden supports patching up other areas.

"Don't ever touch those pillars with your picks," said Amasis, gesturing at them. "Penalty for excavating them is death." Carbo wondered who would be stupid enough to do such a thing.

The access tunnel angled downwards, and Carbo noticed the air getting heavier and warmer. Every so often a shaft in the ceiling allowed ventilation, but Carbo could see how far underground they were by the tiny size of the circle of light at top. The oil lamps set in the niches burned progressively lower as the air became less fresh.

The ceiling got lower still, until Carbo was bent over double, his back getting grazed by the rough surface, muscles stiffening, and the heat increased. The oil lamps gave out a thin smoke, and Carbo found his breathing becoming laboured.

Further along the tunnel was a rockfall. Carbo could see a wooden support had splintered and come down, together with a portion of the ceiling. He noticed a foul smell, and as he walked past, he looked down, and saw a rotting arm sticking out from beneath the rubble. He looked back and saw Sica staring at the same thing in open-mouthed horror.

"Sica," he said to her. She looked up at him, and he held her gaze until he could see she was more composed.

"Come on, you lot back there," Amasis' voice came back to them. "They will get angry if you don't mine your quota this shift."

They carried on, and soon the walls widened out into a gallery. The ceiling was even lower though, and Carbo had to get on his hands and knees. The gallery was a rough, elongated circle. At the furthest end were large boulders.

"These were fire-cracked yesterday," said Amasis. "Now the rocks need breaking. You guys, get to work with your picks. Two of you breaking the boulders into pieces small enough to carry. Two of you work at the face and hack out more rocks where the fire has weakened it. You two little ones, you put the boulders in your baskets and take them back to the bucket in the main gallery. The overseer will check how much you mine and if you don't make your quota you will be punished."

"What's the quota?" asked Carbo.

"No idea," said Amasis. "They don't tell you. Means you just have to work as hard as you can. The shift lasts ten hours. Good luck."

Amasis turned to leave.

"Where are you going?" asked Curtius.

Amasis looked suprised.

"I survived. They promoted me to supervisor. I don't have to do this any more. Thank all the gods." He crawled painfully and stiffly away.

When he was gone, the six of them looked at each other. Curtius laughed and sat down against the wall.

"They send us down here without supervision, and expect us to work our backsides off. They can forget it."

"He said they would punish us if we didn't fulfill the quota," said Meru nervously.

"Screw them," said Curtius.

Carbo sighed and picked up his pick. He surveyed the rock wall before him, focussed on a crack and swung at it. The shock of the impact vibrated up the pick handle, and Carbo nearly dropped the tool. Rock yielded a lot less than flesh when you hit it, he realised. Even less than wood and metal. He drew the tool back and swung again. It was awkward from his half-crouched, half kneeling position, but the second swing was more measured, and he saw the crack he was aiming at widen. A third swing and a chunk of ore fell to the ground. He picked it up and passed it backwards. Phraates took it off him, and used his own pick to break the chunk into small pieces. Sica, who had been holding the basket across her body to disguise her nakedness, looked questioningly at Carbo. He nodded, and she bent down and started loading the pieces into her basket. Orobazes started attacking the already fallen boulders, swinging with gusto, and Meru stepped up and started filling his own basket. Now they were all at work apart from Curtius, who remained seated, watching them all contemptuously.

Soon Carbo was getting into a rhythm, and the rock was building up at his feet as fast as Phraates could take it away and break it up. A sheen of sweat built up on his skin in the warm humid air, and he realised why they had to strip. Working like this all day would bring on heat exhaustion quickly if wearing too many layers.

Carbo's mind emptied, eyes unfocused. The physical activity actually felt good, mindless, repetitive, demanding, taking his thoughts away from grief and despair and loss. After some time, Phraates tapped him on the shoulder. Meru and Sica's baskets were full and they had disappeared down the tunnel to fill up the bucket. Phraates pointed at where Curtius still sat, chin cradled in his hands, staring off into space. Carbo shrugged. He was breathing hard now, finding he had to take deeper breaths in the warm, thick air. Sweat dripped into his eyes, stinging, and he wiped it away with the back of his hand. He paused in his work, enough to let his breathing settle. Meru and Sica returned with their empty baskets, and got back to work on hands and knees, picking up fragments of ore. Carbo turned to the rockface and lifted his pick again.

There was no time in the darkness. Just the rhythmic rise and fall of the pick, the clunk of metal on rock, the coming and going of Meru and Sica with the baskets. Carbo's breathing was heavy, the air not feeling satisfying to his lungs, no matter how hard he breathed, and he found himself tiring easily. The others too, looked exhausted, except for Curtius who sat, watching them work with a wry half-smile on his face. He wondered about forcing the man to help, but he was seized by a deep lassitude, and left him alone. How long had it been anyway? Had they nearly finished for the day?

Meru and Sica returned again with empty baskets, and this time, they were accompanied by Amasis. The supervisor looked at Curtius sitting on the ground with alarm.

"What is he doing? What's going on?"

Carbo stopped, dropping the pick and flexing his wrists to try to work away the burning sensation.

"He won't work," said Carbo, forcing the words out breathlessly through a dry, dust-filled mouth.

"You are well under quota at the moment. And you have only been working for half a morning."

"Half a morning?" groaned Meru in despair.

"If you carry on at this rate, you will be so far under quota they will flog the skin off you all. They won't care who has pulled their weight and who hasn't. That's up to you lot to deal with that kind of thing." Amasis shook his head. "Best of luck to you all. I'm not going to stick my neck out for you though. Sort him out."

Amasis crawled away, leaving the group of slaves looking at each other.

"We in trouble?" asked Sica.

"We will be," said Meru miserably, "If Curtius doesn't help."

Phraates and Orobazes were watching, furrowed brows attempting to understand what was happening. Sica turned to them, and pointed to Curtius.

"He not help." She mimed using her pick. "We in trouble." She pointed to all of them, then mimed a whip. Phraates and Orobazes nodded understanding, then turned to Carbo.

Carbo sighed. Why was it up to him to deal with this? He wasn't a leader anymore. He was a nobody, a failed person, less than a person, a slave. He caught Sica's eye, saw her expectant gaze on him. He imagined her tied up to a tree, her naked back lashed until streams of blood ran in torrents where skin used to be. He shook his head in resignation.

"Take up your pick, Curtius."

Curtius made no move, looking at him defiantly.

"Why should I?"

"Because if you don't," said Carbo, wearily. "I will have to kill you."

Everyone was still. The only noises were the rhythmic drip of water and the far off sounds of pick on stone where another part of the mine was being worked. Curtius reached forward slowly for his pick.

Gripped it tightly and locked eyes with Carbo.

Froze.

Pressed against the side of his neck was a wickedly sharp fragment of rock.

"Or I kill you," hissed Sica into his ear. "You help us, or you dead man."

Curtius hesitated, then lifted the pick. Carbo was aware that if this came to blows the fighting would be awkward, and quite probably absurd, with them both on their hands and knees to avoid the low ceiling, swinging at each other like puppets in a forum show. The moment stretched, then Curtius shuffled forward, holding the pick in front of him like a gladius. Sica watched carefully, holding her improvised blade before her. Carbo's heart pounded, the familiar tension he always felt before battle washing over him. Curtius lifted the pick, brought it down. Carbo tensed, his own pick before him.

Curtius' tool smacked into the rock face, wedging into a crack. He pulled it out with a heave, and chunks of ore came loose. Curtius looked across to Carbo with a sneer, swung the pick again. Carbo watched for a little longer, then went back to work.

# CHAPTER XV

A light drizzle carried by a firm breeze bathed Quintus' face like the spray on a sea voyage. He sat on a stone bench in the covered colonnade that bordered the peristylium, his mood as grey as the sky. His father was out, he didn't know where, and this was somehow a relief. Though he had no intention of discussing his feelings for Marsia with his father, just possessing those emotions in his father's presence felt like Blaesus was intruding. He closed his eyes, cold and damp, and sighed.

A hand on his shoulder made him jump.

"Jupiter, what are you doing out here in the rain?"

Quintus opened his eyes to see Publius' broad face grinning down at him.

"Just sitting, brother. Thinking."

"Any thoughts you want to share?"

Quintus shook his head.

"Well, mind if your big brother joins you?"

"You want to sit out with me in this weather? How drunk are you?"

"Probably just the right amount of drunk, I would say."

Quintus laughed. "Sit then, brother, keep me company."

Publius settled himself next to Quintus on the bench, and took a long drink from a silver cup. For a while they were both silent, staring out into the well-tended garden. At the far end, a slave was weeding the flower beds, drenched to the skin, hair bedraggled.

"Have you ever been in love?" Quintus' words spoken suddenly into the quiet made Publius start. He turned to regard Quintus for a little, then took another drink and shrugged.

"How can you tell?"

"I wish I knew. If it's what I feel, I'm not sure it is a pleasant experience."

"Yes, I can agree with that."

"Have you read Catullus?"

"I'm not really one for poetry, you know that."

"Plato said, 'At the touch of love, everyone becomes a poet.'"

Publius smiled. "Well, in that case I must have never been touched by love."

"Catullus was a very angry man. Love caused him a lot of pain, I think."

"Who is it?" asked Publius. "A rich merchant's daughter? A girl you met in the bars in Nola?"

"It doesn't matter," said Quintus, disconsolately. "It can't happen anyway."

"Why not?"

"She loves someone else."

"Why isn't she with him, then?"

"Well, he is probably dead for a start."

Publius barked out a laugh and clapped Quintus on the back. "Well it looks like you might have an advantage over him there."

Quintus gave a half smile, then stared out into the rain again. Publius' merriment faded.

"You are better off without her, brother. Your Catullus had it right. Love brings pain."

"I thought you had never been in love?"

"I wasn't talking about me."

Quintus waited for Publius to continue. Publius hesitated, seeming to struggle with his next words.

"Father has never got over mother, you know."

Quintus' face twisted in annoyance. "Oh, here we go. I get enough of this from father. How I killed the love of his life. Fine, blame the newborn baby if that makes everyone feel better."

"Don't be so self-centred," snapped Publius. "More happened then than you realise."

Quintus looked at Publius with open curiosity.

"Like what?"

Publius looked down. "I can't say."

Quintus gripped Publius' arm tight, until his brother met his eyes.

"All my life, people have condemned me for my mother's fate. Tell me. What happened back then? I need to know."

Publius looked anguished. "I promised I would never tell anyone."

"I'm family. She was my mother as well as yours. I have a right to know."

Publius took a sip of wine, swallowed hard.

"I'm only telling you now," he said, "because you have come back from Greece changed. You are a man now. And you deserve to know. But remember, whatever I tell you, you are always my brother and I love you."

Quintus stayed silent, barely breathing, hanging on his brother's words expectantly.

"Father had two brothers. The younger, uncle Lucius, and the older, uncle Gnaeus. I sort of remember him. He had a short beard and a very smiley face. He had no children of his own, but he used to play with me. I was very young at the time, but I remember I liked him."

"I didn't know I had another uncle. He died?"

Publius sighed. "Father loved our mother. There was never any doubt about that. But he was away a lot, commanding in the legions. He used to tell me tales of the army, when I was very little."

"He never spoke about it to me."

"No, he stopped. I think he blamed the army for what happened."

"What did happen?"

"Mother used to cry a lot when father was away. Women can become very melancholy after they have given birth apparently. Uncle Lucius was away with father. But Uncle Gnaeus was older, he had proved himself with the legions, and had started on his political career. So he was always around in Rome. When mother was lonely or sad, Uncle Gnaeus used to comfort her."

Quintus paled. "You don't mean…"

Publius fidgeted uncomfortably. "I remember them being close. Remember sometimes being sent away to be looked after by the slaves, when mother wanted to be alone with Uncle Gnaeus. Other things I found out later. Bits of gossip from the slaves. And then one day, after we had left Rome, I was playing soldiers behind a statue in the peristylium, just over there." He pointed to the far end of the garden. "I heard father and Uncle Lucius talking. I learned everything. They discovered me listening, but it was too late. Father was going to beat me, but Uncle Lucius just made me promise not to tell anyone, ever. That bad things would happen to father and to everyone in the family if I did. I was maybe eight years old by then, horrified by what I had heard, but relieved I wasn't getting a beating. I've never told anyone since. Until now."

"Tell what, Publius," urged Quintus.

Publius mouthed something, like he was trying out the words before saying them.

"Father is not…"

"Not what?" asked Quintus, his voice low and dangerous.

"He is not…your father."

He had seen it coming, but was trying not to believe. The actual words hit him like a blow from a watchman's club to his face.

"You're lying," he whispered.

"I'm sorry," said Publius. "It's true. Father…er… Gaius…"

"Call him father," snapped Quintus.

Publius nodded. "Father was away for four months. You were conceived in the middle of his campaign. Uncle Gnaeus was your father."

Quintus stared at his brother, face slack in horror and disbelief. After a few moments, he gathered himself enough to speak.

"What did father do?"

"At first, nothing. Oh, they shouted, screamed, swore bloody murder. Told Gnaeus never to come near mother again. I remember the arguments, the broken crockery thrown across the triclinium. But father loved mother more than anything. She cried, begged forgiveness. And he forgave her.

"As her belly grew, they seemed to come to some understanding. I think mother was genuinely sorry for what she had done, and father knew it. They seemed happy together. And father swore to mother that he would raise the child as his own."

Quintus looked down. "I wonder if he thinks he has fulfilled that promise."

Publius squeezed his arm gently, but didn't answer him. Quintus sighed.

"So, it all changed when mother died."

Publius' took a deep breath. "Do you want to hear this?"

"You seem to be in a sharing mood, brother, why not?"

Publius' mouth tightened, but he carried on.

"It was the worst day of my life, the day mother died. I was old enough to understand, just. I think she developed an infection, or something like that. The physicians couldn't save her. I have never seen father behave the way he did, before or since. He screamed, he tore clothes, he smashed statues. He had the physicians seized and Uncle Lucius had to stop him from killing them. Uncle Lucius tried to console him, but it was no use. One of the slaves took me away, kept me out of sight. You were given to another slave to wet nurse you.

"For a while he refused to believe it was true, wouldn't allow her to be prepared for burial. After he was finally persuaded to allow the funeral to go ahead, he wandered the house, crying out what a terrible husband he had been, how it was all his fault.

"Then one day it suddenly changed. Even now I can remember how he went quiet, in a way that terrified me. He took to whispered conversations with Uncle Lucius, that would stop whenever I came near. Soon after that we had to flee Rome."

"What did he do?" Quintus' voice was a whisper.

"I don't know the details. Just what I overheard, and put together myself. How it happened doesn't matter I suppose. Was it an argument that got out of control, or was it pre-meditated? Either way, Uncle Gnaeus ended up dead, and father and Uncle Lucius fled into voluntary exile before the authorities could take action."

The fine rain had soaked Quintus without him realising, and small drops now fell from his fringe onto the hands clenched tight in his lap. He was frozen in place, eyes wide, a fine tremor running through him. Publius put an arm around his shoulder, tried to pull him close, but the action seemed to break a spell. He angrily shrugged his brother off.

"Quintus…"

"That man," Quintus spat. "Killed my father."

"Quintus, he is your father. He raised you…"

"No! He didn't expose me at birth. He tolerated my existence. He did not raise me as his own. I was a constant reminder to him, of loss and betrayal. I know it now, he really does hate me."

Publius grabbed for Quintus' arm. "That's not true, Quintus, he does love you."

Quintus stood, pulling his arm sharply away from his brother.

"You should have told me before, Publius. You should have told me."

"Quintus, I'm sorry, I swore…"

Quintus regarded his brother coldly, then turned and walked away.

They worked without conversation. At first because of the tension in the air following the confrontation, but soon because the work in the stale air left them breathless. Carbo's palms became numb from the repetitive impact, and he felt his fingers blistering. His front was largely protected by the leather apron, but the skin on his knees rubbed raw, and stone chips shot into his face. His throat stung, his mouth tasted metal and every muscle and joint protested.

Amasis returned, carrying buckets of water. They all threw down their tools and crowded round the supervisor, while he passed out cups. Carbo waited his turn, then drank thirstily, the bland, cold water tasting like the finest Falernian as it moistened his dessicated mouth and washed the dust out. He dipped his cup for another drink, downed that too, and all too quickly the water was gone and the break was over.

"You are doing better," said Amasis, "But Durmius said you are still behind quota."

By the time the next break arrived, Carbo's arms felt as heavy as the ore he was mining. The effort was making him feel nauseous. No longer a cathartic process, working out anger and grief, it was now all about keeping going.

They all drank greedily again, and when the water was gone, they looked at their tools, the rock face and the ore pile miserably.

Amasis shook his head. "You will have to work hard to avoid punishment by the end of the day."

"How much longer do we have to work?" asked Carbo.

"Four more hours till sundown. That's all you have to make up the deficit."

"We can't do it," said Meru, voice cracking with dust and emotion. "We are exhausted."

Amasis gathered up the cups. "I'm sorry, I don't set the targets." And he was gone.

They knelt together in a circle, silent for a while, heads bowed, as if in prayer. Carbo was overcome by a massive inertia, an almost physical inability to move. His mind played over the punishment of the slave they had witnessed, the free use of the whips the guards employed, and he knew that if he didn't get back to work, the consequences would be severe. Still he didn't move.

He felt a sudden pain in his arm and turned. Sica was rubbing her fist.

"Ow. Your muscles hard."

He opened his mouth, surprised.

"Time to work." She looked around. "Time to work everyone."

She bent and started to gather ore fragments for her basket. They all watched her for a moment, then Phraates tapped Orobazes on the shoulder, and they retrieved their tools and went back to the rock face. Meru sighed and joined Sica. Carbo and Curtius looked at each other, then Carbo reached for his pick, and with a grimace, Curtius did the same.

Carbo's shoulders and back cried out to him as he heaved his pick backwards, his muscles begged for mercy as he swung, again and again, but he gritted his teeth, pressed on.

The sounds of work around him became gradually weaker, the thwock of the tools coming less frequently. Carbo worked on through the pain, the rocks around him starting to accumulate faster than Phraates and Orobazes could break them up.

Eventually there was no more room to work. He looked around. Everyone had stopped. Slumped against walls, on the floor, breathing hard, bleeeding from scrapes and cuts, bruised and aching. Meru was crying. Phraates and Orobazes couldn't meet Carbo's eyes. Curtius stared at him defiantly. Carbo let his pick fall and slumped to the floor. None of them could go on. What would happen now, would happen.

Carbo looked up briefly as Amasis emerged from the tunnel, then let his head droop again. Their supervisor looked around in alarm at the despondent group of miners, who were sitting or lying in various poses, tools discarded.

"Oh no." He shook his head. "Oh no, oh no."

Carbo didn't have the energy to speak.

"Why have you all stopped?" asked Amasis.

"Why do you think, you idiot?" snapped Curtius. "We are exhausted. We have been working like mules all day."

"Some of us for longer than others," muttered Meru, earning him a glare from Curtius.

"But...but..." stammered Amasis. "You were already struggling to meet your quota. You have done nothing for the last hour. You are well below an acceptable output. Oh dear. I'm so sorry."

Carbo's head snapped up. "Sorry? Why sorry?"

Amasis just sighed. "It's not in my hands, I'm afraid. Come on, your shift is over."

"What is going to happen to us?" asked Meru nervously.

"It's not my place to say," said Amasis, not meeting anyone's eyes.

"Amasis," said Carbo. "How much trouble are we in? Should we try to carry on working?"

"It's too late," said Amasis, his voice full of regret. "The pit closes for the night, the guards go off duty, you return to your huts. There is no option to carry on. It's all my fault. I should have warned you, supervised you more closely." Amasis let out a deep sigh, and turned back to the tunnel. "Come, all of you. Your day is done."

Carbo followed Amasis out, on his hands and knees. He felt he should be relieved the awful working day was over, but instead his guts were clenched, and even though the air became clearer, the lamps burning brighter as they ascended the sloping passageway, his breathing became tighter.

When they reached the bottom of the ladder, Carbo waited his turn. Sica touched his arm lightly. "What is wrong?" she whispered.

Carbo shook his head. "I don't know. Something bad."

Sica bit her lip and was quiet.

The climb up the ladder was tougher than Carbo expected. Despite the fact that he had been resting for the last hour, his arms felt like the lead he had been mining, and he started to worry he would lose his grip. Halfway up the ladder, a fatal fall below him, a hard climb still before, his heart suddenly started to race. His vision blurred, and he felt he would lose his grip. He stopped, clung on tightly, closed his eyes.

"What's the hold up?" came Curtius' voice from below. "Get moving, you great oaf."

Carbo swallowed, waited for the moment to pass, then clambered the rest of the way up as fast as he could. Once at the top, he reached a hand down to help pull up Sica behind him. Between them, they helped up Meru and then the heavier Phraates and Orobazes. Curtius was last and when he reached the top he extended a hand. Carbo turned his back.

The sun was behind the hills, an orange glow in the west, but the dim light still made them squint and blink. The air was chill. Their sweat-damped bodies quickly lost the excess heat from their work in the hot tunnels, and they all started to shiver. Their nakedness was now more obvious in the twilight than in the dark mines, and Sica drew her arms around herself. Carbo took off his apron and slid it over Sica's neck, and she smiled gratefully.

"What now?" asked Carbo.

"Now, you eat and sleep," said Amasis. "And in the morning…" He shook his head and walked away, towards his own quarters. The same four guards who had escorted them in the morning secured them back in their chains, and then pushed them in the direction of their huts. All around, other groups of slaves were being led away, shuffling, heads bowed. Carbo's workgroup was no different, except maybe showing more shock behind their exhaustion than the others, for whom this daily torment had become their lives.

They were encouraged back into their hut with some cracks of the whip, some of which struck home. Once inside, they all slumped to the floor wordless. After a short while, the door opened again, and Agamede and Pamphile were thrust through, Agamede tripping and sprawling across the floor, landing across Curtius who pushed her away with a curse. Pamphile helped her up, and they found an unoccupied stretch of wall to lean against, arms around each other, shaking.

Time passed, the last light of the day through the cracks in the walls disappearing, and Carbo, despite the exhaustion and the fear, suddenly realised how ravenous he was. Before a battle, he rarely had an appetite, and he was surprised that his anxiety allowed him one now. But the hard physical labour of the day had left him weak, his body craving replacement for the energy he had expended. The thought of food made him salivate, and his stomach cramped painfully.

"Why you not belong here?" Sica asked Pamphile.

Pamphile looked at her, momentarily confused.

"You said you not belong here. Why?"

Pamphile exchanged glances with her sister, who shrugged, looking down at the ground.

"We were taken. Travelling to see a client. Kidnapped and sold into slavery."

Agamede didn't look up, but her shoulders shook.

Pamphile squeezed her shoulder. "It seems so unreal. It has from the moment those bandits jumped out on us, wearing those horrible masks."

Carbo looked up sharply. "Masks?"

"You too?" asked Meru. "They took me! I was travelling from Nola to Rome to learn philosophy. He killed everyone in my group who resisted, took the rest of us as slaves. I'm a freedman, but I was going to make my fortune."

Carbo stared at his fellow slaves.

"Sica? How did you end up here?"

"Was captured when Roman soldiers raided my village. Was with a kind master, a merchant. The bandits killed him, took me."

"The masked ones?"

Sica nodded.

"Atreus and Thyestes." Curtius spat.

"Were you taken by them as well?" asked Carbo.

"Not exactly," said Curtius. "I worked for them."

They all stared at him. Carbo opened his mouth to speak.

The door to the hut opened again, and a guard came in carrying a large cauldron filled with a steaming stew, and another guard brought a jug of water. The aroma of boiled meat was the sweetest smell imaginable. They all stared hungrily at the cauldron, but none moved, awaiting the guard's instructions.

"Did you think we wouldn't feed you?" laughed the guard. "Where would be the logic in that? A farmer feeds his livestock doesn't he?" He set down two clay bowls, and left, locking and bolting the door behind him.

Curtius scrambled forward, but was pulled short by Orobazes yanking on his chain. Curtius yelped, and turned angrily to the fugitive slave, but Orobazes held him firm, and regarded Carbo questioningly.

Were they looking to him as leader? He wanted none of that. If he couldn't look after his own, what good was he to anyone else? But the whole group, starving as they were, waited expectantly for his instructions.

"There are two bowls," said Carbo. "The stew is too sloppy to eat with our fingers. We take it in turns to use the bowls, one bowl each. Then we see how much is left, and share it evenly. The youngsters first, then the ladies."

Orobazes and Phraates clearly didn't understand, but nodded their acceptance anyway.

"Why do they get to go first?" grumbled Curtius.

"Be grateful we are letting you eat at all," growled Carbo. Curtius looked down.

Carbo passed the bowls to Meru and Sica, who took them gratefully, dipped them into the cauldron and then drank from the bowls greedily. Agamede and Pamphile were next, both examining the contents of their bowls with suspicion, before consuming it with as much decorum as they could muster.

"Will you hurry up," groaned Curtius, but he was ignored.

Carbo ate last, with Curtius, and by this time they were down to the dregs. The cooks had measured quantities accurately, one bowlful each. They could scoop the remains from the sides of the cauldron, but the majority was gone. The stew was thin, hot water with corn and small amounts of gristle, which Carbo tried to chew, then simply swallowed whole.

Carbo let Sica and Meru lick the bowl clean, despite Curtius' protests. When it was all gone, they sat in silence, stretching aching limbs, inspecting blisters on hands and feet, grazes on knees.

"I guess you two had an easy day," said Curtius to Agamede and Pamphile. Pamphile looked down, and let out a single sob. Agamede put an arm around her.

"Oh come on," said Curtius. "We were down in the pits, in the dust and heat, working the skin off our fingers. What can you have been doing to compare with that?"

Agamede glared at him and Pamphile trembled.

"What?" pressed Curtius. "I want to know what you did that means you get an equal share of our food."

"If you really want to know," said Agamede, her words clipped, "We spent the whole day treading the boards that operated the water pump, until our legs cramped, and our feet bled. But the kind guards gave us regular breaks, during which they took turns to rape us."

Curtius stared, mouth open. Sica paled. Carbo put his head in his hands.

No one spoke.

Carbo pulled Sica to him, let her rest her head on his shoulder. So much wrong here. The rage that burned inside him started to change. Yes, he wanted revenge, so bad it was a bitter taste in his mouth. But he was beginning to see the extent of the injustice the masked men were committing against the people of Nola. It wasn't right.

But what could he do, destined to die in these mines? Weariness overcame him and he closed his eyes.

## CHAPTER XVI

Lutorius felt conflicted with lust and shame. Not because Calidia was the wife of his commanding officer. He had no great respect for Asellio. The shame came from what he was doing to her. She lay back on the bed, knees up and parted, her hand on the back of his head, grinding her hips against his face as he kissed and licked her. No real man would do this, he thought. The Greeks would, he knew, or the Egpytians, but not a Roman. Yet the taste of her, her cries of pleasure, the way her body writhed at his touch, drove him wild.

She squeezed his head between her thighs and bucked, letting out a wail as her climax arrived. When the convulsions subsided, he kissed his way up her body, over her nipples to her lips. She smiled, then rolled him onto his back, and knelt between his legs. She gripped him tightly in one hand, licked his shaft, then slid her mouth over it. As her head moved up and down on him, he lay back with a satisfied smile. This was more like it. Those Greek bum boys didn't do it like this, he was sure.

When she had swallowed him down, she wriggled herself up beside him, warm body against him, one arm across his chest. He closed his eyes. The patrol through the market had been predictably pointless. They had caught a homeless child in the act of taking a loaf of bread, and caned him publicly before letting him go. Otherwise the market seemed more or less as normal. Maybe a little subdued. Word had got around about the violence in the plaza a few days before. But most of the citizens of Nola figured it had nothing to do with them, and got on with life as normal.

He stroked her hair.

"I love you," he said. What? Where had that come from?

She looked up at him, searched his eyes. He returned the gaze, then when she said nothing, he looked away in embarrassment.

"I'm sorry. Forget I said that."

"No," said Calidia. "It's fine. I just… wasn't expecting."

He sat up abruptly, taking her hand off him.

"I have to go."

"No, Lutorius, not like this."

He pulled on his tunic, slipped into his sandals.

"I'll see you, Calidia."

"Soon?" she asked.

"Sure," he said.

He slipped out of her bedroom, and out of his commanding officer's house. When he was a safe distance away, he slumped against a nearby wall, and thumped his fist into it. What a fool. Of course she didn't love him, she was married, she couldn't. Why did he need to spoil things like that?

But he did love her, and saying it out loud, and not hearing it back, was an unexpected pain. For a moment, he wallowed in his own, self-indulgent misery. Then, he wondered where Carbo was, and his situation suddenly didn't seem quite so bad.

Carbo woke abruptly as the door to the hut flew open with a bang, early morning light flooding in. For a brief moment, he thought he was still in his dream, Rufa and himself, working in their tavern. It didn't take long for all the memories of loss and despair to come crashing back.

A jug of water was brought in, and the bread. Seven loaves. Seven?

Carbo looked at the food uncertainly.

"Why seven?" asked Sica.

Carbo didn't speak. He hoped the obvious answer wasn't the right one. They divided up the food as best they could, though it was hard to divide the seven loaves into eight portions accurately. They had mostly slept remarkably soundly, although they had all been woken by Pamphile suddenly bursting into screams in the middle of the night. When her sister had failed to calm her, a guard had banged loudly on the door and threatened to silence her permanently. Fortunately, Agamede had managed at least to stop the terrible noise, if not provide her sister with any comfort.

When they had eaten, they took it in turns to squat in the corner of the cell in the latrine area. Soon the small room was overpowered with the ammoniacal, farmyard smell of urine and faeces.

The time allotted to breakfasting and toileting was brief, and soon they were being led outside again, blinking in the sunlight, shivering in the cold early morning air, the mine workers naked except for the aprons the men wore, the two women working the pumps allowed short tunics.

The slaves were lined up in their workgroups of around eight workers, and Durmius strutted before them like a cock showing off to the hens. When they were all gathered, he addressed them in a loud, high-pitched voice.

"You all know how things work here. You have jobs to do. You do them, or there is punishment. We don't stand over you, whipping you as you mine or carry or pump or smelt. That is frankly far too much effort. What we do, is ensure that you are motivated enough to carry out the work you are required to do."

He looked up and down the shivering rows of slaves. "Mining work groups have quotas, and when those quotas aren't met, the mine as a whole misses its quota, and the owners become unhappy, and that becomes a problem for me. I don't like problems.

"If you miss your quota by even a tiny amount, you will be punished. If you miss your quota by more, you will be punished severely. One group yesterday missed their quota by one part in eight. This is unacceptable. You will now be given a lesson regarding what happens to lazy slaves."

All the work groups were on edge, terrified they were to be singled out. When Durmius approached Carbo's group, the collective sigh of relief from the other groups was audible.

"I have a bag in here with eight stones. Seven are white, one is black. Take a stone each."

Durmius offered the bag to Carbo first. Carbo didn't know what drawing the black stone would mean, but he knew he didn't want it. He stared at Durmius, hands at his sides, in a brief show of defiance, but the overseer's gaze didn't waver, and Carbo didn't have the fight in him to resist. He reached in and felt around. The stones were all smooth, and there was no indication that one was different from the other. He selected one at random, pulled it out, opened his fist, and sighed in relief when he saw the stone he held was white.

Curtius was next, and he gave a shout of joy when he saw that his stone was white. The two women also drew white, and Phraates and Orobazes, though they looked confused, also showed relief when they found they had white stones.

Only Meru and Sica remained to draw. Carbo looked at Sica, who was trembling from head to foot. He tried to calm her with his eyes, but he knew any reassurance was meaningless. Meru reached in, drew a stone.

Opened his hand.

Black.

"No, no no no," he cried. "It's not fair. What does it mean?"

Durmius offered the sack to Sica, and Carbo tensed. He wondered if Durmius might have been lying about the number of black stones.

Sica drew a white stone.

"It is decided then. Punishment will fall on this boy. Some of you may have served in the legions, many will not. Those of you who have will know there is a time-honoured practice of decimation, a punishment reserved for soldiers who mutiny and desert. The soldiers draw lots in groups of ten, and the unlucky one is beaten or stoned to death by his comrades. I consider a slave who does not work to be the same as a mutineer or a deserter. So the same punishment will be applied here. Although as there are only eight in a workgroup, I suppose we should call it octimation." He chuckled at his own joke, although he was the only one smiling.

"Guards, tie the slave to the stake."

The guards unchained Meru, who had been listening in disbelief. Only as they led him towards a tall wooden stake, buried deeply in the ground near the entrance to the mines, did he start to struggle. The guard's grip was too strong, though, and soon he was bound, hands behind the post, another rope around his neck, holding him tight.

Carbo's workgroup was unchained, and led to a pile of rocks a short distance from where Meru was tied. Meru stared at them, eyes pleading.

"Please, don't do this."

"You will all throw two rocks each. If I deem you have not thrown hard enough, you will be punished and have to throw again. If I still think you have not thrown hard enough, you will be crucified. If he is not dead by the time you have all thrown, then he will be strangled by the guards, the lots will be drawn again, and another of you will undergo the same punishment. I hope that's clear."

Carbo stared at Durmius in disbelief. The threat of decimation was well known in the legion, but rarely carried out. The last time had been in Augustus' reign, as far as Carbo knew. It was a punishment that carried with it fear and humiliation and shame. Carbo was stunned that the overseer would inflict it on slaves. Yet why would he not? All the same reasons it was used in the legions applied here. The threat was so terrible, no one, slave or legionary, would step out of line.

He looked at Meru, who had tears running down his grimy cheeks, his face twisted in misery and terror. Carbo had seen stonings before, and knew they could be prolonged and agonising. Carbo stepped forward, and picked up a fist-sized rock from the pile. This had to be done, but he could end it quickly. He drew his arm back to throw. Meru screamed.

"Stop," said Durmius, his voice penetrating through the murmurings of the onlookers.

Carbo paused. Meru looked over at him, relief flooding his face. A mock execution? It had certainly served its purpose well, in terrifying the boy and the watching crowd.

"You don't go first," said Durmius. "You are too strong, you might kill him outright. That would not be an appropriate punishment. You, girl." He pointed to Sica. "You go first."

Sica looked at Carbo, miserable eyes questioning. He nodded to her, then looked down.

Sica stepped forward, and took the stone off Carbo. She turned to face Meru.

Meru was shaking his head, mouthing soundless words.

"I'm sorry," said Sica. She drew back her arm and threw.

Whether she deliberately threw weakly, or it was her own internal will fighting her, the stone flew gently through the air, and smacked lightly onto Meru's shoulder. He yelped at the impact, but there was little harm done.

Durmius gestured to a guard, who stepped forward and laid his whip hard across Sica's back. A streak of blood across the bare skin traced the whip's impact, and she cried out.

"Try again girl. Remember the punishment for two weak throws."

Trembling, Sica picked up another rock. This time, she managed to impart some force into the throw. It hit Meru in the chest, and his cry of anticipation ended in a grunt as the air rushed out of him.

"Again," commanded Durmius, and Sica threw again, hitting a shin painfully.

"Now, you ladies, please," said Durmius. Agamede threw next, her second throw earning a stripe of the whip. Pamphile threw with more power and anger, her eyes seeming to see someone other than Meru at the stake. Curtius went next. His throws were hard but inaccurate. One impacted Meru's abdomen, the other smashed his shin, causing him to scream, and to keep screaming until one of Phraate's stones caught him a glancing blow to the head, stunning him.

Carbo was last, and by the time he picked up a stone again, Meru was unconscious, bleeding from gashes on his body and his head, one arm, one leg and probably a number of ribs broken. He was clearly still breathing though.

"He's still alive," said Durmius. "This is getting exciting. If you don't finish him off, slave, we get to do this all over again. Fortuna's luck to you."

Carbo weighed the stone in his hand. He had to do this right, he couldn't let anyone else go through this. He picked a point between Meru's eyes, drew back his arm, and let fly with all his strength.

His fatigued muscles let him down, the throw powerful but inaccurate. It crunched into Meru's shoulder, causing him to stir limply in his bonds.

"Last chance, slave," said Durmius, excitement in his voice.

Carbo picked up the largest stone remaining in the pile. He took a deep breath. The watching crowd were hushed. From the corner of his eye, he could see Sica watching him with pleading eyes, hands clasped together.

He threw. The stone hit Meru right in the middle of the forehead with immense force that caved in the young boy's skull. Blood and brain matter oozed out through the hole Carbo had made.

One of the guards stepped forward, bent to listen to Meru's chest. He straightened, called out, "He's dead."

The tension went out of Carbo's body, quickly followed by guilt at the relief he felt.

"Ah, shame," said Durmius. "Still, I think this has been an adequate demonstration. I don't think anyone will be in any doubt about the fate that awaits the work shy. Now, this group is a worker short. I'm nothing if not fair, so one of the women can be transferred from the pumps to the mines. The water level is low at the moment anyway."

"Please, master," said Agamede, "Send Pamphile to the mines."

Durmius raised an eyebrow. "The younger, prettier one? I don't think my guards would be too happy with that choice. No, you shall go. Amasis!" The supervisor scurried over. "Get them to work. And make sure they hit quota today, or I will have to start thinking about whether some punishment for you is in order."

"Yes, master, I will make sure of it."

Durmius turned and strode away. One of the guards took Pamphile's chain and she was led away, looking numb. Agamede reached out for her, and was cuffed away by another guard.

"Come on," said Amasis, "The sooner you start, the better chance you will have of reaching your quota."

He led them down the ladder, back to the sparse air, and the heat, and the body-destroying labour.

# CHAPTER XVII

They worked hard and they worked wordlessly. Agamede copied Sica in collecting the fragments and hauling them back to the central part of the mining complex for lifting back to the surface. Curtius joined in at the rockface with Carbo from the moment they arrived, heaving his pick aggressively, attacking the ore like it was his enemy. Carbo watched him from the corner of his eye as he too worked methodically. Phraates and Orobazes settled back into rock breaking. The workgroup started to develop a rhythm, the ore moving smoothly from rock face to basket, from boulder to fragment. Each of them developed an eye for their work, Carbo and Curtius learning where to aim to harvest as much as possible with each blow, Phraates and Orobazes picking fissure lines that fractured the rocks as efficiently as possible, Sica and Agamede learning to pack their baskets tightly, so they could carry more ore on each trip.

Carbo's arms ached from the previous day's work, and his hands were stinging where blisters had arisen and burst, leaving exposed, weeping sores. He gritted his teeth, ignoring the pain, pictures of Meru's bleeding face swimming before him every time he felt like slacking.

When Amasis arrived with their water for their first break, he watched them work for a little while in approval, before calling for them to stop. They gathered round him, gulping down the liquid, wiping sweat and dirt out of their eyes and from their mouths.

"You are working better today," said Amasis. "More or less on target for your quota. Keep it up."

Carbo glared at him. "What choice do we have? Meet the quota or one of us is killed?"

Amasis looked embarrassed. "I don't make the rules. I'm a slave too, like you. I've been where you are breaking rocks and breaking my back. I was just one of the lucky ones, I survived. You could too, if you work hard, keep your head down. Maybe in a few years, one of you could be a supervisor. Your own room, your own tunic, better food."

"You make it sound so enticing," muttered Curtius.

"We could be like you?" asked Sica.

"If you put the effort in, yes," said Amasis.

Sica spat on the floor. "Would rather die."

Amasis shook his head. "Well, that sort of is the other option." He clapped his hands. "Back to work all of you, if you don't want to be drawing lots again tomorrow morning."

Amasis took the cups away, and the slaves, with sighs and groans, picked up their tools and returned to work.

"Tell me what you did for the bandits," said Carbo to Curtius as they worked.

"Why?" said Curtius.

"Because I asked."

"It's a waste of breath. What does it change?"

"Maybe it will change your destiny. Maybe you won't get your head smashed into the rock face."

Curtius grimaced, but stayed quiet, swinging his pick at the rock. After a while he realised that Carbo's eyes were still on him, and he put his pick down, wiping the sweat from his forehead with the back of his hand.

"I was what you would call a liaison, I suppose. Between Atreus and Thyestes, and the local gangs, like the one Rabidus runs."

"Used to run," said Carbo. "He's dead."

Curtius raised an eyebrow.

"Fat bastards heart gave out, I suppose? Serves him right. We fell out over a payment, and Rabidus double crossed me, told Atreus. So here I am."

"So Atreus and Thyestes are slavers? They steal slaves and free citizens, and smuggle them to the mines for profit?"

Curtius nodded. "Among other schemes they have running. But this certainly seems to make them some money, judging by the lifestyle they lead."

"The lifestyle? You mean you know who they are?"

Curtius' eyes shifted away from Carbo's intent stare.

"No. I mean, not really."

"You're lying."

Carbo grabbed the string around Curtius' neck that held the apron on and twisted. Curtius gasped, gripped Carbo's hand as choking noises came from his throat.

"Tell me who they are!" roared Carbo.

"Stop," cried Amasis. "We don't have time for this."

Carbo looked round, grip not loosening. Sica approached him cautiously, put a hand on his shoulder.

"Carbo, you ask when the work is done. We need him. Or maybe one of us dies tomorrow."

Carbo hesitated, then let go, moving back. Curtius massaged his neck, breathing hard.

"I can't tell you. They have men everywhere, if they found out I had talked…"

"You will tell me. Sooner or later."

"Come on," urged Amasis.

Carbo glared at Curtius, retrieved his pick and resumed work.

As the day wore on, Carbo noticed the rock was getting tougher to break, and the chunks he was mining were becoming smaller. The pick felt heavier as he fatigued, but he thought he was still managing to put as much force into each swing. He looked across at Curtius' rock pile and saw the same thing. Curtius noticed him looking and gestured at the rockface.

"It's getting harder," he said. Carbo nodded, but continued, trying to give each swing as much impetus as he could muster. When Amasis returned with their drinks for the next break, Carbo told the supervisor about the problem.

"Well, of course," said Amasis. "Yesterday, the rockface was freshly firecracked. Now you are getting into the tougher, uncracked rock."

"But that makes it harder to meet our quota."

"Yes it does, though the overseers aren't fools. Quotas are a little less for inexperienced teams. The one you missed yesterday was really very generous. If you had all pulled your weight all day, you would probably have made it without a problem."

Carbo glared at Curtius, who looked down.

"So, keep up your workrate, and you will make your quota. Probably. Yes, I'm sure you will. And tomorrow, they will likely set a fire and crack the rockface again. Right, break over."

Publius wandered the villa disconsolately. Quintus was gone, father was still out. The huge place was completely empty, if you discounted the slaves, which he did. He took a deep draught from his silver goblet, feeling the warmth slide down his throat into his stomach. It helped a little. Not much.

He should never have told Quintus. What good would come of him knowing the truth? And yet, he was his brother. He had a right to know the circumstances of his birth, the reality of his heritage. He thought of his father, and waves of fear and anger rolled over him, pulling and pushing him. If father had kept his temper, if Uncle Gnaeus had lived, they would never have left Rome, they wouldn't live in this boring backwater. He hoped Quintus wouldn't talk to father about what he had found out. It could only have come from Publius himself, and he quailed at the thought of his father's wrath if, despite what had been promised, he knew that Publius had revealed the family secret.

He found himself walking past his father's sleeping chamber. His father's current favoured bedslave, Ipy, was reclining on the bed, asleep. She lay under a light blanket, eyes flickering in some dream, breathing irregular. He thought about taking her, his father's plaything, there in his father's bed. Would that show he wasn't scared of him, give him some measure of satisfaction?

He sat on the edge of the bed, drew back the blankets and looked down at her. She was naked except for a small loincloth, and he admired the swell of her small breasts, the soft curves of her waist and hips. He put a hand on her leg, and felt himself become aroused. She stirred as he stroked the dark skin of her thigh up and down, rolled onto her back. Her eyes opened, slowly at first, a sly smile on her face, then they flew open as she realised who was touching her. She sat up abruptly, arms crossed in front of her breasts, staring at Publius in fear.

"Master? What is it?"

Publius squeezed the thigh firmly, looking at her with eyes narrowed, lust and anger and fear warring inside him. Then he turned away from her, disgusted with himself, though whether the disgust was for what he had been about to do, or for being unable to follow it through, he wasn't sure.

"Get out," he snapped.

Without a word, she grabbed a robe, and fled.

Publius groaned and let himself flop back onto the bed. It was comfortable, the slightly greasy smell of duck feathers enveloping him, competing with the scented candles that Ipy kept lighted. He stared at the ceiling frescoes, semi-naked gods and goddesses cavorting with willing mortals. A wave of drunken dizziness swamped him, and he rolled onto his front with a groan, feeling suddenly hot, reaching beneath the mattress to find somewhere cool to put his hands.

He felt something solid, gripped it, retrieved it. An iron key. He looked at the chest in the corner of the room, and back at the key.

It fit easily, and he opened the lid. Inside were two masks.

Tragedy and Comedy. He picked up the Comedy mask, rotated it to examine it, inside and out. There were flecks of dark blood on the exterior. The leather strap that held it in place was sweat stained. He made to put it on, fiddled with the strap. As it opened, he saw some hair had been trapped in the bronze buckle. He plucked a strand free.

A deep fury shot through Publius. After all he had just shared with his brother, to find he was keeping a secret like this from him.

He rolled the dark, curly hair between his fingers.

Quintus.

Carbo estimated the passing time by the water breaks. By the time each one arrived, he felt he was at the physical limit of what he could do. But around him all the others continued to work, labouring for themselves and for each other, and Carbo kept going. After several water breaks, Carbo felt the day must be drawing to a close, and he asked Amasis how they were doing.

"Lagging behind a little, I believe, but not far. There is just an hour left to work, so if you put your all into it, you should be fine."

Knowing how little time for which they still needed to toil helped, and they attacked the rocks with renewed vigour. Their chests heaved, lungs working hard to draw breath from the heavy air. Hands and knees bled, eyes stung and mouths and noses were choked up with dust. As they worked themselves to the point of exhaustion, Carbo wondered how he could possibly pick up his tools and do this all over again tomorrow. But right now, all that mattered was the finish line, the quota, succeeding and knowing they would live for another day.

Phraates let out a loud cry, and Carbo turned quickly to see what had happened. The large slave was gripping his wrist and shouting what were no doubt curses in his alien language. Orobazes was looking pale. Carbo went over to them. He saw immediately what must have happened. They had been breaking the same rock, and Phraates must have reached out when Orobazes wasn't expecting it, or Orobazes' blow had been badly aimed. Either way, Phraates' forearm now bent at an unnatural angle.

Sica peered round Carbo and stared at the injury.

"Broken," she said. "Bad."

Phraates was slumped backwards against the wall now, breathing hard and trembling as the full force of the pain and the realisation of the extent of the injury set in. Orobazes babbled to Carbo, face anguished. Carbo looked around, realised suddenly that everyone had stopped and was staring in horror.

"Back to work everyone. We don't have much time. Come on."

His words seemed to snap them all out of their trance, and they resumed their labour. Carbo swung his pick with all his might, sending chunks of rock flying. Curtius did the same. Orobazes returned to smashing the rocks, and when the pile that Curtius and Carbo were producing grew too large for the man on his own, Carbo stopped mining and helped him with the rock breaking. Agamede and Sica scurried like worker ants to and fro with their baskets of rubble. Carbo's heart thumped in his chest. He wanted to lie down and die. But he kept on.

Amasis entered. "Your shift is over."

They all slumped to the ground, with groans and whimpers.

"Is it enough, Amasis?" breathed Carbo.

Amasis shook his head. "I don't know." He noticed Phraates nursing his broken arm. "Ah, I see why you slowed down at the end. But you are close, I can see that. Let's just trust to Fortuna. Come on, back to the hut."

Pamphile was already back at the hut when they returned from the mines. When they entered, she didn't look up, just sat in a corner, knees pulled up to her chin, arms tight around her shins. Her face was bruised, her bottom lip split and swollen and bloody. Agamede rushed over and put her arms around her, but Pamphile pushed her back, and turned her face away. When the guards came into the hut to reattach her chains to the rest of the group, she flinched when they came near, though made no effort to resist.

They all sat, exhausted. Curtius eyed Carbo from the far side of the room.

"Tell me who they are," said Carbo in a low voice.

"I can't," said Curtius. "They will kill me."

"Do you really think you are in more danger from unknown informers, or from me?"

Curtius looked into Carbo's eyes and knew the answer.

"Atreus was a man named Blaesus. A wealthy man, has a villa outside Nola. His brother, the one going by the name of Thyestes, is called Lucius."

Carbo gaped.

"You know them already?" asked Curtius.

Carbo nodded. Then a horrible realisation settled on him. If Blaesus was the father, who was the son? Could it be Quintus?

"Who is the one called Menelaus?" asked Carbo.

Curtius looked confused. "Never heard of him. It's just Atreus and Thyestes."

"Thyestes is dead. I killed him."

"Ah," said Curtius. "That explains a lot."

"Now Atreus has a companion called Menelaus, who I think is his son."

"At the time Atreus sold me here, there was no Menelaus. So you think it is his son, Publius?"

"Or his other son, Quintus. He came back from a long stay in Greece recently."

Curtius looked momentarily interested, then sighed.

"Why do you care? Blaesus will go on doing exactly what he has always done. Terrorise, kill, enslave. And we are going to die here."

The food when it came was the same as the night before, stew, with two bowls. They ate hungrily, but quietly, lacking energy for conversation, for anything apart from the things they needed to do to stay alive - breathe, eat, drink, excrete. When the food was gone, Sica shimmied up to Carbo, and fell asleep lying against him. For a short moment, sleep eluded Carbo. He wondered whether they had made the quota, and if not who woud die the next day. He wondered too how it was possible to go on for any length of time. How had Amasis survived so long? Carbo, physically tough as he was, albeit his body worn out from his years in the legions, had struggled to make it through the first two days. How could he make it through a week, a month, a year? And how could someone as delicate as Sica hope to survive?

That was just it, though, he realised. This wasn't about survival. It was about how you died, and when. Blaesus hadn't sent him here to atone for the murder of his brother, to undergo punishment before his return to society. Blaesus had sent him here so that he would die in torment. As sleep gripped him, Carbo realised that was what was going to happen. And as he drifted into a land where Rufa would admonish him, and fallen comrades from the battlefields would haunt him, and Germanic priestesses would threaten torture on him all over again, he realised he didn't want to die.

Publius had already been drinking steadily for most of the day when his father returned home. He reclined on the top couch in the triclinium, picking olives from a plate and sipping from a silver goblet of Falernian.

"Good evening, father," he said. "Had a pleasant day?"

Blaesus regarded him steadily.

"P...pleasant enough."

"Been doing anything interesting?"

Blaesus looked at the goblet, then flicked his fingers. Pharnaces, who had accompanied him, appeared at his shoulder. "Bring me one of those," said Blaesus. Pharnaces inclined his head, and headed for the kitchen. Blaesus sat on the edge of a couch and regarded his son steadily.

"I had some business to attend to in town. Why do you ask?"

Publius took a draught of wine.

"Just showing an interest. A son can be interested in his father's comings and goings can't he?"

"Publius, you're drunk. As usual." The tone was that of a father unsurprised to be disappointed again.

"Does it surprise you, father? Stuck in this backwater, no culture, no career. No opportunity to take my rightful place on the cursus honorum."

"You've never shown any ambition before, son. And as for culture..." Blaesus gave a mocking laugh.

Publius threw his goblet hard against the wall. It clattered to the floor, rolled in a circle, and was still. Pharnaces returned with Blaesus' drink, took in the scene, and froze in the doorway. Father and son ignored him. Publius reached behind him, and drew out the comedy mask.

Blaesus' eyes narrowed.

"You have been in my r...room. You broke into my chest." It wasn't a question.

"There's a tragedy mask in there too." Blaesus regarded him steadily, nostrils flaring with each breath.

"So, the bandits who have been terrorising people around here these last years. You are tragedy, correct? The one calling himself Atreus?"

Blaesus inclined his head. It wasn't quite an acknowledgment, but it wasn't a denial.

"And Thyestes? That was Uncle Lucius wasn't it? Is he dead?"

"Yes," said Blaesus flatly.

"And now they say Atreus has a new partner. Menelaus. His son?"

Blaesus said nothing.

"Father!" The word came out as both a cry of anguish and a plea.

Publius turned to Pharnaces. "Get out, slave."

"Stay, Pharnaces." Pharnaces looked from one to the other, then remained where he was.

"What is it you want, Publius?" said Blaesus.

Publius stared at him for a moment. "Answers. Explanations. Why do you do this? You have no need of money. Do you?"

Blaesus shook his head. "Does it matter?"

Publius slammed his fist onto the table before him, causing the plate of olives to jump, some of the fruits rolling onto the floor. "If it didn't matter, I wouldn't ask," he said, voice tight.

"Yes, we need money. I have wealth, but little income. I enjoy my fine art, my fine wine. I can sell estates and property that I own if I need to, but that is a slow process, and would anyway reduce what meagre amounts we have coming in. So, when we need money, your uncle and I go and take it. He is, w…was, a fine bowman, and after I left the legions, I kept my sword skills sharp training with gladiators, and then when we left Rome, with Lucius."

"I never see you train."

"You have never shown any interest in the arts of war, son. Lucius and I would go into the hills and spar for hours on end, then he would practice his archery while I did exercises. You see me as a weak old man, son, because you never look at me properly."

"But haven't you restored your fortune now?"

Blaesus sighed. "When you are exiled from the great city, boredom is your greatest enemy. No longer proving yourself in politics, in the courts. No groups of clients paying respect at your door every morning. No plays, or chariot racing in the hippodrome, or great gladiatorial displays in the arena. Festivals, markets, religious ceremonies. Rome is life!"

"You think I don't know about boredom, father? Stuck here since I was a child."

"No, you don't know, because you have never h…had it, so you have no idea what it is that was lost." Blaesus shook his head. "Lucius was a loyal brother, he st…stuck by me through everything. But while I lost myself in my art, and my fine living, he looked elsewhere. High class prostitutes and large quantities of wine diverted him for a while. Eventually though, he discovered gambling. He ended up owing a large amount of money to that barbarian, Rabidus. Rabidus demanded repayment of the whole sum, or else face retribution. And he made it clear that retribution would mean the death of loved ones. Of you, since Quintus was away at the time."

"You're telling me you did this all for me, father?" Publius sneered.

"I'm not asking you to believe anything. I'm just answering your question."

"So why do you carry on?"

"Money is power," said Blaesus. "It c…commands the hearts of men, more than wine, more than women, more than family. And power prevents boredom. Boredom, Publius, is death, to the soul. And your uncle and I, we loved being bandits, hidden behind our masks. Powerful, feared, as we used to be in Rome."

"And when uncle Lucius died, even then you didn't stop?"

Blaesus' face darkened. "It is not something you can give up, any more than the drunkard can give up wine. And, there were other reasons not to stop. Vengeance."

"But you needed a partner."

Blaesus nodded. "You can't do it alone. You need someone you can trust."

"And why not me, father?" Plaintive now.

"I already said. You have no interest in, nor ability with, the sword. Besides, you have hardly made any efforts to improve your lot in life. Living off my wealth, no thought for betterment. Not like Quintus, who took himself off to Greece, learned philosophy, learned to fight."

"Father. I thought I was your favourite."

Blaesus shook his head. "No, just the oldest."

For a moment, they looked at each other. Publius felt tears stinging the corners of his eyes, gritted his teeth angrily to hold back any display of emotion.

"Well, father. At least I know what you think of me now. Maybe one day you will change your mind." He turned, the mask gripped tight in his hand, and barged Pharnaces out of the way as he left the room.

Publius cantered along the road to Nola, hands tight on the reins, desperate to be out of the house, out of his father's presence. The tears flowed now there was no one to see them. His heart ached with a sense of betrayal, not because his father had done these things, but because he hadn't trusted his oldest son to be part of them. He cursed Quintus too, who had kept his father's secrets from him, who had gone on these hunts with their father. And not even Quintus' real father at that. Blaesus had chosen a bastard, the product of his brother's cuckoldry, over his own flesh and blood.

Quintus was a cold one, Publius thought. Acting like that Carbo fellow's best friend. Yet if the stories were right, Menelaus had been right there when Atreus had slit his girlfriend's throat. And Quintus had the balls to offer him sympathy.

Publius gripped the hilt of the sword at his belt. He had donned it from habit before leaving the house - it would be foolish to travel the isolated roads alone and unarmed. He drew it, swung it experimentally. His father had exaggerated. Publius had trained with the sword as a young man. He knew how to thrust, cut, parry, how to move his feet, how to read his opponent. But his father had been right that it held no interest for him.

He sheathed the sword again, and looked at the mask, whose strap was wrapped around the wrist of his non-sword arm. Comedy. He had seen some provincial performances of some of the Greek and Latin plays, some tragedies, some comedies. They were mildly diverting. As a child he had found the eerie masks disturbing, and he wondered how it would seem to a terrified traveller to be confronted by a bandit wearing it. He slid it over his head, tightened the strap around the back. The inside smelled of metal and sweat. He stared out of the eye holes, and thought he had an awareness, an understanding of the power and excitement that came with the anonymity and the terror the mask instilled.

He rounded a corner and saw a traveller, walking towards Nola, back towards him, a hundred feet away. As he approached rapidly, the traveller, an older man carrying a sack over his back, turned, and started in alarm. He threw down his sack, extended his arms outwards to show he wasn't reaching for a weapon.

Publius pulled up, dismounted.

"Please, master," said the traveller. "Please don't hurt me."

Publius stared in wonder at the terror on the man's face. It was entrancing, intoxicating. Was this what his father and Quintus felt each time they did this? He drew his sword, slowly, almost contemplatively, and raised it vertically in front of his face. He could see the empty road behind him in the highly polished metal. He looked at the traveller, who sank to his knees.

"I'm a poor man, master," he babbled, clasping his hands together in supplication. "Take what I have. Please spare my life. I have a daughter and a granddaughter who need me. Please, I beg you."

Publius lowered the tip of the sword towards the traveller, and noticed a wet patch appear on the front of his tunic, urine leaking down his leg. He thrust the sword forward, a rapid in and out, penetrating the traveller's neck. It happened so quickly, the traveller almost seemed to have missed it. Then his eyes widened, his hands went to his throat, and blood spurted between his fingers. Eyes fixed on Publius, he fell to one side, gurgling, convulsing. Publius watched until he was still. Then he stepped forward and wiped the blood off his sword on the traveller's tunic.

The sack lay half open where the traveller had discarded it. Publius opened its drawstring and upended it. He kicked through the contents that now littered the ground. Bread, a flask of water, half a dozen copper coins, and a child's rag doll. He stared down for a while, then sheathed his sword, removed the mask and remounted his horse.

Now it was over, he wasn't sure how he felt. The thrill, the climax was over, leaving something of an emptiness. Then he remembered the feeling of power as he leaned over the cowering man, and he knew it was a feeling he wanted again.

Agamede's scream awoke Carbo with such a start he tried to leap up, the chains he was attached to choking Sica momentarily before he realised what he was doing. He slackened the tension, and looked across to Agamede. The first shafts of sun lent dim illumination to the room. Agamede started to moan wordlessly. Pamphile's head was in her lap, but everything seemed dark around her. Carbo squinted to make it out in the gloom.

Agamede slowly lifted her hand so that Carbo could see.

It was caked in congealing blood.

Carbo crawled forwards to Agamede, gently placed his hands on Pamphile, turning the slave woman towards him. Blank eyes stared past him. At the side of her neck was a deep gash, out of which her life blood had poured away, like yesterday's soup discarded onto the street. In one hand, Pamphile still clutched a jagged nail. She must have found it in the hut, or on her way back from her work, and waited until everyone was asleep before using it on herself.

Carbo let her head fall back into Agamede's lap, who caressed her sister's hair while keening softly. He sat back next to Sica.

"She dead too?" asked Sica softly. Carbo nodded.

No one tried to get back to sleep. They sat in silence, staring into the distance, thinking, grieving, or preparing themselves for what was to come.

The door opened, and a bowl of water and some bread was thrown in.

Everyone seemed to hold their breath as Carbo counted the loaves.

Seven.

They breathed out. With Meru dead, there was one each. That surely meant they had made their quota, that they weren't being decimated today. After a short while the door opened, and they were herded out. Pamphile was still chained to her sister, so neither Agamede, nor anyone in the chain, could move. Carbo picked up the body and carried it out into the daylight. The guard took one look at the exsanguinated slave woman, and spat.

"Durmius is going to go nuts."

They shuffled to the assembly area, Carbo still carrying Pamphile. When they were given the command to line up, Carbo gently placed the body on the ground. Durmius stared at Pamphile in disbelief.

"What in the name of all the gods is this?"

"Bitch topped herself," said one of the guards.

"Damned waste, she had a sweet cunnus," said another.

Durmius let his eyes slide across the workgroup, none of whom could meet his gaze.

"You let her die. One of my workers." His voice rose. "No one dies here, unless I order it!"

Durmius' suddenly noticed Phraates. "And what is that?" he screamed, pointing at the broken arm. "Amasis? Amasis!"

The supervisor hurried over.

"I don't know what you have let happen to your workgroup, but if they don't meet their quota today, then you will get to choose a stone along with the rest of them."

"Master, I'm sorry, I..."

"Your workgroup is down to five. That woman will take the dead slave's place in the mines."

"But Master, the one with the broken arm..."

"Enough. Get to work everyone."

Carbo touched Amasis on the shoulder, making him jump.

"How are we going to meet the quota with one of us carrying a broken arm?"

"I don't know," said Amasis miserably.

"You will have to help," said Carbo.

"Me?" gasped Amasis. "I don't labour any more."

"Well, if you don't, and we don't hit the target, you may be the one we stone to death tomorrow morning."

Amasis led them down the mineshaft for the third day. When they reached the rockface, Amasis gathered them round.

"Engineers will firecrack the rock face, around midday today. It will take about an hour for them to heat the rock enough. Then it will be your job to pour vinegar over the rockface to split it apart."

"I can't believe that will work," said Curtius.

"It worked for Hannibal," said Carbo.

"It has been working for miners for hundreds of years," snapped Amasis.

"Is dangerous?" asked Sica.

"No, no, no," said Amasis. "Well. Yes, I suppose it can be. Flying splinters of rock, collapses, asphyxiation."

Curtius growled, but Carbo shrugged. "It's not like we get a say in this, is it?"

Amasis looked surprised. "Of course not. Now, we need to put in a good morning's work to get as near quota as possible. They will make allowances for the time out for the firecracking, but they will still expect a good load from us for the rest of the day."

"Can we do it, Amasis?" asked Carbo. "Make our quota, in these circumstances."

"Oh yes, I'm sure we can."

But it quickly became obvious that it was hopeless. Amasis had been retired from manual labour for a reason. His body was so broken from the years of work that he was all but useless. He was helping Sica in the role that Meru and Agamede had filled the last two days, but he cried out every time he stooped to pick up a piece of rock, and moved at the speed of a slug as he dragged his full basket away. Phraates tried to break up the rocks that Curtius and Carbo mined with his one good arm, but he couldn't get enough force without a double handed grip, and many of his blows glanced ineffectually off the ore. Curtius and Carbo struggled more and more as the rock they tried to mine became progressively denser.

Amasis still brought them their drinks as well as performing his role helping with the haulage. After a morning's work, he returned with water and told them they were finished for the time being. He led them out to the main ladder, and they watched engineers take flammable material down the tunnel from which they had just come. After a while in which they rested and breathed the slightly better quality air gratefully, the engineers emerged again.

"Let the fire burn for one hour," said one of the engineers. "Then extinguish it, and throw the vinegar onto the rocks. Quickly, mind you."

"I know how it works," said Amasis, sniffily.

"Well, it's on your head," said the engineer, and climbed the ladder.

For the next hour, they ferried amphorae of vinegar from the surface down the ladder. When they were on top, they could see dark smoke pouring out of the ventilation shafts, and when they were down below, the thick air was acrid. When all the amphorae were in place, they waited, while Amasis estimated the time. After a period Carbo guessed was near enough an hour, Amasis said, "Carbo, Curtius, take these buckets of water and put the fire out. Make sure you don't splash the rockface."

The two men discarded their leather aprons, which would only be an encumbrance for this task. Carbo picked up two pails, one in each hand, and set off down the tunnel. The smoke from the fire stung his throat, worked its way quickly into his lungs. The poor air quality was worsened drastically by the fumes, and soon he was gasping and coughing. The smoke seemed to cling to the ceiling, so he got on his hands and knees, keeping his head low, searching for clean air. But as the ceiling got lower, the smoke filled the tunnel. Tears blurred his vision, the lining of his nose and throat felt like it had ignited, and every time he took a deep breath, he spluttered it out again uncontrollably. His heart started to race, head swim, and he felt a sudden need to get out, to run. But Curtius was behind him, blocking the passageway, and he knew that running would get him killed.

His experience of fighting panic actually helped him this time. The sensation was familiar, almost like an old friend. He embraced it, and let it propel him forward, even as a darkness started to close in around him.

The air abruptly cleared. At least partially. They had reached one of the ventilation shafts, and the smoke swirled around, mixing with fresh air. Carbo and Curtius breathed deeply, still coughing, but feeling less light-headed.

"This is madness," said Curtius, when he was finally able to draw enough breath to speak. "How do they expect us to do this and survive?"

"They don't care whether we survive," said Carbo, traumatised throat making his voice a husky growl.

"Cocksuckers," said Curtius, his voice also hoarse. "Let's go back."

Carbo shook his head. "We can't. If we don't do this, we will be drawing lots tomorrow morning. One of us will die."

"Better odds that one of us die, than I definitely die down here."

"Curtius, we can do this. We know there are three more ventilation shafts, and the last one is just before the fire. We can make it to each shaft, then rush the last bit to the fire, put it out, and back to the shaft."

Curtius shook his head. "Are you serious?"

"Listen, they may not care much about our lives, but they wouldn't expect us to do this if it was certain death. They need the fire put out, and they must think it can be done. It's unpleasant, but it's possible."

"Unpleasant?" Curtius tried to laugh, then doubled over in a paroxysm of coughing.

"I need you with me on this Curtius," said Carbo. "I can't do it on my own."

Curtius looked at him uncertainly, then nodded.

"Good man. Let's go."

They crawled on, seeking out pockets of fresh air amongst the eddying smoke, like oxen at a trough taking gulps of water. Having made it to the first ventilation shaft, Carbo knew it could be done, and though he still felt the panic of suffocation, he could control it. They reached another ventilation shaft, paused to breathe.

"You still with me?" asked Carbo.

Curtius glowered at him, taking deep, raspy breaths. When his breathing became more settled, he said, "Come on, let's get this done."

Twice more they crawled between the oases of fresh air, each time worse than before, as the air quality deteriorated. Warm as it had been before in the deep mine, the fire blazing ahead of them made it feel like they were headed into Vulcan's home. They paused at the last ventilation shaft.

"How are we going to do this?" asked Curtius.

"Quickly," said Carbo. "The distance to the fire isn't as far as the distance between shafts, so we can get there, throw the water and double back."

"Easy," said Curtius bitterly.

"Let's get it over with."

The last stretch was the worst. The heat was unbearable, the smoke thick. The fire sucked in all the fresh air, and belched out acrid fumes. Carbo emerged into the cavern that for the last three days had been their workspace, to be greeted by a vision straight from Tartarus. The bright glow of the flames was obscured by the dense smoke, giving an eerie quality to the underground room. The heat was intense, scorching his face and bare torso. Chest heaving, he advanced and threw his water onto the fire, first one bucket, then the other. Clouds of hot steam hissed outwards, dispelling the smoke, but doing nothing to improve the breathable air. The fire dimmed, but still burned.

"Curtius," Carbo gasped. "Throw. Now."

No reply. No movement. Carbo turned. Two buckets of water sat by the entrance to the tunnel. Curtius was gone.

Carbo cursed. The heat, the lack of air, the pain in his throat and lungs, filled his existence. He groped for one of Curtius' buckets, heaved it onto the fire. The flames got lower, but still flickered through the clouds. His head spun, ears rang, vision dimming. He grabbed the last bucket, threw it with the last of his strength, saw the water spread across the last of the flames, and the cavern turned black.

Carbo turned to escape, and found he could no longer see the tunnel. He crawled forward, arm outstretched, hitting rock. He moved left along the wall, then noticed the heat from the rockface by the fire was increasing, and moved right. Slowly, as his eyes adjusted to the darkness, he realised the rock face was glowing red, just enough to see the darker patch of the exit tunnel through the smog. He crawled forward, limbs and lungs screaming, head low, bare backside now taking the brunt of the heat from the incandescent rocks behind him. His world became the next step, moving by willpower alone, right hand forward, left knee forward, left hand forward, right knee forward.

The smoke began to clear, but his strength faded faster. His arms would no longer support his weight, and he slumped onto his belly. Still he dragged himself forward, the instinct to survive not allowing him to surrender. But eventually, even the most basic instinct was not enough. He could no longer propel himself. He scrabbled ineffectually at the tunnel floor for a brief moment, before the darkness washed over him.

# CHAPTER XVIII

Carbo opened his eyes, and looked up into Sica's concerned face. She cradled his head in her lap, and there were tears in the corners of her eyes. Carbo stared up at her, dazed. When she realised he was awake, her mouth split in a broad smile. She thumped his arm.

"Stupid man. Scare me." She lifted a cup to his mouth. "Drink."

He took a sip of water, coughed, and took another sip, feeling the cool liquid ease the rawness of his mouth and throat. He tried to sit up, but Sica put a hand on his chest, and he sunk back, weak as a newborn.

"Where?" he croaked.

"You made it to air," said Sica. "Just."

"Yes," came Amasis' voice. "You managed to crawl to the ventilation shaft before you passed out. Enough fresh air near the floor to keep you alive till the smoke cleared."

"Why...did I faint?"

"Not enough air inside you, I guess. Also, some people say when the fire burns underground, it makes bad fumes that can kill you even if there is still enough air to breathe."

"Thanks for...the warning." Carbo made to sit up, and this time when Sica tried to restrain him, he had enough strength to shrug her off. He leaned forward, and found the walls were rushing around him like the wheels on an out of control wagon. He put his head in his hands, breathing deeply and fighting a wave of nausea. Looking through his fingers, he could see that he was beneath a ventilation shaft, a stab of light illuminating the tunnel. The rest of his workgroup was there, all carrying buckets of pungent vinegar. His eyes fell on the man at the back, who looked sheepish.

"Curtius," growled Carbo, and lurched towards him, arms outstretched. Orobazes blocked his way.

"We don't have time for this, Carbo," said Amasis. "We need to get that vinegar onto the rocks before they cool down. Otherwise it won't work, and all this will have been for nothing."

Carbo struggled onto hands and knees.

"Later, Curtius," he said. "We will talk."

The workgroup picked up their buckets of vinegar, two each. Carbo reached over to take one of the buckets off Sica, but she slapped him away. Inside, he was grateful. He needed all his strength just to keep moving.

They made their way down the tunnel, and Carbo saw how they all sweated as the heat from the rocks increased. The others shot him glances, wondering how he had made it so far in this heat, with the tunnel full of smoke.

They came out into the cavern, flinching back from the intense temperature. The air was still thick with lingering fumes, and they all spluttered and gagged.

"Everyone gather round the rock face," said Amasis. "This needs to be done right. We all throw our vinegar at once. The rock has to cool very quickly to crack."

"Like throw ice in hot water," said Sica.

"Exactly," said Amasis. "Are we all ready? On my count of three. One, two, three!"

They all hurled their buckets against the rock face together. There was an enormous hiss, a great cloud of vinegar-scented steam, and then a violent cracking sound. As the steam cleared, they saw the rockface in front of them was crisscrossed with fracture lines. The group let out a small celebratory cheer, and Amasis beamed at them.

"Well done, everyone," he said.

More cracking sounds came from the wall, and a few turned to look, expressions becoming nervous. Amasis chuckled. "Don't worry. It's just the rocks settling and finding their new positions."

An almighty crack rang out like the sound of a thunderclap overhead, making their ears sing, and a fissure appeared in the ceiling. Amasis looked up, opened his mouth to speak. The ceiling split wide open, and rocks crashed down into the cavern, the roar of the collapse mingling with terrified screams, some of which cut off abruptly.

All light vanished, as the lamps were extinguished by the gust of wind from the falling rocks, and the clouds of dust that were thrown up. Fist-sized clumps of rock impacted Carbo's head and shoulders, small sharp pebbles with the speed of slingshots cut his skin. He curled into a ball, hands over his head, and waited for the bombardment to abate.

The noise died away as the collapse ended, the rocks settling into position. There was a shocked silence. Then a woman started to scream. "Help me. Oh Juno, help!"

A man, Carbo recognised Orobazes, plaintively called out for Phraates. That was it, no other voices.

"Sica?" he called out. "Sica!"

No reply, just the woman screaming for help, and Orobazes yelling for his lover.

The darkness was complete. It must be like being struck suddenly blind, he thought. Lights swam before him, but he knew they were phantoms, the false patterns you see when you shut your eyes. He turned his head rapidly from side to side, but there was not a hint of illumination in any direction.

Carbo felt around him, calling Sica's name. His hand grasped a leg, and he felt his way upwards. As he reached a hairy upper thigh, a hand gripped his wrist.

"That's far enough," said Curtius.

"Curtius," spat Carbo. "Trust you to survive. Help me find the others."

"Why?"

Carbo resisted the urge to punch him. "So they can help us dig ourselves out, you fool. Or had you not noticed we are trapped down here?"

Curtius sighed, and Carbo heard him shift onto hands and knees, and start feeling around the fallen rocks. Carbo moved along the rubble, exploring, and soon his hand touched a protruding leg. He squeezed it but there was no reaction. The shin he was holding was muscular and hairy.

"Orobazes. I've found Phraates."

The foreign slave recognised the names, and hurried over. Frantically he started digging, throwing rocks over his shoulder, causing Curtius to curse as one glanced off him. Carbo moved further along, and found an arm. It was warm, and he could feel a pulse in it. He followed it up to find the chest was covered, but further up the head was exposed. The skin on the face was smooth, the hair long, the eyes closed. He could feel warm breath on his palm, and he slapped the face lightly.

"Sica. Sica! Wake up!"

The girl stirred beneath him, groaned. She tried to draw in air, coughed, tried again.

"Can't...breathe."

"Hold on, Sica, I'm getting you out." He grabbed heavy rocks and pulled them away from her chest, hearing her respiration ease as the weight lifted. She gripped his knee tightly as he worked, and breathed in and out through gritted teeth. Carbo realised she was in some pain, but she made no complaint, unlike the woman still screaming.

"Curtius, can't you help that poor woman?" snapped Carbo.

"I'm looking for her," Curtius shot back.

"Look harder!"

Carbo worked Sica's body loose from the rubble, and pulled her gently out. She gasped a little as her legs came free, and forgetting decorum, he checked her for injuries. She winced when he felt her ankle, but he was satisfied.

"Nothing broken, Sica. Not even a rib. You are a tough girl."

She squeezed his arm.

"Carbo, get over here," yelled Curtius.

"Will you be alright if I go to help?" asked Carbo.

"Carbo!" yelled Curtius.

"Go," said Sica.

Carbo groped his way over to Curtius, following the sound of his voice and the crying woman, stubbing a toe and grazing a knee painfully on the way.

"What is it?" asked Carbo.

"It's Agamede," said Curtius. "Feel."

Carbo reached out, finding Agamede's face, working his hands downwards over her chest. He reached her abdomen, still not encountering any rubble, and wondered why she was whimpering and gasping in obvious agony. Then as his hands explored lower they bumped into something solid. His fingers told him that an enormous rock had landed on Agamede's pelvis and upper thighs. Gentle probing beneath showed that her lower body was completely crushed.

In the pitch black, Carbo could not exchange a wordless look with Curtius, could not silently confer over the seriousness of the injury.

"We need to lift the rock," said Curtius. "It will take both of us."

"No," said Carbo.

For a moment, Curtius said nothing, his shock palpable in the dark.

"You're the do-gooder, the moral one who shares the food out and won't let us have fun with the girls. Help me, man. She needs us."

"She will die if we lift that rock," said Carbo.

"What?"

"I've seen it before. I'm no medicus. But I've been in ambushes where rocks were rolled down onto the enemy. Been on both sides of that. When the lower body is crushed, and then the weight is lifted, the person dies straight away."

Agamede groaned in pain and terror.

"Why?" asked Curtius.

"No one knows. Some of the physicians say it is because of the blood loss, some say it is the sudden release of evil humours, some say it is just the will of the gods. But it always happens."

156

"So what do we do? We can't just leave her like this."

"I don't know," snapped Carbo.

"Lift...the rock," gasped Agamede.

Carbo instinctively looked down, though he could make out nothing. He placed a hand on her cheek.

"Agamede, if we lift the rock, you will die."

"I know. But...it will be quick, you say?"

Carbo nodded, then remembered she couldn't see him. "When I've seen it before, yes, very quick."

"I'm broken, Carbo. Even if they could heal me, I would be useless as a worker. They would kill me. Besides..." She tensed, body spasming, clutching at Carbo, and let out a moan. "Besides..." she tried again. "What have I to live for? This miserable existence. I want to join Pamphile."

Carbo squeezed her shoulder.

"Are you sure?"

"Please, Carbo."

Carbo took a breath. "Curtius?"

Curtius' voice broke as he replied. "I'm ready."

They took one end of the rock each, and lifted. It took all their combined strength to ease it off her, and as the weight came off, Carbo heard a crack of shifting bones, and Agamede shrieked, the horrific sound filling the cavern. They heaved the rock away sideways, let it crash to the ground. Agamede abruptly stopped screaming. Her breathing became erratic, laboured. Carbo knelt beside her, took her hand. She squeezed him, once, weakly. Then her hand went limp.

The sudden silence in the cavern was as disconcerting as the screaming had been. Even Orobazes paused his digging for his friend momentarily. Then he went back to work, heaving stones and rocks out of the way. Carbo knew when Orobazes finally uncovered Phraates. The foreign slave started to cry uncontrollably, repeating Phraates' name over and over.

Carbo made his way over to Orobazes. He was clutching his friend's body to his chest and weeping. He put a hand on his shoulder, but Orobazes shrugged him away. Carbo returned to Sica, and called for Curtius to join them.

"Four of us still alive," said Carbo. "Agamede and Phraates are dead. I presume Amasis is dead too, buried deep under the rubble."

"They will have to give us a break, won't they," said Curtius. "They can't expect us to fill our quota after this."

"Curtius," said Carbo gently. "Do you hear digging?"

Curtius listened.

"No. Do you?"

"No," said Carbo.

"My ears are still ringing from all the noise. They must be working at the other end of the collapse by now."

"No digging," said Sica.

"But...why not?"

"It's not worth their while," said Carbo.

"What...what do you mean?"

"Think about it Curtius. This tunnel would have to be re-excavated, cleared, engineers make it safe again. Why would they bother? They will just mine another tunnel."

"But what about us?"

"It's economics," said Carbo. "Our value as labour is not worth their effort to rescue us."

"You're saying we are going to die down here?"

"No!" said Carbo firmly. "What I'm saying is we are on our own. It's up to us to dig ourselves out."

There was quiet as the words sunk in.

"Can we do it?" asked Curtius.

"I don't know," said Carbo. "But it's our only chance."

"We have air?" asked Sica.

"I don't know, for Jupiter's sake!" snapped Carbo, then sighed. "I'm sorry. This cavern is large, it should sustain us for a while. And it isn't too far to the first ventilation shaft. Maybe some air can get in that way. Whatever, we need to get on with this. Curtius, you and I will clear the large rocks. Sica, you try to move back what you can from behind us, roll it away, however you like, just make sure we have a clear space to throw the rubble into."

"What about Orobazes?" asked Curtius.

"Let's hope he starts to help."

They set to excavating, and soon settled into a rhythm, just as when they had been mining. The work was tough, and painfully slow. It wasn't clear at first if they were even digging in the right direction, but then Carbo caught a draught of cool air between some of the rocks, and knew they were headed towards the ventilation shaft.

After a short while, they uncovered Amasis' body. The supervisor's skull had been crushed. They heaved the body out of the way, wordlessly and unceremoniously, and carried on. Orobazes came to join them, saying nothing, just heaving the debris behind him. From time to time they encountered a rock too large for one of them to move, and then two or three would manhandle it out of the way. Curtius had found his pick, and when they came across one rock that was large and too wedged to remove, they managed to break it up, taking it in turns to wield the tool. When it came loose, the rocks shifted with an ominous groan, and they all held their breath. When no collapse followed, they breathed out.

"We have to go easy," said Carbo. "It's unstable."

"You're telling me we have to heave these heavy rocks out of the way gently?" asked Curtius.

"Just…be careful."

They carried on. And on. No light. No water breaks. No hut to crawl back to at the end of the day, if they didn't free themselves. As they worked their way into the tunnel, they had to use a chain system, like the chains of water buckets the vigiles used for extinguishing fires, passing the rubble backwards, as there was only room for one at the front. They rotated the front person regularly as they became fatigued, all having to crawl backwards into the cavern to accomplish this. Twice, removing rocks caused fresh collapses, and they had to retreat hurriedly, and then start that section again.

Eventually, Carbo saw a glimmer of light through some cracks in the rock.

"I can see light," said Carbo. "The ventilation shaft is ahead."

They worked with renewed vigour, and as more debris was cleared, they found they were able to see a little - tiny shafts of light illuminating blackened, exhausted faces. The light began to fade though, and by the time they reached the shaft itself, dusk had fallen.

They paused for breath, staring at the narrow shaft leading up to safety, to the outside world.

"How much further do you think the collapse goes?" asked Curtius.

Carbo shrugged. "Could be five feet, could be five hundred."

"If only we had a ladder up that shaft."

"I can climb," said Sica.

Carbo turned to look at the slight girl in surprise.

"You can get up there?"

"Yes."

"And how will that help us?" asked Curtius sourly.

"Maybe it doesn't," said Carbo. "But at least one of us will survive."

"Help me," said Sica. Carbo lifted her into the ventilation shaft. It was narrow enough that she could lean her back against one vertical wall, with her feet pressed into the opposing side, supporting her weight.

"I come back," she said. Then she started to lever herself upwards, one foot, then the other foot, then using her arms to support herself as she elevated her back. Carbo watched her ascend, heart racing each time she slipped, or missed a foothold. But with amazing agility, she pulled herself to the top, and over the lip of the shaft. He sighed in relief.

"I couldn't do that," said Curtius bitterly.

"Me neither," said Carbo. "Come on. We'd better get back to digging."

They got back to working on the rubble filling the tunnel ahead of them, starting to edge their way forwards once more. When Curtius was taking a turn at the front, he hauled a rock clear, then let out a curse.

"What is it?" called Carbo.

"It's the tunnel walls. They have shifted. It's not just rubble here, it's solid rock face. We are going to have to mine ourselves out."

"With one pick, excavate a whole new tunnel from solid rock? That would take days."

Carbo groaned and slumped to the floor.

"What, are you giving up?" asked Curtius.

"What's your plan, then?" asked Carbo.

"I don't know, I just…you have all the ideas."

"Not for this," said Carbo.

The three of them sat in silence. Carbo's craving for water was intense. His mouth and nose were clogged with dust, and despair and extreme exhaustion overwhelmed him.

Something tumbled down the ventilation shaft. Carbo looked round. The end of a thick rope dangled in front of him.

Vespillo and Marsia finished a light lunch of sardines in garum and bread and walked back down to the docks, where they had spent most of their time in Neapolis for the last three days. They wandered slowly along the seafront, watching the slaves and sailors at work. Tar was reapplied, sails patched and sewn. Cargoes unloaded, new cargoes reloaded. Regularly, boats and ships landed and departed.

Each time a new arrival docked, Vespillo quizzed the captain as soon as the gang-plank hit the dock. So far, no Zosimus, and none had encountered him, or had news of when he was due back.

A tatty boat with ragged sails appeared over the horizon and drew close. Vespillo watched its approach, hoping that this was the one. The chariot races that the captain had mentioned were being held tomorrow. If Zozimus wasn't back by then, maybe he didn't intend to return. Maybe after he had dumped his cargo of slaves, he had found another lucrative job, and departed to some far flung part of the Empire, Egypt or Africa or Hispania.

The boat docked, sailors threw ropes to the dockers, and it was hauled side-on to the dock. The sailors heaved a gangplank into place, and Vespillo leaped onto it and boarded the ship, Marsia close behind.

The captain strode over to him, a short, round, bearded man, and said in a deep, Greek-accented voice, "Who by Hades are you?"

"Are you Zosimus?" asked Vespillo. The captain pursed his lips.

"I ask again, who are you?"

"My name is Lucius Vedius Vespillo, tribune of the vigiles of Rome."

Zosimus frowned as he tried to place the description. "Vigiles? You mean the firemen? The ones that work in Rome? What right does that give you to board my ship?"

Vespillo cursed inwardly, he had hoped the mention of an official position might have awed the captain a little, but no such luck.

"I am here in a private capacity, investigating a disappearance. Please, are you Zosimus?"

"I am," said Zosimus.

Vespillo breathed a sigh of relief. "May I buy you a drink, captain, in exchange for some information?"

"You can pay for my first whore. It's been a long journey. Then you can buy me a drink and we can talk."

Vespillo and Marsia leaned against the wall outside the brothel, listening to the guttural male groans and the simulated female cries of pleasure from within. A togate woman approached Vespillo, eyes heavily shadowed, cheeks lead-whitened, lips cherry red.

"Why are you waiting out here, handsome? Plenty of room inside."

"Thank you, no," said Vespillo.

"I bet an experienced man like you knows a thing or two about pleasing a lady. I bet I could teach you some new tricks myself though."

"Really, I'm just waiting for a friend."

The prostitute's face dropped. She pointed at Marsia. "Are you doing him al-ready? This is our patch."

Marsia's face remained impassive.

"I'm talking to you, bitch." She brought a hand around fast to slap Marsia's face.

Vespillo caught her wrist. "She is my personal slave. She is not a whore. Now go away, or I will beat you."

A flash of fear twisted the prostitute's face. She spat, and retreated back inside.

Fortunately, a few days at sea had deprived Zosimus enough that he didn't need much time in the brothel to see to his immediate needs. He wandered out, doing up the belt on his tunic, a satisfied grin on his face.

"Now, about that drink," he said.

He led them to the nearest bar, and ordered the most expensive wine they stocked, which fortunately wasn't at all expensive. They sat together around a table and watched Zosimus drain his cup in one long draught. Marsia was fidgeting, itching to speak, but Vespillo restrained her with a subtle squeeze of her thigh. Zosimus signalled to one of the slaves for another drink, and while she was filling his cup, he turned to Vespillo and Marsia and said, "Right, what do you want to know?"

"We are looking for a man who has been wrongly arrested and enslaved. We think he was on your boat when you sailed last."

"Really. There were a lot of men on my boat when I sailed last."

"Tall man, very well built, black hair, scarred body, walks with a limp."

Zosimus sipped his drink, slower and more thoughtful this time.

"Doesn't ring any bells," he said.

Marsia looked downcast. "But we were told..."

Vespillo slid a silver denarius across the table.

"I think maybe I can hear something tolling in the distance," said Zosimus. He looked at the coin. "It's a very faint sound though. Might just be the wind."

Vespillo opened his purse. "How many coins do I have to throw at this bell to get it to make a noise?"

"I've always liked the sound of gold against bronze." Vespillo pulled out a gold aureus and gave it to him.

"That's better," said Zosimus. "Now, where were we? Large chap, scars, limp, black hair. Yes, I do remember now, he was on my ship. Chained with the other slaves."

"He's not a slave," said Vespillo.

"Well, he looked like one to me, that's all I can say."

"Who sold him to you?"

"The man didn't give his name. Old chap, not from round here, needed a quick sale to get money for his fare home to some foreign country."

"Where did you take the... slave?"

Zosimus cocked his head on one side, put a hand to his ear. Vespillo sighed, and gave him another aureus.

"Sicily," said Zosimus.

"Why?"

Zosimus looked at the purse expectantly. Vespillo snapped his hand out and gripped Zosimus' wrist tightly.

"I've paid you more than enough for information. Tell me."

Zosimus looked down at Vespillo's hand contemptuously, but replied anyway.

"He was with a group, bound for the lead mines."

Marsia gasped, put her hand to her mouth. Vespillo looked grim.

"You would know which one?"

"I believe I heard their destination."

"Take us there."

Zosimus looked surprised. "I'm a cargo boat, not a passenger ferry."

"Your boat looks fast enough. It might take us days to find someone going in the right direction, or willing to take us."

"It will be expensive."

"Our friend has some means. We can pay. Name your price."

Zosimus named a price about three times more than the already exorbitant figure Vespillo had in mind. He managed to beat him down to just twice as much as exorbitant and shook hands.

"Let me unload. We have to wait for the tide anyway. We can depart this evening. Be ready, with the money."

Vespillo nodded, stood to leave.

"And don't forget to settle my bar bill before you go."


Carbo looked up, and could just make out the form of Sica at the top of the shaft waving to him.

"Climb," she called.

Curtius was the first to react. He grabbed the rope, gave it a tug to check it was secure, then hauled himself upwards, hand over hand, feet against the wall. The shaft was tall, and Curtius' progress was slow, with curses echoing down everytime a rock came loose or his foot slipped. In time though, Curtius disappeared over the top of the shaft. Carbo offered the rope to Orobazes. The foreign slave nodded, accepted the rope, and with some assistance from Carbo to get him started, he climbed.

When it came to Carbo's turn, there was no one to help him, so he had to start his ascent with hands and feet on the rope, heaving his muscular frame upwards. Once he was into the shaft proper, he could use his feet on the wall to work his way up as the others had done, and this eased the strain on his arms. Progress was slow, though. His arms, his legs, even his fingers felt drained of all strength, after his exertions before and after the cave-in. His lungs still protested at the effort. Around halfway up, he stopped.

"Climb, Carbo," called Sica, beckoning him. "Nearly here."

He was exhausted, and yet terrified. A fall from this height would be fatal. Yet the shaft above him seemed interminable. He remained frozen, arms gripping the rope, legs jammed into the shaft wall, feeling the strength ebbing, waiting for it to fail completely. Why didn't he just let go, end all this pain? What even awaited him at the top of the shaft? The hut, and then another day of labour, then another, then another, until he died of exhaustion or cold or despair.

"Carbo," called Sica again. "Please. I need you."

He shook his head. She didn't need him. He was no help to anyone. He couldn't protect, couldn't save, couldn't even avenge...

Rufa's face appeared before him, from the gloom. He hadn't seen her for the last couple of nights, his exhausted sleep dreamless. Now the sudden manifestation of his lover's lemur nearly caused him to lose his grip on the rope.

She looked into his eyes, with affection, and longing and sadness. Her mouth moved, and though he heard no sound, he could read the words her lips formed. "I love you. I love you, Carbo."

Tears sprang to his eyes, and he clung tightly to the rope, staring at the pale face of the only woman he had ever loved.

"I love you, too, Rufa," he whispered.

"Carbo," called Sica. "Please climb. For me."

For Sica? Maybe. For Rufa? Yes. He could do that.

He moved one hand further up the rope, took a step up the wall, moved his other hand. His fingers cramped where he had been gripping the rope so tightly. But he gritted his teeth against the pain, poured every ounce of his will into the climb. Rufa's face faded away, but he kept climbing, not looking up, the next step all that mattered, then the next one.

Suddenly strong hands were grasping him, hauling him up and over the edge. Curtius and Orabazes heaved him onto the ground at the top of the shaft, and he lay there, limp, breathing hard.

Sica jumped on him, knocking the air out of his chest, and kissed him on his cheek and forehead and nose, beaming broadly.

"You did it," she cried. "I knew you could."

Carbo sat up, looked around. They were a few hundred feet from the main shaft to the mine. Night had fully fallen, and the area was deserted. Further away, Carbo could see guards patrolling the staked wooden fence that marked the perimeter of the mining complex.

"Well, I guess Durmius is going to be surprised to see us," said Curtius

"We're not going back," said Carbo flatly.

Curtius looked at him in surprise.

"What are you talking about? We are still stuck in here. They have a fence, guards. I've heard the dogs barking at night. Even if we get out, they will come looking for us, track us down. Where would we go?"

"They think we are dead," said Carbo. "If we can get out of here unseen, they will never know. We would be free."

Curtius looked at him thoughtfully. Orabazes regarded them both patiently, uncomprehending, waiting to follow them, whatever they decided.

"It has to be all of us," said Carbo. "If one of us returns to them, they will know the others escaped."

Sica took Carbo's hand. "I come with you." She turned to Orabazes, pointed to each of them in turn, then pointed to the fence. Orabazes' eyes widened, then he nodded.

"Curtius?" asked Carbo.

Curtius hesitated, then nodded. "You're going to get us all killed. But right now, that feels better than the alternative. I'm with you."

CHAPTER XIX

Vespillo looked around the boat, while Marsia remained at the side rail, watching the Bay of Neapolis recede. There was a pleasant smell of wheat, the main cargo that vessels brought out of Sicily. But underneath were more earthy, visceral smells. Faeces. Urine. Blood. Fear. He opened the hold and looked down, and the smell slapped him in the face, even more powerful. He descended the ladder, looked around, squinting into the darkness.

As his eyes adjusted, he saw a long wooden bar across the floor of the hold. Attached to it were rusty iron chains with wrist and ankle cuffs. The floor was still slick with human excrement. He gagged at the sight, and shook his head in disgust. Poor Carbo, chained here like the lowest farm animal. He climbed back up the ladder, and found Zosimus at the prow, surprisingly sober, keeping a steady look-out ahead.

Vespillo put a hand on his shoulder, turned Zosimus to face him. "You kept them chained up in their own filth?" he said. Zosimus shrugged the hand off.

"I'm busy."

"I've seen pigs treated better. These are humans!"

"They are slaves," spat Zosimus. "And not just any slaves, but the lowest slaves. I don't know what they have done to deserve their punishment. I don't ask. But I can guess. They are thieves, runaways, rapists. They are being sent to die in misery for their crimes. Why should I treat them well?"

"Maybe they are innocent," said Vespillo. "Maybe they shouldn't be slaves at all."

"Someone else made that decision. I'm just taking them to their fate."

Vespillo stared at him angrily, but knew there was nothing more he could say. "How long till Sicily?" he asked, curt.

"Unladen like this, with tide and wind in our favour, two days."

Vespillo nodded, then went to join Marsia at the side rail.

They approached the perimeter fencing cautiously, bent over so their silhouettes could not be seen against the faint light of the cloud-strewn night sky. Carbo led the way aiming for a point on the fence halfway between two sentry huts. The night air was bitter, and all four of them, naked as exposed babies, shivered violently.

Motion caught Carbo's peripheral vision, and he looked round, trying not to look directly at the movement, to make the most of his night sight. It was a guard, on a casual patrol along the inside of the perimeter. Carbo gestured for everyone to get down, and they flattened themselves to the ground, barely daring to breathe as the guard wandered within feet of their position. Once he had passed, Carbo beckoned them forward.

When they reached the fence, Carbo looked up. It was a ten foot palisade, made of sharpened stakes. He grabbed one and shook it experimentally, but it was well built, probably by the legionaries or veterans. He put his hand out, and Sica gave him the rope that she had found discarded. He made a loop at one end, and tossed it up so the loop caught over one of the stakes. He pulled on it hard, then passed the rope back to Sica. Nimbly she scaled up and gracefully disappeared over the top. They barely heard her land.

Curtius was up next, and the short climb caused him no problems. Orobazes was slower, and his landing was heavier. Carbo looked around. He saw movement again, the guard returning. The pace was still slow, showing no sign of alarm. Carbo gripped the rope. Though the climb was short, his muscles screamed protest at being put to use again so soon. When he reached the top, he swung his leg over. For a moment he found himself straddling the fence, his whole weight on his hands, a sharpened stake pointing directly at his bare genitals. He closed his eyes as he swung his other leg over, then let himself drop.

The tip of a stake grazed a buttock as he fell and he gritted his teeth as the sting hit him, even as he rolled on the hard ground to soften the fall.

"Where is rope?" hissed Sica.

Carbo cursed.

"Great," said Curtius. "I thought they were supposed to think we were dead. We might as well have scrawled graffiti on the fence saying 'escaped slaves this way.'"

"I get it," said Sica.

"Wait," said Carbo. He pressed his face to a gap in the fence, saw the approaching guard. How observant was he? Carbo wondered, praying to Fortuna. The guard strolled past, not slowing, not looking around, the rope that hung against the fence concealed in shadow. Then he stopped, turned to the fence, hitched up his tunic and started to urinate. Carbo watched, waited as he shook, put himself away. The guard took a few steps away from the puddle he had made, then sat down, back to the fence. He reached into a pouch on his belt and brought out an apple, which he started to crunch loudly.

Carbo cursed to himself, then gestured to the others to move quietly away from the fence. When they were out of earshot, he said, "The guard has settled himself in. We can't get the rope."

"Then we're in the shit," said Curtius.

"Not necessarily," said Carbo. "They won't see that rope till dawn, it's too concealed. And even if they do, they won't know who put it there."

"I think they will have a pretty good guess," said Curtius bitterly.

"Well, let's just make sure we are long gone by then. Come on."

They followed him, picking their way tentatively through the rocky terrain, balancing speed and a desire to put as much distance between themselves and the camp, against the fear of a twisted ankle or lacerated sole that could leave them unable to flee. Still, they made steady progress, and soon the camp was a shadow in the distance.

"Where are we going?" asked Curtius.

"We need to find shelter," said Carbo. "Keep your eyes open for any signs of civilisation."

Carbo had no real idea which was the best way to head. He had a rough idea of the direction they were going in, from the north star which appeared from behind the clouds from time to time, and he kept them heading north east, on the assumption that they had landed in Sicily at the nearest port to mainland Italy, and that would be the quickest way back. Before they contemplated leaving Sicily though, they needed water, food, clothing. And most importantly, they needed to rest, to just stop, and sleep, and maybe start to come to terms with their suffering over the last few days.

They kept on, Curtius muttering complaints, Orobazes and Sica silent. The rocky ground turned to grass beneath their feet, making the going less painful. A few sheep milled around, grinding the grass down, looking up with bored curiosity as the strangers passed. The wind chilled them, and Carbo started to worry about exposure. He was chilled to the core himself, but Sica was trembling all over. How ridiculous, he thought, to survive all they had, and then freeze to death for want of a tunic or blanket, a hut or cave.

"There," said Sica, pointing. Carbo peered into the distance, could make out nothing. But Sica was insistent, and her younger eyes proved accurate. Out of the darkness loomed a small wooden hut, smoke curling out from a hole in the roof. Carbo put a finger to his lips as they approached it. When they reached the door, he held up a hand, and counted down from three on his fingers.

When his last finger curled down, he barged the hut door open, entering with the roar, the other three hard on his heels.

A young boy screamed at the sight of four demons bursting into his hut, naked, dirt-smeared, yelling for his blood. Carbo grabbed him, pressed him up against a wall, retrieved a short knife from the boy's belt, then looked around him. A small fire glowed in a hearth in the centre of the room, smoke drifting lazily upwards. A pot bubbled over the fire. Blankets were strewn on the floor. A shepherd's crook stood propped up in a corner.

"Is there anyone else nearby?" asked Carbo, voice dripping with menace.

The boy shook his head, eyes wide with terror.

"How far to the nearest village?"

"About...half of an hour's walk."

Carbo released him, then said to Curtius, "Tie him up."

Curtius nodded, and bound the shepherd boy's hands behind his back, using strips of torn blanket, then hobbled his ankles.

They all moved near the fire, mesmerised by the heat and light.

"Carbo." Orobazes held up a jug. He took a sip, smiled, took a deep glug, then passed it to Carbo. Carbo drank, the cheap, watered, vinegary wine which tasted like the finest Falernian. He passed the jug to Sica, who drank and passed it to Curtius.

The pot on the fire contained a rich mutton stew. Only meant to feed one for a full meal, but enough to ease the hunger cramps that the smell of cooking had instantly induced.

They huddled together around the fire, and for a moment, Carbo thought he had never been so happy. To have his most basic needs met, warmth, drink, food, rest, was not what he had imagined happiness to be. Now he knew better.

"I'll take watch first," said Carbo. "The rest of you get some sleep. Use those blankets. Tomorrow we can cut holes in them to make tunics, until we can find some real clothes."

"Then what?" asked Curtius.

"Then, we are going to find our way back to Italy. I have unfinished business there."

Durmius looked thoughtfully at the rope. He gave it an experimental tug, noted it held fast. He looked at the ground, saw scuff marks in the dirt.

"When was this noticed?" he asked.

"At first light," said the Cominius, the guard captain. "When the shifts changed, the new patrol saw it straight away."

"The guard that was patrolling this section at night. Have him whipped."

"Yes, sir," said Cominius. "Do you think someone has escaped?"

"No, captain, I think some of the prisoners have been practicing wall climbing for exercise, because they have too much energy left at the end of the day."

"Really sir? I thought they were usually tired by the end…"

"Captain, how did you get this job?"

"Well, my mother's aunt was…"

Durmius held up a hand. "That's enough information. Which of the prisoners are unaccounted for?"

"None, sir."

"None?"

"All the prisoners were in their huts at morning head count. No one unaccounted for. Apart from the dead ones of course." The guard let out a chuckle.

Durmius looked thoughtful. "When did the engineers intend to clear out that tunnel that collapsed yesterday?"

"Not for a few days, sir. They said they wanted anything that was unstable to have found its position before they started messing around with it."

Durmius put a hand to his face, and chewed on his lip. "It's that Carbo, I'll bet. I knew he was going to be trouble."

"You think he survived?" asked Cominius.

"I think if anyone could, it would be him."

"What do we do then? If he is already counted as dead, surely we don't need to put ourselves out recapturing him."

"It's the principle, captain. Nobody escapes from here. If word got around it was possible, your men would be fighting off escape attempts every night."

The guard captain sighed, shoulders slumped, knowing what was coming.

"Organise a party. Get the dogs. You will lead."

"Yes sir." Cominius scurried off to obey his orders.


"Listen," said Sica.

They had left the shepherd boy tied up, after a brief debate over whether he would be found before he starved to death. They decided if he didn't return home, his family would likely look for him in good time, so decided the low risk of him dying a slow painful death was outweighed by the high risk of him reporting them to the authorities. Now they trudged roughly north east, wrapped in makeshift clothes made out of blankets, though still bare-foot except for Curtius who was wearing the shepherd boy's rather snug sandals.

Carbo paused to listen, turning his head so the noise from the whistling wind was minimised. For a moment there was nothing. Then he heard the barking.

"Merda. Dogs."

"They hunt?" asked Sica.

Carbo nodded. "We need to find water to disguise our trail."

"Water?" asked Curtius. "But it's freezing out here."

"Would you rather be cold out here, or warm back in there, awaiting your punishment?"

Curtius shivered and Carbo knew it wasn't from the cold.

"Let's get going."

After maybe a mile, they found a stream snaking down the hillside. Carbo led the way, wincing at the bite of the ice cold water on his feet. They all followed, Curtius loudly complaining, Sica and Orobazes silent. The stones on the bed of the stream were sharp, and the pain of treading on them was intense, until the cold began to numb their feet. Then Carbo began to worry what damage his feet may be taking without him realising.

When they had travelled what Carbo judged a reasonable distance, they exited onto the far bank, and carried on. Their wet feet did not warm up, and they all stumbled frequently. The sound of barking dogs receded as they travelled, and Carbo felt his anxiety ease. He looked up. The sky was overcast, dark, threatening rain. They would need shelter if they got caught out in a downpour, but the hilly countryside offered little - no caves, no overhanging rocks, not even any trees of a size big enough to huddle beneath to wait out a rainstorm.

Orobazes, who was leading the way, stopped and pointed. "Carbo."

To one side of their intended route, there was a small collection of huts. Three, Carbo counted, and some barns and other outhouses. How many would live there? he wondered. Say it was three families, with slaves, that could be easily twenty or thirty people. But the huts looked small, poorly maintained. Probably no slaves then. These were likely subsistence farmers. Husband, wife and some children. And maybe some of the men would be away, working the fields or tending flocks.

"We need food, we need shoes, and we need proper clothing," said Carbo. "We go to the village."

"And they will just give it to us?" asked Curtius.

"No. And we have nothing to trade. We will have to take what we need."

"Armed with just that little fruit knife you took from the boy?"

"It will be enough," said Carbo.

"The men with dogs?" asked Sica. "They will ask at village. Find us."

Carbo nodded. "I know. But they will find our trail again soon anyway. We will be faster with food inside us and proper clothes and footwear. The decision is made. Follow me."

They approached the village warily. Some geese hissed at their approach, and as they got closer, an elderly dog, tied up to a pole between the huts, opened one eye, realised that intruders had got closer than they should, and jumped to his feet, barking furiously.

A woman came out from one of the huts, baby clutched to her breast. She took one look at the four escaped slaves, and retreated into the hut, slamming the door shut and barring it.

Carbo reached her hut, rattled the door, and realised it wasnt going to open easily. He turned to the next hut.

"Let's try this one."

This one was unlocked, and Carbo threw the door open and entered, knife extended.

A toothless lady sat in a chair at the far end of the single room, her sewing on her lap. She stared at them, masticating a morsel of something soft.

"Apologies for the intrusion," said Carbo. "We are in desperate need of food and clothes. Can you help us?"

The woman continued to stare, chewing noisily.

"I don't think she is all there, Carbo," said Curtius. "Let's take what we need and go."

They looked around, found a man's tunic that was too small for Carbo or Orobazes, but fitted Curtius, found a shawl that Sica wrapped around herself, and found some dried meat and fruits. They ate these hungrily.

Sica looked at the old lady's sandals, then looked at Carbo, conflicted. Carbo nodded to her. Sica approached the lady, untied the laces that held them in place. As she started to take them off, the old lady seemed to awake from a trance, and started to smack Sica around the head, cursing her in accented Latin. Sica stepped back, looking distressed. Orobazes took the old lady's wrists, and held, them, gently but firmly, allowing Sica to finish.

"Sorry, lady," she said in a small voice, and put the sandals on.

"There's nothing else here," said Carbo. "Let's try the other hut."

The last hut was locked but not barred, and a shoulder barge from Carbo broke the lock open. This hut was unoccupied, and they quickly looted it. A little bread, which again they ate immediately, and some more dried meat, which they stored. Two larger tunics meant that they all now had some extra clothing against the cold, and one pair of very worn caligae. Carbo wondered if these belonged to a veteran, or whether they had just been picked up when some legionary had discarded them. Either way, despite the holes in the soles and the perished leather uppers, they would be a godsend. Carbo picked them up and looked at his own feet, blistered and bleeding. Then he handed them to Orobazes. The large barbarian smiled and put a hand on his shoulder.

There was no more to be had here, so they went back outside. They searched the outbuildings, but found only a grumpy looking ox, animal fodder and agricultural tools. Carbo took a solid looking axe, and a small hacksaw but nothing else. He looked at the barred hut that the mother and child had retreated into.

"We need more," said Curtius. "More food, more shoes, more warm clothes."

Sica nodded agreement. Orobazes pointed to Carbo's bare feet.

"I know," said Carbo. "But how do we get in?"

"Burn them out," said Curtius.

"Great plan," said Carbo. "Then we burn everything of use inside."

"What do you suggest then?"

Carbo studied the door. The builders obviously had security in mind. It was heavy wood, with a sturdy metal handle and an iron lock. The handle was bolted securely to the door. He thought back to the outhouse he had just been in.

"I have an idea."

With help from Orobazes, who proved adept at animal handling, they led the ox out by its nose ring, and harnessed it with some fencing rope, so that the rope ran through the door handle. They then shouted and smacked the stubborn beast, encouraging it to pull. For a moment it seemed oblivious to their urgings, then it started to pad forward. When the rope reached full tension the ox paused. But it was trained to the yoke, and besides, it was stubborn. It put its head down, and strained.

The door handle creaked, one nail popping out, but the rest remained fast, and the door and the frame it was attached to began to bow. Suddenly there was a loud crack, and the door flew open. Carbo rushed in quickly, knife held out, Orobazes behind him with the axe.

A woman screamed, which started a baby howling. In the dim interior light, Carbo could see a young boy, maybe ten years old, pointing a sword at them. His arm trembled with the weight, and Carbo could see he would not be able to keep it raised for long.

"Put it down, boy," said Carbo, holding up a hand to restrain the others. "We don't want to hurt anyone."

"Go away," said the boy. "Touch my sister and I will kill you."

"Where are your parents, boy?"

"Nearby. They will be back soon."

Carbo doubted it, but it was possible.

"We just want food, clothes, shoes."

"Get out!" The boy's voice had risen to hysterical pitch, and he moved forward, waving the sword in Carbo's face.

Carbo took one step, grabbed the boy's wrist and pulled it forward so the sword passed by his body and was trapped under his muscular arm. In one smooth movement he placed his foot behind the boy's leg, then pressed firmly into the boy's face with the palm of his face. The boy tripped over Carbo's foot, and fell backwards heavily. Carbo retained control of his arm, and with a squeeze made him drop the weapon.

The girl had backed into a corner, looking terrified, clutching the baby like it was about to be taken away. The baby screamed.

"Search the place, quickly," said Carbo, putting a foot on the boy's chest so he couldn't rise.

Orobazes found two tunics, holey and waiting for stitching, and a sheepskin cloak.

Sica went to a small wooden chest and threw the lid open. She pulled out a knife, the sort used for skinning and dicing meat, and looked at Carbo questioningly. He nodded, and she made a hole in her cloak to slide it into. She reached in again, and this time drew out a pair of large walking boots. She smiled and tossed them over to Carbo. Orobazes came over to restrain the boy, allowing Carbo to pull the boots on. He winced as the leather chafed on his sore feet, but he knew that now they were all shod, they would make much better progress.

Curtius opened some parcels wrapped in cloth and found cheese, bread and nuts.

"We'll take that with us," said Carbo. Curtius looked at the food wistfully for a moment, then wrapped it back up. "Anything else here?"

Curtius walked over to the woman, who shrunk away from him. Roughly he patted her over, taking time to run his hands over her breasts and buttocks.

"Nothing on her but her clothes," he said. "Do we take them?"

Carbo looked across to Sica, who looked at her makeshift tunic, then at the stola the woman wore. She sighed and shook her head.

Carbo took inventory. They now all had footwear, none were naked, they had eaten and had a little spare food to take, and they even had weapons - two knives and an axe.

"It's enough. Time to get moving."

"Moving where?" asked Curtius.

"To Messana. It's where we arrived, and it's the quickest way back to Italy."

"Why should we go back to Italy?"

Carbo looked at him in surprise. "It's where I am from. My farm, my tavern, my friends."

"I have no yearning to return to Italy. Rome has done me no favours. And what about these two? They aren't Romans. Enslaved and taken from their countries. Sica, don't you want to go home?"

Sica stared at Curtius, then turned to Carbo, confusion in her eyes.

Carbo's expression hardened.

"I am returning to Italy. I have business with the man who sent me here."

"Then you are on your own. I'll take these two into the heart of Sicily. We can hide out, live off the land, maybe steal enough so we can afford to get back into society. And there have been slave rebellions in Sicily in the past. Imagine if we could get the other slaves to rise up with us!"

"Those rebellions didn't end well, if I remember correctly."

"Who cares? We can look after ourselves. With or without you Carbo."

Carbo looked around at the others. Orobazes looked confused, as usual. Sica looked torn. Curtius folded his arms.

Carbo picked up a leather sack, and stuffed a loaf of bread and the hacksaw into it. He made a length of twine into a belt, and put the knife through it. Then he walked to the door, opened it, and started walking, a marching pace, without looking back.

He had maybe gone twenty yards before he heard light, rapid footsteps behind him. Sica appeared at his side, gave his arm a squeeze, and walked with him. Shortly afterwards, heavier footsteps came, and Orobazes ran up, puffing from the exertion.

"Wait!" Curtius voice carried to them. Carbo turned, and Curtius approached, shoulders down, expression resigned. "You win, I'll come."

Carbo regarded him. "What if I don't want you?"

Curtius looked taken aback. "But, you need me."

"No, I don't," said Carbo. "Ever since we met, you have been a boil on my arse. The food, the women. Always moaning. Not pulling your weight. Meru is dead because you didn't help us meet our target."

"That's not my fault," said Curtius defensively. "We were never going to hit that quota."

"We don't know that. We might have made it, or at least close enough to avoid the stoning."

"Come on, Durmius had it in for us. He was going to make an example of us from the moment we arrived."

Carbo shook his head. "You aren't a team player," he said. "We are better off without you around."

"No," said Curtius, his voice rising in pitch and volume. "You need another man who can fight if you run into trouble with the guards or locals."

"You abandoned me!" roared Carbo into Curtius' startled face.

"No, I..."

"You left me, in the tunnels. You ran and left me to die. Now you are on your own." Carbo turned away.

"Go then," yelled Curtius. "See how far you get. You are only getting rid of me so you can fuck that girl in peace."

Carbo whirled, a solid punch connecting squarely in the centre of Curtius' face. One blow was enough to knock him onto his back. Carbo stood over him, fists clenched.

"Get up," he roared. "Get up and say that again."

Curtius cowered back, holding his broken nose as it poured blood.

Sica placed a hand on his arm. He pushed her away angrily, then saw her alarmed expression. He took a deep breath, unclenched his fists.

"I'm sorry, Sica." He looked down at Curtius. The stricken man looked up at him anxiously.

"Please, Carbo. I can't do this on my own." He held out his hand. Carbo looked at it for a while, then grabbed it and heaved Curtius to his feet.

"From now on, you do as I say," said Carbo, voice low but firm. "And if I need you, you had better damn well be there."

"You're the boss, Carbo," said Curtius gratefully.

Carbo nodded. "It looks that way." He turned and resumed his march.

# CHAPTER XX

Vespillo stepped down from the carriage Zosimus had helped them rent in Messana, and held a hand out for Marsia. She ignored him and jumped down, a little heavily, sending up a splash of mud. Vespillo rolled his eyes at the mule driver that Zosimus had insisted accompany them. The mule driver motioned for them to stay by the cart and approached the guard at the gates of the perimeter fence surrounding the mines. He passed the guard the letter of introduction that Zosimus had told them he would provide, then beckoned them over. Vespillo addressed the guard in a firm voice.

"Who is in charge here?"

The guard eyed him suspiciously. "Who wants to know?"

"Lucius Vedius Vespillo, tribune of the vigiles."

The guard wasn't as well informed as Zosimus about the limits of the vigiles authority, and he looked impressed.

"Durmius is the overseer. He runs the place."

"What's your name?"

"Lartius, sir."

"Take me to him then, Lartius." Vespillo's tone was military and brooked no argument.

"Yes sir."

Lartius led them through the compound. Vespillo took in the lines of dirty, exhausted slaves marching to work, the thick fumes belching from smelting furnaces, the ramshackle huts he presumed served as accommodation for the workforce. His gut clenched at the thought of proud Carbo, reduced to a slave, working in these conditions. Hopefully, his bondage would soon be at an end. Horrendous as the conditions were, they weren't enough to break a man like Carbo in such a short space of time. Maybe in weeks, or months, he would succumb, but not yet, not Carbo.

Lartius took them to one of the few stone buildings and knocked. Another guard opened the door, and Lartius said, "There is a tribune here to see the overseer."

They were shown into a small atrium, where they stood. After a few moments, a bald, hook-nosed man appeared. He looked them up and down, then beckoned them into his tablinum. He offered them both seats, then sat behind his desk. The guard passed him the letter, which he took without reading.

"I am Durmius, head overseer. What can I do for a tribune of the legions?"

Vespillo wondered whether to correct him, and decided against. This looked like the sort of man who would be impressed by rank.

"I am Tribune Lucius Vedius Vespillo. I have come to find the whereabouts of a man who was wrongly enslaved."

"They all say they were wrong enslaved, Tribune. Can you be more specific?"

"His name is Gaius Valerius Carbo."

Durmius broke the seal on the note that Zosimus had sent, scanned the contents, then put it to one side.

"You travelled with Zosimus, who recommends I listen to you. So what is your interest in this Carbo?"

"That need not concern you. All you need to know is that he was enslaved in error, and I want him freed."

Durmius pressed his palms together and touched the tip of his fingers to his long nose.

"It's not as simple as that, I'm afraid. Error or not, if he is a slave here, it is not in my power to release him. That would involve a loss of money for the mine owners, and they would not tolerate it. His emancipation would require an edict from Rome."

"We can compensate you financially. And by 'you' I mean both the mine owners, and you personally. I will take care of the emancipation myself."

"I see. And how much 'compensation' might be involved?"

"The going rate for a mine slave, for the mine owners. The same again for yourself, for your trouble."

"Well, I'm sure we could arrange something. Carbo, you say?" He pulled a scroll from a drawer, unrolled it, and ran his finger down the page, reading.

"Ah, Carbo. Oh. Oh dear. I'm very sorry."

"What is it?" asked Vespillo, an ominous tension rising inside him.

"I'm afraid your Carbo is dead. A mine collapsed, three days ago. Killed the entire working party."

Marsia let out a cry, pressed her hand to her mouth. Durmius looked at her curiously.

"I'm sorry your trip has been wasted."

"Dead?" Vespillo shook his head incredulously. "He can't be, not Carbo."

"Mining is dangerous. These things happen. It's tragic."

"I want to see the body," said Marsia.

Durmius raised his eyebrows. "And you are...?"

"Never mind who she is," snapped Vespillo. "The body."

Durmius shook his head sadly. "Regretfully, they were all buried under tons of rubble. It hasn't been safe yet to try to dig them out."

Vespillo sat back, squeezed his eyes shut, put a hand in his hair. Was it really over? After all the two of them had been through together?

"It's not true," said Marsia.

"Marsia," said Vespillo, his voice soothing. "I know what he meant to you."

"No. He is not dead. This man is lying."

Vespillo stood, taking Marsia by the arm.

"I'm sorry, Durmius. Grief easily turns to anger and blame. Thank you for your time." He shook the overseer's hand, then ushered Marsia towards the door.

"I just wish I had had happier news for you. Safe journey home."

Vespillo guided Marsia out of the overseer's house.

"No, Vespillo. He isn't dead. I know it, here." Marsia thumped her chest.

Vespillo sighed, and Lartius escorted them back towards the gate. The grim industry all around, the human misery and the desecration of the landscape summed with the despair in his heart, and he fought the urge to just fall to his knees and scream. Instead, he forced himself to make conversation with Lartius.

"The guards here are all legionaries?" he asked.

"No," said Lartius. "This mine is privately owned, so we are employed by the mine owner. Some senator who lives in Rome and never visits."

"I've been to some harsh places in my time in the legions, but this has got to be one of the worst."

Lartius looked despondent. "The pay is good. The slave women are a bit rough, but we are isolated out here. Can't exactly nip out to the local brothel after the shift finishes. I'm just doing this until I have saved enough to set myself up in business. I'm a carpenter by trade."

"I can see this isn't a job you would want to do for long."

"It's pretty dull. Unless we get an escapee. Then some of us get out of here for a while. Not me this time, though. I wasn't chosen for the seach party."

Vespillo looked at him sharply. "Someone has escaped. Do they know who?"

"Maybe. If they do, they haven't told me."

They reached the gate. Marsia was trying to catch Vespillo's eye, but he was carefully avoiding her gaze. He stopped and leaned against the fence casually.

"How do they go about tracking the escapees down then?"

"The dogs follow the scent if they can. Otherwise they just spread the net as wide as they can, question the locals. There isn't much shelter nearby, so there are only so many places they can go."

"Think you will catch this one?"

The guard shrugged. "There are a few of them apparently. They've been gone three days, that's longer than most. But I think they are closing in on them. One of my mates was in the search party. He twisted his ankle, so he came back this morning. He said they passed through a small village, to the north east, a couple of days ago. Not moving very fast. I guess you wouldn't, not without decent shoes, and knowing where you are going, and what with trying to stay out of sight and everything."

"North east? Towards Messana."

"I guess so. Nearest port. Why are you so interested?"

"Just talking." Vespillo mounted the carriage, held out a hand to Marsia, who ignored him and pulled herself up to sit beside him. He picked up the reins.

"Good to meet you, Lartius. Hope you get out of here soon."

"Me too, sir, me too."

Vespillo flicked the reins, and the horse pulled away.

Durmius re-read the letter that Zosimus had sent him, and shook his head at the captain's stupidity. He had brought this interfering Tribune right to the heart of their criminal enterprise, no doubt taking decent money to do so, and then told Durmius to take him and his slave into captivity and put them into the mines. And then he had had the cheek to demand half of their value, for delivering them to him.

The note had clarified that Vespillo was a Tribune of the vigiles, not of the legions, and so had virtually no power. There was almost nothing he could do to hurt Durmius, and the setup they had. Even if he managed to trigger a more formal investigation, he would get wind of it from his contacts before it started. He could quietly dispose of the less legitimate workers here long before an official could arrive to start asking questions, and leave the legally acquired slaves to man the mines until the investigation was over.

Yes, almost nothing to hurt him. Unless he found Carbo. A living witness, a survivor of the mines, who had been wrongfully imprisoned. That could make things very difficult.

But it was in hand. Naked, unarmed, in inhospitable terrain, pursued by his men and their dogs. Carbo had no chance of escape.

Pinaria walked stiffly home from her shift, through the dark streets of Nola. Her back was aching, between her legs was stinging, and there was a taste of bile and alcohol in her throat, where the wine had failed to stem her nausea. Still, her purse jangled with a healthy amount of new coins.

She hated working in the brothel, hated coming home to her husband too tired and sore and frankly revolted by the thought of any more sex to attend to his needs. She knew that he knew where she went, that it shamed him that he could not earn a living for her and their children himself, that she had to be a prostitute by night, as well as a seamstress by day. But she didn't blame him. He had lost an eye and a hand fighting for Rome, and she would continue to support him, even if Rome did not.

She heard a noise behind her. She stopped, and the sound stopped. Footsteps? Was someone following her? She turned, but could see nothing in the shadows that the faint starlight cast. She carried on, breath quickening, and heard the distinct sound of padding steps behind her. She hurried her pace, and the steps quickened too. She began to run, and heard the steps galloping, closing. It was obvious her follower had her outpaced, so she spun to face her assailant.

A large, skinny dog stepped out of the shadows, bared teeth white in the dim light. It stopped before her, legs gathered beneath it, ready to spring. It gave out a low growl that seemed to permeate her body.

Her foot twisted on a loose cobblestone, and she nearly stumbled. She tottered for a moment, kept her balance, then reached down and picked up the stone. The dog leaped, and as it did so, Pinaria brought the stone round in a wide swing, connecting with the dog's head. Its leap missed her, and it landed clumsily, yelping. It spun to face her again, lips pulled back, eyes blazing. It seemed to calculate the odds for a moment. Then it turned, and slunk away.

She leaned back against the wall at the corner of the street, closing her eyes and saying a brief prayer of thanks to Fortuna.

A woman's scream came from around the corner. Fearfully, she peeked around. A few short feet away, illuminated by the glow of a lamp from a high window, a man wearing an actor's mask and holding a bloody knife stood over the sprawled body of an elderly man. She knew immediately it was one of the bandits that had been the talk of the town. The young woman with him screamed again, the scream turning to a gurgle as the knife plunged into her chest.

Pinaria put a hand to her mouth, desperate to run, but unable to tear her eyes away from the scene. The masked man knelt down, rummaged through the man's clothing, and came up with a small purse. He pushed the mask back onto the top of his head, to give him a better view of his prize.

Pinaria took in an involuntary but soundless gasp of air. That man had paid for her services only the night before. She pulled her head back around the corner, and hurried away before she was discovered.

Carbo stroked his fingers around his neck, trying not to pick at the long scab. Orobazes had not been gentle when he had sawn off Carbo's neck collar, and had opened up a long wound in the skin. They had all used the hacksaw to work at each other's shackles at hands and feet and throat during rest periods. It was tough, slow work, and they had to be careful not to break the small saw. But they were finally all free of the trappings of slavery. At least the most visible ones. Orobazes had a brand on his upper arm, but his tunic concealed it.

Carbo thought he could smell sea air. They were staying off the roads, avoiding the small towns nestling between the hills in the rugged terrain. The rocky countryside and scrub afforded them some shelter at night, but more than once they had heard the baying of hounds, and had had to find hiding places during the day, cowering beneath bracken and bramble like mice evading a prowling owl. Although travelling at night made sense regarding avoiding their pursuit, the treacherous footing made it impractical. Their food had run out the day before, and hunger pains wracked them all.

Finally though, Carbo thought their journey, or at least this stage of it, might be drawing to a close. Seagulls wheeled overhead, and in the distance, he could just make out the smoke from a substantial settlement.

"Messana," he said. "It must be."

The others were too tired and hungry to respond. They trudged along behind him, watching where they placed their feet to avoid sprains and breaks. He looked up at the sky. The sun was past its zenith, descending towards the horizon. He hoped they could make it before nightfall.

The sound of howling dogs reached him, closer than he had heard since the time they had disguised their scent in the stream. Sica looked at him in alarm. Orobazes turned in the direction of the sound, scanning the horizon.

"Let's move it. We need to reach the town, before they find us. We can lose them there, and then start looking for a boat."

The four fugitives put their heads down, pulled their cloaks and tunics tighter against the wind, and resumed their march. They followed goat trails around rocky hills, fought their way through scrubby bushes, slid down slopes of scree. All the time the sounds of pursuit grew closer.

"They are definitely onto us," said Curtius, a hint of panic in his voice.

"It won't be much further," said Carbo, remembering his mother telling him the same when she took him on shopping trips to the Forum Holitorium near the Campus Martius, where she said the best value vegetables in all the Empire were on sale.

There was no reply, as they all conserved their energy. The fast pace Carbo had set them would be a stroll for a seasoned legionary, but these were civilians, weakened by their recent ordeals, without the benefit of the time it takes for those ordeals to toughen them up. Carbo himself was no legionary in his prime either. Marching made the old spear wound in his leg ache, and his limp became more exaggerated.

They crested a hill, and suddenly, below them, was Messana. The outskirts of the port were maybe two or three miles away, he judged. Beyond was the part of the Mare Nostrum known as the Straits of Messana and beyond that the Italian peninsula. The sun was out, visibility was good, and he could clearly see the lighthouse.Even, if he squinted, he could imagine the statue of Neptune standing on the dome that topped the tower.

A cry carried to him on the wind, and he turned. He raised a hand to his eyes to shade the sun, and saw, standing on the peak of a hill behind them, a guard, holding back a large dog. As he watched, two more joined him, both with dogs, and they pointed towards the fugitives. Carbo realised that they were exposed, outlined against the clear sky behind, and cursed his carelessness. The guards started to descend at a run, the dogs barking excitedly and straining on their leashes. Three more guards appeared behind them.

"We have to run," said Carbo. The others looked at him hopelessly.

"We can't," said Curtius.

"Run or die," said Carbo, and set off.

The pace he set was a slow jog, the equivalent of a double time march. There was no way any of them could maintain a higher speed for the distance they had to travel. He hoped it would be enough.

After maybe half a mile, he risked a glance backwards. The guards who had been less than a mile away when they were spotted had already closed the pace. Fit young men, no blistered feet, daily physical training, but not to the point of exhaustion and bodily damage. With the threat of punishment for failure to capture the fleeing slaves. Carbo knew he was in the race of his life.

His heart pounded, his feet bled, his legs burned, his injury screamed protest at new damage. His lungs cried out for more air, though he was at least grateful he wasn't in the sparse atmosphere of the mines. His injured leg came down on a loose rock, which slid away, causing him to take a heavy tumble. He lay, breathing hard, knowing he must get up, but using the fall as an excuse to get his breath back, even if it was just for a moment.

Two pairs of hands hoisted him unceremoniously to his feet. He looked around at Curtius and Orobazes. Orobazes pointed to Messana, and started to jog again. Stiffly, Carbo followed. Sica settled in beside him, and Carbo now realised that despite his earlier contempt for the marching abilities of the civilians, his age and injuries counted against him, and Sica was actually slowing her pace to his. The sound of barking dogs and excited shouts from the guards drew nearer, but he didn't turn.

"If you can run faster," he gasped, "Run."

Sica shook her head. "Going nowhere without you."

He set his eyes on the port, which drew closer at a painfully slow speed.

"Over there," said Sica, pointing.

In a depression between two hills, Carbo saw a cart track. It wasn't cobbled like a proper Roman road, but it was smooth enough for wheeled traffic, and that meant more than smooth enough for pedestrians. There was no need to avoid frequented routes now they had been spotted, and as they would reach the track before their pursuers, it might give them enough of an edge to reach the town before they were caught.

"This way," said Carbo to the others, and they ran towards the track. By the time they reached it, the guards were no more than a hundred yards behind them, but the gap had increased a little by the time the guards themselves were on the track. The track wound through hills rising either side, so Carbo couldn't judge how far the port was, but he knew it must be less than half a mile, from the last view he had had of it. They rounded a corner, nearly stumbled into a surprised traveller carrying a heavy sack of vegetables, ran on as he stopped and watched them with curiosity.

The guards rounded the corner, not fifty yards behind. Carbo tried to make his legs move faster, but they had nothing left to give him. Curtius ran faster, pulling away from them.

"Keep going, Carbo," said Sica. "Nearly there."

Like his mother, thought Carbo, wryly. He had never believed her either. Curtius leading the way, they rounded another corner. Suddenly, Curtius came to a stop, and Carbo stumbled into the back of him, nearly knocking him over.

"What...?" Carbo looked up, saw what Curtius had seen. Four guards, lined across the road, gladii out. Behind, the pursuers slowed to a walk, and four drew swords, the other delegated to hold the dogs which were obviously trackers not fighters. Carbo looked at the verges of the road. The hills on either side were almost sheer. They could try to climb, but the guards would be on them before they got halfway up.

The guards in front started to advance on them slowly.

"I not go back," said Sica.

Orobazes looked grim, and patted the shaft of his axe into his palm.

The weaponless Curtius hesitated, then reached up to an overhanging tree and snapped off a thick branch. Carbo drew his knife.

"I'm sorry," he said. "I tried."

Curtius nodded to him respectfully. Orobazes put a hand on his shoulder. Sica impulsively threw her arms around him.

"You gave hope, Carbo," she said. "Don't be sorry."

He squeezed her back briefly, then pushed her away, and turned to the guards in front of them.

"We rush these ones," said Carbo. "On my command. You don't need to kill them. Just knock them down, incapacitate if you can, then keep running. Don't stop, for anything."

They gripped their weapons, readied themselves.

"Charge!" roared Carbo, and they ran, as fast as their energy reserves allowed, the three men in front, Sica just behind them. The oncoming guards hesitated at the sight of the onrushing fugitives. They were unarmoured, armour not having been considered necessary for the pursuit of some escaped slaves. One of them gave an order, and they lifted their swords, but these were not trained legionaries, they had no discipline.

As Carbo reached them, he swung his knife two handed, batting away the outstretched sword of the guard he had targetted. He dropped a shoulder and hit the guard in the chest, hurling him backwards three feet. Carbo stooped, and thrust his knife into the guard's throat, then pulled it out to release a bright red spray of arterial blood. To his right, Orobazes swung his axe, cleaving the guard's sword in two. He gripped the man's tunic, and headbutted him in the middle of the face, sending him unconscious to the floor. Curtius pushed past his opponent, neither disarming nor incapacitating him. The guard let Curtius pass, and grabbed Sica who was behind him instead.

Sica thrust out with her knife, nicked the guard's forearm, but the fourth guard who had not been targeted took hold of her arms, and pinned them behind her. The guard she had slashed looked at his bleeding arm.

"Little bitch," he swore, and, too far away to intervene, Carbo watched helplessly as the guard drew his sword back to run her through.

With a loud curse, Curtius threw himself onto the guard's back, grabbing the sword arm and wrestling with him. The guard twirled around, trying to shake Curtius loose, but he gripped him like a wolf on a deer.

The guard holding Sica hurled her to one side, gripped his sword two handed, and plunged it into Curtius' back. With a cry, the thief let go, dropping flat onto the dusty track. Carbo hurled himself forward, knife outstretched, and stood over Curtius' writhing form. The two guards swung at him, but he ducked one blow, parried another with his knife, then twisted his arm, so his knife slid off the guard's blade, and buried with force through the astonished man's mouth and out of the back of his neck. As he stiffened and fell, Carbo released his grip on the knife and grabbed the gladius, by the blade. Though it bit into his hands, drawing blood, he gripped it tight, and swung it in time to parry another swing from the guard still standing.

Untrained, he thought, analysing the fighting, even as he flipped his sword into the air and grabbed it by the hilt. A thrust might have finished him off, as every legionary knew. The swing could be parried. The guard swung at him again, and this time Carbo, holding the sword in both hands, feet set apart in a defensive stance, met the blow with such fury that the guard dropped his weapon in shock. Carbo didn't hesitate and thrust his sword into the guard's unprotected chest, pulling it out and turning to face the next threat.

He stopped.

Orobazes looked ashamed.

"I'm sorry, Carbo," said Sica.

The four pursuing guards, and the one with the dogs, had reached them, encircled the barbarian and the young girl. Three swords pointed at Orobazes' chest and the guard holding Sica had the blade across her throat. As Carbo watched, the guard with the dogs approached, and took Sica's knife and Orobazes' axe from their unresisting hands. Carbo recognised him as Cominius, the guard captain from the mines.

"You run, Carbo," said Sica. "You go free."

"Drop your sword," said Cominius, "Or they die right now."

Orobazes shook his head. Sica beseeched him with tear filmed eyes. Carbo tossed the sword into the dirt.

One of the guards left Orobazes to stand behind Carbo, pressing the tip of his sword painfully into Carbo's back, over his kidneys.

"What shall we do with them?" asked one of the guards.

"Orders were 'dead or alive', weren't they?" said Cominius. "It will be hard work bringing them back alive."

"Yeah," said another guard. "And what if they escape along the way? Then it will be our lives forfeited."

"We're agreed then?" said the Cominius. "Finish them off?"

"Aye," the other guards all chorused.

"Fine. Kill the men first. No point hurting the girl until we have had some fun with her. And yes, Modius, I know you would prefer some fun with the men, but that's too risky."

The other guards chuckled, and Modius, who was restraining Carbo, flushed angrily. "Go suck your own cock, Cominius."

"Get to it then," said Cominius. "The big one first, he is most dangerous."

"Stop!"

The voice was distant, but carried unquestionable authority.

The guards turned. Carbo squinted in the direction of the voice, which emanated from the direction they had arrived. A short, broad man, flanked by a young woman, was running towards them, puffing hard.

"Damn you to Hades, Carbo, why do you always do things the difficult way?"

"Vespillo?" Carbo gaped, incredulous.

Marsia ran full speed at Carbo, flinging her arms around his neck and holding him in a bearhug.

"Master," she wept into his neck. "I told them. I knew you were alive."

The guards stared at the two newcomers.

"Excuse me," said Cominius, frowning.

"Excuse me, sir," corrected Vespillo.

"Excuse me, sir," said Cominius. "But, by Juno's tits, who are you?"

"Tribune Lucius Vedius Vespillo. I'll take things from here."

"But...by whose authority?"

"How dare you question me?" roared Vespillo. "I'll have you and all your men strung up by your balls. This is what happens when you let the mines be run by private companies. Far better when the legions were in charge. Now, I will take custody of this man, unless you want me to summon my first century, and have them instil some legion style discipline into you all!"

"Of course, sir," said Cominius, backing away and nodding to Modius to release Carbo. "It is just the one prisoner that you are taking charge of, is that right?"

"Yes," said Vespillo.

"No," said Carbo.

Vespillo shot Carbo a glance, warning him not to push too far. Carbo stood his ground.

"I believe these prisoners also fall under your juridisction, sir," he said. "They are in a similar position to myself."

Vespillo gave a sharp nod. "As you say. I will take charge of all these prisoners."

"This is...completely unprecedented," said Cominius. "What will I tell the overseer?"

"Tell him that Lucius Vedius Vespillo appreciates his openness and his help, and that I hope I can pay him back one day."

Cominius frowned, searching for a hidden meaning or threat in the statement, but Vespillo regarded him with a neutral expression.

"Do you need any help escorting them further?" asked Cominius, with clear reluctance. "They are very dangerous. They have killed some of my men."

"You have no need to worry on my account," said Vespillo. "Now gather your things, and take your men for burial. I will deal with everything from here."

Carbo bent down to Curtius.

"Curtius. Can you stand?"

"Hurts like a bastard," groaned Curtius through gritted teeth. Carbo turned Curtius over, probed the wound through the rent in his tunic, causing Curtius to swear.

"It's bounced off your ribs and sliced open your shoulder muscle," he said. "You are going to be fine, you lucky bastard." He put a hand under his shoulder, and heaved. Orobazes moved to the other side and helped him get Curtius to his feet.

"Let's get on our way," said Vespillo in a low voice. "Before anyone with more authority shows up."

They left the camp guards trying to rouse their unconscious colleague, and attempting to work out how to get the three dead bodies back to the mining compound. Marsia remained glued to Carbo's side, and Sica and Marsia exchanged suspicious looks.

It wasn't far to the outskirts of Messana. They passed a small cemetery and entered the port. The first tavern they reached, Vespillo ushered them inside, finding a table around which the six of them could sit. The fugitives slumped into the wooden seats as if they were feather padded couches. Curtius groaned as he settled into place, but Carbo saw his face was flush, not pale, and the blood loss seemed to be minimal.

A slave girl came over to take an order, looking around at the dirty, dishevelled group with concern.

"Wine for everyone," said Vespillo, producing a few sestertii. "Not too much water. And bring some food, whatever you have that is hot." The slave girl took the coins, and showed them to the barman, who looked over at the group, then nodded. She returned with six cups of wine. Carbo took a glug. They had been fairly heavy on the water, despite Vespillo's instructions, but Carbo didn't care, and he thirstily drained the cup, feeling the wine warm his guts. Sica took a sip, wrinkled her nose, shrugged, then drank deeply.

Sloppy stew appeared in bowls, with some loaves of bread on a plate. The fugitives ate ravenously, silent apart from the noises of swallowing, chewing and belching. As Carbo mopped up the last of the sauce from his bowl with a piece of bread, he looked up. A sudden realisation hit him, shock and exhaustion having delayed its arrival in his head.

"Vespillo. Am I free? Really?"

Vespillo reached out and gripped his forearm.

"Really, friend."

Marsia grinned and threw her arms around him again, kissing his face, then sitting back down, embarrassed. Sica tutted.

"Would now be a good time for introductions?" asked Vespillo.

"Of course," said Carbo. "This is Orobazes. He doesn't speak Latin. He comes from somewhere in the east. Maybe Parthia? This is Curtius, he is an Italian. And the young lady here is Sica, from Dacia."

"And you were all prisoners in the mines together?"

"We were. This is what remains of my workgroup."

"The rest died in the cave-in?" asked Vespillo.

"How did you know about that?"

"I met that pleasant overseer, Durmius. He told us you had died in the cave-in."

"We didn't," said Curtius.

"I can tell," said Vespillo.

"And how did you find us?" asked Carbo.

"One of the guards was talkative. We heard there were one or more escapees. I didn't know it was you, wasn't sure even whether to follow it up. But Marsia is quite persuasive when she puts her mind to it. We were able to catch up with the search party, then follow at a distance. They outpaced us when they caught sight of you though. I'm just glad we got to you in time."

"So are we," said Carbo.

"Thank you," said Sica. She looked at Marsia. "Both." Marsia inclined her head grudgingly.

"So how did they all end up in the mines?" Vespillo asked Carbo, eyes narrowed. Carbo looked at his fellow escapees. The thief, the fugitive, and the girl who cut off her master's genitals.

"It is of no importance," said Carbo. "Not anymore." Carbo locked eyes with Vespillo, held them.

Vespillo nodded. "No importance," he agreed. "Does anyone want more to eat or drink? We have a boat waiting for us."

"You did what?" yelled Durmius.

Cominius flinched. "He was a Tribune. How could I refuse?"

"You aren't in the legions, you fool. You aren't subject to orders from the military. You don't even know he was a Tribune anyway. He could have been anyone!"

"He had a certain air about him…"

Durmius slapped him round the face, the white mark he left on Cominius' cheek turning slowly red.

"So you just let four slaves go, because he had 'a certain air about him?'"

"Well, yes, sir."

"After the slaves had killed three of your men."

"Well I wasn't happy about it. But he said he had spoken to you."

Durmius looked at him sharply.

"Did he, indeed. And what did he say?"

"He said Lucius Vedius Vespillo appreciates your openness and your help, and that he hopes he can pay you back one day."

Durmius looked thoughtful. How had the man seen through his lies? Had he made himself a formidable enemy? Maybe it was prudent to chalk this one up to experience.

"Shall I go back, sir. See if I can intercept them?"

"No, Cominius," said Durmius. "I think there has been a misunderstanding somewhere. You can go about your duties. In future, though, don't use your own initiative, or obey orders from someone else. You answer only to me."

"Yes, sir." Cominius left, looking relieved.

Durmius mused briefly on Carbo's signficance. He had arrived mysteriously, and had been rescued by someone of minor importance. There was nothing further he could do. But chances were that was the end of it. The vigiles had no jurisdiction here.

His mind moved back to the mine workings. The water table was rising, he would need to allocate more slaves to the pumps. He was a little short of labour after the cave-in and escape, but he had a score more slaves due in a few days. He would just make the ones he had work a bit harder in the meantime. Also, one of the older women was struggling to keep up. She was becoming more of an expense to house and feed than she was worth in labour. He would deal with her in the morning, in front of the other slaves. He smiled at the thought.

# CHAPTER XXI

Carbo and Vespillo walked slowly along the docks, the others limping along behind. They had spoken little since Vespillo's intervention had saved them, Carbo more intent on restoring his energy with food and a good wine. Now, as they got nearer to the boat Vespillo had organised to take them home, he felt himself tremble at the thought of being off this accursed island.

Vespillo noticed and put a hand on Carbo's shoulder. "How bad was it?" he asked.

Carbo said nothing, eyes fixed on the horizon. Vespillo sighed dropped his hand.

"It was bad," said Carbo.

Vespillo waited.

"I'm a strong man, Vespillo. You know what I have been through. I don't think I would have lasted much longer there."

Vespillo kept silent, waiting for his friend to talk in his own time.

"The people down there, the slaves. They are treated worse than animals. Worked to death, then thrown into a pit, while new meat is shipped in to replace the losses. All so we can have our silver cups and our fountains supplied by lead pipes."

"It's meant to be like that, Carbo. For most there, it's a punishment. A death sentence, just like being thrown to the beasts. Except slower, and less entertaining for the crowds. But more use to the rich."

Carbo shook his head. "Many of them there were free, or slaves that had been stolen from better circumstances. But regardless, no one deserves to live like that. Or die like that."

A seagull wheeled overhead, raucous cry answered by nearby companions, drowning out the shouts of the dockworkers.

"I wondered at first why he didn't just kill me," said Carbo. "But he had a reason He wanted me to know utter defeat, and pure suffering, before I died."

Vespillo looked at Carbo. "He? Who? You know who did this?"

Carbo nodded. "Curtius, used to work for him."

"Who is he, Carbo?" asked Vespillo urgently. "Who is Atreus?"

"Blaesus," said Carbo.

Vespillo sucked in his breath.

"Blaesus, the nobleman in the villa on the next farm?"

Carbo nodded.

"Blaesus, the father of Quintus?"

Carbo nodded again.

Vespillo bit his lip, the implications churning through his mind.

"So let me get this straight. Blaesus is Atreus, the bandit who attacked us when we first arrived. Whose brother you killed. Who murdered Rufa!"

Carbo nodded. Another awful thought dawned on Vespillo

"Who now commits his crimes with his son? Oh no. Could it be...?"

"I've been turning it over in my head. Over and over, as I slammed my pick into the rock, as I stared into the darkness in my workgroup's hut. Blaesus has two sons. Menelaus could be either one."

"Surely not Quintus? That boy thinks the world of you. He fought alongside you against the bandits."

"That was coincidental. The bandits weren't to know Quintus was with us when they spied us from afar. He had been abroad for years, and grown a beard, so Blaesus may not have recognised him immediately. But he certainly spared him. At that point, I'm sure Quintus knew nothing. But when Blaesus' brother died, and he wanted another partner, who else could he trust but a son?"

"But Quintus helped us."

"Did he? He wasn't with us when I was taken. Maybe he was there though, wearing a comedy mask. And how did Blaesus know about our ambush in the plaza in advance, so he could turn it against us?"

Vespillo gritted his teeth, shaking his head in denial.

"But he seems so earnest. So true."

"They wear actors' masks. I think their dramatic abilities run deeper than that. Look at Blaesus, to all the world a hedonistic, frail old man. I can tell you, matching swords with him, he is not frail. He is strong and swift. You know, even his stutter disappears with the mask on."

A sudden thought struck Carbo. "Does Quintus know you came here to look for me?"

"Actually no. Marsia and Quintus seemed to have something of a falling out. They had started to get strangely close, you know. Anyway, since then, I have seen less of Quintus, and when we found out you were in Sicily, I didn't think to send word back to Quintus and Lutorius. Just as well, I suppose."

"If it was Quintus, I will kill him, Vespillo."

"Blaesus has another son," said Vespillo. "It could be him."

"I really hope so," said Carbo. "But I will find out."

They reached the boat, and Carbo stared in disbelief.

"You came here on this?"

Vespillo grimaced. "I'm sorry, I know you might not want to travel in this boat again, but it is the quickest way home. The captain was very helpful, once I had paid him enough."

A portly man strode down the gangplank, caught sight of them, and blanched.

"Captain," said Vespillo. "Our mission was successful. Thank you for your help. We are here for the return journey we paid for."

Carbo stepped forward and punched the captain hard on the jaw. Zosimus' legs buckled, and he crumpled to the deck heavily. From out of nowhere, Sica appeared, leaping on him like an angry cat, clawing at his face, biting his ear. Vespillo hauled her off with difficulty, receiving a couple of scratches himself in the process. He pressed her into Carbo's arms, who hesitated, then clutched her.

Marsia had materialised at Carbo's side. Sica's fury evaporated as quickly as it had appeared, and she leaned into Carbo's chest and started to sob. Marsia took her hand, and led the girl gently away.

Vespillo gaped at Carbo. "What was that about?"

"He was in on it, Vespillo. He is part of the whole system. Blaesus gave me to him, and he paid off the dock official to keep him quiet. He shut us up in that stinking hold down there, let us suffer in unspeakable conditions. He threw a slave overboard just to bargain for an extra price. And then he handed us over to rot in the mines. Vespillo, he deserves to die."

Vespillo stared at the recumbent captain.

"And what about Marsia and I, captain? You looked surprised to see us. Weren't we supposed to return from our visit to the mines?"

He kicked the man hard in the chest, causing him to roll up and groan.

It was Marsia who stepped forward, and gently calmed the two outraged men.

"We need him. To get us back to Neapolis. Let the stationarii deal with him when we are home."

Zosimus was clutching his ribs and moaning softly.

"I'll kill you," said Zosimus. "You and that little savage girl."

Carbo put a foot on his chest.

"No," said Carbo. "You will sail this boat back to Neapolis. And if you get us there quickly, and you keep out of my sight, I will possibly let you live. Possibly, mind you."

A movement in the corner of his eye caught Carbo's attention. A sailor had crept up behind Vespillo and Carbo, out of the field of view of Marsia and Sica. In his hand he held a short, sharp blade. But he was unmoving, eyes wide. Carbo looked beyond the sailor, and saw Curtius behind, his own blade jammed up under the sailor's ear. Curtius smiled at Carbo, and Carbo acknowledged his help with a dip of his head.

"That goes for everyone on this ship," said Carbo, raising his voice to the men on the vessel. "Do your jobs, get us home, and you have nothing to worry about. Upset me and, well…" He looked around, catching the eyes of as many of the sailors as he could, though most had their gazes cast down on the deck. "Well, let us say, little has happened to me lately that would give me cause to be merciful." He looked down at Zosimus. "Am I understood?" Zosimus looked momentarily defiant, but Carbo leaned forward so his weight transferred to the foot on Zosimus' chest. He felt ribs protesting beneath his shoe.

"Yes, yes," gasped Zosimus. "Understood."

Carbo let the weight rest there a moment longer, then stepped back. Zosimus sat up, gasping for breath, holding his chest. Carbo turned back to hold the side rail, and watched the horizon once more.

Lutorius held Calidia's hand tight, looking earnestly into her eyes.

"You are absolutely sure about this?"

"Yes," she said, dabbing her eyes with a small cloth. "Pinaria is a very sound woman. An excellent seamstress. You should see what she does with Asellio's old tunics. As good as new."

"Being a good seamstress does not make her a reliable witness."

"But she was right there. She saw him kill that man and his daughter, just feet away. Saw him take off his mask."

"And it was Publius Sempronius Blaesus. He is Menelaus?"

"It was Publius, yes. He is Menelaus if you say so."

Lutorius let out a whistle. "Then Atreus is that grumpy old sod in the villa near Carbo's farm, Gaius Sempronius Blaesus."

"Again, if you say so." Calidia squeezed Lutorius' fingers. "My love, you must do something."

"But what can I do? You have already taken this to Asellio. What was it he said exactly?"

"He just dismissed everything. Said there wasn't enough evidence. That even if there was, it was not the concern of the stationarii. And even if it was, he didn't have the manpower to deal with it."

"So what do I do?"

"You are an optio in the stationarii. You must be able to do something."

"Well, he hasn't spoken to me about this, so he hasn't given me a direct order not to do anything."

"There, you see. I knew you would come up with a plan. Lutorius you are wonderful."

She kissed him hard on the lips, and he took the prize, even as his mind started to turn over the situation. If only Vespillo was here to help. If only Carbo wasn't missing, presumed dead. But she was right, he was an optio. He had some authority. He just had to use it without being countermanded by Asellio. Well, he had had some practice sneaking around behind Asellio's back. He would work this out.

Tomorrow.

He pushed Calidia back onto her bed, and slid her dress up around her waist, rolling between her legs as his lips sought hers.

Lutorius waited in the beautiful atrium. The afternoon sun cast a beam of light through the impluvium, brightly illuminating part of a fresco on one wall. He tried to keep himself erect and professional-looking, eyes straight ahead, though his heart was hammering with excitement and nerves in his chest. The two stationarii he had bought with him looked around in wonder, however, taking in the marble busts, the Sileni statues, the statuettes of agricultural youths, and the statue of Pan indulging in grotesque bestiality, with slack jaws.

Publius entered. Lutorius recalled being introduced to Blaesus' son in the past, and recognised him, though they had exchanged few words. There seemed to be something alive and vibrant in Publius' expression as he reached out and shook Lutorius' hand.

"Optio Lutorius. How may I help the stationiarii?"

"Thank you for agreeing to see me, sir. May I ask you a few questions?"

"Of course." Publius sat on a stone bench, putting one foot up, and flicking his fingers for his slave to bring him a cup of wine. He made no move to offer a seat or a drink to his guests.

"Where were you the night before last?"

Publius expression took on a vague air of irritation.

"What business is it of yours?"

"I'm investigating a crime, sir. I would be very grateful if you would answer."

Publius waved a dismissive hand. "I don't recall precisely. That seems a very long time ago. I stayed at home I believe."

"Can anyone else confirm that?"

"I'm afraid my brother Quintus has taken himself off somewhere in a sulk about a woman. And Jupiter knows where my father is, some business deal no doubt. The slaves can tell you I was here though."

"They will testify to that under torture?"

Publius' eyes narrowed. "Slaves will testify to whatever you want them to, when they are tortured."

"Publius Sempronius, we have testimony from a witness. You were seen assaulting and murdering a woman in Nola the night before last."

Publius gaped. "It's not possible. It was dark, no one could have seen… I mean, it was night time, you said so, the person must have mixed me up with someone else."

"I think we should ask you further questions at the statio. Men, bind his hands."

Publius rose to his feet, face twisted in outrage. "How dare you? Do you know who I am? Who my father is? I'll talk to your commanding officer, have you flogged to death for this disrespect."

The two stationarii took his arms and pinned them behind his back, tying his wrists together efficiently.

"Stay with him," said Lutorius. "I'm going to take a look around."

The villa was enormous, with its huge peristylium, its ample triclinium, its numerous rooms for slave accommodation, its well-equipped kitchen. But the part in which Blaesus' family lived was actually relatively modest - a bedroom each, a small tablinum. Lutorius rifled briefly through some papers in Blaesus' study, but they seemed to relate mainly to business matters, and the odd piece of personal correspondence was uninteresting. He found the master bedroom, and reclining on the bed was a beautiful Egyptian looking slave. She sat up at the sight of him, drawing the bedsheets around her lightly clad form.

"Is this Blaesus' bedroom, slave?" asked Lutorius.

She nodded. He looked around, and his eyes lighted on a chest. It was unlocked and he flipped the lid. Just a few items of clothing and jewellery.

"Where is Publius' room?" he asked.

"Publius is in trouble?" she asked, timourous.

"Maybe. Show me his room."

The girl stood, her breast band and loin cloth the only clothing concealing her stunning body. Lutorius tried not to stare, feeling suddenly guilty about looking at another woman than Calidia, then feeling stupid given Calidia was married to another. The slave girl took him to another bedroom, and showed him in. There was little to see on a cursory glance, luxurious bed, erotic frescoes, ornate oil lamps, another chest at the foot of the bed, which again contained only jewellery and clothes. He sighed in frustration. He didn't know what he was expecting, but he feared the testimony of the prostitute was never going to be enough to convict Publius.

The girl studied him for a little while, then bent over by the bed. He couldn't help admiring her round buttocks protruding from beneath her loin cloth, and he bit his tongue to help him concentrate. She twisted two knobs that were part of the decoration of the frame that supported the feather mattress. A small drawer slid out. Lutorius stepped forward, reached inside, and drew out a small knife, its blade dark with congealed blood. Next to it was an actor's mask. A comedy mask.

Lutorius picked the items up and returned to the atrium. He held them up for Publius to see.

"Publius Sempronius, I found these in your bedroom. Do you have anything to say?"

Publius paled. "No, they aren't mine, you planted them."

"Publius Sempronius Blaesus, I am arresting you for murder. Come on lads, let's get him back to the statio."

CHAPTER XX

"You did what?" roared Asellio.

Lutorius stood straight, not flinching at the furious tone.

"I arrested Publius Sempronius Blaesus on suspicion of murder, sir. And I believe he is the one going by the name Menelaus, the bandit."

"Publius Sempronius Blaesus? Son of Gaius Sempronius Blaesus, the richest man in the area?"

"I have good evidence, sir. A witness, and the knife and the mask."

"I don't care if you have the high priest of Jupiter Optimus Maximus testifying against him. You need to let him go."

"I can't do that, sir. Besides, I suspect that his father is the other bandit, the one called Atreus."

"Of course he is," snapped Asellio.

"Sir? You knew?"

"I have my sources."

Lutorius knew that wasn't true, Asellio was a lazy and ineffectual commander, with no interest in investigative work. His eyes widened as realisation hit him.

"He paid you off!"

"What? How dare you?" But Asellio wouldn't meet Lutorius' eyes.

"Release him," said the centurion. "You don't have enough evidence."

"No, sir. The courts can decide on the evidence."

"Are you disobeying an order?"

Lutorius leaned forward, putting his hands on Asellio's desk so he could look down at him.

"Don't push me, sir. If I take my doubts about you to the town council, would you really want them looking into your affairs?"

"You would love that, wouldn't you?" yelled Asellio. "Have me arrested too, disposed of, so you could carry on with my wife? Oh, you may think me stupid and blind, but I do have ears, and at least some of my subordinates remain loyal to me."

Lutorius stood, speechless. There was a knock at the door, and one of the stationarii entered.

"Letter for you, sir, the delivery boy said it was urgent before he shot off."

Asellio ripped open the letter, read, then tossed it onto his desk, slumping backwards in his chair.

"It's too late," he said. "Blaesus says let him go, or he is coming to get him. And he says if he has to come and get him, then afterwards he will let his men loose in the town. "

"Sir, we have a century of stationarii. Trained legionaries. What does Blaesus have, but a group of hired thugs?"

"Let him go, Lutorius."

"No. Sir."

"Then you are on your own."

Asellio stood.

"What do you mean?"

"The men are getting unfit and lazy. It's time I took them on maneuvres. I think

I will lead them on a day's route march. Toughen them up."

"Are you serious?"

"Yes, I'm serious," snapped Asellio. "If you want to punish this man so badly, then it's on your head. The fate of the town, and my whore wife, will be down to you."

Asellio marched out of the room, leaving Lutorius staring into space in disbelief.


"He'll kill you, you know. And not in one of those good ways. Cut throat. Blade in the heart. Nothing quick and painless. If I know my father, the upset to his pride will require a rather more... sophisticated approach."

Lutorius sat outside the cell, gripping his balled fist with his other hand in an effort not to show his tremors. He couldn't believe Asellio had really done this. He had always suspected his superior officer was useless, but corrupt? Or was it cowardice, or even his own way of getting revenge on Lutorius and Calidia?

Publius laughed, and the laugh echoed around the cellar that had been converted into the holding area for the stationarii when they had requisitioned this house for their headquarters. Lutorius pulled out a whetstone and ran it along his gladius, the familiar routine going some way to calming his nerves. The statio was ridiculously inadequate for defence, had never been conceived as any sort of fortress. It was merely an administrative headquarters and barracks for the legionaries detached to keep peace in the area. There had been no military action on the Italian peninsula for decades.

So how was one man supposed to hold the place against an army, even if it was only made up of brigands, bandits and thugs. And what of the townfolk? Would Blaesus really follow through with his threat to sack the town after he had rescued his son. Now he knew that Blaesus and Atreus were one and the same, he feared that he would. His stomach suddenly cramped at the thought of what that would mean for Calidia. Had his stubborness brought this awful fate down upon the woman he loved?

A loud hammering came from the main double doors upstairs. Lutorius jumped, and Publius laughed again through the barred window of his cell door.

"Like a frightened kitten," he said. "And now my father is here, and it's all over. You had your chance to let me go, your chance to run. Now you are a dead man."

"If I'm a dead man, then maybe I should kill you now." Lutorius hefted his gladius and advanced towards the cell. Publius backed off, sudden doubt in his eyes. "Come on, Publius. Or Menelaus, if you prefer to hide behind a name and a mask like a coward. Tell me, what have I got to lose."

"You would have to open the cell door and come and get me."

"Is that supposed to scare me? You think that I, a seasoned veteran of the legions, armed with a freshly sharpened sword, couldn't make short work of an unarmed, out of shape, bored little rich boy like you?"

The hammering came again, more urgent. He heard shouts. Lutorius sighed. If he was going to kill him, he would have done so by now. He wanted to see justice done, not murder. He supposed he had better face Blaesus. The man still had to break down the barred statio doors. Maybe he had some breathing space to negotiate. To threaten Publius, to escape with a sword at the young man's throat.

He ascended the stone steps from the cellar, walked past the deserted sleeping quarters, and the open door to Asellio's empty office, and approached the main entrance. The hammering came again.

"By all the gods, Lutorius will you open these cursed doors, you cocksucker!"

Lutorius hesitated. That voice. It wasn't Blaesus. It sounded like...

He put his eye to the crack between the two doors. The light was occluded as a face appeared before his own, separated by the thickness of the wood. He smelled sea salt and garum and onions.

"Carbo?"

"Lutorius," yelled Carbo. "Are you deaf? Get these doors open."

In disbelief, Lutorius heaved the wooden bar out of the way, and yanked open the doors, noon day sunlight flooding into the gloomy interior, making him blink. Carbo stood before him, complexion grimed, hair unkempt, eyes tired and haunted. Beside him stood Vespillo, regarding him with a lopsided smile. Relief flooded over him.

"Lutorius," said Carbo. "Tell me, by Hercules' cock, what is going on."

Carbo had waved away all Lutorius' questions about his whereabouts and his escape, and Vespillo told him to leave well alone. Vespillo told Lutorius that they had come to the stationarii to tell them about Blaesus, and found the town shuttered, and the statio door barred.

The three of them sat in Asellio's office, and Lutorius told them about how he had caught Publius, the witness, and the mask.

When Carbo heard that Publius was Menelaus, he had exhaled, his shoulders relaxing as at least one burden was taken from him.

"I was sure it was going to be Quintus," he said. "I shouldn't have doubted the lad."

"You have precious little reason to trust at the moment, Carbo," said Vespillo consolingly. "Don't blame yourself." Vespillo looked at Lutorius. "Where is Quintus anyway? He wasn't at the farm, and you said he wasn't at Blaesus' villa."

"I don't know," said Lutorius. "I think he had given up hope. Hope of finding you, hope of... well, there was a woman. He has taken himself off like a wounded wolf, and if Fortuna is with him, he is a long way from here."

"So, Publius will be tried? Executed?" asked Carbo.

"It's not as simple as that. Asellio has gone."

"What do you mean gone?"

"Left. Departed. Training exercise, with all the men."

Carbo and Vespillo looked at each other. "Why would he...?" began Vespillo.

"Blaesus," said Carbo. "He's coming for Publius isn't he? So is Asellio corrupt or a coward?"

"Corrupt at least. Maybe a coward too."

"And the reason that all the shops and houses are closed and shuttered?" asked Vespillo.

"They will have seen the stationarii leave, and word will have got out that Blaesus is on his way. He plans to sack the town, once he has rescued Publius. For revenge, or reward for his men, or pleasure. I suppose it makes no difference to the women raped and the old men and children slaughtered."

"Why haven't people fled?"

"I'm sure many have. But it's not easy to evacuate a whole town. Some can't be moved, some won't believe in the threat, some will stay to defend their property."

"How many men has Blaesus got?" asked Carbo.

Lutorius shook his head. "I have no idea. There are as many rough men available as he can afford to pay, so I guess as many as he thinks he needs. With the stationarii gone, maybe he won't be expecting too much of a fight, but I'm sure he will still bring more than enough to finish the job."

"Will the townsfolk help us?"

The optio shook his head. "No chance. They are terrified. They have either fled, or barricaded themselves in their homes."

Carbo considered for a moment, then looked at Vespillo, cocking his head on one side.

"This place isn't defensible," Vespillo said. "It's surrounded by narrow alleys and overlooked by houses. They could burn us out, they could take out those doors with a couple of good axes in moments. Then they could overwhelm us with their numbers."

"I agree," said Carbo.

Lutorius looked from one to the other. "Are you saying we should run?" he said in amazement. "Let Blaesus take back his son?"

Carbo's eyes blazed. "Do you really think I would let the man who helped kill Rufa go free?" he said coldly.

Vespillo put a conciliatory hand on his shoulder. "You know us better, Lutorius. We take Publius to Carbo's farm."

"The farm? How is that better?"

"Firstly, it will draw Blaesus away from the town. It will help keep the citizens safe. And secondly, well. Lutorius, I know you are a legionary, but you haven't seen a lot of active service have you?"

Lutorius grudgingly shook his head.

"Then prepare to witness a Roman army entrenching."

Carbo bucked and jolted on the horse, gripping the reins tightly, despite Vespillo consistently yelling at him to ease off. He knew how to ride, but wasn't a natural, and didn't choose this mode of transport unless desperate. He consoled himself that Publius, gagged and bound hand and foot, and slung over the horse in front of his saddle, was having a considerably more uncomfortable time of it. Carbo had to restrain himself from worsening the young man's discomfort. But he had promised himself he would savour the man's punishment when the time came.

Vespillo rode beside him at an easy trot, and on the other side rode Lutorius, who like Carbo looked uncomfortable, but had the bonus of his woman's arms wrapped around him. Lutorius would not leave without Calidia, and Carbo had reluctantly conceded it made no sense to leave her behind where she could be used as a hostage. If Asellio was corrupt, and knew about Lutorius and Calidia, then he would likely have told Blaesus all about the two of them as well.

"How long till they come for us?" asked Vespillo.

"However long it takes for Blaesus to round up his gang, get them to town, discover we aren't there, grab some poor townsperson to ask which way we went, then head over."

"They will be on foot," said Carbo. "And they aren't legionaries. Getting them to move with any speed will be like herding cats."

"We have at least a few hours then," said Vespillo. He squinted at the position of the sun. "Maybe the rest of the day. If they haven't got to us before sundown, do you think they will attack at night?"

"They are thieves and murderers. I'm sure of it."

Vespillo nodded with satisfaction.

"Good."

Lutorius looked from one to the other, shaking his head.

"I know you two are veterans, and believe me I know you can fight. And I know you have a plan. But do you really think the three of us are a match for the numbers Blaesus is bringing with him?"

Carbo's face was grim, but determined. Vespillo smiled broadly. "The Fates will decide. But in any case, we number more than three."

# CHAPTER XXIII

Dusk had turned to night, the grey clouds that had covered the earlier sunlight now black. There would be no moon tonight. That was a mixed blessing, Carbo thought. But more of a blessing than not. His mind turned to his preparations. Were they adequate? How observant were Blaesus and his men? How many would he bring with him?

Vespillo watched him, and Carbo knew he was reading his mind, was thinking the same things. They had both been in battle many times before, as besieged and besieger. Maybe it wasn't as terrifying as his first time. But usually in battle, they weren't defending their own loved ones.

Severa, Fabilla, Calidia, Theron and Thera were in the cellar, the hatch barred from below, Publius tied up securely with them. They would be safe, while the battle lasted. If the battle was lost though, Blaesus would find them and...

Carbo repressed the thought. It wouldn't help him in the coming fight. He studied his sword, checking the edge was keen. It would be no use to him in the first part of the action to come. Ranged weapons would be more important when defending a position, but that sort of fighting, at a distance, was for auxiliaries. Legionaries fought sword to sword, looking the enemy in the eye and screaming into his face.

They had raided the armoury of the statio before they left. Asellio had taken most of inventory with him, but they had liberated a handful of javelins, two bows and around two score of arrows, as well as three somewhat rusted and blunt gladii. Carbo looked around him. To his right, peering out of one of the windows in the atrium, into the darkness, Vespillo held a bow. He didn't look comfortable with it, but had handled one before.

Sica held the other. With her free hand, she twiddled an arrow in a rapid circle, throwing it in the air still spinning, then catching it on its descent and with one swift movement notching it and drawing the bow. Carbo might have thought she was showing off, but knew that it was just her way of dealing with her nerves. He had been reluctant to let her take part in this fight, but when she had taken one of the bows from him and split an onion at a hundred paces, he had conceded she might be useful.

Of course, if Sica was fighting, Marsia would not be left with the women, children and the old man. She hefted a gladius, patting it into the palm of her hand, face set. Brought up in a martial Germanic tribe before her enslavement, Marsia too could prove important. Carbo's pride was going to take a dent from fighting alongside women, but if the Romans' ancestors, the Trojans, could fight alongside the Amazons, he supposed he could live with it.

To Carbo's left, Orobazes waited stoically, gripping the shaft of a sledgehammer that Carbo had found in a shed. Sica had spent some time explaining what was happening, mainly with sign language. Carbo wasn't sure he had really understood much, but he knew a fight was coming, and he was willing to help.

"Where are they?" muttered Curtius. Curtius also held one of the short swords. The legionary and veterans had helped sharpen them as best they could. When Lutorius had complained they couldn't make gold out of lead, Carbo and the former mine slaves had gone quiet, and Vespillo had cuffed the stationarius around the head for his thoughtlessness.

"Do you think they stopped to sack the town before coming here?" asked Marsia. "We are too far to see the fires aren't we?"

"Man come for son," said Sica. "Not stop for anything else."

Marsia shot her a withering look, but didn't retort.

The front door crashed open, and Lutorius burst in.

"They're coming," he gasped.

"How many?" asked Carbo.

"It was hard to tell in the dark. But I counted ten torches. I think one torch for every four men."

Carbo sucked in breath between his teeth. Forty men? That was surely like taking Orobazes' hammer to a small nut. Blaesus wasn't taking any chances.

But then, Blaesus didn't know what they had prepared for him.

"How far?"

"A quarter of a mile."

"Time for me to go and say hello, then."

Carbo picked up a bright torch, turned, and felt everyone's gaze upon him. Curtius looking shaky but resolute, Orobazes looking calm. Sica and Marsia, looking worried about him. Lutorius looking uncertain, but trusting. Vespillo, like a rock, as always. He held each one's gaze for a moment, then stepped out of the door.

His family was cursed. Atreus knew this, had known it for many years. Since the loss of his wife, the loss of his position, the… loss… of his brother. That's why he had chosen the name Atreus, when he had started his alternative life as a part time bandit. Because they were cursed, just like the House of the Atreides.

He had dared to hope the curse had lifted. With his fortunes restored, his sons becoming adults, maybe the curse would stop with him. Then Carbo had arrived, and killed his other brother.

And now this.

He was sure he had been avenged on Carbo, with a vengeance worthy of Nemesis. He was sure he just had to walk into Nola to collect his eldest son, since he knew Asellio would be gone. And he had walked through the open doors of the statio, to find it empty. Just a note, pinned on Asellio's desk with a knife.

"Come and get your son. You know where I live. Carbo."

His stomach roiled with anger even now at the thought of it. How had the man escaped? He wanted to lash out, to scream. But he didn't. He retained his composure, like the true Roman aristocrat he had been born as. He looked out of the eye slits of his mask, into the darkness, past the circle of light shed by the torchbearers, straining to catch his first sight of Carbo's farm, where he would finally end this. He supposed strictly the mask was superfluous now that his identity was known. He would deal with that problem another time. Asellio would help. For now, the mask felt like part of him, gave him the confidence to be what he needed to be. Tonight, he wasn't Blaesus, he was Atreus.

Around him some forty of the worst men Febrox could find walked with him. Cutthroats, thieves, beggars and murderers. All looking for money, a fight, and then torture and rape.

To his left walked Febrox, his feral grin illuminated by the flickering torchlight to give him a demonic air.

To his right, wearing a comedy mask that Atreus had inconveniently had to find to replace the one taken when that idiot Publius had been captured, was his other son.

Atreus put a hand on Menelaus' shoulder, and gave it a squeeze.

He peered forward. There was a building ahead, and a light. Was that a figure holding a torch?

A loud voice cut through the night air.

"Stay where you are, Blaesus."

Atreus gritted his teeth.

Carbo.

Carbo saw the bandit army approach, making no effort to conceal their presence or their number. They had no need he supposed, with their overwhelming numerical superiority. As they drew nearer, he saw the leader, wearing his tragedy mask. And to Blaesus' right, he saw another figure wearing a mask. A comedy mask. His heart plummeted.

Oh no. Quintus.

It didn't make sense. Quintus and Publius were both Menelaus? Publius was pretending to be Menelaus? There was no time to comprehend it. He took a breath, called out loudly.

"Stay where you are, Blaesus."

He saw Blaesus hold up a hand for his men to stop, saw them raggedly come to a halt.

"Carbo," called back Blaesus. "You are a surprise. This time though, there will be no escape. No prolonged punishment. This time, I will kill you."

"Go back," called Carbo. "Publius will be tried for his crimes. The stationarii will deal with you."

"Give me my son, Carbo, and I will make the deaths of all your loved ones merciful. If I have to fight my way in there, my men will torture and mutilate every man, woman and child that they find. And, I'm sorry to say, some of these men have had a lot of practice at that sort of thing."

"This is between you and me, Blaesus. I killed your brother. You killed my woman. Let's fight it out, man to man."

"How gladiatorial. No, I think I prefer the odds I currently have, which as you can see, are considerably better than one to one."

"Last chance, Blaesus. You will die at my hands, but if you leave now it won't be tonight."

Blaesus turned and muttered something to the figure at his side, that Carbo could now see was Febrox. Febrox gestured, and half a dozen men advanced on Carbo's position at a jog.

Before they had covered half the distance, one of them cried out and clutched his foot, then another. The others stopped, looking down uncertainly.

"Caltrops?" Blaesus laughed. "You will have to do better than a few nails in my men's feet to stop us."

Carbo held his torch up high, then brought it down sharply. At his signal, two flaming arrows arced from the house. One fell short, but the other landed at the feet of the men who had advanced. There was a moment of silence, then a noise like a sharp exhalation as the naphtha soaked dry straw at the men's feet ignited. The men screamed out, tried to run, stepped on more caltrops in their panic and tumbled to the ground. The flames engulfed them as they rolled in terror and agony. Their screams seemed to last an eternity, before the last ones died away. Soon after, the flames died down, the oil and straw rapidly burning itself out. Through the smoke, Carbo saw that Blaesus had not moved.

"You've sealed the fate of everyone in that farm, Carbo," said Blaesus. "And I will keep you alive long enough for you to watch what happens to each one, before I kill you."

Carbo turned and walked back to the farm, Blaesus watching him go in impotent fury. From inside the farmhouse, Carbo watched Blaesus send forward some more men, who stepped gingerly, slowly picking their way through the bent nails they had twisted and scattered that afternoon. Carbo could see in the light of the torches they held up that they were avoiding the sight of the charred corpses around them.

Carbo looked to Marsia. "Are you sure you want to do this?"

Marsia gave him a stern look. "Go then," he said. "And wait for the signal."

Marsia slipped quietly out of a side window, and headed up the steep hill in front and to the right of the farmhouse. She was soon lost in the darkness.

Carbo watched the torches approach, two torchbearers with another six men accompanying them. Reconnaissance in force, they used to call it in the legions, he reflected.

The others were watching Carbo intently as the bandits got closer.

"Do it," hissed Curtius.

"Not yet," said Carbo. "Closer."

"I can hit them from here," said Sica, flexing her bow.

"Save your arrows," said Carbo. "Wait."

He calculated the distance again. It was hard in the dark, but he must not spring the trap too early. They had to get the numbers they were facing down if they were to have any chance.

"Carbo," said Vespillo, seeing the men getting closer still.

"Wait. Wait. Now!"

Sica sent a flaming arrow, the tip wrapped in cloth and soaked in oil, then dipped in flame, high into the air. The advancing men paused, watching to see where it would land, nervously waiting for another conflagration. When the arrow landed and fizzled out, they looked at each other, and Carbo could hear them laugh.

A low rumble reached them, getting louder, from the hill to the right. The advancing bandits turned, looked towards the sound. From out of the darkness, a dozen tree trunks rolled down on them, from where Marsia had cut the ties binding them. They were still gathering speed when they crashed into the screaming men, breaking bones, caving heads and snapping spines.

Carbo could imagine Blaesus' frustration. Would he stop his advance now, wait for light? Carbo doubted it. This wasn't a disciplined legion, this was a bunch of criminals who would scatter if their boredom levels got too high.

In confirmation of Carbo's question, Blaesus sent scouts to the left and right of his position, checking for any more traps that might take them in the flank. The bandits reached bowshot range, and Sica looked at Carbo questioningly. He held a hand up. The bandits drew closer.

"I think I can hit them now," said Vespillo.

"Wait," said Carbo. He could see the nervous bandits, looking around them, wondering where the next assault would come from. But as nothing happened, he saw them gaining confidence, their backs straightening, moving more surefootedly.

"Carbo," said Sica, pulling her bowstring to her ear with two fingers and sighting down an arrow.

Carbo estimated the distance, the wind, factored in the darkness, and the torches that lit up the targets.

"Fire!"

Vespillo and Sica loosed simultaneously, Vespillo's arrow having the distance, but flying wide, Sica's taking the lead bandit straight in the centre of the chest, pitching him backwards with a cry. Before Vespillo had notched another arrow, Sica had released her second into the bandits, the despairing gurgle confirming another kill. Vespillo's next arrow coincided with Sica's third, and this time both struck home. The unshielded bandits hesitated in their advance. If they broke now, Carbo knew, Blaesus would have a hard time of it getting them back together.

"Charge!" yelled Blaesus. Febrox and Menelaus lifted their swords, and front and centre of the bandits, broke into a run, yelling as they ran full speed towards the farmhouse. To their left and right, the rest of the bandits cheered and charged too.

Sica and Vespillo continued to fire, but in moments the bandits had cleared half the distance back to the house.

There was a loud crack, then another, followed by a crash, and screaming. Menelaus and Febrox looked back. To both sides, a deep ditch filled with sharpened stakes that had been concealed by branches had claimed the lives of the front row of bandits. Only those far enough back to halt their momentum, and those running right down the centre pathway that had been left for Carbo's retreat, were spared.

Shrieks filled the air, men writhing, grasping at the stakes that impaled limbs, abdomens and chests. The charge faltered. Febrox looked back towards Blaesus and the remaining bandits. Still maybe a score in total. Sica picked off another. One less. Carbo looked at Blaesus' figure, standing at the back, hesitant.

"On me!" yelled Menelaus. "Stay to the centre. Torch bearers hold your torches high. We are nearly at the door, there can be no more surprises."

Without looking back to see if he had support, Menelaus ran towards the house. The ditch had been around thirty feet from the building, and he covered the distance in seconds, flattening himself against the wall near a corner, where arrows could not reach. The other bandits saw him reach safety and ran together. Sica and Vespillo claimed two more, and Carbo and Curtius launched javelins that wounded another two, but the bandits had arrived. Carbo had no more tricks up his sleeve. Now it was steel on steel.

There was a strange stillness, a hiatus. Blaesus had options now. He could fire the house, force them to come out. But they could retreat to the interior, to the peristylium and then the bandits would still have to come in and get him. He could force entry in the front, or look for another entrance. There were no more doors, and they had boarded the windows, but they would not hold for long.

Blaesus and his men would be coming soon.

Carbo looked around the room. Curtius, Orobazes, Sica. Lutorius the stationarius. Marsia, his loyal slave. Vespillo, his best friend. They all looked at him with fear, held in check by belief. What had he done to deserve such friendship, such confidence. Should he say something? He opened his mouth.

A crash interrupted. The struts of the front door splintered as an axe impacted from the outside. Pause, another crash. Carbo drew his gladius, saw the others grip tight to their weapons. A third crash and the head of the axe came through the wood. Then another crash, this time from behind them. Someone was hacking at the boarded up kitchen window.

"Vespillo, Lutorius, go," said Carbo, and the two men rushed to the back, weapons out.

The door in front of him splintered again, the axe and the hand holding it coming all the way through. Carbo slashed down, and his evilly sharp-edged gladius took the hand off at the wrist. Blood spurted into the room as the bandit screamed, dropping the axe and retreating.

But others joined the assault on the door now, kicks and clubs and sword hilts rattling the frame.

Suddenly, one well-aimed or particularly hard blow connected in just the right spot. The door flew off its hinges, crashing down into the atrium. Carbo had to jump back to avoid being squashed by the flying timber. As it tumbled to the floor, Carbo found himself face to face with a furious bandit. They stared at each other for a heartbeat.

The bandit charged at Carbo with a roar, sword raised, then collapsed with an arrow in his gut. Sica, standing in one corner, was already notching another arrow, but the next bandit was on Carbo before she had a chance to shoot. Carbo parried a sword swipe as four more bandits entered. Curtius stepped forward to engage one, Orobazes another, but the third leapt on Sica as she was about to loose. The slight girl disappeared beneath the bulky bandit, and Carbo, fighting for his life, saw a dagger raised, about to plunge.

Sica's assailant yelled in frustration as a figure leapt onto his back, grabbed the dagger hand. Marsia wrestled him like a Fury, the dagger thrashing around in the air wildly. Her gladius lay beside them on the floor, forgotten in her desperate defence of Sica.

Another slash from Carbo's opponent, another parry and stab from Carbo, then time for another quick glance towards Sica and Marsia, a sick feeling in his stomach. Marsia had been thrown to the floor, and the dagger remained in the bandit's hand. As he moved towards her with a growl, the winded Sica grabbed the gladius and thrust it through the bandit's chest, skewering him from side to side.

Carbo's opponent took advantage of his distraction, thrusting towards Carbo's midriff. Carbo, wearied from the day's work, half broken in the mines, was slow, and though he twisted, the blade sliced over his ribs, tearing muscle and drawing a gush of blood. He gasped, staggered back, barely parried another blow before it gutted him. This time though, the opponent's thrust left him unbalanced. Carbo reached up to grab the man's hair, using his momentum to propel him forwards into the wall behind Carbo. He hit it head first with a resounding crash, and before he could recover, Carbo turned and slid his sword deep into the back of the man's chest. The man slid to the floor as Carbo pulled his sword free with a tug and a gush of blood.

For a moment, Carbo had no opponent and he looked around. Orobazes had pushed his opponent back and out of the door with wild swings of his sledge-hammer. His enemy's blade was broken, and he parried wildly, ducking and stumbling to avoid the hefty blows. Then his foot caught on a rock and he tumbled backwards. Orobazes lifted his hammer high and brought it down on the man's head, which split apart like ripe fruit.

Carbo suddenly saw the danger, but was too far. Concealed by the wall, Menelaus had let Orobazes pass him, and he stepped up behind the large barbarian. Even as the escaped slave was holding his hammer high in celebration, Menelaus thrust his sword into his back, the tip emerging from the front of his chest with a gout of blood. Orobazes' legs buckled, and he plummeted forwards, head first, twitching and gasping as he bled out. Carbo roared out, "Quintus!" and started forwards. Menelaus turned, masked eyes meeting Carbo's for a moment.

From behind Carbo came a cry for help. Curtius was down, bleeding from a leg wound. A large bandit stood over him, hacking downwards with fury. Curtius fended the blows off with upraised sword, but one sneaked through, piercing his chest. Carbo started towards him, but with his attacker's blade trapped, Curtius thrust upwards, his rusty gladius spearing through the bandit's chin and into his brain. The bandit stiffened, and toppled to one side.

Carbo bent to Curtius, who was bleeding freely from his two wounds, and breathing heavily through gritted teeth. Carbo gripped his good shoulder, looked into his eyes.

Curtius returned the stare resolutely. "Leave me, Carbo. The battle isn't over."

Carbo hesitated, nodded, then turned to the front door again. Menelaus was nowhere to be seen. The sound of fighting came from behind him. Lutorius and Vespillo were fighting a retreat, shoulder to shoulder, as half a dozen bandits, with Febrox behind, forced them backwards. Carbo stepped forwards to reinforce them, ushering Sica and Marsia behind him to guard their backs. But they had lost the narrow doorway as a defence, and had to step back into the atrium. The three legionaries, one serving and two veteran, fought side by side. Sica had picked up a javelin and with Marsia jabbed over their shoulders and heads at any bandit coming too close. But they were tired, the bandits fresh and angry and scenting victory.

Thrusts and stabs and clubs started to find their way home. A bandit fell to a stab from Carbo. Then came a slash to Vespillo's upper arm. A thrust slicing the skin on Carbo's thigh. A club, glancing off Lutorius' head, sending him tumbling to one side.

The stationarius' fall left a gap in the line, and Sica stepped forward. Carbo wanted to tell her to step back, but he had no breath, was fully occupied with the men in front of him.

Febrox sighted on Sica's chest and drew a knife, pulled back, threw. Sica cast her spear at the same time. Febrox, flinching at the spear coming towards him, aimed off target, the knife catching Sica in the abdomen instead of the neck. Sica did not flinch. The spear sailed through the air, and caught Febrox in the neck.

The bandit leader grasped the shaft, eyes wide in disbelief. His mouth opened, and blood gurgled out and down his chin. He fell forward on the spear, the weight of his fall thrusting the tip through his spine.

The five remaining bandits hesitated.

"Carbo!"

Carbo half-turned, keeping his gladius forward. Behind him, Atreus stood, the tragedy mask frowning at Carbo. He held Marsia around the throat, knife to her neck.

Carbo's head spun. Marsia's face changed into Rufa's. Her eyes pleaded to him for help. She was going to die. Just like before, and he was helpless again.

Carbo and Vespillo stood in the centre of the room. Five bandits before them, Menelaus and Atreus behind them. Carbo looked at Vespillo in despair, started to lower his sword, even as Vespillo shook his head.

"Get him Melanchaetes!" The voice was a child's, a little girl's. From out of the dark, a huge shape bounded forwards and landed on Atreus, knocking him sideways, sword flying free, mask loose.

In panic, the unmasked Blaesus tried to keep the giant dog away, as Melanchaetes went for his throat. Huge teeth sunk into Blaesus' arm, and he cried out.

Menelaus stepped forward, and sunk his sword into the dog's chest. Melanchaetes didn't cry out, just turned, bit at the blade buried in him, then tried to leap on Menelaus. The faithful beast's legs betrayed him, and he collapsed, sides heaving, sucking sounds coming from the chest wound.

"Melanchaetes!" came Fabilla's anguished cry. Menelaus turned towards her.

"Fabilla, run!" yelled Carbo. The little girl hesitated, but when Menelaus took a step towards her she fled.

Menelaus started to pursue, but Blaesus called him back. "We can kill her at our leisure. Slowly. We need to dispose of these three first."

Vespillo and Carbo locked eyes.

"On three?" asked Vespillo.

Carbo nodded. "Three!"

They charged into the five bandits before them with a roar, ferocity and bulk knocking them backwards. Two fell to the first gladius thrusts, a third to an elbow in the throat from Carbo. The last two turned and ran.

A crash, and Vespillo grunted and toppled to the floor, the well-aimed rock that Menelaus had thrown at the back of his head rolling beside him. Carbo turned slowly. Comedy-masked Menelaus and naked-faced Atreus, now just plain Blaesus, stood before him. Blaesus face was twisted in fury.

"Y…you…" The stutter was back, the words coming with difficulty. "Y…you have d…destroyed so much."

"The destruction started with you, Blaesus," said Carbo wearily. "You drew first blood, with your attack on my family and friends."

"Y…you k…killed my brother. Everything since has been v…vengeance."

Carbo looked around. So many dead. The bandits. Orobazes. Curtius no longer moving. Vespillo breathing but unconcious. Sica clutching a belly wound. Marsia unharmed, but held at bay by Menelaus' outstretched sword.

"So take your vengeance old man. Here I am. Wounded, exhausted, nothing left to live for." Carbo held his hands out to the side, gladius pointing downwards. "Do it!"

Blaesus charged at him, leading with the tip of his sword. Carbo swung his sword, gripping it with two hands, parrying Blaesus' thrust weakly. His arms were leaden, he felt faint from blood loss and tiredness, and his legs barely held him up. He parried and parried, not attempting to counter. It felt like going through the motions, putting on a decent show before the inevitable - Blaesus killing him, or if he was incredibly lucky and survived the fight, Menelaus finishing him off.

They circled, and he retreated, step by step, forced out of the farm door, backwards towards the ditch of spikes. Menelaus looked on, laughing at the spectacle. Carbo could see Marsia's anguished face, illuminated by the torchlight from within the farm, but even the sight of her misery and loyalty could not spur him to a greater effort.

A cut made its way through Carbo's defences, just a graze, but an indication he was flagging. Blaesus was a skilled swordsman, his up-to-date training and his freshness from his lack of effort in the fight so far compensating for his age. Carbo reached the edge of the ditch and knew he could retreat no further, nor fight any longer. A hard blow forced him to one knee

"Carbo."

Fabilla's voice was near. Too near. She hadn't run.

"Kill him. Please. For mummy."

Blaesus turned to the voice and laughed. He slashed down, twisted, and Carbo's sword flew off into the spiked ditch.

Blaesus looked down at the helpless man before him.

"Now you l…lose. Everything."

He lifted the sword for the last time, brought it down hard.

With the last reserves of his strength, Carbo grasped the descending sword arm and the wrist. Pulled.

With a cry, Blaesus tumbled forwards, screaming as he plummeted, arms flailing, into the ditch, a wet sound emerging as multiple spikes impaled him.

The cry choked off, and for a moment there was silence.

"No!"

Menelaus' heartbroken scream echoed off the hills. He ran towards Carbo, sword held high. Carbo bowed his head, nothing left to give. He closed his eyes.

The sound of metal on metal rang above him. He opened his eyes, looked up, blinked in confusion. Holding back the blow from Menelaus, was…

"Quintus?"

Quintus pushed Menelaus backwards, and laid into him with a fury. Menelaus fought with equal ferocity, and the match was a blur of thrust, slice, parry, stroke and counterstroke.

Finally a sword thrust found its way home. The two men clutched each other, faces almost touching. Then Menelaus slid backwards, falling off Quintus' sword, to lie supine on the ground, staring at the sky.

Quintus knelt beside him, and with a strange gentleness, removed the mask. Carbo saw the face of Pharnaces, twisted with pain.

"You were always his favourite," said Pharnaces. "Not your stupid elder brother. Nor me, the son he got from his best slave." Pharnaces stiffened, body wracked in pain, then relaxed. Carbo thought he was gone, but Pharnaces spoke again.

"He loved you, you know, though you were not even his. He just couldn't cope with the knowledge that you were both his beloved wife's most precious thing, and the cause of her death."

"I'm sorry, Pharnaces. Brother. I wondered, but was never sure. I should have treated you with more…kindness."

Pharnaces reached up to hold his brother's hand, slave and free united in this moment on the edge of death. Then Pharnaces sighed, and the arm went limp.

Quintus leaned over him, and wept.

CHAPTER XXIV

Severa apologised over and over again for letting Fabilla escape from the cellar. The willful girl had slipped the latch when no one was watching, and had gone to help. Now the little girl sat, face buried in Melanchaetes fur, motionless.

Severa and Marsia tended the injured, with Theron and Thera handing out drinks and food. Curtius and Orobazes were dead. Vespillo was dizzy from his latest blow to the head, but otherwise unharmed, leading to some wry comments from Severa about the thickness of his skull. Sica's abdominal wound had not penetrated beyond the muscle into the guts, and when Marsia had cleaned the area, rather too vigourously, and then poured the strongest wine they had onto the raw flesh, she had pronounced that Sica would live.

Lutorius' head had a lump the size of a duck egg on it from the club blow he received, but he had recovered quickly, and had retrieved Publius from the cellar, double checking his bonds, before taking great delight in telling him the outcome of the battle.

Quintus now came face to face with Publius, and they gazed on each other with sadness.

"I thought it was you," said Publius. "I was so angry, that father had overlooked me. I always felt you were his favourite, though it made no sense to me. When I found the mask, with a dark curly hair of the type we Blaesus men sport on it, I believed you were Menelaus. I had no idea that Pharnaces was our brother."

"I'm sorry, Publius. For everything I have brought on this family, from the day I was born."

"You are blameless, brother. You always have been. That might be the most galling thing about all this."

"You know there is nothing I can do to help you, don't you? Even if I wanted to?"

Publius nodded, and looked down.

Marsia tightened a bandage around Carbo's cut ribs, pulling it tight, making Carbo groan. The slave looked up into Carbo's eyes with concern, and more.

"Why did you return, Quintus?" asked Carbo.

Quintus looked embarrassed. "I went away for a few days. I did some drinking. Then I did some thinking. I thought about what I wanted. What I should take for myself, if I was a real man. I had just found my courage, and I had come to buy Marsia from you."

He looked at the slave girl, who was blushing furiously, avoiding his gaze. "I know you like me, Marsia," he said. "But you love someone else more, and I could never compete with that. I was a fool to try."

Carbo looked between Marsia and Quintus, a puzzled frown on his face. He opened his mouth to speak, but Vespillo caught his eye and shook his head, and Carbo closed it again.

"What will happen to my brother?" asked Quintus.

Lutorius sighed. "He should be executed. Beheading, as befits his rank. But the victims didn't have any connections or much wealth. With the right bribes, he will probably just be exiled. A small island in a remote province no doubt, with enough slave girls and wine to keep him occupied."

Lutorius looked like he had swallowed something sour.

"There is one thing I don't understand though," said Vespillo. "When they ambushed us, in the square. When Carbo was captured. How did they know? The only people who knew our plan were myself, Carbo, Lutorius and Quintus. And I think we have all proven ourselves."

"The only free people, you mean," said Marsia.

Carbo looked at her, then round at Theron, who had frozen in the act of pouring a drink for Lutorius.

"And the same one who told Blaesus about your plan, would be the same one who told him about your trip into town with Mistress Rufa," said Marsia.

Thera, who was holding a tray of flat breads, stared at Theron.

"Father?" she said in a small voice.

Theron looked at his daughter, face twisted in guilt and grief.

"I had to," he said. "I have known Blaesus a long time. Have passed him information about travellers all the time he has been a bandit." He turned to Carbo, beseeching. "We needed the money. The farm brings in so little. But I didn't betray you for money."

Carbo stood slowly and picked up a knife.

"Master, please."

Carbo looked at the sticky dark fluid congealing along the edge of his blade. So much blood shed. He looked at the old man, who had sunk to his knees. The reason Carbo had gone to the mines. The reason Rufa was dead, Fabilla orphaned.

"He said he was going to kill Thera," begged Theron. Fabilla had walked over, and now stood beside Carbo, slipping her hand into his, staring at Theron with blank eyes.

Carbo lifted the knife.

Thera gasped. "No! Father!"

"Rufa would have done the same," pleaded Theron. "For her, for Fabilla, her mother would have done anything."

Anger, grief and guilt warred inside Carbo against a terrible weariness, a desperation to see the end of the violence.

His fingers relaxed.

The knife fell to the floor.

Theron's shoulders slumped in relief.

Fabilla knelt down, picked up the knife, and plunged it into Theron's heart. As he fell, Thera's scream ringing through the air, she walked away from him without a backward glance. She knelt, and once more buried her face in Melanchaetes' warm, still body.

Asellio marched into the statio, confusion and anger warring inside him. The town was intact, and as he marched his men back through the streets, the citizens jeered them, threw rotten fruit and stones, and spat at them. He left a small guard party at the door, and accompanied by two of his stationarii, strode into his office, determined to make sense of what was happening.

Carbo sat in his chair, feet up on the desk. Vespillo was rifling through a drawer, examining personal possessions. As Asellio watched, Vespillo held up a jewel-studded gold bracelet. "Look at this one, Carbo. Must be worth a fortune. I don't remember being able to afford this sort of trinket on a centurion's salary, do you?"

"What in Hades are you doing?" roared Asellio. "Get out of my chair. Leave my belongings alone. I'll have you arrested, flogged for... for..."

"For what, centurion?"

Asellio turned. He had not seen the figure standing behind the door when he entered. He blanched.

"Tribune Gemellus? Why... what brings you here?"

"I was informed there was some unrest. I thought I would see for myself how you were handling things. It appears you are serving the citizens of Nola by absenting yourself in their time of need."

"No, tribune, it's not like that." He was floundering, dread gripping him. He pointed at Carbo. "It's his fault. That man stirred up the bandits, incited thugs to run amok. Actually I suspect he has conspired with them to destabilise the region, for his own profit. When I heard there was trouble, I marched my men straight back from the exercises I regularly put them through to keep them in top shape." Asellio gestured to his men. "Arrest him!"

"Do no such thing," said Gemellus. "I think you and I should have a talk, Asellio. And if everything that Carbo and Vespillo tell me are true, I think we can safely conclude that your career will be... cut short."

"You can't believe a word he says."

"Really? Why would I not believe the word of the best pilus prior I ever served with?"

Carbo inclined his head at the compliment, then returned a hard stare to Asellio.

"Besides, Carbo says your optio, Lutorius will confirm everything."

"Where is he, then? And where is my wife? They were having an affair, you can't believe what he says either."

"Ah yes, your wife. She has been very forthcoming too. Gave me a lot of details about your finances, which I found very interesting."

Now Asellio started to shake. He turned to his men, eyes appealing, but they faced forwards, avoiding his gaze.

"As for newly promoted centurion Lutorius, I have given him a task of his own. You, guards. Put him in a holding cell, while he awaits trial on charges of corruption."

The two guards led the shocked Asellio away, somber faced and still studiously avoiding looking at him.

Gemellus turned to Carbo and Vespillo.

"Maybe you two amateurs could get the authorities involved at an earlier stage if you get wrapped up in something like this again, rather than trying to play the heroes."

Carbo grimaced. "I can assure you it was never my intention to play the hero. We thought the proper authorities were involved. I didn't know how deeply Asellio was into this shit."

Gemellus nodded. "It's good to see you again, Carbo. I'm going to return to my legion in the morning. What are your plans?"

Carbo looked into his bleak future, and said nothing.

The woman was tied to the stoning post, sobbing quietly. Her workgroup colleagues' faces showed overwhelming relief and crushing shame, as they picked their rocks. They knew how this worked, had seen it before. She had to be dead by the last throw, or it would start again.

They didn't even think they had missed their quota. They had worked as hard as any other day, had been as exhausted as always. Maybe Durmius was bored. Or he was still angry about the escape of that Carbo fellow, curse him. The furious Durmius had made it horrific for everyone since that day, with increased quotas and arbitrary floggings, whippings and stonings. The slave population of the mines lived every moment in constant terror, a supplement to their normal anxiety, exhaustion and despair.

A young girl picked up the first stone, tears running down her face, hand trembling violently. She looked at Durmius, who looked back coldly, one eyebrow raised at the delay. The girl pulled her arm back.

The throw was feeble, the stone bouncing off the woman's shoulder, causing her to yelp more in anticipation of injury than the pain itself. A burly slave, with a grizzled beard, shoved the girl roughly out of the way, and picked up the largest rock in the pile.

He hefted it in his hand calculating the distance and the point on the woman's body that would be most likely to kill her, most likely to end this quickly, and more importantly make sure that there was not another round of stoning with another one of them. He prepared to throw.

"Stop!" came a commanding voice. "Put the stone down."

All turned at the newcomer striding towards the group, a soldier in centurion's uniform, accompanied by half a dozen armed and armoured legionaries. The slave stared, dropped his stone in surprise.

Durmius gawped at the intruders, and marched up to them.

"Who are you, and what are you doing in my mines?"

"Are you Durmius, the overseer of this establishment?"

"I am. I ask again, who are you?"

"Centurion Lutorius, on detachment from Nola. I carry orders from Tribune Gemellus for the arrest of Durmius the overseer, on charges of bribery, corruption, and illegal imprisonment of free Roman citizens. You are to be taken to Nola, where you will be tried with your confederates, Asellio the former centurion, and Zosimus the captain. Take him."

The legionaries stepped forward and grabbed him by both arms.

"You can't do this," gasped Durmius. "Guards, help me. Stop them."

Some of the guards let their hands fall to clubs and knives, but Lutorius drew his gladius halfway from its scabbard, and the guards stepped back, hands away from their weapons.

As Durmius was led away, a noise started up around the camp. Low at first, then building in volume. Lutorius looked around him. The noise came from hundreds of slaves. Cheering in delight, for the first time in a long, long time.

Carbo held the urn of ashes. It seemed too small to hold all the earthly remains of a human body. The local potter had made a decent job of his assignment. The handiwork was professional, the geometric pattern decorating it seemed symmetrical, and the handwriting on the insciption was neat. "To the spirits of the dead, Rufa, mother of Fabilla and beloved of Gaius Valerius Carbo."

He looked up, to see Fabilla watching him closely, wide eyes dark-rimmed from the nightmare-disturbed sleep Carbo knew she experienced.

"Are we taking mother home?" she asked.

Carbo nodded. Nola was no place for them now. He would hire a new steward, buy new slaves to work the farm. He had emancipated Thera, and Quintus had found her an apprenticeship as a seamstress in the town. The young girl had not thanked him, had not said a word to him or Fabilla, understandably, except to forbid them to attend her father's funeral.

Carbo placed the urn delicately in the cart with the rest of their luggage, making sure it was well-cushioned, and wouldn't fall or tip. Then he turned to the small group of people gathered around.

Quintus and Lutorius had come to see them off. He shook both of the men's hands in turn, firmly, exchanging looks that needed no words. Quintus gave Carbo a half smile, that he knew covered up grief, guilt and shame. Lutorius' smile was more heartfelt. Life was good for him now, promotion, prestige, and the woman he loved. Carbo tried not to resent him.

Severa held Fabilla's hand tightly. The maternal instinct there was strong, and he knew he would not have to raise Rufa's daughter without help. Beside them stood Marsia and Sica. Carbo had requested Sica to be acknowledged as free with a quiet word to the town council, which they had quickly confirmed. Carbo had turned down all other gifts from the grateful people, despite suggestions of a festival and a monument in his name. He didn't feel like he had much to celebrate.

Vespillo patted Carbo on the shoulder. "Let's get moving, or we won't get many miles under our feet before it gets dark."

Carbo looked around, surveying the farm that was to have been his new home, his new start, with his new wife. He tried to picture his life without Rufa, and felt a wave of panic rising inside him. He took out a flask of unwatered wine, and took a long draught. The warmth of the drink calmed him a little. He shook his head, and set his sights on the road to Rome.

# HISTORICAL NOTES

Being condemned to the lead mines, damnatio ad metalla, was one of the worst punishments in the Roman Empire, a lingering death sentence. Mining was reportedly forbidden on the Italian peninsula, but central Italy was relatively mineral poor anyway. Most of the metal resources for Roman needs were met from outside Italy, particularly Spain and Britain, but also other parts of the Empire including Sicily.

Pliny the Elder and Diodorus of Sicily gave detailed descriptions of Roman mining techniques, and Plutarch supplied the information that the rock pillars used to support the mines were not to be touched on penalty of death, though why anyone but a suicidal slave would do so is hard to understand. Pliny, Vitruvius, Diodorus and Livy mention fire cracking and vinegar. Although vinegar is unlikely to have been superior to any other cold liquid, it would have performed the task well, and this technique was used in mining until the invention of explosions. Hannibal may have known of the technique as Livy tells us he used it to blast a way through a blocked pathway in the Alps.

Roman mines must have been truly hellish places. The heat forced miners to work naked or simply protected by a leather apron. They performed backbreaking labour for long hours in darkness and poor quality air, with the constant risk of death from collapse or suffocation, and the mortality rate must have been tremendous. Water accumulation was a constant problem, and the Egyptian screw invented by Archimedes is described by Diodorus and Vitruvius. Valuable slaves were never sent to the mines unless as a punishment.

Banditry was a problem throughout the Roman Empire, with no real police force to combat it. At different times the level of banditry and unlawfulness varied, and in Tiberius' reign the Pax Romana meant the countryside was probably not desperately dangerous, allowing people to travel in some degree of safety. However, the ancient writers imply that banditry was ubiquitous, and certainly Rome had no way of ensuring the safety of travellers beyond what they could do for themselves, notwithstanding the detachments of soldiers sent to the provinces to maintain order known as the stationarii. Desperate men through history have always done whatever they needed to survive, and Rome had plenty of men outside society who needed crime to survive, such as escaped slaves and starving poor, as well as those who would rather choose a life of banditry than work for a living.

The bandits in this book are of a slightly different ilk, being led by nobles. Noble Romans who commit crimes could escape punishment by going into voluntary exile. Exile was also the punishment imposed by the courts as an attempt to avoid capital punishment, and for a Roman who identified himself so much with the eternal city, this was actually a severe punishment in itself. I hope my readers can see how an exiled nobleman would feel both desperate to restore his former wealth, and to find a way to restore his dignitas and auctoritas, even anonymously.

A glossary of the Latin terms used here will be available on my website, www.romanfiction.com

Carbo has been through a tough time again, but his suffering is sadly not over. The next book in the series, provisionally titled Killer of Rome, sees Carbo's despair causing him to lose everything, while a murderer stalks the streets of Rome. Killer of Rome will be published in 2016.

## ACKNOWLEDGEMENTS

Thank you to the numerous people who commented on parts or all of this work, in particular S. J. A. Turney, Jerome Wilson, Brandt Johnson, Paul Bennett, Robin Levin and Irene Hahn. Thanks to the Roman History Reading Group for listening to me during the writing process, and to our fearless leader Irene for running the group. Thanks to Ben Evans again for the professional and thorough editing work. Thanks as always to friends and family for supporting me.

Alex Gough, Somerset, 2015

If you have enjoyed this book, please leave a review on Amazon. Reviews really are the life blood of independent authors, and even a sentence or two can make all the difference!

For random Ancient Roman blogging, reviews and news of new books, please follow me at

www.romanfiction.com

twitter: @romanfiction

Facebook: Alex Gough author

## WATCHMEN OF ROME by ALEX GOUGH

Read the first book in the Carbo of Rome series, Watchmen of Rome.

Rome, AD 27 Gaius Valerius Carbo has returned to the heart of the Empire after 25 years serving in the legions. He just wants to retire in peace. But his friends are gone, his family are dead, and his home now belongs to someone else. When local thugs attack the tavern where he is resting, he finds himself caught up in the fight, and inadvertently becomes the new owner of the building - and the enemies that come with it. His world is turned upside down when he is confronted with a face from his past. He had sworn to protect and look after his childhood friend Rufa after her father died alongside him in battle. But now she has been sold into slavery, and is on the run from her mistress, Elissa. Elissa is a powerful priestess who is organising a cult to try and destroy Rome from within. Can Carbo protect Rufa - and Rome - from Elissa's evil plan? Or will her following be too strong for the Watchmen of Rome?

"It's a superb piece of work. Excellent characterisation, great action, lovely attention to detail, storming plot and a really nice ending." - SJA Turney, author of the Marius Mules series.

"The author has given us tale filled with action as well as a tale filled with emotional strain and anguish." - Hoover Book Reviews

"Watchmen of Rome is a fast paced, exciting novel which reveals a multitude of details about daily life in Ancient Rome, centered, for once, in the realm of the lower classes rather than the wealthy. The novel offers everything you might want in a work of historical fiction." - Robin E. Levin, author of Death of Carthage

## CARBO AND THE THIEF AND OTHER TALES OF ANCIENT ROME
## by ALEX GOUGH

Want more Carbo? Try the short story collection, Carbo and the Thief and Other Tales of Ancient Rome:

Six tales from Ancient Rome. Carbo journeys back to Rome after his retirement from the legions, unaware of the dangers that await him there (described in Watchmen of Rome). On the way he has to solve a mysterious theft of a bulla, and meets and old friend in a town getting ready for a gladiatorial combat. In other stories we learn more about characters from Watchmen of Rome, Elissa and Vespillo. The Battlefield tells the story of a young boy's first encounter with war, and the Wall tells of a new recruit's posting to Hadrian's Wall.